FOCUS ON THE FAMILY PRESENTS

Adventures in
ODYSSEY®

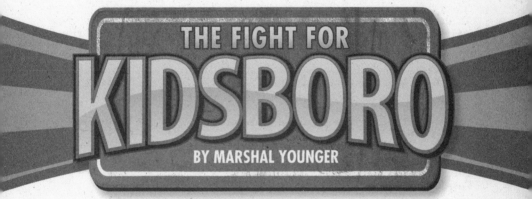

THE FIGHT FOR KIDSBORO

BY MARSHAL YOUNGER

Tyndale House Publishers, Inc.

Carol Stream, Illinois

A Focus on the Family book published by
Tyndale House Publishers, Inc., Carol Stream, Illinois 60188

Editor: Kathy Davis
Cover illustration: Gary Locke
Cover design: Jacqueline L. Nuñez

Library of Congress Cataloging-in-Publication Data
Younger, Marshal.
  The Fight for Kidsboro / Marshal Younger.
    p. cm. — (Kidsboro ; 1)
  At head of title: Adventures in Odyssey
  A Focus on the Family book—T.p. verso.
  Previously published as: Battle for control, The creek war, The rise and fall of the
Kidsborian empire, and The risky reunion.
  Summary: As mayor of Kidsboro, Ryan Cummings faces losing his office, a war against
Max Darby's Bettertown, an economic crisis, the threat that a dangerous secret will be re-
vealed, and citizens' concerns about taxes and the services they provide.
  Creek war.
  Rise and fall of the Kidsborian empire.
  Risky reunion.
  ISBN 978-1-58997-675-7 (alk. paper)
  [1. Politics, Practical—Fiction. 2. Conduct of life—Fiction. 3. Christian life—Fiction.
4. War—Fiction. 5. Honesty—Fiction. 6. Secrets—Fiction. 7. Municipal finance—Fiction.]
I. Title. II. Title: Adventures in Odyssey. III. Title: Creek war. IV. Title: Rise and fall of the
Kidsborian empire. V. Title: Risky reunion.
  PZ7.Y8943Bat 2011
  [Fic]—dc23
                            2011015568

Printed in the United States of America
1 2 3 4 5 6 7 8 9 /17 16 15 14 13 12 11

CONTENTS

*To Stephanie, who worked so hard to
keep a roof over our heads
while I sat at a computer and wrote
a bunch of stuff that will never sell
(and a couple of things that did).*

■ ■ ■

BOOK 1

Battle for Control

PROLOGUE

THE BIRTH OF A CITY

CAREER DAY WAS A BUST. There were tables lined up end-to-end across the Odyssey Middle School gym, and as soon as our teachers let us loose, we all dashed around like 300 mice scrambling for six pieces of cheese, eager to sign up for the fun jobs. If we signed our names on the list fast enough, we had a good chance of working in whatever occupations we wanted for a day. Most everyone wanted exciting things like working at the fire department or police station. At one point, I saw Alice Funderburk, a rather large girl, shove people out of the way as she steamrolled to the police station table. The crowd of people parted for her like the Red Sea. She was the first one to sign up.

I didn't worry too much about getting on the list quickly, because I figured there weren't too many people interested in what I was interested in—politics. I wanted to be the mayor. I wanted so badly to meet with, work with, and *think* with the mayor of Odyssey. I strolled casually to my table, all the while watching people clamor and fight for their own tables, and sure enough, when I got there, no one had signed the sheet. I signed my name, *Ryan Cummings, age 12.* I could hardly wait to walk up the City Hall steps in the only suit I owned, ready to dazzle the mayor of Odyssey with my knowledge of government and politics.

It was not worth the wait.

When I got to City Hall later that morning, the mayor wasn't even around. The secretary showed me his office, and I sat at his desk. There were stacks of papers in front of me that I wasn't allowed to look through. I tried to answer the phone once and I got yelled at. I just sat there and waited for three hours, and when I finally met him, he shook my hand, had a picture taken of the two of us, and told me he was very sorry but he had a meeting to attend. I was dismissed shortly afterward. If all I had wanted was a photo, I could've posed with the cardboard cutout of himself that he still had in his office from his election campaign. I was bitterly disappointed. I wanted to work with him. I wanted to, for a few moments, *be* the mayor.

When I went to Whit's End that afternoon, I found some comfort in the fact that my friends had much the same experience I'd had. We all sat at the counter of the ice cream shop, complaining about our day. John Avery Whittaker, or "Whit" as most adults called him, was the owner and operator of the ice cream shop and discovery emporium and had the misfortune of having to listen to us whine.

Jill Segler had gone to the *Odyssey Times* to find out what it was really like to be a news reporter. She'd had dreams of uncovering some big business scandal.

"I went to Dale Jacobs's office," she began, knowing everyone would recognize the name of the editor of the *Odyssey Times*, "and the first thing he tells me is, 'It may be a slow news day.' Come to find out, it was not a slow news day. It was a *no* news day. I ended up helping a guy write a story about how celery prices have risen 5 percent in the last two weeks."

Mr. Whittaker chuckled.

Scott Sanchez, my best friend, had a similar experience. He had signed up to learn how to be a private detective. Unfortunately, his mentor was Harlow Doyle, a private eye in Odyssey who may have actually been a worse detective than Scott was.

"We spent two hours filling out my paperwork. All he had to do was sign the form to prove that I showed up. First he couldn't find a pen, then he couldn't decide whether he should sign his middle name, then he couldn't remember his middle name, and then he confused my name with his own. It was unbelievable."

Alice Funderburk also had a frustrating story. She was angry that they didn't give her a gun when she checked in at the police station. She spent most of the morning riding around with a police officer and handing out parking tickets. But when Alice threw a jaywalker up against a wall, she was forced to go back to the police station and do paperwork for the rest of the day.

The only person who had a positive story was Nelson Swanson, who worked with Eugene Meltsner, an employee at Whit's End. Eugene was the resident genius, and Nelson was his protégé. Eugene had helped Nelson conceive and build some of his best inventions, of which he had many. Eugene and Nelson had spent the day building a solar-powered air conditioner. Everyone felt sorry for Nelson when he told this story—until we realized that he had actually enjoyed doing it.

We all whined some more. I said, "How are we ever going to know if this is what we really want to do with our lives if we never get a real opportunity to try it?"

Mr. Whittaker didn't answer. Instead, he began to stare at nothing, which made us think that the wheels were turning inside his head.

"Mr. Whittaker?" Scott said, waving a hand in front of his face.

"You know what?" he said, breaking out of his trance. "If you really want practical experience at these jobs, there may be other ways of getting it."

"How?"

"Why don't you create your own jobs?"

None of us knew what he was talking about, and maybe he didn't either, because he paused and stared into space again. "Better yet . . . why don't you create your own *town*?"

Still, we weren't getting it. "I'll get you started," he said. "You can form a community. Each of you would have a different job—whatever you want to be. It won't be exactly the same as real life, but it might give you a taste of what you're looking for."

I nodded more and more as he went on explaining his idea. I loved it! We could create our own town!

■ ■ ■

And so Kidsboro was born. We started off with five of us: Jill Segler would start the *Kidsboro Chronicle*, a weekly newspaper. Alice Funderburk chose to be the chief of police. She had no police to be chief *of*, but no one was about to argue with her. Nelson wanted to be a small-business owner, selling his inventions. Scott wanted to be a private detective, though I couldn't imagine what kinds of cases he would be called on to solve in a town of, presently, five. And none of us were criminals.

Me? I wanted to be the mayor . . . and no one had any objections. The others seemed to think I was the perfect choice, and this made me feel good. I liked my title—mayor of Kidsboro.

The five of us became the city council, and with Mr. Whittaker's help, we wrote the city charter, or the Kidsboro Constitution. All the laws of the land would be laid down in this document.

After we wrote the city charter, we decided that if we were going to do this, we would do it right. "I think we should have actual buildings," I said in our first city council meeting.

"What do you mean?" Jill asked.

"Mr. Whittaker owns the woods behind Whit's End, and he told me we can use it. I think we should build clubhouses for our offices and bigger clubhouses for meeting halls."

"Build clubhouses?" Scott said. "With what?"

This question led us to another question. Was our new town going to be just the five of us, or would we allow other people in? The clubhouse question answered this for us, because we ran into an immediate problem: none of us had any kind of building materials. Mr. Whittaker didn't want to supply our materials, because he wanted us to come up with our own solutions.

We all knew someone who had a supply of wood, and admitting him as a citizen would solve our problem. Max Darby's father owned a construction company, and Max had easy access to wood scraps. I was worried about asking Max to be a part of Kidsboro, though, because he was known for getting into trouble at school. But having him as a citizen would make it easy for us to get the wood we needed to build our town.

We asked Max, and he loved the idea of becoming a citizen because he thought it could make him rich. He would make us pay for the wood. That's when we decided to set up a money system for Kidsboro. Max would get Kidsboro money (instead of real money) for his wood: tokens (about five cents) and starbills (20 tokens, or about a dollar).

Everything sold in Kidsboro would have to be paid for in Kidsboro money. Mr. Whittaker decided that everyone who became a citizen would be given a certain amount of Kidsboro currency to start off with: enough to buy a house and have a little money left over to spend around town.

Over the next couple of weeks, with Max's help, we built a clubhouse for each of us. Eugene Meltsner was closely involved with the layout of the town, making logical decisions about where everything should go based on proximity to neighbors, quality of soil, and drainage. We also built a meeting hall, which was an open-air pavilion 10 times as large as any of the clubhouses. It was a multi-purpose city council meeting hall and entertainment center.

The next step was to build up our population. We began a search for citizens. Everyone we talked to seemed excited about the idea of being part of a kids' town, so we didn't have much difficulty finding interested people. Everyone was welcome to come to Kidsboro, but it was simply impossible to allow everyone to become actual citizens. We couldn't build that many clubhouses.

We decided that the requirements for citizenship in Kidsboro should be high. We wanted people of reasonably high standards so that we could build up a strong community. The city council would vote on each candidate. I disagreed with a couple of the selections: Valerie Swanson, for one. She was Nelson's sister and a very manipulative girl. But she was voted in despite my arguments against her. That's because she was the prettiest and most popular girl in school. I knew that most of the guys at Odyssey Middle School had secret crushes on her.

Mr. Whittaker gave us advice whenever we really needed it, but for the most part, he held back. He wanted us to get the experience of solving our own problems, and I appreciated this. I doubted that I would ever go to him for advice on a mayoral problem, but I knew that I could if I needed to.

So we had our little town. We started off with 20 people and added more over the next couple of months. Things went smoothly at first. Most Kidsboro citizens came to the town after school through the early spring months, and a lot of us spent our weekend days there. People obeyed the laws; businesses were set up and seemed to be prospering. And I was the mayor.

Which also made me the prime target.

1

THE PIT BULL AT MY DESK

MY FOOT SEEMED TO HAVE a life of its own as it tapped uncontrollably on the ground. I pressed it flatter against the ground in an attempt to stop it, but I couldn't. Fortunately for me, the desk hid my foot's nervous dance from Valerie. I've heard that in the presence of vicious animals, you should never show fear, because it's the first thing they sense. I forced myself to look at her, stone-faced. She would not see me flinch.

She spoke, an evil smile crossing her otherwise perfect face. "I don't care if you *are* the mayor, Ryan. If I don't get what I want, I'm gonna take over this town and run you out."

I felt the blood drain out of my face. I tried to return the smile, even though I knew that was silly. Valerie's smile didn't convey friendship or kindness. The fact that Valerie smiled was worse than if she had frowned or gritted her teeth. A frown would've meant she was serious about crushing me into tiny little bits. A smile meant she would also enjoy it.

She stood up without taking her eyes off of me. She leaned over my desk until her long, brown hair was almost swinging in my face. It smelled like strawberries, and for a split-second I was distracted. But I shook off the momentary crush and stared at her eyes, which were half-closed like a lion ready to pounce.

"Ashley gets in," she said. She turned around and left, her work here done.

Whew! I could finally exhale. I wiped the sweat from my forehead with a sleeve and paced around the office, trying to work off some nervous energy. Most of the guys in our school, including me, actually admitted to being afraid of Valerie. The guys who wouldn't admit it were lying. And crushing me under her cruel thumb would be as easy for Valerie as crushing an ant with her foot.

We had grown to 29 citizens in our short two-month history, and we were planning to accept a new person into our town to make it an even 30. That afternoon, Valerie's best friend, Ashley, would be reviewed by the city council for possible citizenship. Valerie was trying to ensure that Ashley got the votes required to get in. One thing about Valerie: It was horrible being her enemy, but it was great being her friend. Having power in your corner has many advantages. Valerie knew that the five council members had to vote on Ashley. If Ashley didn't get an 80 percent majority vote (meaning four out of five people had to say "yes"), she didn't get in at all. No doubt Valerie pretty much knew how the voting would go: Ashley had three votes in the bag, and one vote against her. I was the wild card. If I voted yes to Ashley, she got in. If I voted no, she didn't.

The problem was, I didn't like Ashley. She called me "Dummings," a less-than-clever variation of my last name, Cummings, plus she got into trouble a lot in school. I'd seen her cheat on tests and copy other people's homework assignments. She was not the type of person I wanted in my town. Kidsboro was a community filled with good citizens who followed rules. After all, this was not a real city—we couldn't actually force anyone to pay a fine or stay in jail, so everyone had to follow the rules on his or her own. A person like Ashley wouldn't take the laws seriously. I was sure of that.

So here was my choice: I could put the town in danger by allowing in a person who might ruin it; or I could put *myself* in danger by tugging on the chain of a fierce pit bull named Valerie.

Politics.

■ ■ ■

I went to the meeting hall pavilion where the city council met. All five members of the council gathered around the table.

Scott Sanchez was talking to himself, muttering the phrase "Walk the dog" over and over, which most likely meant that he was supposed to go home and do that right after the meeting. He would probably end up forgetting anyway, as he usually did.

To Scott's left, *Kidsboro Chronicle* reporter Jill Segler had her notebook out and a pencil resting on her ear. Next to her, Police Chief Alice Funderburk was jerking her head back and forth to crack the bones in her thick neck.

Finally, Nelson Swanson was studying a chart he had created on his computer. At the top, the heading was "Voting for Ashley." Below the heading were two columns—a list of reasons for voting "yes" and a list of reasons for voting "no." In the "no" column were all the things that I would've had in *my* "no" column—that Ashley was not very nice, that she was a dishonest student, and so on. In the "yes" column was one phrase, typed in the biggest font Nelson could fit on the sheet of paper: "VALERIE WON'T KILL ME!" Nelson was Valerie's brother and the only one smarter than her in town. But unlike her, he used his intelligence in positive ways.

They sat there staring at me, knowing exactly what was going through my head. Ashley's future in Kidsboro, and possibly *my* future as a living, walking human being, depended on my vote. Jill and Alice would vote for Ashley because she always invited them to her birthday parties. Ashley lived on Trickle Lake and her birthday party always included boating, swimming, and water skiing. It was the best party of the year. So Jill and Alice would vote for her simply because they wanted that invitation in their mailboxes.

Nelson would end up voting for Ashley. Getting Valerie mad at *me* was one thing. But actually living with her every day in adjoining rooms like he did, where she had easy 24-hour access to his neck, would be a nightmare.

I knew Scott would vote against Ashley. Scott had never liked Ashley, and he would do anything to keep her out, even if it meant putting his life in danger.

So the vote would be three to one. If I voted yes, the vote would be four to one, and Ashley would have the required 80 percent.

We went around the room. "Yes," Alice said.

"Yes," Jill said.

"No," Scott said.

"Yes," Nelson said.

No surprises. They all sat up in their chairs and gazed at me. I could almost feel Valerie's hands around my neck, ready to squeeze. I took a long breath, still not quite sure what I was going to say. I closed my eyes tightly. Sweat began to drip down my face. Not a sound came from the other four members of the council as I opened my eyes and let the word slide off my tongue.

"No."

2

DANGEROUS CHOICES

I REMAINED SEATED AS EVERYONE filed out of the meeting hall past me. Nelson looked at me the way a priest would look at a man who was about to be executed. He adjusted his glasses and put his hand on my shoulder as if to say, "Bless you, my son," and that he'd pray for my soul. Scott, being my best friend, probably thought he should be supportive, and so he said, "The town thanks you." Then he went to his clubhouse, obviously forgetting that he was supposed to go walk the dog. Jill smiled as if she just might have a homicide to report in the next edition of the newspaper. Alice offered her protection. I think she was joking, but I'm not sure.

As I left the meeting hall, I expected Valerie to jump around the corner immediately, but she didn't. This frightened me. I figured I would be okay as long as I could look her in the eye. But if she lurked in the shadows, I'd probably go nuts. Maybe she knew this. Maybe her plan was to drive me crazy by *not* acting. It would certainly cause everyone in town to wonder whether they should have a mayor who was insane. Then, when she had everyone thinking I should be locked up, she would take over. That was probably her plan . . . and it was working rather well so far.

■ ■ ■

My stomach was in knots, so I walked to Whit's End to get something to drink.

"Hello, Ryan," Mr. Whittaker said from behind the counter.

"Hi, Mr. Whittaker."

"Is something wrong?" he asked.

"Why?"

"You look a little pale."

"My stomach hurts."

"Are you sick?"

"No," I said, "but I may be dying."

"What?"

He made me sit down and spill the whole story of Valerie and Ashley and the city council vote. He smiled and said, "You made the right choice, even though it could make things difficult for you. I wish *all* of our political leaders had your standard of ethics. So, who are you going to nominate next?"

I hadn't thought about that. Since Ashley didn't get in, I had to come up with a new candidate for citizenship. I had a few ideas off the top of my head.

"I've been thinking about Larry Mankowicz." He was a track star at Odyssey Middle School—a very popular guy who would put Kidsboro on the map just by being there. "Also, Mary Burgess," I said. Mary was the second prettiest girl in our school, in my opinion, next to Valerie.

"Oh . . . okay," Mr. Whittaker said, bowing his head and suddenly becoming very interested in cleaning a glass. He knew both of these people, and though he didn't say it, I could tell he disapproved of my choices. I saw him glance over to one of the booths, and I followed his look. Sitting in the corner by himself was Roberto Santana. I barely knew him, though I knew he had moved to Odyssey from the Dominican Republic about two years earlier. He didn't appear to have many friends. I knew what Mr. Whittaker wanted me to do, though he refused to say it. I felt a little ashamed. I was picking people based on what they could do for Kidsboro, not for what Kidsboro could do for them.

"I catch your drift," I told Mr. Whittaker.

"What?" he said innocently.

I smiled and left. I had to get council approval.

■ ■ ■

"There he is," I said to Scott as we ate lunch in the school cafeteria. I pointed to Roberto, sitting alone at the very last table. He was eating at lightning speed so he could run to the library, where he could be by himself and not have everybody staring at the kid who was sitting alone. He did that every day.

"Roberto Santana?" Scott asked. "Are you sure?"

"He's perfect," I said.

Scott dipped a French fry into his ketchup. "Excuse me for bringing this up, but you do know his dad's in jail, right?"

"That's just a rumor." I hated the way kids believed anything they heard. The latest gossip was that Roberto's dad was in jail. No one knew exactly why, but everyone had a guess. Roberto denied all of it. I believed him, though I had no evidence on my side either.

"Maybe it's a rumor, maybe it isn't," Scott said.

"Yeah, but even if it is true, which I doubt, why should that matter?"

Scott shrugged, his ketchup-soaked French fry dangling limply from his hand. "We don't want any trouble in our town, do we?"

"What Roberto does and what his father may or may not have done are two different things."

"So maybe we should ask him," Scott said.

"Ask him if his father's in jail?"

"Yeah. The city council's gonna want to know."

"Why should it matter?" I asked.

"I don't know. You don't think it matters?"

"No."

Family matters were private. I knew this especially, because I wanted my own family matters to be private. My mother and I had moved from California to Odyssey when I was eight. No one knew anything about my life before I came to Odyssey, and I was determined to keep it that way. It was something I never talked about, even with Scott. Roberto had a right to keep his mouth shut too.

"Pardon me for breathing," Scott said, "but does he even wanna be in Kidsboro?"

"I told him about it," I said, "and he seemed to think it was a cool idea."

■ ■ ■

The next day I presented Roberto's name to the city council. I was met with a less-than-enthusiastic response.

"Do you really know him?" Jill asked.

"No. But I know he's smart. He got the best grade in my history class."

"How is knowing history going to help us?" Scott asked, still not convinced of Roberto's worth.

"I don't think he knows how to speak English," Alice said.

"Yes he does."

"I'm just trying to figure out how he's going to help Kidsboro," Jill said.

"We didn't ask that question about any other candidate. I mean . . . we've got people in this town who have almost no positive qualities at all except that they're somebody's friends. Now why does Roberto have to live up to higher expectations?"

They all exchanged looks.

Nelson was the only one brave enough to speak up. "I know this may not be a reason to keep him out, but you do know about his dad—"

"Yes!" I answered angrily. "I know what people say about his dad. What does that have to do with *him*?"

Nelson adjusted his glasses. "Some studies indicate that criminal behavior is genetic."

"Have any of you ever seen Roberto steal anything?" I asked.

They shook their heads.

"Have any of you ever seen him destroying property? Getting into a fight?" More heads shaking. "Then we have no evidence that he is anything but a good student. *That* we have evidence for."

"I agree," Jill said. "We can't keep him out because of his father. But I think he should have a probation period. A couple of weeks to show us what he's got—since nobody really even knows him."

Everybody around me nodded. I was against this, but I was confident that Roberto would soon show everyone that he could be an asset to the community. So I agreed. Roberto would become a citizen of Kidsboro, but he would be watched very closely.

I gave Roberto the news (though I didn't mention the probation), and he seemed happy about it. I had a feeling he was just thrilled to be a part of something.

Scott and I showed Roberto around the town, including his new clubhouse. Usually, new citizens were given a plot of land, and then they were responsible for buying the wood to build their own houses. But our town builder and handyman, Nick, had built this one for Jeffrey, a boy who had come in about two weeks before, but had moved away suddenly. We gave Roberto the choice of buying this clubhouse or building his own. He decided this one was fine. It was just like everybody else's anyway. It was a rectangular box made of scrap wood that was big enough to stand up in, with about a foot and a half of head room for most people. If you stretched out both arms, you could touch either wall at its width, and its length was enough for two people to lay end-to-end. You had to duck your head to get through the door.

"Very nice," he said, and we exchanged smiles.

Then we showed him the business district—the newspaper office, the church, the police station, and the bakery. We saved the bakery for last because it was the most successful business in Kidsboro.

We turned the corner around the meeting hall and saw the sign for Sid's Bakery. Sid, one of two African-Americans in Kidsboro, made muffins, donuts, cookies, and cakes—all himself. He used ingredients that he bought from Mr. Whittaker. We could all buy smaller items from Mr. Whittaker with tokens, and he would buy ingredients or parts from the store with real money. Obviously, this meant Mr. Whittaker would be spending his own money and getting nothing in return since he couldn't use the tokens anywhere but Kidsboro, but this was one of the sacrifices he made in order to keep Kidsboro going.

Sid's business had thrived. He had one advantage in that kids are never too picky about freshness, so he could frequently sell a three-day-old donut. The bakery was not much bigger than a regular clubhouse, but Sid always had a table full of pastries inside. I hadn't been there in a while, and I thought I would buy a cinnamon-raisin donut for Roberto as a "Welcome to Kidsboro" gesture. But when we got there, Sid was leaving.

"Where are you going?" I asked.

"You're too late. I just threw away my last donut," Sid said. Roberto was visibly disappointed.

"You're closing already?"

"Yep. Forever." Sure enough, there on the outside of the door was a sign that read "Going Out of Business Sale." Sid closed the door behind him. "We had muffins for a token apiece," he said. "You should've been here."

Sid's muffins were usually four tokens each—and everyone in Kidsboro would agree that they were worth it. Most people in town had some vague idea about what they wanted to be when they grew up. Sid didn't just have an idea. He had a destiny. At age 13, he was a fine chef in the making. He was already better than my mom—not that my mom was a bad cook. He was just a master—a pastry artist. Closing his bakery was like Michelangelo deciding to go into real estate.

"Why are you shutting down?" I asked.

"It's not worth it. Hardly anybody buys anything anymore."

"*We* were just coming to buy something," Scott said.

"Great. But where have you been? You know how much stuff I sold last week? Two donuts, three cookies, and a bear claw. I can't survive on that."

"So what are you gonna do?" Scott asked.

"I don't know."

"You can't leave!" I shouted, sounding more desperate than I meant to. "Maybe it was just a slow week. People'll be back."

"I can't wait for that. I'm wasting too much good food."

"Okay, okay. You can go for a while. Then everybody will miss you, and you can come back."

"Maybe." And with a look that seemed to say, "I'm going to France to find people who appreciate my talents," he left.

"I don't understand," Roberto said. "He had good donuts, but his business is over?"

"I don't understand it either, Roberto," I said. I looked at Scott. "I'm gonna miss the bear claws. Did you ever try those? They were incredible."

"Nope. Never tried one. I never bought *anything* from the bakery."

"Why not?"

"I don't have any money."

I didn't want Roberto to get the impression that life was tough for citizens of Kidsboro. He had just met someone whose business had tanked, and another person who was broke.

But it was true. Scott had never earned a single token with his detective agency in the two months of Kidsboro's existence. Of course, there hadn't been much need for a private investigator.

Like every other citizen of Kidsboro, Scott had been given enough tokens to start off with. He had probably already used that up-front money and never made any more.

I wondered if this was true of more people in Kidsboro. Citizens were responsible for making their own living in whatever ways they wanted. As mayor, I was paid by the city. This meant that every month the residents paid 10 percent of their income for taxes. This money went to pay me, Alice, and Corey, the garbage man. Tax money also went to build special buildings, like the meeting hall. So far, I had not had to worry about making a living.

Alice, in addition to being the police chief, was also in charge of collecting taxes. She was an obvious choice because no one would dare try to cheat her for fear of their very lives. Alice took care of all of this herself, so I didn't know how much anyone made at all. Were there a lot of people out there not making any money? Was that the reason Sid was going out of business?

We dropped Roberto off at his clubhouse and left him there to consider what his place would be in Kidsboro.

■ ■ ■

The next night there was a buzz in the air about some kind of meeting or rally that was taking place at the meeting hall. I figured I should check it out. When I got there, the place was packed.

Valerie stepped to the front and stood behind a music stand. Oh, no. It was Valerie's rally. I bit my lip to keep it from quivering as she began to speak.

"Here I have the city charter," she said, holding up a 10-page booklet. "Let me read some of the rules we have in this town. 'No one is allowed to be in the city after eleven o'clock on weekends and nine o'clock on school nights.'" She flipped a page. "Here's another. 'There will be no fires or fireworks inside the city limits.'" She flipped through some more. Her eyes widened as if she saw a really offensive one. "And it goes on like this for 10 pages." She paused for dramatic effect. "Is it my imagination, or has our city council suddenly become our parents?"

Heads began nodding in approval. She continued. "These people think they can tell us how to live our lives. They don't think we have enough rules. But don't we? I mean, we have rules in school, we have rules at home, we have rules at church and on the street and in the grocery store. We're kids! Shouldn't there be a place we can go where we are free to do what we want to do?"

More and more heads were nodding. The meeting hall began to buzz with protesting murmurs. Valerie raised her fist with confidence, shouting, "We don't need the city council and the mayor to be our babysitters!"

An unidentified voice shouted, "Yeah!" and others followed with the same exclamation. Most of the crowd were sitting high up in their seats, ready for a revolt. Four people were notably *not* sitting up in their seats. Me, of course, and three other members of the city council. Alice was standing in the front corner with her hand on her hip (where a real police officer would have a gun), poised to extinguish a riot if she needed to.

Valerie was about to continue when someone ran up. "Hey, come on! There's been a break-in at Marcy's house! The new kid did it!" Everyone rushed past me to see what all the excitement was about. I was the last one out.

■ ■ ■

When I arrived at Marcy's, the scene was clear. She was standing in the middle of her house, looking at all of her stuff. It looked as if someone had clobbered the room with a baseball bat. No one kept anything expensive in their houses, but she had a chair, some pictures, a few books, and a clock that were destroyed. Her walls were cracked in several places as well.

"Are you okay?" I asked her.

Her mouth was open in disbelief. "Yeah. Why would anybody do this?"

"I don't know," was all I could say.

Roberto was there too. Alice grabbed him and started searching him, just in case he was actually carrying a weapon. She stood him straight up facing the outside wall of the clubhouse, bending his arm across his lower back, and read him his rights (which she'd memorized for just such an occasion as this).

I went up to her. "What happened?"

"Marcy came home, and the door was wide open. The whole place was trashed. When I got here, this little punk was still standing here like the cat that ate the canary," Alice said, bending his arm farther toward his head. Roberto winced.

"You saw Roberto trashing your place?" I asked Marcy.

"No. But he was here. Standing right outside the door."

"Roberto, were you in Marcy's house?"

"Yes," he said, "but . . . I-I did not do it."

The crowd, all ready to hang somebody after Valerie's speech, didn't believe him. Alice took Roberto away and put him in the town jail.

3

ROBERTO TAKES THE FALL

THE CITY CHARTER STATES THAT if anyone is arrested, he or she must go to jail until an investigation can be completed. This was the first time in Kidsboro's short history that we had to use this page of the city charter.

Alice would do the investigation, Roberto would be put on trial, and then if he were found guilty, the jury would have to decide what the punishment should be. If Roberto were convicted, there would be no other choice for us but to kick him out of town. This was a serious crime.

Scott started to argue with Alice about who should do the investigation, but Alice put a stop to that right away. "Are you a member of the police force?" she asked, pushing up her sleeves.

"No," Scott said.

"Well, this is official police business."

"I'm a private investigator. I can investigate for you."

"If a private citizen hires you, you can investigate. Until then, this is a crime scene. Get back."

Scott backed off without another word. This was the first real police work Alice had had the opportunity to do. No way was anybody going to move in on it.

Alice looked over the crime scene, took statements from Marcy and Roberto, and checked around to see if there were any other witnesses.

There weren't. Things didn't look too good for Roberto. In fact . . . I was beginning to think he might actually have done it. I wanted to believe him, but frankly, all the evidence pointed in his direction. I went to the jail to talk to him.

■ ■ ■

Roberto was obediently sitting in the cell, which was barely larger than a closet. The bars were made out of thin tree branches, and anybody with the strength of a kitten could get out, but the understanding was that you wouldn't try. I guess all of our rules were pretty much this type of understanding.

Roberto barely looked up when I walked in. He acted like a guy who'd just missed a million-dollar free throw. Being a part of Kidsboro was his chance to fit in somewhere, and it looked like it was slipping away.

I sat at Alice's desk outside the cell and looked into his eyes. He stared back at me blankly. I decided to be up front. "Did you do it?"

"No," he said sincerely. He explained in his accent, "I was in my house putting pictures on my walls. Then I heard someone call me. So I went to see who, and I saw this girl Marcy's door was open. I thought that maybe the voice came from inside. So I went in and saw the whole place was torn up. Then I turned around and Marcy was there watching me. She yelled. I did not know what to do. Then that big police girl came and pushed me up against the wall."

"You said you heard somebody call out your name. Was it a boy's voice or a girl's voice?"

"Boy."

"Did you recognize it?"

"No."

"Did you tell Alice all of this?"

"Yes, but I do not think she believed me." He looked at me sadly and asked, "Do *you* believe me, Ryan?"

It suddenly occurred to me that my opinion might be important to him. Maybe I was the only person who had ever given him a chance. Now my answer to this question would do one of two things: show me to be a true friend, or lump me in with all of the other kids who distrusted him because of his father's reputation. Maybe the way I answered this was more important to him than being a part of the city. "Yes, I believe you," I said. I think I meant it, but to be honest, I'm not sure.

— — —

I was on my way to ask Alice about the investigation when I saw a crowd of people gathered around Jill. She was holding up a newspaper and everyone around her was waving their money to get one. "Special edition! Five tokens a copy! Read all about the Kidsboro Burglar!"

The normal price for an issue of the paper was three tokens. This was the biggest story ever to hit Kidsboro, so five tokens was probably a bargain. Unfortunately for Jill, there was not a lot of news to report in a town of

30—especially when the crime rate, before now, was basically zero. A donut had been stolen from Sid's Bakery a couple of months earlier and Jill had had a field day with that. It was front-page news for three issues. She did extensive interviews, took photographs of the crime scene, wrote feature stories on the history of the bakery and the history of donuts and the history of stolen donuts—and then Sid remembered that he had eaten the donut. Jill had got a lot of ribbing for that. I was sure that she wanted to save face now with this new story.

I went up to Jill and took five tokens out of my pocket. "How did you do this so fast?"

"Ryan, dear, old news is no news. And this is the biggest story in the history of Kidsboro."

"Yeah, but how did you get all the information already?"

"You wanna know what made the front page of my last issue? Alice's new police badge that she bought at a carnival," she said, rolling her eyes. "Let's just say I was inspired."

I smiled and looked at the story. She had certainly made headway in the last two hours. She had summaries, interviews, pictures of the scene (apparently she'd gone to a one-hour photo place), biographies of all the people involved . . . Wait a minute!

My face turned hot as I flipped to page two of the story. Jill had made her way down the street and was giving change to someone. I stormed over to her.

"What is this?" I shook the paper.

"What?" she asked innocently.

"You mentioned that Roberto's father is in jail!"

"Yeah."

"First of all, that's a rumor. Second, how dare you *print* it!"

"It's a fact related to the story."

"It has nothing to do with the story."

"Don't you think it's important?"

"No, I don't!" I shouted. "It has nothing to do with whether he broke into Marcy's house!"

"He did it, Ryan. Everybody knows it."

"*I* don't know it. In fact, I'm beginning to doubt that he had anything to do with it. The point is, he hasn't had a trial yet. He's innocent until proven guilty in court."

She breathed heavily a few times, then realized she had no comeback.

"Don't tell me how to do my job." She charged off.

- - -

The trial process was a little sketchy, but it was outlined in the city charter. There were three lawyers in town. One was Pete Marvison, whose only qualifications were that he liked the idea of being a lawyer and watched a lot of lawyer television shows. Pete was Roberto's lawyer.

Pete was smart enough, and I didn't doubt that he might actually make a good lawyer. The problem was that his opponent was none other than Valerie Swanson. Valerie could make anyone look dumb, and Pete knew it. He knew he would be no match for her, and everyone could tell he was more than a bit nervous about opposing her.

Pete came into the courtroom with a huge stack of disorganized papers, and, of course, as soon as he stepped through the door, he dropped all of them. He fell to his knees and scrambled to retrieve them before too many people noticed.

I knew Pete was really in trouble when he shouted, "Objection!" before the trial even started. Amy, the judge, said, "What are you objecting to?" and Pete slid back down in his chair and sheepishly answered, "Never mind."

Valerie spoke well. She used big words and concepts like "reasonable doubt." She even threw in some Latin at one point, and I could tell this made an impression on the jury. Her first witness was Officer Alice. Alice obviously thought Roberto did it. Later on, Valerie had the nerve to mention Roberto's father. I glanced at Pete, hoping for an objection, but he was sitting in his chair, trying to get chocolate off of his sleeve.

Pete asked Alice a few questions too, but they were completely beside the point. He asked her if she really thought girls could be police officers. Alice, and pretty much everyone else in the room, was offended by this question. Alice rolled up her sleeves like she was going to deck him, but before she could, Pete quickly said, "No further questions, Your Honor," and backed away.

The five-person jury went outside to discuss the case, but everyone knew the verdict was already decided. They returned in 30 seconds to declare Roberto guilty. And just as I had figured, the punishment was banishment from the town.

- - -

After the trial, I stepped over to the defense table. Roberto had his head in his hands.

"I'm sorry," was all I could say.

He stood up. He wouldn't look me in the eye.

"Hey," I said. "We're still friends, okay?"

He thought for a second, chuckled, then said, "Were we friends before?"

"We will be now."

I don't think he believed me, but he managed a smile anyway. "Yes. I'm sure we will." I think he assumed that I would never talk to him again.

■ ■ ■

I was hoping to look further into the crime, but I felt like I had to get on with some mayoral duties first. I had several appointments with Kidsboro citizens who I thought might be in the same predicament Scott was in—they were broke.

The first appointment was with a boy named James—a puny little kid who was probably the only person in town who would lose to Scott Sanchez in a fight. He didn't even have to duck his head as he came through the door into my office. He stood in front of me, a nervous look on his face.

"Hi, James," I said, trying to set him at ease.

"Hi."

"Sit down." He sat. "I'm having meetings with a bunch of people today just to get some idea of how everything is going. How you like living here, how you like your job, whatever. I'm always trying to get new ideas for ways to improve things." He seemed to loosen up a bit and I went on. "So how *is* everything going?"

"Good."

"You like being a citizen here?"

"Sure."

"How's your job going?" He looked at me as if I had just asked him why he didn't hand in last night's homework.

"Fine."

"What is it you do again?"

"I'm a doctor." This was the scariest thing I think I ever heard.

"Really? And have you . . . treated anyone?"

"No," he answered and I breathed a subtle sigh of relief. "You know, I only do first aid anyway. No surgery or anything."

"Of course."

"I figured since we're in the woods, somebody might get hurt. So I got this medical kit at the store. It's got bandages, antiseptic, stuff like that. And I took a CPR course, too. I'm pretty good at it."

"Congratulations."

"But nobody trusts me. A few people have gotten hurt, but they won't let me put anything on it, not even a Band-Aid. You remember when Max fell out of that tree and hurt his ankle?"

"Right."

"I went over and tried to help him, but he wouldn't let me. He called me a quack and limped home."

"So, you've never actually used any of your medical skills?"

"Just on the dummies at school."

"Then you've never made any money since you've been here."

"No."

"No side jobs?"

"No."

"So, you've never *bought* anything in town?"

"At first, with the money I had left over after I bought my house. But not for a couple of months."

"Hmm." I tapped my lips with my pencil. "Okay, James, that's all I need. If you ever have any suggestions for making the town better, just let me know, okay?"

"Sure." He turned around and left.

I wanted to think that James was not the norm. James was, after all, known for being a pretty lazy person. Surely the others would be vital participants in the town's economy.

I was wrong. All of the interviews were the same. I talked to 10 people, and eight of them had never made any money in two months. I had to do something about this.

■ ■ ■

I told the city council what was going on, and they agreed we needed to make sure that everyone had a legitimate job. I proposed that we establish a law where every person had to find some way to make at least 10 tokens a week. Those who failed to do so three weeks in a row would lose their houses for a month. I thought this was tough, but fair. I called it the Everybody Works program.

Making 10 tokens a week should be a cakewalk. All these people needed was incentive. I knew that every citizen of Kidsboro had enough creativity and intelligence to come up with ways to make money. But until now, there had never been anything there to push them to do so. This program would force them to think for themselves and become productive members of society.

After some tough discussion, the city council voted four to one that we enforce this law for the good of the people, so that what had happened to Sid wouldn't happen to others. Scott voted against it, undoubtedly because this meant he would have to find a way to make some money himself. Scott needed a kick in the pants more than anyone.

I left the meeting feeling as though I had accomplished something. The Everybody Works program seemed like a good long-term idea, even if it wouldn't win me any popularity contests at first. I was working for the good of the city, so popularity was not my top priority.

■ ■ ■

A couple of days later I headed to my clubhouse office. Valerie and a few others were gathered out front in what looked like a press conference. Jill was there, writing down everything Valerie said. The others were listening intently.

"I don't know about anyone else," Valerie said, "but I'm embarrassed for our mayor. What is this Everybody Works program? Now he's *forcing* us to work? Don't we work enough at school and at home without having to worry about the daily grind in Kidsboro? This guy is in love with rules. And another thing, he selected Roberto to be a member of our community, and not two days after he was voted in, Roberto committed the biggest crime ever in Kidsboro. I'm beginning to think the mayor doesn't really know what's best for the city anymore."

Valerie spotted me as I walked up. She smiled that evil smile of hers. "Well, hello, Mr. Mayor." Jill stopped writing and looked up at me as well. I guessed she was still mad at me because she smiled her own version of an evil smile. She obviously planned on printing Valerie's every word in the next issue.

Valerie continued the press conference. "Like I was saying, I'm beginning to lose my trust in a mayor who votes to put criminals on our streets. . . ."

I turned away, realizing that her vision to destroy me was only just beginning.

Suddenly, it dawned on me. Of course! Valerie wanted to disgrace me in front of the whole town. What better way to do it than to disgrace one of the people I had chosen to join the town! Valerie set Roberto up! I stepped into my office. The investigation was reopened!

4

SUPER SLEUTHS

OFFICER ALICE HAD ALREADY DECLARED that the investigation was over, so I couldn't ask her for help. I decided to go to the Scott Sanchez Detective Agency. I realized Scott had never actually done any detective work before, but another set of eyes and brains wouldn't hurt, no matter how untrained the eyes and brains were. Plus, I had promised Scott after we passed the new law that I would help him find work. Keeping my promises—what a great elected official I was!

When I walked through his doorway, Scott was sitting in a lawn chair reading a comic book. It never even occurred to him that I might be a client. "Hey," he said. "What's up?"

"I'm here to hire you," I said.

"You what?"

"I want to hire you."

"Pardon me for being dense, but I don't follow."

"Aren't you a detective?" I asked.

"Sure."

"I need a detective."

He dropped the comic book as if his hands had suddenly gone numb. He acted like he had no idea what to do at this point. Should he ask a bunch of questions? Should he get his magnifying glass?

"How much do you charge?" I asked as I pulled a few starbills out of my pocket. Scott seemed clueless.

"How much? Um . . . I don't know. I—I used to have this written down somewhere. Hold on." He began to rummage through a shelf. It was filled with comic books, cereal box tops, and a paddleball game. You know— important detective equipment. He stopped looking and faced me again. "I'll tell you what. Since you're a friend, I'll forget the rates and give you a discount."

"Sounds fair," I said, knowing he was winging it.

"How about half a starbill an hour?"

This rate was a little steep, but I thought I'd give him a break.

"It's a deal."

"Great. Okay." He nervously looked around, probably hoping by some miracle that there might be something lying around his office that would tell him where to start.

"Listen," I said as he continued to search. "I don't think Roberto broke into Marcy's house. I think we should reopen the investigation."

"Here it is," he said triumphantly. He held up a plaid hat, like the one Sherlock Holmes wore. He returned to his shelf. I hoped that he wasn't searching for a pipe.

"Great. Did you hear me?"

"Yes. Marcy's house. Who do you think did it?"

"I have my suspicions, but I'd rather not say right now."

"Okay," he said. I waited for him to suggest a course of action, but I was torn. I wanted to give him the chance to lead the investigation, but at the same time, he was charging me half a starbill an hour for this. I wanted to get started on it.

"Why don't we go to Roberto's old house?" I said finally.

"Good idea." He started out the door.

"Um," I said, "are you going to wear that hat?"

He stopped and thought about it. "You don't like the hat?"

"It's just . . . a little . . . goofy."

He seemed offended and, for the first time, showed me who was boss here. "I'm leading this investigation, thank you. Come on."

■ ■ ■

Roberto's house had been left just as it was when the burglary took place. He hadn't come back for any of his stuff. He probably didn't want to risk running into anyone and having to explain himself. There were magazine pictures scattered all around.

"Wait a minute," I said. "He told me he was putting up pictures when he heard someone call his name."

"That looks possible," Scott said. "Some of these pictures are tacked up, some aren't." This was obvious to both of us, but since I was paying him, I guess he felt he ought to observe something.

We continued looking around, but we were interrupted by a ruckus outside. Several people were running past the door. "What's going on?" I asked one of them.

"There's been another break-in!"

- - -

It was Nelson Swanson's house. The place was littered with blueprints, ideas, sketches, and a number of different gadgets that Nelson had invented. It looked as if someone had trashed it just for the sake of trashing it.

"Did anybody see anything?" I asked Alice.

"No," Alice replied, having a little trouble concentrating on my question because she was staring at Scott's hat. "Nelson said that nothing was stolen."

"Why would somebody go to all the trouble to break in, trash the whole place, and not steal anything?"

"I don't know." She raised her eyebrows as if she *did* know. "Revenge, maybe?"

"You think it was Roberto?" Scott asked.

She lowered her voice. Scott, who was listening up to this point, backed away as if he sensed he wasn't invited to the conversation. "This place was wired with an alarm—and whoever did this managed to do it without setting it off. This is the work of a professional. He knew what he was doing. And Roberto's father being who he is . . ."

"I don't want to hear any more," I interrupted. She was jumping to a wild conclusion, and she knew it.

"Where's Nelson?" I asked.

"Outside. I was just about to ask him some more questions," she said. We followed her out.

Nelson was sitting by a tree, looking troubled and holding a metal gadget. Eugene Meltsner was trying to console him.

"I don't believe your efforts were in vain, Nelson," Eugene was saying to him as we walked up. "The difficult work has already been accomplished, such as the intellectual labor that went into figuring out exactly how it could work."

"But I was so close," Nelson replied.

"As far as the rebuilding process is concerned, I believe it should go much faster now, since you know the basics."

"Hello, Eugene," Alice said.

"Greetings."

"You mind if I ask Nelson a few questions?"

"Not at all."

Alice looked at Nelson. "What's that you've got there?"

"A broken automatic door opener. All I had to do was adjust the sensitivity . . ."

"Is it worth anything?"

"Not much. Just the parts."

"You still haven't discovered anything missing?"

"No."

"Do you have any enemies?"

"No."

"Competitors?"

"No."

"Anyone you owe money to?"

"No."

"This alarm you installed. Did it malfunction often?"

"No. That's what's so strange. I can't understand why it didn't work."

"Neither can I," Eugene said. "It worked consistently in the trial runs."

A voice with a Southern accent came out of nowhere. "Kinda makes you wonder if *anybody's* safe, doesn't it?" I looked up and saw Max Darby. Max had moved to Odyssey from Georgia a few years ago, and hadn't even begun to lose his accent.

Max always seemed to be up to something. He wanted you to think he was your best friend—in fact, everybody's best friend—but his real best friend was himself. "I'm sorry," he said. "Am I interrupting something?"

"I was done anyway," Alice said, moving her investigation back to Nelson's house.

"You know what you need, friend?" Max said. "You need something that'll keep you high and dry when the rest of the world is floatin' down the river."

"What are you talking about?" Nelson asked. I wished he hadn't asked.

"I'm talkin' peace of mind," Max continued, "restful nights. I'm talkin' about preparin' for the future."

"Okay, sure, but . . . what *specifically* are you talking about?"

"Insurance. The one thing that'll help you out if this ever happens again."

"Max," I interrupted, "this isn't the time."

"Oh, I disagree. I think this is the perfect time."

Nelson said, "Go on."

Max knelt down next to Nelson and put his hand on his shoulder. He had him. "You'll never have to go through this again if you have Darby Insurance. Buy one of my policies at my limited-time, special-price offer, and if tragedy ever strikes again, I'll pay you enough money to fix all the damages."

By the time Max was through with him, Nelson had bought a home-owner's policy. The way it worked was that Nelson would pay Max a star-bill every month, and if something ever happened to his house or furnishings again, Max would pay to replace everything. Leave it to Max to make money off a tragedy.

But, to be honest, insurance wasn't such a bad idea for Kidsboro. In fact, Marcy, with her trashed house, probably wished she'd had insurance as well. Apparently, a lot of people saw the benefits of it. Max sold five policies right there at the scene of the crime. He sold one to Scott, and he told him his hat would be insured as well. Scott was already spending the money he was going to make off of me. I didn't buy one simply on principle. I wasn't about to give my money to Max.

While Max introduced Scott to the details of his new policy, I sat under a tree and thought about the situation. The break-in just didn't make sense. If Valerie was responsible for the first break-in, why would she do this one as well? She would risk getting caught, and she had already made her point. Everyone in town thought Roberto was a crook, and that I was wrong for selecting him. She had already convinced everyone that I had poor judgment. So why would she do it again?

After the crowd had thinned around Nelson's house, Scott and I went back in to look around. Alice was off questioning other possible witnesses or suspects, and I thought it would be the perfect opportunity to do some investigating myself.

Eugene was standing in the middle of the mess, scratching his chin. The place was trashed in an unusual way, but it was hard to put my finger on what was so strange about it. I asked Scott what he thought, and, of course, he had detected nothing.

"This is very odd," Eugene began. "The alarm is still set. Not only did it not go off, I don't believe it was ever even tripped."

"But how could somebody get in here without tripping the alarm? The wires are all over the floor, on the door, around the window . . ."

"So where did they break in?" Scott joined in, probably feeling either awkward or guilty that he hadn't discovered anything yet.

Eugene scanned the floor and the walls, then his eyes stopped at the ceiling. We all looked up. He raised his arm and pushed up on the wood. It lifted easily.

"They broke in through the roof!" I exclaimed.

"Ingenious," Eugene said.

Scott looked around again. "So, they broke in through the roof, knocked over the chair, broke a few gadgets, laid these books down on the table, threw a couple of pieces of paper around . . ."

"Wait a minute!" I shouted. "That's it!"

Scott seemed pleased that his summary had helped jar something in my brain. "What?"

"These books. Look at 'em. They're laid down on the table like somebody was getting ready to study. If someone was coming in just to make a mess, wouldn't they be thrown everywhere, on the floor, laying open? And look at this chair. It looks like it was carefully laid down on the dirt."

"Precisely!" Eugene said. "The person who vandalized this clubhouse was making extreme efforts not to trip the alarm."

"Get Nelson!" I said.

Scott left to earn some of his money and came back with Nelson.

"Nelson, were these books already lying on the desk like this?" I asked.

"No, I always put them up on the shelf. I assume the burglar did that."

"Tell me about your alarm system," I said, playing a hunch.

"Well . . . I set up wires around the room, on the walls . . ."

"Around the circumference of the window as well," Eugene added.

"And if someone bumps it, it releases a high-pitched noise. Pretty much everybody in town would be able to hear it."

"Is there any way somebody could've gotten in here and not tripped the alarm?"

"No. The alarm must have malfunctioned . . . or maybe I forgot to turn it on, I don't know."

"Impossible," Eugene said.

"What if the burglar came in through the roof?" I asked.

"Well, sure, I didn't have any wires on the ceiling, but if somebody came in here and was throwing books and stuff around, there's no way they wouldn't hit an alarm somewhere."

"But that's just it," I said. "These books are *not* thrown around. Look at this chair. It's laid down so nicely, not touching any walls, not tripping any alarms."

Nelson was beginning to see where I was going with this. Scott still didn't have a clue. "You're right," Nelson said. "So whoever broke in must've known where the alarms were set."

"Exactly," I said. "Did anyone besides you know where you put the alarms?"

"Well," Nelson began thinking. "I've had people in my house before. I suppose someone could've noticed where the wires were."

"Who?"

"Well . . . you."

Scott suddenly woke up. "You're accusing Ryan?!"

"No. I'm just trying to think who's been in here. My sister . . ." This one caused my eyebrow to raise a little.

"Didn't someone assist you with the installation?" Eugene asked.

"Oh, yeah, Nick did that."

Nick's father worked in a tool shop, and Nick knew how to build club-houses and just about anything else.

"Nick?" I asked. "How exactly did he help you?"

"He stapled the wiring to the walls." Nelson's eyes lit up as if the mystery was solved. "He knows the whole system—where all the wires are placed, how much pressure is needed to set off the alarm—he knows everything!"

I looked at Scott. He said in perfect TV detective fashion, "I think we need to take a little trip to Nick's house."

There was a knock at the door. It was Alice.

"Nelson, I need to take an official statement . . ." she stopped suddenly when it dawned on her why Scott and I might be in the room. "What are you guys doing here?"

"We're just, um . . ." I began, not sure if I should tell her. "We're talking to Nelson."

"About what?"

"Nothing," Scott said quickly, making it obvious that we were, indeed, talking about something. Scott's face paled.

Alice looked at Scott. "Does wearing that hat mean you're doing detective work?"

"Well, I . . ."

She looked at me. "This is *my* investigation, Mr. Mayor."

"Look, Alice . . . I just have this hunch . . ."

"And you think your hunch is better than mine?" Her neck muscles tightened. Scott started to sway as if he were going to faint. "You think you can do this better than me?"

"I'm just . . ." I began. "No."

"Didn't think so. Now go do some mayoral work and let me do my job."

Scott was out of the house in about three milliseconds. I followed him.

■ ■ ■

On the way to Nick's house, Valerie stopped us. "Mr. Mayor, how lovely to see you," she said. Scott had taken enough ribbing about the hat and had taken it off. "And you have your little elf with you too. How nice."

"We're kind of in a hurry, Valerie. Did you want something?"

"I just wanted to invite you to my press conference. I'm holding it in the meeting hall in about 10 minutes."

"You mean you have something *else* to say to the newspaper?"

"Oh, something very important," she said with that evil smile.

"What is it?"

"I'm running for mayor."

5

THE TRUTH REVEALED

I WAS VERY PROUD OF myself for not letting my mouth quiver in front of Valerie when she said she was running for mayor. I bit my lip until it hurt. But as soon as she left, I felt my face turn cold. Valerie was the most popular person at Odyssey Middle School. I wasn't even in the top 50.

Desperate, I went to Whit's End to see if we had put anything in the city charter about regular elections and I had just forgotten about it. I knew it was a slim chance, since we had only written the charter less than three months before, but I figured my only hope was that a spontaneous, midterm election was unconstitutional.

Mr. Whittaker scanned through the pages of the city charter and shook his head. "Nope. Nothing," he said.

"But we can write something in now," I said.

"I agree that there needs to be a section about a mayor's term, but you can't write it in now just because it serves you well."

"So what can I do?"

"You have to beat her, Ryan," he said. "Then, as your first act as the newly reelected mayor, you can add a clause in the city charter about regular elections."

If the election were held that day, I thought I had a chance. Yes, Valerie was popular, but that didn't necessarily make her a good political leader, and I hoped people knew that. Not to brag, but people in the town trusted me. Besides, I was the one who had given them their start. And, with the exception of the serial burglar and Sid's Bakery closing, everything had run pretty smoothly from the beginning.

However . . . Valerie wasn't done campaigning, and something told me she was saving her best for last. She had told me she was scheduling a debate. That would be a challenge for me. She had a way with words. I knew she could manipulate people one-on-one, so I assumed she could do the same with a crowd.

One thing that would really help me win the election would be to solve this burglary case and clear Roberto's name. Then I couldn't be accused of letting criminals into the town. Linking Valerie to the break-ins would be a bonus.

I needed to focus my attention on the one person who could get me out of this jam—Nick.

■ ■ ■

Nick was outside in his T-shirt and overalls, busily putting on an addition to his clubhouse when Scott and I walked up. Most people had built small houses to begin with, but the ones who were making money were starting to add on. They put on extra rooms, built extra tables, added shelves, and so on. Max Darby, of course, had the biggest house in Kidsboro. He had four rooms, including a rec room that actually had a working air hockey table. Nelson had helped him create it. They poked holes in a sheet of heavily waxed wood and put a fan underneath it so the air would come out. It worked okay, but it had taken a while to get the bugs worked out. One time the puck caught too much wind and flew off the table, smacking Joey, the town minister, in the forehead. There was a circular mark on his forehead for about a week.

Nick had knocked out part of a wall and was building a new room when we walked up. "How's it going, Nick?" I asked.

"Pretty good."

"The place is looking great," I said. And it was. Nick was a great builder. I decided not to waste any time. "Did you hear there was another break-in?"

"Yeah, I heard something," he said.

"Nelson's house."

"That's too bad," he said, not looking up from the board he was hammering.

"Burglar got right past his alarm. Can you believe that?"

"Pretty wild."

"It almost seemed like the burglar knew exactly where the alarm was set."

"Really?" he said, making a great effort not to look at me.

"Nelson said that you helped him install his alarm system."

He paused before he answered. "I don't know what you're talking about." Ah! So he denied it. Now we were getting somewhere.

"So you didn't help him with it?"

"No."

"Have you ever seen Nelson's system?"

"No."

"Have you ever been in Nelson's house?"

"No."

"Did you ever talk to Nelson at all about his alarm system?"

"No. Look, I don't care anything about Nelson. I've got nothing to do with any of this. I've been working on my house all day." Annoyed, he sent a nail all the way in with one hit.

"But—"

"Just get outta here," he interrupted. "I'm not answering any more questions."

I was satisfied with this meeting. I had obviously rattled him, and this made me pretty certain he was guilty. I was confident I could get proof somewhere along the line. I started to back away.

"Pardon me for being born, Nick, but . . . I don't believe you," Scott said suddenly. Scott hadn't uttered a word during the whole interrogation, so I was shocked that he even spoke, much less said something aggressive. Scott continued, stammering nervously, "Nelson said that you . . . he said you helped him with his alarm. So, you're saying he's lying?"

"Yeah. He's lying."

"You didn't?"

"What?"

"Help him?"

"No."

"Well . . . you see, I don't understand something. P-Pardon me for intruding, but . . ." Scott began, walking over to a roll of electrical wire that was lying on a stump, "we found this same type of wire in Nelson's house."

"You can get that wire anywhere. He probably just bought it in a store." This was a perfectly good answer, but it looked as if Nick was beginning to come unglued. For the first time, Nick stopped hammering and started paying attention to Scott. Scott must have sensed he was getting to him, because confidence entered his eyes.

"You know, you should've seen how well this alarm was placed in a hole in the wall. It looked like a professional did it. With professional tools," Scott said, holding up a staple gun. "Kind of . . . well, kind of like this one." I wanted to applaud.

Nick brushed a drop of sweat from his forehead. "Lots of people have staple guns."

"Wow, look at this," Scott said, holding up a screw. "We found these very same screws in Nelson's house."

"Ha! That's a lie!" Nick shouted. "His walls are too thick for that screw."

"But I thought you said you've never been in Nelson's house."

Bravo! Scott looked at Nick, who was breathing hard and appeared to be thinking harder.

"Well, maybe I did go in there once. I don't remember."

"So, you're saying you remember what type of wood he has for his walls, but you don't remember if you actually stepped foot in his house?"

"Okay, I've been in his house a couple of times. He's invited me in."

"So, you're friends?"

"Yeah, sure."

"But I thought you said a couple of minutes ago that you didn't care anything about Nelson."

My chin had dropped to the ground about two minutes before, but now the rest of my body was about to join it. Scott was amazing. Maybe endless hours of watching tough-guy detective shows had finally paid off for him. Scott grilled him for a while longer until Nick finally got sick of getting caught in lies and confessed to breaking into Nelson's and Marcy's houses. He also confessed to setting up Roberto. I told him that he would probably be kicked out of town for this. He acted like he didn't care.

Scott and I walked away. I felt so proud of him. Scott seemed unaware that he had just done something incredible. He casually told me that he needed to go home for dinner. But as he walked away, I spotted him putting his hat back on.

■ ■ ■

Something still bothered me, though. I couldn't understand why Nick would do it. Scott had tried to ask him about this too, but by that time Nick had had enough and wasn't about to answer any more questions. What possible reason could he have for breaking into two houses and not taking anything?

This, of course, led me back to Valerie. Did she hire him? I could understand the first break-in. She was trying to frame Roberto to make me look bad so that she could take over as mayor. But the second house made absolutely no sense. She *had* to have done it, though. Who else would have anything to gain by breaking into two houses?

Suddenly, like a message from above, I got my answer. As I was walking back to my office, I noticed Max Darby surrounded by a crowd of people. He was selling insurance. I was pretty sure this didn't happen in real life—an insurance salesman having to fight people off.

Of course! Max was getting rich because people were scared of being robbed or vandalized! *Max* had something to gain! Max must have paid Nick to break into the houses! This would explain how Nick got the money and the wood to build a huge addition to his house. That was it! It was an insurance scam!

After the crowd around Max dwindled, I approached him. "Selling a lot of policies?"

"Fourteen total," he said. "Seems to be the hot item. Change your mind about it?"

"No thanks. I'm sure glad someone is benefiting from this rash of crime."

"Oh, I'd never want to benefit from something like that."

"I'm sure you wouldn't," I said, knowing full well he would love to benefit from something like that. "I just found out who did it."

"Well, partner, I think you're a little late. Everybody else in town has known for days. It was that Roberto kid you brought in."

"No, it wasn't." I paused for effect here. I wanted to be able to read guilt in his eyes, so I watched closely as I laid the bomb on him. "Nick did it."

He didn't flinch, blink, or blush. "Really? Never woulda suspected him. Good guy, that Nick. Quiet, shy type. That's always a good type of person to sell insurance to."

I could suddenly picture Scott and his merciless grilling of Nick, and I decided to go in for the kill. "You paid him to do it."

Max smiled and chuckled a little, as if the thought had never occurred to him. I expected him to deny it, but instead he offered a much more interesting idea. "Prove it," he said.

He had me there. I could accuse him all I wanted to, but unless Nick admitted Max's involvement to me point-blank in front of witnesses, I had no case.

Max took another unexpected turn. "Now, I know you didn't mean that. You're just fishin', I know. But let's pretend for a second that I *did* commit this tragic crime. What exactly can you do about it? Kick me out of town? I know how politics work, and banishing your most valuable citizen doesn't look too good come election time."

"You think you're our most valuable citizen?"

"Where else you gonna get wood, buddy? You banish me, and you've got no future. You can't build anything. And it's not like you paid for this wood with real money. It's pretend. Which means I can take it back. I can rip apart these houses faster than they went up. And you know, it's real cute to see you acting like this is some kind of great democracy you're runnin' here, but when it comes down to it, this town is just a bunch of clubhouses in the woods. You lose me, you got nothing." He smiled again and turned away. I watched him walk quickly over to a clubhouse and knock on the door. He had insurance to sell.

6

FRIENDS AND FOES

I WENT BACK TO NICK'S house. He was packing up his things, figuring that he was going to be kicked out of town. We talked for a while, but he would never admit to being hired by anyone. He never denied it either. He had learned his lesson from our last interview and wouldn't answer any of my questions with anything more than a "yes" or "no." I told him I would ask the council not to banish him if he would tell me who had hired him, but he wouldn't budge. He said he wasn't a rat. This was, of course, evidence to me that there was someone he could be ratting *on*.

But I still had no real proof.

■ ■ ■

We held a city council meeting after school the next day. Jill, Nelson, Alice, and Scott filed in. Everyone knew why we were there—to discuss Nick's punishment. A trial wasn't necessary since he had confessed in front of two of us. After a short discussion, we voted unanimously that Nick had to be banished and Roberto would be cleared of all charges. Alice felt quite embarrassed by the whole thing, since this meant she had put an innocent man in jail. But she didn't protest. She'd made a mistake and was ready to move on. I think she was still mad at me, though.

Before everyone got to their feet after the meeting, I made an announcement. I wanted to vote on the punishment of Max Darby.

"What?" Jill asked, speaking for the whole group.

I cleared my throat to show them I was serious, then said, "I have reason to believe Max hired Nick to break into the houses so that he could sell insurance policies."

They stared at me in disbelief. Finally, Jill was able to speak. "Do you have proof?"

"Well . . . no. But I'm pretty sure about it."

"Did he confess?"

"No."

"Well, we can't banish him just because you *think* he did it."

I was losing them. "I'm asking you to trust me."

Alice shook her head as if I were crazy. "Sorry, Ryan. No can do. Not without a trial."

That's what I wanted them to say. "What if I get him to trial? Let me tell you why I think he's guilty, and then you tell me if you think he'll lose in court."

"Wait a minute, wait a minute," Jill interrupted. "I don't wanna hear this."

"Why not?"

"I don't want you bringing him to trial. What if he's found guilty?"

I was confused by the question. "Well . . . then justice would be served."

"Would we banish him?"

"Sure, I guess."

"Then where would we get our wood?" she said. Alice and Nelson nodded in agreement.

My heart sank. I never expected anyone on my city council to place more value in wood than in justice.

"Wood?" I asked weakly.

Jill continued, "I mean, I'm for justice being served and all that, but if we banish Max, we're in deep trouble. We can't build anything. We can't add to the population. We have to think about the future of the town."

"The future of the town?" I asked, my voice raising. "What kind of future are we going to have if people like Max know they can get away with stuff like this? What happened to our laws? Who cares about the quality of our houses? What about the quality of our people?" This was a great line, and if I hadn't been trying to make a point, I would've written it down and saved it for the debate.

Jill thought for a minute, but then shook her head. "Maybe we should let this one pass. Sorry, but like it or not, we *need* Max."

"She's right," Alice said. "I hate crime, but we gotta have wood."

Nelson nodded along with her. Scott had been completely uncommitted from the moment I started talking. My mouth hung open in shock. I had nothing else to say. I turned around and left, defeated.

— — —

I talked to Roberto the next day at school and told him he was welcome to come back to town. He was hesitant, saying that he didn't feel comfortable coming back right now. I could tell it still hurt him that people had jumped to the conclusion that he was a criminal. I understood and said that I'd be back to ask him again soon.

The election was to be held on the first day of May, and I felt that the past week had been a definite victory for me. I'd been right about Roberto. My approval rating was probably up, and Valerie had lost her whole "He's letting criminals into town" argument. So even though I was disappointed in my city council, I had something to keep my head up about.

I headed over to Jill's office to see how she was planning to cover the Nick/Roberto story in the newspaper. As I approached the newspaper office, I heard two angry voices coming from inside. I rushed in to see what was going on. It was Jill and Marcy. Marcy had one hand on her hip, and with the other she was shaking a pencil in Jill's face.

"You just think you're Miss Journalism, don't you?" Marcy said, not seeing me yet.

"I'm not running your story," Jill said. "That doesn't mean I won't run other stories."

"It's a perfectly good story."

"There are finally some things going on in this town. We don't need fluff. Nobody cares about your canary." Jill glanced over at me. "Ryan, do you care about Marcy's canary?"

I'd seen Marcy's canary. It was cute. Would I throw myself in front of a bus for Marcy's canary? No. But did I *care* about it?

"Are you gonna answer the question, Ryan?"

"Oh . . . uh . . . I don't know. Why?"

"Well, you see, Marcy's my new assistant. I'm paying her 10 tokens a week so she can keep her house."

Hey! The Everybody Works program in motion! I thought.

"So I told her to write a story," Jill continued. "Well, she came back with a story that I don't think works very well for our newspaper."

"But it's great!" Marcy said. "It could become a regular column: 'Citizens and Their Pets.' I think Nelson and Valerie have a Siamese cat."

"Great. We'll make it a double issue," Jill said sarcastically.

"This is not *The New York Times*. We're kids."

"It's lame, Marcy."

"It's not. But even if it was, so what? At least it fills up space."

"Let me explain something to you." Jill squared her shoulders as if she was about to teach her pupil something. "There are only two ways that this newspaper makes money—people subscribe to it, and people advertise in it. Okay, right now I have 11 subscribers and one advertiser—Max and his scary insurance ads. Now if any of those people decide that your canary story is too lame for them to keep spending money on this newspaper, I'm doomed. Do you understand?"

Marcy's shoulders fell. "Fine. I'm leaving. Maybe somebody'll murder me on the way home and you can have your great story." Marcy left.

Jill turned away from me and crumpled up the piece of paper in her hand. "Maybe we should rethink this Everybody Works thing. I didn't know it would cause this," she said.

"You don't think she'll work out eventually?" I asked.

"She's a really good friend . . . but she doesn't have a clue about the newspaper business."

"Then why'd you hire her?"

"I had to. She was desperate. She didn't want to lose her house, so she came to me. I couldn't turn her down. She's my friend." She sighed, but then her eyes brightened. "I want to have another city council vote on the Everybody Works law."

"We can't back out on it yet. Just give it a little time. It'll work." Little did I know that the problems between Marcy and Jill were only the tip of the iceberg.

■ ■ ■

"Everybody Works Doesn't Work," part two, occurred the next day when I ran into Pete and Nelson. Nelson was walking quickly, trying to get away from him, but Pete kept up the pace, jumping in front of Nelson to force him to make eye contact.

"But . . . how do you *feel* about the break-in?" Pete asked.

"I don't feel anything," Nelson said impatiently. "It just happened. They already caught the guy. It's over."

"But don't you feel emotional distress or anything?"

"No. Now go away." Nelson insisted. I was terribly confused by this conversation.

"What about future stress? Do you think you'll have to go into therapy because you'll never feel safe in your own home again?"

"Listen, I'm working on a spanking machine, and I won't hesitate to make you my first guinea pig."

"What's going on?" I asked.

"He's trying to get me to sue somebody. But there's nobody to sue," Nelson explained.

Pete was unmoved by my presence. "Okay, let's forget the break-in. What about your life? Has anybody discriminated against you recently? Maybe someone defamed your character?"

"I'm in middle school. Everyone defames my character."

Pete's eyes lit up. "Okay, okay. Now we're getting somewhere."

"Forget it, Pete."

I stepped in. "Look . . . there's no place for this. We can't have lawsuits against each other."

"Can I sue the government?" Pete asked.

"No."

"Well, what else am I supposed to do? I've never made any money by being a lawyer. Now with this wonderful new law you've passed, I have to find a way to make some money or I lose my house."

"There are better ways than this."

"I'm a lawyer, Ryan. I love the law." I could tell he got that line from a TV show, as well as the next one. "If I do anything else, it's like cheating on my girlfriend."

I rolled my eyes. Pete remained undaunted and looked at Nelson. "Now are you gonna listen to me or not?"

"No."

"You're missing out on almost certain riches, my man." Pete shook his head sympathetically, and then took off to badger more potential clients. I looked sheepishly at Nelson.

"We should've seen this coming," Nelson said. "And you know what? Somebody's gonna end up suing. And if it works . . . everybody's gonna want a piece of the action. It'll be a litigation free-for-all."

Something told me Nelson was right.

7

EVERYBODY WORKS

I SAT IN MY OFFICE, banging a pencil against my card-table desk. History is filled with leaders who had to make tough decisions under pressure. I'm sure plenty of people asked George Washington, "Why are we crossing the Delaware? It's a dumb idea to cross the Delaware. Let's just go around the Delaware."

I picked up a pen and began to drum it against the desk as well. I knew that nobody would blame me if I decided to change my mind about the law. If I took the idea back to the city council, they'd choose to forget the Everybody Works program had ever happened. The town wasn't too thrilled with it—I knew that. But I also believed it would work over time. In a few months, when the economy had picked up, people would be telling me what a brilliant idea it was. The thought passed through my brain that I could take back the new law, get reelected, then pass it again. But I knew that wouldn't be right. Maybe I could get reelected just on the basis of my integrity—the fact that I wouldn't take back the law, even if it meant possibly losing the election. George Washington stuck to his guns. So would I. Maybe people would reelect me because of that.

Fat chance.

Jill burst in without knocking. I jumped when she slapped a piece of paper down on the desk in front of me.

"I'm being sued!"

"What?"

"Yesterday's paper had an interview with Corey Hawkins." Corey was the neighborhood garbage collector. "You know how Corey wants to start having recycling bins in town?"

"Right."

"So I let Marcy do the interview. And she writes in the article that after he picks up our garbage, he uses some of it to decorate his room."

"What?"

"Exactly what I said. I asked her, 'Are you sure he told you that he decorates his room with garbage?' I asked her that three times. She swore up and down that's what he said. So I did what you told me to do—I figured I would give her a shot. I ran the story. Well . . . as it turns out, Corey doesn't decorate his room with garbage. He simply *knows* someone who decorates his room with things that other people would *consider* garbage."

"That's a pretty bad misquote."

"Apparently Corey's the laughingstock of the town now. He told me that one kid gave him a moldy donut and a nail and asked him if he wanted to hang it up on his wall."

"So he's suing for libel."

"And he's got a case."

"For how much?"

"Thirty starbills. I don't have it."

"I can't believe this."

"Do I have the authority to call a city council meeting?" she asked without hesitation. She had obviously already given this some thought.

"I'll talk to Corey. I'll ask him not to sue."

"That's not the point. This program isn't working. It's making people too desperate for money."

I leaned back in my chair. She had a point. "I'll look into it." She gave me a long, hard stare, nodded her head, and left without another word.

■ ■ ■

It was time for some more appointments. When in doubt, make an appointment. I needed to find out if this program was working at all. So I spoke to all the people who had been "forced" to get jobs, 10 in all, and they agreed to meet with me in my office to discuss their progress. It had been two weeks since I had set up the Everybody Works program, so if anyone was having trouble finding work, this was his or her last week to come up with something.

I thought I'd begin with the one person who I knew would have the biggest problem with the new law—James the doctor. It's rumored that one summer he faked sunstroke to get out of mowing the lawn. He'd looked it up in some medical journal and acted out the exact symptoms. Then after his father finished the lawn, he faked a miraculous recovery. He was actually admired for how good he was at being lazy. If anyone was going to fail at finding work, it was James. That is, unless he was pushing people down cliffs so he could give them medical attention and charge them afterward. The way things were going, that sort of thing didn't appear to be beyond the people of this town.

James came in with a much different look on his face than when he had come in before. He actually seemed excited to talk to me. Of course, the cliff theory immediately came to mind.

"So, James, how are you doing?"

"Great. Thanks."

"Are you finding any work?"

"Sure."

I swallowed a lump in my throat. "What kind?"

"I sold some lemonade and juice and stuff. See?" He reached into his back pocket and pulled out two starbills. My mouth fell open. "Remember how it was so hot the other day? I guess people were pretty thirsty, huh?"

"You made two starbills selling drinks?"

"And change. Sold about 40 cups."

I smiled. "You're kidding me. That's great!"

"I just thought about what you said about being a productive member of society and participating in the economy. So I figured I should do this."

"I'm impressed. I guess you're gonna keep this lemonade thing going, huh?"

"Definitely. Especially this summer."

"Well . . . I'm sorry for ever doubting you. You really came through. I was beginning to think this new program wasn't working for anybody, but . . . at least it worked for you."

"Yeah," he said.

"Well, I'll tell you what. Go on and keep doing what you're doing. In a few weeks, I'll check on you to see if you're still making money. Okay?"

"Sounds good."

James left, and I held my chin up high. I felt like a father whose son had just hit the home run that won the game. I imagined turning to the other parents in the stands, saying, "I taught him that swing."

■ ■ ■

Much to my delight, most of the interviews went just as well. Out of the 10 people I talked with, only three were displeased with the new law. Five had gone out and gotten new jobs or figured out new ways to make money. A couple of them, like James, had rarely lifted a finger in their lives. But I guess with the right incentives, people can produce. I began practicing the speech

I would give before the U.S. Congress in 25 years: "Ladies and Gentle-men, I have two words for you—Everybody Works . . ." (Applause.) "Thank you . . ." (More applause.) "Thank you . . ." (Standing ovation.) "Thank you . . ."

■ ■ ■

The first thing I did after the interviews was tell Scott, and he immediately took the wind out of my sails.

"James sold lemonade?" he asked.

"That's what he said."

"Do you believe him?"

"He had the money right there."

"But do you know for sure that's how he got it?"

"I have no proof, no. You don't think he sold lemonade?"

He picked up a pipe from the table. It wasn't a real pipe, it was a bub-ble pipe, but he claimed it helped him think. "That doesn't sound like James."

"I know it doesn't. That's what's so great."

"And the others. How did they get their money?"

"Different ways." I looked at him and grabbed the pipe out of his mouth. "Oh, come on. You think they're all lying?"

"Pardon me for raining on your victory parade, but it sounds suspi-cious," he said as he grabbed the pipe back. "I think I should investigate." I guess he figured he was on a roll, detective-wise.

"I'm not paying you."

"I know that. I'll do this one for you on the house."

I rolled my eyes. He had never liked the new law. I assumed this was his way of trying to prove it didn't work. He picked up his magnifying glass and hat.

And as he opened the door, someone started screaming.

8

BAD JUSTICE

THE SCREAMING WAS COMING FROM Jill's house, which was next to Scott's. Jill was pointing her finger in Marcy's face, and Marcy wasn't backing away. They were both yelling at the same time, listening to nothing but themselves. Others were gathering around to watch the fight, but Marcy and Jill didn't see them. All they were seeing was red.

"I never should've hired you!" Jill shouted.

"I wish I'd never asked you to!" Marcy replied.

"Fine. Then go ask Corey for a job. Start picking through our trash cans. I hear he needs a decorator for his kitchen!"

"If I'd known what a jerk you'd be for a boss, I would've done that to begin with."

"*I'm* a jerk? You've been my employee for three weeks and you may have just bankrupted us!"

"You take this dumb newspaper too seriously."

"Well, thanks to you, that might not be a problem anymore."

"I hope it does go bankrupt. At least you'll be human again."

This was too much for me to stand back and watch. I felt responsible for some of this, and the verbal zingers were getting way too personal. I stepped in. "Hey, hey. Wait a minute."

"Go away," Jill said to me.

"I'm quitting this town," Marcy said.

"Marcy—" I said.

"No, wait. I'm not quitting yet. I'm gonna stick around long enough to vote you out of office, then I'll quit." She stomped away.

Jill turned away from me and headed back into her house. I debated going in the other direction and letting her cool off, but I wanted to defend myself now. I opened the door. She was sitting at a table with her head resting on a stack of papers—the issue in which Corey was misquoted.

"Jill . . ." I whispered.

"*You're* the cause of all of this!" she shouted without looking up.

"You two will work this out."

"She was a good friend, Ryan. I slept over at her house when we were in *kindergarten*! I've *never* fought with her like that."

"That's why you'll be okay."

"Please! Let me call a city council meeting!"

"It's not the law, Jill. The program is working. We just need to work out a few of the kinks."

"You're putting the town before friendships."

"I'm not, I—"

Her head popped up as if it were attached to a spring. "Then how come I just lost one of my best friends?" She brushed her hair away from her face. Her eyes watered like she might cry, and she stared at me, waiting for an answer to this unanswerable question. She breathed in sharply. "There are things that go on outside these woods, Ryan," she said.

"I know," I replied.

"Then maybe you should stop being so much of a mayor and just be a kid." Jill laid her head back down on the stack of papers.

"I'm sorry." I didn't know what else to say, so I turned and left.

The crowd that had gathered to see the cat fight between Marcy and Jill had not yet dispersed. They all looked at me, searching for some look on my face that would tell them what had happened. Scott ran up to me.

"What's going on?" he asked.

"Nothing," I said.

"Well, hey," he began, excited. "Guess what I just saw." I looked at him as if to say, "I'm not guessing."

"I saw James going into Max's house." I failed to catch his point, and he noticed. "Come on! James and Max? They're not friends. They're not even *close.*"

"Scott, would you please get to whatever point you're trying to make."

"I think Max is up to something."

"So, what's new?"

"No, I mean, with all these people suddenly making money, like James. I think Max is responsible."

"You think he's hiring them for something?"

"I don't know. But it seems possible, doesn't it?" I hated to admit it, but this did sound like something both James and Max would do. "Let's go investigate," Scott said, leading the way.

■ ■ ■

I think Scott sensed that if he was going to uncover something here, he was going to have to do it primarily on his own. I did not want to find anything. I wanted James to be telling the truth.

We sneaked toward Max's house and watched from behind a tree. James was nowhere in sight. We tiptoed a little closer, making more noise than we would have if we had just walked, but that wasn't important. Scott was on the prowl. We were behind the tree closest to Max's house, and we could hear voices from inside.

"Is that James?" I whispered.

"I can't tell," Scott said. The leaves crunched under Scott's feet as he inched closer. Suddenly, the door swung open. He scurried back to the tree.

James came out of the house. "It's due Monday," Max said to him from inside. James had a thick book in his left hand.

"Okay," James replied like a servant to his king. James closed the door behind him.

"Let's get him," I whispered.

"Wait," Scott said. "Let's just follow him for a minute."

James went through the downtown area and stopped at one of the two picnic tables that made up our park. He sat down and opened the book. He pulled a pencil out of his pocket and began to work.

Scott was ready. "Okay, let's go." We pretended we were on our way to the other side of town and just happened to see our good friend James there.

"James!" Scott said with a smile pasted on his face.

"Hi."

"What are you doing?" Scott asked as he sat down across from him at the picnic table. I slid in next to Scott.

"Just a little homework."

"Oh." Scott lifted up the corner of the thick book to read the title. "Algebra. Tough stuff. Especially for a sixth grader."

James pulled the book toward him and suddenly became very interested in his homework.

"You know, Ryan, I don't know any *sixth* graders in algebra. That's a seventh grade class, isn't it?"

"I think so," I said, knowing exactly what Scott was up to and playing along.

"I'm in an advanced-placement class," James said, stuttering over every word. This was actually not that far from believable. James was definitely smart enough to be in an advanced-placement class. The problem with him was that he would be too lazy to do all the work required. I didn't believe him, and neither did Scott.

"Oh, I didn't know that. But I guess I could've just asked the algebra teachers. I have them for math. In fact, maybe I'll ask them at school tomorrow."

"Well . . ." James was thinking fast. "I'm not actually in the class. They didn't want me to be in a seventh grade class, you know, because I'm a sixth grader, but I'm doing the work at home. I have a tutor." This was very good. James seemed flustered as he closed his book. "I gotta go," he told us.

"But you just got here," Scott said.

"I know, but I just remembered something I have to do." James spun out of his seat and practically ran away from us, stumbling over a tree root as he went.

"So, what do you think?" Scott said.

I hated to admit this. "I think Max is paying him to do his homework."

"Pretty obvious."

"But that doesn't mean Max is paying *everybody*. Max doesn't have that much homework—and he's smarter than most of those kids. There's no way he'd *let* them do his homework."

"That's what investigations are for," Scott said, scratching his chin and raising his eyebrows.

At least *someone* was enjoying his job.

■ ■ ■

I felt obligated to go to Jill's trial, though I didn't really want to witness it. Jill didn't have much of a chance, in my opinion. Pete was the opposing lawyer, and I hoped that he would panic again like he had before. But he wasn't up against Valerie this time; Jill was defending herself. I had no idea what to expect from Pete.

Corey was suing for 30 starbills, which was a lot. Nobody in Kidsboro had 30 starbills lying around, except maybe Max, who probably had 30 starbills under his sofa cushion at home. Rumor had it that if Pete won the case, he'd get a third of the winnings. Ten starbills would be enough for him to live off of for a pretty long time.

And Jill was right when she said that Marcy may have bankrupted her. Jill didn't have 30 starbills to pay. Obviously, she'd used her father's computer and paper to create the newspaper, so she didn't actually have to cease production. But this would mean that all future profits she made at the newspaper would go to Corey for a long, long time. Jill wouldn't have anything for general expenses. She would be no better off than James the quack doctor. Plus, the newspaper was a business, and businesses were required to pay special business taxes. She would end up owing the city a lot of taxes after a while.

The jury would not be thinking about that, though. They would probably be thinking about doing something cool. Like nailing the press.

Court was called into session, and Pete made his opening statement. He basically just stated the facts—that the *Kidsboro Chronicle* had been irresponsible for printing something that was not true, and that Corey was going through public humiliation because of it.

Jill made her own opening remarks, admitting that she'd made a mistake, but that we all make mistakes. She offered to print a retraction stating that Corey did not, in fact, decorate his room with garbage.

She also questioned the amount Pete was asking for. "Thirty starbills? The paper doesn't make that in a whole year!" I noticed a couple of the people in the jury nodding their heads when she said this. Thirty starbills was too much. Jill had a good chance of getting the amount reduced to 15 or even five. Five she could handle.

Pete called his first witness. "I'd like to call Corey Hawkins to the stand." Pete and Corey had obviously rehearsed this. Corey pretended to be very upset with the way people were treating him. He was practically in tears as he told a story about how somebody glued soda cans together to form a swan and put it in his front yard. It wasn't a pretty story, but the performance was so fake that I think it turned some of the jurors off. It was looking as if Jill might have a chance.

That is, until Pete called his second witness.

"I'd like to call Marcy Watson to the stand." Marcy stepped up, ready to tell her story. The bailiff swore her in. "Marcy," Pete began, "How would you describe your relationship with Corey?"

Marcy looked surprised by the question. "My relationship?"

"Yes. Are you friends?"

"Well . . ."

"Do you like him?"

She shrugged her shoulders. "I don't know."

"Have you ever had him over for dinner? Done homework together?"

"No."

"So you're not friends."

"No. I guess not."

"Are you enemies?"

"I wouldn't say that."

There wasn't very much space for anyone to move in the meeting hall pavilion, but what room Pete did have, he made use of. He began to pace in little 12-inch circles, like a buzzard ready to feast.

"But isn't it true that in the third grade, you had a little . . . argument?"

"I don't know what you're talking about."

"An argument about a doll?" Marcy's eyes went to the floor. She knew what he was talking about.

"Marcy, didn't Corey steal your Baby Wetty doll and throw it down the sewer?"

Marcy flipped. "Are you trying to say I did this on purpose?" There was a murmur from the crowd.

"Just answer the question, please." I had a feeling Pete had been waiting to say that.

"That was years ago!"

"Answer the question."

"I forgot all about that."

"Yes or no."

"Yes, but . . ."

"And didn't you say, Marcy, and I quote, 'I'll get you back for this if it's the last thing I do'?"

"I don't remember."

"Is it possible that you said that?"

"I guess."

"No further questions."

Marcy stood up. "I didn't do this on purpose. Why would I still care about something that happened four years ago?"

The judge asked Marcy to sit down. I looked over at Jill, who had her head down.

When it was her turn, Jill called Marcy back up to the stand. She tried to make it clear that Marcy had no intention of getting back at Corey for something that had happened in the third grade. I didn't know if it was working or not.

The lawyers made their closing statements, and then left the decision to the five-person jury. After 10 minutes, it looked as though the jury would be arguing for a while, so I left. Jill was outside facing the opposite direction from Marcy. They still wouldn't speak to one another. I couldn't look at Jill as I passed her.

- - -

The jury came back in 45 minutes, and I honestly didn't have a clue what the verdict would be. I slid back into my seat and held my breath as one of jurors read off a slip of paper he held in his hand.

"The jury finds for the plaintiff, Corey Hawkins. For the full amount of the suit." All 30 starbills. Corey and Pete gave each other high fives while Jill immediately left the room. I ran after her.

"Jill!" I shouted. I finally caught up to her.

"Go away," she said softly.

"Jill, I'm sorry."

She stopped suddenly and I almost ran into her. She looked at me with her hands on her hips. "Thanks a lot." She took off and I didn't follow her.

9

FALLING APART

I WAS SITTING IN MY office, staring at the wall, when Scott came bursting in. "You gotta see this," he said, and didn't wait for me to get up.

We ran to McAlister Park, which was on the other side of Whit's End. There was a gathering of about 20 kids, some Kidsboro residents, some not. I wasn't quite sure what was happening, but Max and several of his friends were pushing five other kids (all Kidsboro residents) on the merry-go-round. The riders didn't appear to be having fun—but Max and his friends did.

"What are they doing?"

"Max and his friends have been pushing these guys on the merry-go-round for about an hour now, nonstop."

"An hour?"

"It gets worse. About 15 minutes ago, they went into phase two. They forced them to eat greasy potato chips. A full bag each."

"*Forced* them? How?"

"You tell me. Why do you think these guys owe anything to Max?"

"You think they all borrowed money from him?"

"I've got no proof. But it sure looks that way."

Scott left to go sneak around a bit. No one noticed me as I moved a little closer. The five boys on the merry-go-round were looking very green. A large piece of cardboard with writing on it was propped up near the merry-go-round. As I studied it more closely, I realized it was a sign asking for predictions on which kid would throw up first. No one had done so yet, but by the looks of the victims, that wasn't too far away. There was also another friend of Max's videotaping the entire thing and giving a play-by-play commentary.

I wondered what I should do. Since they were not within the Kidsboro city limits, there was nothing that I could do legally. I had no authority over

Max. We were both just kids in a park. But there had to be another way that I could make him pay for his cruelty.

Scott ran up and handed me a piece of paper. "Look at this," he said. "I found it in James's backpack."

"What are you doing going through people's backpacks?"

"It was open."

I looked at the paper. "What is it?"

"A loan contract between James and Max. Max gave James a loan of five starbills, at 50 percent interest, compounded monthly."

I quickly did some math in my head and soon figured out that James would owe Max about 16 starbills in just three months. Max was the only person in Kidsboro who could afford to pay off 16 starbills.

"And look at this right here," Scott went on, pointing to the bottom of the page. "It says that if James doesn't make monthly payments, then Max will decide how payment will be made."

"Meaning James will have to be his slave."

"Bingo."

"Meaning he'll have to do his homework and play along with him and his friends while they put him on the vomit machine."

"Exactly."

I couldn't figure out how someone as smart as James could be so naïve. Maybe he was so desperate to hold on to his house that he temporarily lost his common sense. Max was using my program to humiliate people.

"Okay. Max can't get away with this." I stomped over to him. He was pulling a six-pack of soda out of a black box. He seemed happy to see me, which annoyed me a lot.

"Hey . . . my good friend Ryan! You're just in time. We're fixin' to go into phase three. The warm soda phase." He laughed. "Won't that be the coolest?"

"I need to talk to you about this, Max." I held up the contract. "It was in James's book bag."

"Hey! What are you doin' goin' through people's book bags?"

"It was open."

Max looked at the paper and smiled. "Oh, yeah. One of my little goodies. What a great idea this turned out to be, huh?"

"You can't do this."

He didn't stop smiling. "I can't?"

"You can't make him pay back his loan by spinning him on a merry-go-round for an hour."

"Oh, but you know what? Strangest thing. Right here in the contract. See that? That right there says I can."

"I don't care what this lousy contract says."

His smile disappeared. "The city charter states that all legal documents are binding. This is a legal document, signed by me, James, and a certified lawyer of Kidsboro." I looked at it again. Pete's signature was at the bottom. Another person I needed to scold. "According to this *legal* document, I can charge any interest rate I want, and I can collect it however I want."

He was right. He could make these kids spin until their eyeballs faced the backs of their heads, and I couldn't do anything about it.

"How many people have you got under contract?" I asked, not wanting to know.

"Five," he said smiling. "Hey, we're going into phase three. You're welcome to stay." He took off with the warm soda.

Five. And if my memory served me correctly, that was exactly the number of people whose lives had been "saved" by the Everybody Works program.

The first thing I had to do was call a city council meeting. Whether it looked like a political move or not, I had to recall the new law. It wasn't working, and it was threatening to destroy the town.

■ ■ ■

The city council met, and by a vote of four to one (Alice being the lone "nay"), we agreed to repeal the Everybody Works program. Everybody could go back to living in their clubhouses, while all the businesses in town went bankrupt because nobody was making any money.

I was planning to spend the rest of the day preparing for the debate, which was the next night, but when I got back to my office, I was too depressed to think about it. Maybe Max was right. This wasn't a town. It was just a bunch of clubhouses in the woods.

10

THE DEBATE

ON APRIL 30, I WROTE down the 10 things I would least like to be doing that night. Number one was getting dragged behind a car through a field of cactuses. Debating Valerie in front of the whole town was number two, but not by much.

The election was the next day after school, and I wasn't sure if I could turn the tide in one night. In a town of only 28 people (down from 29 after we banished Nick), you can pretty much figure out who's going to win if you simply know the people. I knew I had my own vote (unless Valerie was so good in the debate that she convinced me not to vote for myself), and I knew I had Scott's. He was, after all, my best friend. After that, I had no idea if I had any more votes. Max would vote for Valerie since he obviously had no regard for me whatsoever. Alice was mad at me for humiliating her about the Roberto investigation. Jill was mad at me for ruining her life. Nelson was a possible vote. Then again, being Valerie's brother, he had to live with her wrath if he happened to be the vote that caused her to lose. I knew a few of the boys who would vote for Valerie because they were secretly in love with her. I didn't think I could count on any girls being secretly in love with *me*, but that was a possibility.

All Valerie needed was 15 votes, and I could count six or seven that she definitely already had. And, of course, I was sure she had quite a performance planned for the debates. Put Valerie on stage in front of a bunch of people and she could persuade an Eskimo to put central air conditioning in his igloo.

When I got to the meeting hall, I counted the people. A crowd of 28 including me and Valerie. This *would* have to be the event nobody missed.

I sat in front, facing the crowd. Valerie was already there, smiling at all the registered voters. She was dressed as if she was going to church, and looked quite pretty, actually. Jill sat in front with us. She'd been chosen to be the host and moderator for the event.

Valerie showed her "good sportsmanship" by coming over and shaking my hand. She smiled sweetly and said, "Good luck, Mr. Mayor." She quickly looked around the room to make sure everyone saw this "gracious" gesture, then returned to her seat.

Jill began by welcoming everyone and introducing the participants. Then she asked us both to begin with an opening statement.

Valerie stood up and gave everyone a big smile. There was a lot of applause. She stood behind a music stand in front and began. "Ladies and Gentlemen, I have decided to run for this office not because I don't respect our current mayor. Our mayor has run this town as best as he can. He has done exactly what he thinks is best for us, and for that, I respect him." I hoped I wasn't the only one who could see how phony she was. "But I also think, somewhere along the road, our mayor lost touch with the people. He *wants* to do what's best, but he no longer *knows* what's best. And I believe I *do* know. Thank you."

There was scattered applause, and then everyone looked at me. I was never told how this debate would go, so I hadn't really prepared an opening speech. I definitely didn't have anything as polished as the one I had just heard. But I stepped up to the stand.

"I also respect my opponent," I said, hoping people couldn't detect how phony *I* was. "And I respect her right to challenge me for this office. After this is over, if I'm reelected, I'll make sure regular elections are put into the city charter. But do you really think this town needs a different leader? I have always made my decisions based on what I believe will help the town prosper. If you think I have done that, I'd appreciate your vote."

Again, there was scattered applause. I looked into the crowd and spotted Nelson. He had told me that he was bringing a new invention—an applause meter—to the debate. A few people were huddled around him, looking at it. They were checking to see if Valerie's applause was louder than mine. I wondered too.

Jill went ahead with questions. Her first question was how we planned on making the city better if we were elected. Valerie, of course, started in on her "fewer rules" campaign, except she called it "more freedom to do as we choose."

"Our mayor actually tried to force people to work. His Everybody Works program should've been called, 'Everything Works, But This Program.'" Some laughter. "Of course, yesterday he repealed this law, but then again, he also knew there was an election coming up. How convenient." I figured she would use that against me. "But let's be honest, people. The economy is in shambles. Businesses are going under, and it's not because people don't want to work. It's because there are no jobs out there. As your new mayor, I will start a program that will introduce new jobs into our community. But I promise that I will never tell you that you have to work or you'll lose your house." Some applause. I could sense from the crowd that they liked this idea, and in fact, Valerie made it sound great.

When I got up, I responded to Valerie's "more freedom" thing and said that even though rules weren't something we liked, they were still something we needed. I sat down. It was obvious Valerie received more applause after this segment of the debate.

Jill then asked a question about new ideas we might have for the coming year. I decided to take on Max here.

"There are people in this town who seem to be taking advantage of the freedom they do have. I consider that a *crime*." I didn't mention any names, but everyone knew who I was talking about. By now, they had all heard about the merry-go-round incident. I detected a smile from Max in the back. "I believe we should crack down on this stuff before it gets worse and people get hurt." Little applause.

It was Valerie's turn, and she stood up confidently and smiled at me as she went to the stand, as if to say, "This is where I lock up the election."

She began. "I believe this town has a lot of potential. A lot of potential for growth and learning and for just being a place to have fun. But I don't think our current mayor realizes this potential as much as he should. I think we should be more open-minded about who we allow to become citizens of Kidsboro. We can have a *different* assortment of personalities here and, therefore, become a city of variety and new ideas." My eyebrows rose. What was she going to suggest?

"For example . . ." she started, glancing my way to make sure I was listening carefully. She had my full attention. "Luke Antonelli. I believe most of us know him." Yes, everyone knew him. He was in Rodney Rathbone's gang, "The Bones of Rath," and was one of the biggest troublemakers in our school.

"I know for a fact that he would like to become a member of this town. My question is, why shouldn't he be allowed in?"

I had a few hundred reasons, actually. I wasn't sure where she was going with this. No one in his right mind would want Luke Antonelli living next door.

She went on, "I believe that Luke has a lot to offer our town. For one thing, his father owns a swimming pool store. Luke has told me that if he were allowed to join us, he would get his father to give us a small, used pool. Now wouldn't it be nice to have a public pool in our town?"

I looked into the crowd and saw some heads nodding. I couldn't believe this! She was promising a pool! "There are many others who can offer so much to our town. Jerry Wilmott, for instance." Jerry Wilmott! He was a three-time convicted shoplifter! She continued, "Jerry's mother works for the city and can get access to all the equipment and property within the city parks. Wouldn't it be nice to be able to go to the nearby baseball fields and play a game there any time we want—under the lights, even? As a matter of fact, I think Kidsboro could field a pretty good team," she said with a playful chuckle.

By the time she finished answering the question, Kidsboro had a paintball field, a snow-cone shop, and a recreation center that included a pool, volleyball court, and refreshment stand. I had no idea how she could deliver these things, but the crowd seemed to think that she could. They were drooling faster with every word that came out of her mouth.

By the time my turn came, there was nothing I could've said that would even get anyone's attention, much less change their vote. I pleaded with them not to allow our town to be filled with hoodlums, but they didn't seem to care. They wanted a pool.

The next day, I went to the meeting hall and cast a vote for myself. I figured it might be the only one I'd get, besides Scott's.

11

AN UNEXPECTED MEETING

Twenty-eight votes is not a lot to count. The polls closed at seven o'clock that night, and at five after seven we were all gathered in the meeting hall to hear the outcome. Alice counted the votes, since she was the highest ranking city employee next to me. Also, she was considered trustworthy by pretty much everyone. She read the little slips of paper and made tally marks in her notebook. After a couple of minutes, she rose and went to the front to make the announcement. Valerie and I sat in the same seats we had sat in for the debates. Alice approached the stand. She cleared her throat, and the hall went immediately silent.

"The winner, by a vote of 25 to 3, is Valerie Swanson." There was applause and whooping and hollering from some of Valerie's most loyal fans. Valerie showed very little emotion, however. She smiled and came over to me and shook my hand.

"I always keep my promises, Ryan," she said before she went to the stand to address her town. Indeed, she had kept her promise. She had promised she would take over the town . . . and now it was hers.

■ ■ ■

I was actually a little bit excited by the fact that I got one more vote than I had expected. From whom, I couldn't guess, but at least somewhere out there I had a fan I didn't know about.

For the next week, I spent very little time in Kidsboro. I cleared out my office the day of the election, but after that I pretty much stayed at home—my *real* home. Valerie seemed to have the city running pretty smoothly. I heard a rumor that she was going to put Luke Antonelli (and his pool) up for a vote soon, along with a few others.

I did make one trip to town that week. We actually have a church in Kidsboro. It's not a building, but rather an area next to the creek that runs along the edge of town. I went to real church every week with my mother. When we first came to Odyssey, we never went to church, but then we met Mr. Whittaker and he took us. I didn't like it too much at first, but over the next two years, I really began to enjoy it. I became a Christian a year after we started going.

The "preacher" of Kidsboro, a 10-year-old, African-American boy named Joey, held a service for anyone who was interested. Joey's father was the pastor of the liveliest church in Odyssey. The singing in that church could drown out a low-flying aircraft.

I'd only been to a couple of services at the Kidsboro Community Church, and there had never been more than three people in attendance, including the preacher himself. Mr. Whittaker sometimes came to show his support, but I could tell it made Joey nervous to have him there. It would be like me making a political speech with Abraham Lincoln in attendance.

The service was about 15 minutes long. There was always a song, a short sermon, and an offering, but no one ever put anything in the offering plate. Joey was always hopeful, though. He never missed a week, either. He always had something to say.

Mr. Whittaker was already sitting down when I got there. We were the only ones there. Joey was glad to see me. He said he was sorry about the election, and that he would pray for me. Oddly enough, this was kind of nice to hear.

Joey led the three of us in a chorus of "Seek Ye First," which I knew. Mr. Whittaker knew it too. Joey wanted to try it in a round, but I told him that would be kind of weird since there were only three of us.

Joey then launched into a sermon. This day he spoke about the Ten Commandments. I knew all of them already, so I kind of sat back and let him go through the list, smiling and nodding but not getting much of anything new out of the sermon.

But then he said something that struck me. He said, "Wouldn't it be a great world if everybody followed the Ten Commandments?" How true. No stealing. No killing. No lying. None of that. The Ten Commandments—now those were some rules you didn't mess with.

I was so struck by Joey's statement that I didn't really listen to the rest of the sermon. After he was done, Joey prayed with his arms raised, then passed the offering plate. I took it and stared at it for a second. He wasn't quite sure what I was going to do with it, and neither was I. But then I reached into my pocket and took out 12 starbills—everything I owned—

and placed it into the offering plate. He looked at the money as if it were the Holy Grail. I patted him on the shoulder and said, "Thanks, Joey." He was still staring at the money when I started to leave.

"Good sermon, huh?" Mr. Whittaker said.

"Yeah," I replied. We headed to Whit's End together in silence. I was considering the perfect world that Joey had described.

I'm not exactly sure why I gave everything I owned to the church. Maybe it was because the church was the last thing in Kidsboro that I felt I could have faith in.

◼ ◼ ◼

The following week, right out of the blue, the impossible occurred.

I was at Whit's End with Scott on the first day of summer vacation. We had been spending a lot of time together, mostly away from Kidsboro. Without me, I guess he didn't have any reason to be there either.

"You wanna take an Imagination Station adventure?" Scott asked. The Imagination Station was Mr. Whittaker's most popular invention. It was like a time machine, where you could visit places in history and people from the Bible. I wasn't really in the mood for an adventure, but Scott got in and started pressing buttons.

"How about the Boston Tea Party? You wanna go there?"

Just then, I noticed a boy in a leather jacket glancing over at us. I couldn't see his face well, but every now and then I would look over and he would quickly turn the other direction. It was as if he was staring at me, but didn't want me to know it. I looked in at Scott.

"Oh, let's do the Lewis and Clark adventure! That's so cool!"

I tried to listen to Scott, but heard footsteps behind me. I turned.

"Jim Bowers," he said, looking at me. A lump settled in my throat.

"W-W-What?"

"You're Jim Bowers," he said.

My leg was shaking uncontrollably. "You . . . you're mistaken. My name is Ryan."

"Gimme a break, Jim. I'd know you anywhere. What, in four years you've already forgotten me? Jake Randall."

I glanced at Scott to see what his reaction to all this was. He was half concentrating on his list of adventure options and half on me. I turned toward the machine. "I don't know what you're talking about," I said.

"Don't be an idiot, I know who you are."

Scott shifted in his seat to get a square look at this kid. "Pardon me for being on Earth, but you've got the wrong person. His name is Ryan Cummings."

"Ryan Cummings?" he said with a chuckle. "Get real, Jim. Stop the game. I know it's you."

I turned around, showing a little more anger than I probably should have. "Listen, I don't know what you're talking about. My name is Ryan, and this Jim is probably somebody that just looks like me, okay? Now would you please leave us alone?" I quickly became very interested in the Imagination Station.

From behind me, I could sense he was deep in thought. "I don't know what you're doing. Maybe you think I'm mad at you or something. I'm not. I'm okay. But I'm staying here with my grandmother until the end of the summer. I'll find out what's going on." I watched him in the reflection of the computer screen inside the cockpit. He stood there for a second, then left. I exhaled.

"You know that guy?" Scott asked.

"No. Never seen him before."

I ran my fingers through my hair and took a deep breath. Jim Bowers. I hadn't heard that name in four years.

— — —

I felt bad about lying at Whit's End, but I had panicked. It was a matter of personal safety, and I didn't know what to do. One day I would have to apologize to everyone for my deception. But for now, I tried to forget about it. I had a feeling it wasn't over, though.

Reports had it that things were going great in Kidsboro. All of Valerie's friends had become citizens. Somehow she got her pool, and it was the hot spot, even though it hadn't gotten quite warm enough in Odyssey to really require a pool. The pool was three feet deep and only 15 feet in diameter, but she packed them in there like sardines. Last I heard, she was working on the volleyball court. I couldn't imagine that she wouldn't get it.

I read a lot of books in my bedroom that week. Before we had started Kidsboro, my summers had always been spent reading alone in my bedroom. I would read about 20 books a summer. So in a way, it was kind of nice to get back to that.

I would take trips into Kidsboro just to see what was going on, but I'd never spend more than a few minutes there. Nobody said a lot to me as I passed them on the streets. I guess they didn't want to disturb my grieving process—or maybe they just felt guilty for not voting for me. Whatever the case, I didn't feel much like I was a part of the community anymore. But I still had my books.

I was reading a good one when my mom told me I had a visitor. I went to the front door and looked through the screen. It was Jill. "Hey," she said softly, smiling.

"Hey," I replied the same way.

"Whatcha doin'?"

"Reading. What are *you* doing?"

She shrugged. "Just thought I'd stop by. Haven't seen you in a while."

"Yeah . . ." I looked out at the front porch swing and motioned to it. We sat down. "I haven't spent a whole lot of time in Kidsboro lately."

"I know," she said, pushing her hair away from her eyes. I was wondering if she had a point to this visit, but it didn't matter to me if she didn't. It was nice just to see her.

"Marcy and I made up," she told me. I thought there was a slight tone of forgiveness in her voice, and I eased up a bit.

"Good."

This was not her point. She had another one. "So, have you decided that you don't want to be our friend if you can't be our mayor?" This was not the point I expected. I expected one about a thousand times less blunt. She backed off when she saw me practically swallow my own tongue. "I'm sorry. I shouldn't have said that. I know you're just . . . depressed or whatever." She looked at me deeply, like she was trying to sense what I was feeling. "You feel like you're losing your town?"

By this point, I had pretty much recovered from the first question, so I answered her. "I guess a little bit."

"Well, you're not. We miss you. And we need you."

"You need me? Why?"

"I don't know. There's just something not right about everything when you're not there."

"You mean it's a lot more fun when I'm not there," I said.

"Oh . . . Valerie's done some good things, I won't lie. The pool's a blast. She's got about a hundred other ideas, too. The place is gonna be Disneyland by the time she's through. She's even gotten a few people new jobs in the rec center she's building. But . . . it doesn't have the same . . . I don't know, *feeling* to it. We used to be such a family, you know? Well, the stuff that happened with me and Marcy kinda stunk, but still . . . deep down we were all friends, and we liked being around each other."

"And now?"

"Now . . . well, for example, Luke Antonelli's planning on moving next to Nelson. And Nelson's scared of him. He doesn't even want to live there anymore. He says he's gonna build another house somewhere else. And two of Valerie's friends had a fistfight the other day. Stuff like that never happened before. Makes me think it's because you're not around."

"I'm surprised you'd say that. I thought you'd be thrilled to have Valerie as your mayor. No lawsuits. She probably lets you print whatever you want in the paper."

"Sure, but . . . I'd rather have you."

"Really?"

She pushed her hair away from her face again and blushed a little. She looked at me. "*I* was your third vote." She cocked her head and laughed. I laughed too, because I never would've guessed that.

"Why?" I asked.

"Because you were right. I never should have printed that story about Roberto's dad. And you were right about Roberto being innocent. And even though it didn't work out the way you wanted it to, that jobs program was something you thought would be a good thing for the town. And if we had given it more time, I think it probably would have worked. You're always thinking of the town first. You're always doing whatever's right. You're the only person I know who does that. And I want somebody like that as my mayor."

"But I lost."

"Come back anyway."

I thought about it for a second, and the next logical question came to my mind. "What am I gonna do for a living?"

"I don't know. You can work with me. Be my sports editor. You won't get paid. I'm still paying off Corey. But we've got a volleyball court coming, you know."

We laughed for a second, and then decided we had other things to talk about. We sat and talked until the sun went down.

PLAYING WITH FIRE

I DECIDED JILL WAS RIGHT about coming back and being a productive member of society, so I went back to Kidsboro. But I still wanted to ease back into it, so I figured I would take a job in which I wouldn't have to do any work. The perfect job immediately came to mind. I would work for the Scott Sanchez Detective Agency!

Scott was excited about having me as an employee, not just because he had his best friend with him, but because he liked the idea of being my boss. Of course, he didn't have any real orders to give me, but every now and then he would make something up. "Wipe off my magnifying glass," he would say.

I was pulling up weeds in front of the agency when I saw someone walking toward me. I couldn't believe my eyes. It was Rodney Rathbone, the biggest bully in school and a mortal enemy of mine. He had on swim trunks and had a towel draped around his neck.

"Cummings!" he said, smiling like he was my best friend. "Thought you quit this place."

"I just . . . took a vacation."

"Well, how about a little swim?" I didn't like being in the same zip code as Rodney, much less a place that introduced the possibility of drowning.

"No thanks."

"Oh, come on. What, you can't swim or somethin'?"

"I can, but I'm gonna stick around here."

"Be that way then," he said and started to leave. As if he regretted missing a perfect opportunity to pound me, he flicked his towel at me and stung my legs before he was out of reach.

After he was gone, I went inside to see Scott. "What is Rodney Rathbone doing here?"

"Oh, yeah," he said. "I've been asking myself the same question. He just made it in last week."

"He's a citizen?"

"Valerie thought he could help out with getting electricity in the houses, since his Dad owns the Electric Palace store."

"He'll never pay attention to the rules here."

"He probably doesn't know there are any."

"He asked me if I wanted to go to the pool."

"Yeah," Scott said. "I don't go to the pool anymore. Valerie's friends always hog it. And they splash water in your face and dunk you and stuff."

"What about everybody else? Do they go to the pool?"

"No. All the original people kinda stay away from Valerie's friends. Pardon me for being blunt, but nobody really wants to be around them."

My heart sank. I had to go to the pool and see this for myself.

■ ■ ■

Just as Scott said, Valerie's friends were the only ones there. They seemed to be having fun, doing stunts and tricks they would never be able to do in a regular city pool with paid lifeguards. There wasn't an original member of the town in sight.

I was about to go back to Scott's place when I spotted someone out of the corner of my eye. It was Valerie, watching her friends in the pool. She looked worried, as if she knew she was losing her grip on things. She turned and saw me. We stared at each other for a second, and for the first time I found myself feeling sorry for her. I wanted to help her, if not for her sake, then for the sake of the town.

I walked over to her and we watched her friends in the pool for a few seconds. She didn't look at me, as if it were illegal for us to be talking to each other.

She finally broke the silence. "I appreciate your concern, but don't worry. I'm gonna fix this." She left quickly.

■ ■ ■

Valerie called for a meeting, and the entire town gathered for it. The meeting hall had never been this packed. If everyone crowded under the roof, it would hold about 30 people. Today there were 35. All 28 pre-Valerie members of the town, plus seven of Valerie's friends. A few people stood out from under the roof.

No one knew why the meeting was called, but everyone (except for maybe Valerie's friends) was aware that there was a problem in the town. We figured this would be Valerie's solution for it. Valerie stood up on stage and got everyone's attention. She was all smiles, as if everything was just peachy.

"Thanks, everybody, for coming. I won't keep you long, I just have one announcement. I've decided we should do something to celebrate the new era of Kidsboro." Of course, this meant the era that started when she got me out of the way. "We've had a lot of newcomers recently, and it doesn't seem like we know each other very well. I think we should have a get-together. So this Thursday, we're going to have a campfire." This was met with a few smiles. Other people exchanged looks and shrugged their shoulders as if to say, "I guess there are worse ideas."

Valerie went on. "It'll just be a time to hang out. We'll have some organized games, each of us will bring hot dogs and marshmallows . . ." Valerie's friends suddenly paid attention. Food was involved. "And at some point, we'll all introduce ourselves and get to know one another." Most of the crowd seemed to approve of the idea, and Valerie grinned. "Any questions?"

There were none, and she dismissed us.

- - -

I'm not sure what Valerie expected to happen at the campfire. I imagine she had dreams of people holding hands around the fire while singing "Kumbayah." Maybe Luke Antonelli and Scott Sanchez locked in an embrace of unity. I thought it was a good idea to try to bridge the gap between the two groups of people in the town, but I doubted it would actually happen. I figured I should show my support for Valerie by actually attending, at least for a little while. But I was not in the mood to bond with Rodney Rathbone.

The night was perfect. The sky was clear and the stars were bright. There was a cool breeze blowing through the woods so that when the fire started going, it would provide just the right amount of heat to make us all comfortable. Rodney had already picked the spot for the fire—a place in the middle of town. Everyone arrived with food, even the bullies, which surprised me. People had marshmallows and hot dogs and buns and potato chips and dip and soda and cookies and lots of other things. Everyone seemed to be taking this seriously. This was a great sign for Valerie, who I knew had to be nervous.

We all ate, and the groups sort of naturally separated themselves. Valerie's friends were huddled in one group on one side of the fire, away from everyone else. There was some interaction, but it was limited. At one point, I saw

Luke Antonelli squeeze ketchup on Nelson Swanson's hot dog. Valerie saw it and smiled. This was quite a victory for her, I knew. She must have had a talk with Luke beforehand.

I sat next to Scott as we ate, but we talked little. We both kept a close eye on Rodney and his friends, frankly because we didn't trust them to be nice for any length of time.

Near the end of dinner, Valerie brought us all closer to the fire and suggested that we introduce ourselves. We were to say our names and what positions we held in town.

"I'm Valerie Swanson," she began, "and I'm the mayor." She chuckled artificially, obviously very proud of being able to say that.

We went around the circle. "I'm Ryan Cummings, and . . ." Everyone waited to see what I would say and how I would say it. "I work for Scott, here, at his detective agency." I tried to say that with all the dignity that I could muster, but it just didn't sound right. Rodney and his friends chuckled.

Then we got to them. "I'm Rodney Rathbone, and I'm the town drunk." This was met with hilarious laughter from his group but no one else. I could tell Valerie was bothered by it, but she put on a straight face.

"Rodney is going to take my place as one of our town lawyers," she said.

"Oh, yeah," Rodney said. "That's right. I'm doing that on the side." More laughter from his crew.

They went on. "I'm Luke Antonelli. Pool maintenance." More laughter. This was hardly a real job. Then again, neither was being Scott's assistant.

Rodney and his gang of laughing hyenas continued, each making up a position and receiving a lot of laughs for doing so.

After the introductions, Valerie suggested we all play a game. As everyone was scurrying around getting ready, Scott and I took the opportunity to leave. I had put in my appearance, showing I supported and approved of our new mayor and her harebrained . . . I mean, *good* ideas.

■ ■ ■

Scott and I sat in his clubhouse and talked for a while. As we did, we heard encouraging sounds from the campfire area. People were laughing and having fun. I couldn't believe it, but Valerie's idea seemed to be working. She had brought together two groups of people that I never thought could've been brought together.

"So, what if this works out?" Scott asked.

"What do you mean?"

"Will you be happy or sad?"

"I'll be happy," I replied, and meant it. "Maybe Valerie knows what's she's doing. If it works, we've all made some new friends and the town is better for it."

We sat for a little while longer, listening to the sounds coming from the campfire. Just as I was contemplating going back to the fire to get a refill of my drink, we heard a noise that didn't sound encouraging. It was a scream!

Both of us dropped our cups and ran outside. There were a few more screams as we approached the campfire. Nelson was running toward his house like he'd just seen a bear.

"What's going on?" I shouted.

"They're going crazy," was all he could say as he kept running.

We ran as fast as we could toward the campfire. Several people were backed up against a house, acting as if they were being rushed at by angry wolves. Then I saw what they were so afraid of—Rodney and Luke were holding burning sticks and poking them at people.

Rodney was waving his torch and laughing. Luke rushed at Reverend Joey and came within inches of burning his face. Everyone screamed. People were paralyzed with fear, afraid that if they attracted attention to themselves, the two boys would pick them as their next target.

"Come on, everybody! I'm not gonna hurt you. Come over here and let me show you how friendly I can be." Rodney waved his torch wildly, and sparks fell to the ground. "Come on, you can trust me."

Luke went over to a group of people and scared the daylights out of them. The rest of Rodney's crew were getting some big laughs out of this. Alice was motioning for kids to run.

"Drop your weapon!" she shouted at Rodney. He just laughed.

Valerie was standing to the side and suddenly seemed to realize she was responsible for doing something about this. She stepped forward. "Rodney, stop it! Luke! Cut it out, right now! Put down the torches!"

Rodney chuckled and said, "Uh-oh, Luke. Look out. Our mayor is telling us what to do."

Luke joined him gleefully. "Yeah, we'd better obey or she's gonna throw us in jail!"

"I mean it, you guys!"

"Oh," Rodney said, "She *means* it! Luke, I didn't know she *meant* it. I guess we'd better *mean* it too."

With that, Rodney ran toward her angrily and poked the torch close to her stomach. Everyone screamed. Valerie backed away from him, but he kept after her. I've never seen such fear in anyone's eyes as I saw in Valerie's.

"Come on, Ms. Mayor. I heard somewhere that you *liked* playing with fire."

She started backing away more quickly, but he lunged at her. Dodging the flame, she fell. He came right at her with the torch!

Without thinking, I dashed toward them. The flame was inches from her stomach. Just as Rodney turned to me, I dove at the torch, knocking it out of his hand. He jumped on top of me and we wrestled on the ground. Luke saw what was happening to his friend, dropped his torch, and ran to help. He tried to pull me away from Rodney. Scott ran over and tackled Luke, sending him sprawling to the ground.

Rodney was much stronger than me, and he had me pinned. Just as he was about to send his fist through my skull, he glanced to his right. His mouth dropped open. The fire had spread and a house was in flames!

We suddenly forgot about beating each other up. "Get off!" I yelled and pushed Rodney off of me.

"Scott!" I shouted. "Go to Whit's End! Mr. Whittaker has a fire extinguisher!" He ran to get it. "Alice, call 911!" She obeyed. "You people!" I pointed to a group of kids. "Find some buckets or something and get water out of the pool and dump it on these flames!" They all scurried off. "You guys!" I shouted at Rodney's gang. "Help me put this out!"

I frantically kicked dirt onto the fire. It had climbed all the way up the wall of a house and was making its way along the roof.

Mr. Whittaker and Scott ran back with the fire extinguisher. Mr. Whittaker charged the burning house and sprayed. The fire died wherever he hit it, but it had spread too far already. The house was consumed by flames.

A dozen people came back with glasses, buckets, hats, and anything else that would hold water, and began to pour it on the flames. But it was like trying to stop a tidal wave with a garbage can lid.

The spray ran out of the fire extinguisher, and we had nothing left to do.

"It's too dangerous!" Whit shouted. "Everybody get out of here!" He waved his arms, signaling all of us to move away from the town. I had a fleeting thought in the back of my mind. *What if the fire spreads to Whit's End?* We watched the flames from a hundred feet away, and waited for the fire department to arrive.

The fire department got there in five minutes, but had some problems getting back into the woods, so it was 10 minutes before they were able to do anything to the flames. By that time, four houses were already consumed by fire. Whit's End was saved, but not by much.

■ ■ ■

We got a stern talking to from the fire department. Scott told the fire chief what had happened, and then the fire chief took Rodney and Luke aside and lectured them for a while. Besides the four houses that were burned to the ground, two others were damaged. No one was hurt, though. Everyone just wanted to go home, take a bath, fall asleep, and forget about this night.

I wanted to go home too, but on my way I saw Valerie. She was sitting on a stump, all alone. She was shivering with a blanket draped around her. She looked in the direction of the burned houses, but probably saw nothing but the memory of a flame being shoved into her face. I sat on the ground next to her.

"Are you okay?" I asked. She nodded. Just about everyone else had gone by this point, and the crickets were starting to chirp as if nothing had happened. "Maybe you oughta go home," I said. She nodded again. I guess she didn't feel much like talking. Neither did I.

"Thank you," she said suddenly, "and I'm sorry." Probably the two hardest things she'd ever had to say to anyone, and she accomplished them both in one sentence.

"That's okay," I replied.

We sat for a few more seconds, and then she began again. "I'm resigning." This shocked me, even under the circumstances. "This is your town. I'm giving it back."

"Are you sure?" I said, not knowing what else to say.

"Yes." She stood up, now ready to go home. "Are you gonna start rebuilding the houses tomorrow?"

"We'll do something tomorrow, I'm sure."

"Okay. I'll be here." Valerie started to leave.

"Valerie," I said, and she turned around. "You did some good stuff. The rec center, that's great. You did something else I didn't do. I was trying to force people into jobs that didn't exist. But you *created* jobs. I'm going to use that."

"Thanks."

"I might need you in the future. You know, to help me brainstorm ideas."

"Sure." She gave me a half-smile and left.

I got ready to leave too, but then I saw that I wasn't the last person there. Jill was looking at her house, which was one of the ones that had burned down. She was on the verge of tears as I walked over to her.

"The very first issue of the *Chronicle* was hanging up on the wall of this house," her voice trembled. "Now it's gone."

I didn't know what to say, so I just patted her on the shoulder. She didn't react.

"Come on, I'll walk you home," I said. She looked at me, and then we turned and walked toward our real homes.

"Pretty wild night, huh?" she said.

"That it was."

"I guess I'll be starting from scratch tomorrow."

"Well . . . as for your house," I said. "Don't worry about it. You've got insurance."

13

BACK TO THE BASICS

THE NEXT DAY I TOLD Max that he owed six people insurance money, and he informed me that he already knew this. He had to cough up about 100 starbills to pay for all of it, since his policies didn't just cover the wood, but also everything inside the houses. Some of the 100 starbills would go right back to him when people started rebuilding their houses with his wood. But he was still out a lot of money. The look on his face was all I needed to see. Justice had been served after all.

I put Max back up for another vote before the city council. I thought the others would feel, like me, that what he did to those kids on the merry-go-round was grounds for banishment. They disagreed, saying that he had a legal contract and we had to honor that. Plus . . . we needed wood.

Well, I'd given it a shot.

- - -

A week later, the town held a new election, and I was voted in unanimously. It wasn't a terribly glorious victory since there was no one opposing me, but it was sweet anyway.

Rodney and the rest of Valerie's friends told her that they weren't interested in coming back to town, so banishing them was not an issue. I'd been afraid that was going to have to be my first act as mayor.

Over the next month, we got the rec center going. We had a pool table/ping-pong table that was donated by someone's parents, and it became the featured activity there. You could also use other sports equipment in a room next to it. People who used the facility had to pay a small monthly fee, just like a real health club. The fees would help pay the salaries of any employees who worked there. James was the first employee, and he enjoyed taking care of the place. He handed out equipment and refreshments and kept the ping-pong players on a time limit. He was very happy with his new position.

The city council also voted on more government jobs. People took jobs mowing around the trees and building "streets" made out of thin pieces of plywood so that people could ride their bikes up to their houses. Under enormous pressure from people dying for a good cinnamon bun, Sid decided to reopen his business. With more people working now, he felt confident that he would have more customers. He was right.

Kidsboro suddenly seemed like a breath of fresh air.

■ ■ ■

One of the first things I did after I was reelected mayor was to persuade Roberto Santana to once again be a citizen of our town. And he agreed.

He moved into the same house he had before, and everyone welcomed him back. Some even apologized for accusing him of something he didn't do.

Roberto chose his job as well. He decided he wanted to work with Jill at the newspaper. I was surprised, because she had written about his father being in jail, but he told me that she had apologized to him and he had forgiven her. He didn't seem to have any hard feelings, and he really wanted to work on a newspaper.

Jill was more than happy to have Roberto on her staff, since he actually had some newspaper experience working for a school newspaper and she was running out of ideas for news. She had bought Max's extended insurance, so she was able to pay Corey back a good portion of the 30 starbills she owed him. She couldn't afford to pay Roberto much until she paid Corey off completely, but he wanted the job just the same.

At the end of the day, Roberto came into my office and told me about his first day on the job.

"I had a good time," he said. "Jill's very nice, and she let me write an article about how it feels to be a new citizen."

"Great."

"I even put a part in there about you. About how you believed in me."

"Well . . ." I blushed. "You didn't have to do that."

"I just wanted to come by and say thank you and that it's nice to be here."

"I'm glad you're with us," I said.

He started to leave, but then turned back around. "There is something that I should tell you."

"What?"

"My dad . . . he really is in jail." I felt deeply honored that he would trust me enough to tell me this. It almost made me want to share my own secret, just to show him that I trusted him as a friend too. But I didn't. I couldn't.

Instead, I looked into his eyes and said, "That doesn't matter."

He smiled and turned toward the door.

"Welcome back, Roberto," I said.

"Welcome back, Mr. Mayor."

THE END

For Bryn, my firstborn.
The day you were born, the day you were baptized,
and the day you first spelled "photosynthesis" backward,
are still three of the best days of my life.
Thanks for giving those to me.

■ ■ ■

BOOK 2

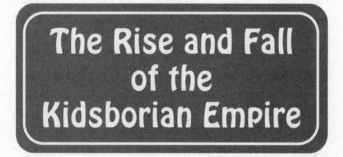

The Rise and Fall
of the
Kidsborian Empire

1

THE MAD AND THE GLAD

SNAP! MAX BROKE THE STICK he was holding. I glanced at him, and he looked at me with narrowed eyes and clenched fists. I couldn't help but smile, and this made him even madder. He glared at me one more time, and then left the crowd to go mourn the end of his reign as the most powerful man in Kidsboro, a community run by kids in Odyssey. Five of us had started Kidsboro months ago and our population had grown. We'd built clubhouses and small businesses in the woods behind Whit's End, an ice cream shop and discovery emporium owned by Mr. John Avery Whittaker, or "Whit" as most adults called him. And I, Ryan Cummings, was the mayor of Kidsboro.

Mark continued his presentation, pulling out a pocket-knife and cutting a window out of the tarp. The crowd around him watched with undivided attention. I was the only one who noticed Max leave. I had to follow him. I couldn't help it. I would enjoy seeing him squirm.

Max was forever tricking people out of their money. He always had at least three schemes going at one time. I couldn't understand how he was able to keep up with all of the lies he told.

Because his father owned a construction company, Max had a practically unlimited supply of scrap wood, which he sold to Kidsboro citizens for high prices. Of course, he was paid in Kidsboro money: starbills and tokens.

Max was not only the richest citizen in Kidsboro, he was also the most powerful. No matter how many schemes he pulled, I could never get the city council to kick him out because we needed wood. He could get away with pretty much anything.

But now . . . O glorious day! Now, we had just voted in a new citizen: Mark. His father worked at an awning company. At this very moment, he was showing us how to make the walls of our clubhouses out of plastic tarp instead of wood. Tarp had a lot of advantages over wood. First, there were no cracks that people could see through. Second, it was better for keeping the weather out. Third, it was easier and cheaper to build with.

People loved the idea. If everyone decided to go with the tarp, then we wouldn't need wood anymore and Max would be out of business. Plus, if he tried another one of his schemes and we found out, no one would hesitate to kick him out. At last I could be free of Max.

I caught up to him. "So, Max . . . what do you think about this tarp idea?"

"Go away, Ryan."

"Looks like you may actually have to make an *honest* buck for once."

He stopped suddenly and pointed in my face. "Do you really think I care diddly squat about this tarp guy?"

"It looked like you cared when you demolished that stick back there."

"Let's just keep one thing in mind, partner. The thing that makes me the most powerful man in Kidsboro ain't the wood. It's the fact that I'm 10 times smarter than any of you. This tarp thing is a bump in the road. I'll be back. I'll own this whole place. And when I do . . . you'll be the first person I crush."

He took off toward his home and I didn't follow. I knew he would live up to those words. I was in for a war.

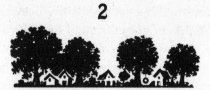

THE BIG IDEA

MAX'S MELTDOWN WAS THE most exciting thing that had happened in Kidsboro for at least three weeks. School had been out for summer vacation for about a month, and it seemed like we didn't have enough going on to fill up the time. As mayor, one of my duties was to hand in weekly Kidsboro reports to Mr. Whittaker. Lately, he had commented on how boring the entries were.

My daily entries had been getting less and less interesting as the summer wore on. For a couple of days the only thing I had written down was, "I bought a raisin bun at Sid's Bakery."

"It seems like everything has come to a screeching halt," Mr. Whittaker noted.

"I guess we're in a rut. We're all just doing our jobs. Nobody knows what else to do."

"I suppose that's not too much different from real life sometimes. But I certainly didn't think you'd be bored with Kidsboro in just five months."

"What do you think I should do?" I didn't usually ask this question. As the elected official for Kidsboro, I wanted to solve things on my own instead of asking Mr. Whittaker for advice. He wanted us to solve our own problems too, so for the most part he wasn't involved with running the town. But this was a question I had been mulling over for a week. I figured I could use some help.

"It sounds like you need something to stir things up," he said, scratching his chin. "Maybe a new government project, or a new business, or . . . something the whole town could be involved in."

I agreed with him, but I had no idea what steps to take to make that happen.

"That's the coolest thing I've ever seen!" my best friend, Scott Sanchez, shouted as the car stopped right in front of him. It was Nelson Swanson's newest invention: a computer-programmable toy car. Eugene Meltsner, a college student and Odyssey's resident genius, had helped Nelson create the car. But he stepped back and allowed Nelson to soak in the limelight.

"Now watch this," Nelson said, kneeling down next to the car. He began to punch numbers into a calculator that was glued to a couple of pieces of plywood on wheels. From the top, it looked very basic. But underneath was a sophisticated system of wires and computer circuits that would boggle the mind of anyone in Kidsboro—except Nelson. "I'm going to program the car to go to Sid's Bakery and return with a donut," he said.

"What?"

"I enter number 12 for Sid's Bakery . . ."

"Um . . . excuse me for living, but," Scott said, "you just tell the car to go to Sid's Bakery, and it knows where it is?"

"I had to preprogram it, of course. You see, yesterday Eugene and I spent all day surveying the dimensions of Kidsboro. I know exactly how many feet specific locations are from this spot right here." He pointed to an X painted on the ground. "So we programmed the car to go 42 feet forward, three feet to the left to get around that tree, and then turn right and go 14 more feet right up to Sid's Bakery."

He looked toward Eugene. Eugene handed him a tiny wagon. "Don't forget to activate the voice player," Eugene whispered to him.

He hooked the wagon onto the back of the car and put three tokens, the price of one donut, into it.

Nelson punched some more buttons and stood up. "Now, instant delivery service."

My mouth fell open as I watched the car go forward 42 feet, turn left and go three feet, and then turn right and go 14 feet. It stopped right in front of Sid's Bakery . . . and beeped its horn! Sid heard the beep and came out of his shop. He looked around confusedly, and then saw the car sitting in front of his door. The car said in Nelson's voice, "Could I have a glazed donut, please?" Sid obeyed without a word, as if this was a customer with arms and legs and absolutely no calculators glued to him. He came back with a glazed donut and placed it in the wagon, taking the tokens in return.

Sid looked around to see if there was a human responsible for this, and waved when he saw Nelson. He smiled. Now it made sense. We all expected things like this from Nelson. Nelson waved back. His voice came out of the car again, "Press the red button when you are done." Sid obeyed, and the car backed up and retreated along the exact path it had taken to get there. It stopped right in front of Nelson's feet. Nelson casually bent down, picked up his donut, and took a bite.

"Nelson, that's amazing," I said.

"How'd you get it to talk?" Scott asked.

"It's all in the programming."

"It is precisely the same concept as an answering machine," Eugene piped up, obviously unable to control the urge to explain something.

"I can't believe you made that," Scott said to Nelson.

"It's definitely your best invention yet," I added.

"Thanks. I've been working on it for about six months."

"Do you think you could make me one of those?" Scott asked. "I'll pay you for it." I wasn't sure where Scott was going to get the money for this. He was usually broke, but had made a little money with his detective agency during the spring. In a town as small as ours, there wasn't a huge need for a detective, but Scott had actually cracked a couple of cases.

"Sure," Nelson said. "I can have one for you next week." Eugene cleared his throat. Nelson turned and looked at him. "What?"

"Nelson, I believe I will be experiencing a very busy week at the college. Unfortunately, I do not think I'll have much free time to help."

"Oh, okay," Nelson turned back to Scott. "I guess it'll take me a couple of weeks."

"No problem. You know, you could use this car for anything! You could deliver mail with it, or . . ." His eyes lit up. "I could use it in my detective work! I could rig it with a microphone and secretly drive it up to somebody's house and record criminals as they make their plans."

"That would be illegal," I reminded him.

"Who said?"

"It's in the city charter. We have privacy laws." Scott's shoulders drooped.

"You still want the car?" Nelson asked.

"I guess," Scott said.

There were plenty of legal uses for Nelson's car, and I was certain others would see that as well.

■ ■ ■

The next night as I was leaving to go to my real home, I was surprised to see a light on in Nelson's clubhouse. Nobody really wanted to hang around town that much at night, be-cause it got awfully dark in the woods. I knocked, but Nelson didn't answer. Thinking he might have left his battery-operated light on accidentally, I opened his door. Nelson was fast asleep. His head was flat on his desk, his glasses pushed over so that his right lens was over his left eye. He was holding a red wire, poised to place it somewhere on the underside of a computerized car on his desk. Four empty cans of caffeine-enriched soda lined a window ledge.

I tapped on his shoulder, first gently, then with more force. He awoke with a start. "I can't do any more pull-ups!" Nelson shouted and stood up, his face full of utter terror. Obviously, he was having a gym-class nightmare.

"Nelson, it's me."

"What?" he said, straightening his glasses and looking disoriented.

"It's Ryan. You were having a dream."

"Oh." He sat back down at his desk, shook his head, and without missing a beat, put the red wire into a hole near the back end of the car. He began to screw it tight.

"It's late. You need to go home."

"Is it curfew?"

"Pretty close."

"Okay, I'll work until curfew. I'll see you tomorrow."

"How long have you been working on this thing?"

"Since about five . . ." he cleared his throat, "this morning."

"That's . . . 16 hours!"

"I've got it worked out. If I come in here at five o'clock every morning for the rest of the summer, I'll be able to fulfill all the car orders I have by the time school starts back, depending on—"

"Car orders? What do you mean?"

"I did a little demonstration for a group of people yesterday after I showed the car to you. Several of them wanted their own—just like Scott."

"How many?"

"Twelve."

"So you're going to pull 17-hour days until school starts in order to get this done?"

"I'm giving myself Sundays off. And the Fourth of July."

"Are you crazy? You'll be brain dead by August."

"These people are paying top dollar. I could end up as rich as Max."

"How much are you charging?"

"Twenty starbills a car."

My chin dropped. Twenty starbills was an incredible amount of money—and Nelson was planning on making that 12 times over. He could practically buy a *real* car for that. He could buy his own *company* and make . . . Wait a minute! Mr. Whittaker's words flashed into my head.

"Nelson . . . why don't you start your own company?"

"How?"

"With that much money coming in, you could start a factory right here in your clubhouse. You could hire people to do this work *for* you."

"I don't have any money to hire people."

"You could have investors. Ask people for money up front to start your business. Then when you start selling lots of cars, they can share in the huge amounts of money you'll be making."

"So, I could have employees?"

"Sure. Is there anything you could teach other people to do, like attaching the wheels or something?"

"Yes. I mean, with some training, pretty much anybody can do the body work and some of the easier circuitry."

"So, why not?"

Nelson stood up, as if the ideas flying around in his head had lifted him off his chair involuntarily. He turned to me and smiled.

■ ■ ■

And so was born Kidsboro's first mega-business. The next day, Nelson went around to some of the richer citizens of Kidsboro and asked them if they were interested in investing in Nelson Motors, Inc.

"Nelson Motors?"

"Yes," I overheard Nelson say to a potential investor. "I'm planning to start mass-producing the computer cars. I already have 12 orders at 20 starbills apiece."

"What do you need me for?"

"I need your money so I can start the company and hire employees."

"So you want me to give you money."

"Not give. Invest. You see, if you invest in my company, you share in all the money I make off the cars. For example, if you give me 10 starbills right now, I estimate you would get 20 starbills back after I sell my first 12."

"I give you 10, I get back 20. That's it?"

"That's it. And that's just for the first batch. I plan on selling many more after that."

"So I can double my money without doing anything?"

"Absolutely."

This was the pitch Nelson gave to everyone, and it worked! He collected 50 starbills in about two hours. He was ready to start his business.

His search for employees wasn't too difficult either. Everyone liked the idea of making cars. In fact, much to his surprise, several people offered to share their ideas about how to improve the cars. For example, Nelson wasn't too concerned about style, and one of his potential employees offered to make the car look "cooler" with new colors and shapes. He suggested they could even take custom orders. If a customer wanted a race car, a truck, or even a minivan, Nelson Motors would give him exactly what he wanted.

By the end of the week, Nelson had four employees: two builders, one designer, and one tester.

The wheels were rolling—so to speak—both at Nelson Motors and Kidsboro itself.

3

TAKING OFF

PEOPLE SAW THE SUCCESS OF Nelson's new business, and suddenly everyone wanted their own. Ideas were popping up everywhere. Jill and Roberto, the editors/reporters of the weekly newspaper, the *Kidsboro Chronicle*, created a new magazine. It would include stories and poems written by Kidsboro citizens, features about people and places in and around Kidsboro, and general interest articles. The first issue included a *Romeo and Juliet*-type short story about a boy falling in love with a girl that his parents didn't like. Jill wrote this story herself, and it was a favorite among the girls in the town, though the boys wanted more "explosions or something." I personally didn't see an appropriate place in the story for a bomb, but I must admit the action did drag a little bit before page 15 or so.

Kidsboro also had a new attraction—a nine-hole miniature golf course created by Mark, the tarp guy. Mark, like every other Kidsboro citizen, had been given a certain amount of Kidsboro money in order to build his house and get established in the community. And by using tarp instead of having to pay Max for wood, he'd had enough money left over to start his business.

Mark bought a piece of property next to his house and brought in some wood to build boundaries and obstacles. He used actual golf balls and clubs. From the way he described it, it sounded like it was going to be one of the favorite activities in Kidsboro.

Then I tried it. He let me play the first round ever. The course went over dirt and around rocks and tree roots. He told me it would be challenging. He didn't want kids to get bored with it too quickly, but he had no idea just how challenging it was. On hole number four, the golfer had to clear the creek to land on the green where the hole was. The green was only about four feet wide—a dinky target. If you hit the ball too softly, it went into the creek. If you hit it too hard, it plummeted down a 15-foot cliff. I, of course, overshot the green and went down the cliff. It took me 18 strokes to get it back up, then the ball went into the creek. Mark just watched and chuckled.

Holes five through nine weren't much better. Hole eight had a working windmill, with turning blades and everything. However, the rotation of the blades was much too fast. If your ball had the misfortune of getting hit by a blade, it would be thrown about 30 feet out of bounds and into the creek. By the end, it had taken me 104 shots to complete the course, a three-hour round of golf. I told Mark I appreciated the challenge, but I was afraid the course might frustrate players more than challenge them. He agreed to take another crack at it.

The most promising new business was the Kidsboro Cineplex: an outdoor movie theater with a small concession stand. Pete, one of two lawyers in town, was a movie buff. His parents owned a huge collection of videos. Mr. Whittaker allowed Pete to use an old video projector that belonged to Whit's End. Pete strung up some bed sheets between trees for the screen, and everyone would bring their own blankets or lawn chairs and watch the movie. It only cost three tokens to get in. Pete had to put up some more sheets to prevent people from peeking in when they hadn't paid. Then he discovered that kids were climbing a nearby tree and watching the movie over the sheets. So Pete hired Alice, our five-foot- eleven policewoman who had biceps thicker than some tree trunks, as a bouncer to keep an eye on the trees around the theater. If she found anybody trying to take a free peek, she would shake the tree until the offender either fell out or surrendered. Pete also hired someone to work at the concession stand, selling popcorn and sodas to moviegoers.

It became a nightly tradition during the summer—every weeknight there would be a new movie and practically everyone in Kidsboro attended. No matter what the movie was, kids would come to the theater just to be with everyone else. It became a time when all of Kidsboro came together as a sort of family. It made me proud to be a citizen.

The only problem was that at the end of the movie every night, Pete would hold a discussion about the film. I think he mainly did this to show off his impressive film vocabulary. One night, after watching a mindless movie about a guy whose family is taken hostage by bad guys while he's in the garage (as it turns out, he bests them with a weed whacker), the discussion among the boys became quite passionate.

"That was so cool when the trailer blew up!"

"The hero was awesome!"

"That was an incredible fight at the end!"

"Great movie, man!"

Then Pete took the floor and announced, "The cinematography was a bit uninspired," and went on and on about it. This, of course, took the wind out of the sails of anyone who had actually enjoyed the film. This happened pretty much every night. The crowd would talk about how much they loved the movie, and then Pete would get up and explain why the editing was uneven or whatever. It was actually getting a little annoying. Then one night someone finally had the guts to challenge him.

"I found the Jane character to be one-dimensional," Pete said. "She was merely a piece of cardboard. And what was the point of having the grand-mother come back? I found that to be a very implausible plot twist."

"Oh, yeah?" came a voice out of the crowd. "You think you can do any better?"

Pete was totally thrown off by this. No one ever challenged him. "What?"

"You haven't liked a single movie you've shown here. So why don't you make one yourself?"

Pete's body twisted and it looked as if he was going to lose his balance. "Well . . . I'm not a filmmaker."

"You act like it," the boy said as others nodded.

"I don't have the equipment . . ."

"Your dad has a video camera, right?"

"Yes."

"You've got a whole town full of people who can be your actors. What else do you need?"

Pete swallowed and looked out at the crowd. He took a deep breath, and then nodded. "Okay. I will. I *will* make a movie." Suddenly, he stood up straight and, as if he were announcing his candidacy for president, said, "And it'll be better than anything you've seen so far."

The crowd was both excited and skeptical. It was certainly a fun prospect to be involved in a movie.

And so began a new industry in Kidsboro: filmmaking.

4

BLACKMAIL

I WAS WALKING TOWARD MY office when someone snuck up from behind and tricked me.

"Jim!" he shouted.

On impulse, I turned around. I immediately wished I hadn't.

"Gotcha!" he said, laughing. It was Jake Randall—a face from the past I had hoped was out of my life forever. "I knew you were Jim."

"My name's not Jim," I said. "It's Ryan."

"But you turned your head when I called you Jim."

I had to think fast, before he noticed how nervous I was. "You were 10 feet behind me and you screamed something. I would've turned around no matter what name you called."

"What a lie," he said, bumping me with his shoulder.

He was right. I was lying, but I had good reason. My real name was Jim Bowers, and he was the only one in Kidsboro who knew it. I had known Jake since we were kids in California, before I moved to Odyssey. There was a secret surrounding my life in California, and Jake knew some of it. Now he was spending his summer in Odyssey, harassing me here just as he had done in California. Since the day I had run into him again after four years, I had tried to act like I didn't know what he was talking about when he called me Jim. But he knew my real name, and he knew I was running away from it. He didn't know everything—at least I didn't *think* he knew everything. I had to prevent him from finding out the whole truth. It would be too dangerous for my family.

I continued walking toward my office. I was hoping he would go the other way. He didn't.

"I've heard about this nice little . . . like . . . *town* you've got here. Cute little clubhouses everywhere. And I hear you're the mayor or something?"

"Yes."

"How many people have you got livin' here?"

"Thirty."

"Wow. Congrats. Leader of 30 people—five months before you're even a teenager." He leaned down and whispered in my ear, "Notice how I know your exact age?"

"Good guess. Maybe you can get a job at a carnival."

"Yeah, this little town's nice and comfy. Got a bakery, a newspaper . . . I ran into your police chief back there. That girl's a tank." He was referring to Alice, of course.

"I wouldn't say that to her face."

"You think I'm nuts?"

"You know," I said, "I have some things to do. I'll see you around." I sped up and ducked my head into my office. He didn't take the hint. He followed me in.

He sat down in a chair and put his feet up on my desk. "I was thinking about maybe becoming a citizen myself. Where do I sign up?"

For the first time, I looked directly at him. My veins turned to ice. If Jake became a citizen, I wouldn't be able to sleep at night. I would be constantly looking over my shoulder and checking behind trees.

"You know, it's pretty hard to get in," I said. "You have to go through a screening process, and you have to win an 80 percent majority vote in the city council. It's not really up to me."

"I see," he said. "So, you don't think I have a chance?"

"Well . . . you're new here. I don't really know you, and I don't think anyone else on the council does either. It might be a long shot."

"But you're the mayor. You can make things work out for me, right? Or don't you want to?" I didn't answer. "You know what? I've got something that might make you want to. Come with me."

"Look . . . *Jake*, is it? I don't have the time. Maybe . . ."

"I think you're gonna want to see this." I looked up and saw him smiling. He had me. I didn't know how, but he had me. I was compelled to follow him. Without a word, he headed for the movie theater. Pete was setting up for that night's feature. We stepped across the series of extension cords that led from the woods to Whit's End and approached him.

"Ask him if we could use the video projector for a bit." I did, and Pete agreed. He turned the power on, and then went back into his office/house. Jake and I were alone.

Jake pushed a videocassette labeled "Tenth Birthday" into the projector. "After our last little encounter, I did some research. I had my mom send me this video from California. I think you'll find it very interesting."

The screen lit up and showed a birthday party. The cake said *Happy 10th Birthday, Jake,* and in the background was a 10-year-old Jake. He puffed up his cheeks and blew out the candles as everyone clapped. Then the camera panned and caught a little boy wearing a purple superhero shirt—an eight-year-old me. The person operating the camera said, "Jim! Make your funny face." The eight-year-old me scrunched up his face as though he had just eaten a box of lemons. Jake pressed the pause button, crossed his arms, and glared at me.

"You know," Jake said, "that kid looks . . . like . . . *exactly* like you. But . . . they called him Jim. I wonder why."

"I guess his name is Jim," I said as calmly as I could. "I admit, he sure looks like me. Thanks for showing me that. It was interesting." I started to head back to my office.

"You want to see another coincidence?" he said, stopping me in my tracks. He pressed a button and the video started up again. I was still making faces, and there, coming up from behind me, was my mom. She hugged my neck. Then she looked right into the camera and the two of us smiled. Ten-year-old Jake came into the picture and called her "Mrs. Bowers."

"You see, that's what's weird," Jake said. "That kid's mother looks just like *your* mother. And yet her name is Mrs. Bowers. Can you believe that coincidence?" He paused for effect. "No. You don't believe that's a coincidence. And neither will anybody else. Can you imagine how awful it would be if, for some reason, this tape accidentally got switched with the tape Pete's going to play at the Cineplex tonight? You would have a lot of explaining to do, huh?"

The tape was still rolling. There were only five or six kids at the party that day. Jake was not real popular. He had invited me only because he had very few other friends. My mom and I were sitting together as we watched Jake open his presents. I got excited when he opened the one I gave him— one of those super water guns. Jake immediately ran to the bathroom to fill it up. I smiled at my mom and said, "I told you he'd like it." Times were much simpler then.

"So what's your story, Jim? Why are you hiding out here with a bogus name? It's not because you're scared of *me*, is it? Surely you don't think I'm still mad about that whole detention center thing."

Just a few months after that birthday party, Jake had taken me out to the woods and showed me his father's gun. I got scared, and I ran and told my mom. She called the police, and they came and picked him up. Of course, the gun episode hadn't been the only reason Jake had been sent away, but I sensed he blamed me anyway.

"Surely you didn't move away just because I had to spend the next three months in a juvenile detention center." Jake said. He was telling me now, four years later, that he wasn't mad about it. But I couldn't imagine that he had put it behind him. I was sure he wanted revenge.

"You know what? I don't think that's it," he said. "This is a long way to come just to get away from me. I think you ran away from California for a different reason." I swallowed a lump in my throat. "It was a weird thing. Nobody in our old neighborhood could figure it out. You and your mom just suddenly disappeared. Not even your father knew where you were." He smiled. "I think you were running away from *him*."

He knew it all. When I was eight, my mother and I gathered up our belongings and left the house in the middle of the night to escape an abusive husband and father—my dad. If he had known we were leaving, or where we were going, he would've found us and maybe hurt us even worse than he had before. He was an alcoholic and we never knew how violent he would turn at any given moment when he was drinking. So we left that night and went to an abuse shelter, where they helped us start our lives over. They gave us new names, a new address thousands of miles away, and a new life. They told us not to tell anyone in Odyssey about our past, not even our closest friends. Now . . . my worst enemy knew.

"Jake, you can't tell anybody."

"Oh, I don't plan to. You know, as long as you keep me happy."

He had me. I had to give him whatever he wanted.

"What do you want?" I asked him.

"I want to be a citizen."

"Why?"

"I haven't gotten to know many people here. I think it'd be nice to settle down in a small town . . ." This part I believed. Jake was never one to make friends easily. But I didn't believe this was the only reason he wanted to be a part of my town.

"I told you, it's not completely my decision," I told him.

"Then you'd better hope your friends follow your lead and vote for me."

"They don't even know you."

"Tell them about me. Tell them what a good pal I've always been to you." In other words, lie.

"I can't guarantee anything," I said.

"Sure you can."

"I'll do my best."

"That's the spirit."

But don't ask me any questions, I thought. *You don't need to know anything else.*

■ ■ ■

I rolled back over onto my stomach. I could never sleep on my stomach, but I wasn't sleeping anyway. I thought about waking Mom up and telling her everything, but I didn't want her to panic and insist that we move out of Odyssey. I liked it here.

I also considered telling Mr. Whittaker. He was the only person in Odyssey besides my mom and I who knew the truth about our situation. When we moved to Odyssey, we immediately knew he was a person we could trust. He helped us out a lot, and was responsible for my mother and me becoming Christians. I wanted to tell him, but I knew he would want me to tell my mom, and I didn't want her to worry. Why did Jake have to show up and ruin everything?

I couldn't imagine Jake being a citizen of Kidsboro—to look across the way and see Jake eating a donut from Sid's Bakery, attending a movie at the Cineplex, talking with all of my real friends. I would be constantly wondering what the topic of conversation was . . .

I would have to look straight into the faces of the city council members and tell them that Jake would be a wonderful asset to our community. I had no choice.

■ ■ ■

I called a city council meeting first thing the next morning. Everyone was there—Scott, Nelson, Alice, Jill, and me. None of them knew why I had called the meeting.

"I want to vote in another citizen," I said, my stomach turning.

As I expected, Jill immediately objected, "I thought we were going to stop at 30 for the rest of the summer."

"That's right. We did say that at the last meeting," Alice agreed.

"Then someone must be leaving," Nelson said.

"Who's leaving?" Scott asked.

"No one's leaving. There's just someone I think we should consider."

"Who?"

I took a long breath. "Do you guys know Jake Randall?" I got blank stares.

"Never heard of him," Scott said.

"He's from California. He's visiting for the summer—staying with his grandmother or something."

"He doesn't live here?" Jill asked with an exaggerated shrug of her shoulders.

"No, he doesn't. But I think he could turn into a very valuable citizen."

"Why?" Jill asked.

"Because," I could tell that I hadn't rehearsed this well enough. "Because . . . he's . . . smart . . ."

"That's it? He's smart?"

"No, that's not it."

Jill wasn't going to let up. "Well, you're going to have to make a better case for him than that. None of us knows the guy. How do you expect us to vote for him?"

Alice spoke up. "Can we ask some questions about him?"

"Sure."

"Does he have a record?" she asked, without a hint of a smile.

"You mean, is he a *criminal*?" Did Alice have a sense about these things, or was this just a standard question? I didn't answer.

"Do you mind if I do a check on him?"

"Um . . . no, go ahead."

Alice wrote something down in the notebook she kept in her shirt pocket.

"You say," Nelson said, "we could benefit from him being a citizen. How?"

"How? Well . . . like I said, he's smart. I could see him starting a new business."

"We have tons of new businesses."

"True. You're right, we do. But . . . his business could really . . ." I looked around at the confused faces around me. They weren't buying it. I didn't want to resort to this, but I had run out of options.

"Listen," I began, swallowing a lump in my throat, "do you think you could maybe just . . . trust me on this one?" Jill and Nelson exchanged looks while Alice and Scott stared at me through squinted eyes. "I can't explain right now. I just . . . need for you to vote for this guy. Okay?"

There was silence as I scanned the faces of my friends. Jill looked down, fiddled with her ear, and finally said, "Okay. I trust you. I'll vote for him."

"Me too," Scott said. Nelson and Alice followed.

"All right then," I said sheepishly. "Jake's a citizen." I let out an unintentional sigh of relief and Jill glanced at me. "Thanks. Meeting adjourned."

"Do we get to meet Jake at some point?" Jill asked.

"Sure. Um . . . he'll be around. I'll introduce him." We all filed out.

As I headed back to my office, I noticed that Jill and Scott had remained in the meeting hall. When I looked back, they saw me, and their conversation came to an abrupt halt. They both gave me an awkward smile and pretended, badly, that nothing was going on. I turned back around and tried to act like I wasn't affected by this scene, but I had a feeling that their level of trust in me had taken a hit.

■ ■ ■

I hadn't attended the Kidsboro Community Church for several weeks, but I decided to go, hoping that Reverend Joey might say something to inspire me. When I arrived, he and Mr. Whittaker were the only ones there. Joey preached, banged his fist on the music stand a couple of times, and led us in a couple of songs. With the Fourth of July coming up, I think he preached on appreciating America. To be honest, I wasn't paying much attention. It was when he asked if anyone wanted to come to the altar to pray that I woke up.

I walked up to where Joey had laid out a couple of milk crates for an altar. I knelt down and almost started to cry. I felt terrible for deceiving people that I really cared about.

"Lord, please forgive me for lying. But I don't know what to do. I don't want to keep lying, but I can't tell them the truth, either," I whispered.

Mr. Whittaker startled me with a tap on the shoulder. "Are you okay, Ryan?" I wanted to tell him everything, but I couldn't.

"I'm okay."

"Would you like me to pray with you?"

"No. I'd just like to pray alone for now."

"Okay, Ryan. But let me know if you need to talk." He hesitated, waiting for me to take him up on his offer. Seeing that I wasn't going to at this point, he slowly backed away.

I finished my prayer with one more sentence, "Please, God, show me what I can do."

I didn't get an answer immediately, but I figured one was coming. God had never let me down before.

■ ■ ■

Jake was all smiles when the city council greeted him as the newest citizen of Kidsboro. He was building his house very close to my office, and the sight of it gave me an instant headache. I stood at a distance while Jill, Scott, Nelson, and Alice shook his hand, one by one.

The only good thing about this scene was the fact that Jake's house would be the second to use tarp, thus continuing the demise of Max's chokehold on the city.

■ ■ ■

Even though Jake was now a citizen of Kidsboro, I couldn't help but smile when I saw how far the town had come in such a short time. Everywhere I looked, people were involved in businesses of various kinds. Pete had no problem finding investors for his movie. Just as with Nelson's cars, we all knew the movie would make a lot of money. Everyone figured that people would pay to see it simply to watch themselves onscreen. Pete raised 40 star-bills almost immediately. That would be plenty to pay all the actors and crew members.

But I also noticed that something disturbing was going on. People who couldn't get investors for their businesses were borrowing money from each other. I didn't like this going on between friends, because if someone couldn't pay a friend back, it might hurt the friendship.

So I discussed an idea with the city council: We needed to start a bank. "People will put their extra money in the bank, so they can earn interest. Interest is money the bank pays you because it gets to use your money for a while. It's a form of investing. I figure people will go for it because they will be making money for doing nothing," I explained.

"On the flip side, people can also *borrow* money from the bank if they want to start new businesses. On a loan, they'll have to *pay* interest. The longer they take to pay back their loans, the more money they'll have to pay back. Hopefully, once the borrowers get their businesses going, they'll be making enough money to pay back their loans pretty easily." Everyone on the city council agreed it was time for Kidsboro to open a bank.

■ ■ ■

As soon as we announced the opening of the Kidsboro Savings and Loan, people began to gather up their extra cash and deposit it in the bank. I appointed Marcy to be the bank teller. She had always had trouble finding a job, plus she had a laptop computer, so she was a natural choice. Nelson brought his newfound wealth and deposited all of it. Before lunch, a total of 182 starbills had been deposited into the bank. Once there were funds in the bank, people were able to take out loans to start their own businesses. And from the crowd of people outside the bank that first day, it looked like the bank was turning out to be a good idea.

5

THE GOLDEN ERA

I TOOK A LOOK AT Pete's movie script before the filming started. Not that I could've stopped him from making the film, but I told him I wanted to see the script so that I could decide whether or not I could support it as mayor. I didn't want the citizens of Kidsboro imitating Hollywood morals in one of its own productions.

I was pleased to discover that everything in it seemed harmless. The plot was fun and exciting. It might not be a classic, but I wouldn't withhold my support just because I thought it wasn't going to win any awards.

Pete held auditions for all the roles in his film. He told everyone that it was an action/adventure movie and that there were plenty of parts to audition for. Anyone who did not get an acting role could be hired as a crew person—cameraman, assistant director, sound technician (microphone holder, as it turned out), and so on. Practically everyone in Kidsboro showed up to audition. I sat and watched part of it, though I didn't audition myself. Pete sat in a director's chair. He had on sunglasses and held a megaphone, though it was an overcast day and he was only 15 feet away from the actors.

"Next," Pete said through his megaphone. Scott stepped to the front. "Name?" Pete asked.

"You know my name," Scott said.

"Name?" Pete insisted.

Scott rolled his eyes. "Scott Sanchez."

Pete wrote something down in his notebook. "Is that with an *S*?"

"Yes, two of them."

"And what part will you be reading for?"

"I'll be reading for the part of Rock Bockner."

"Oh . . ." Pete said, shaking his head. "I'm sorry, I've already cast that part."

Scott instantly objected, "Well, excuse me for using up oxygen, but am I not the first guy to audition? How could you have cast the part already?"

"It was a pre-production decision. Why don't you try out for Dead Guy number two?"

"Who got the part of Rock?" Scott demanded. At this point, other guys who were waiting their turn moved in to see what was going on.

Pete noticed the sudden invasion. "Would all other auditioners wait behind the curtain, please?"

"We want to know who got the part of Rock!" one boy demanded.

"Rock Bockner is . . ." Pete began quietly, then with all the confidence he could muster, he looked him straight in the eyes. "Me."

The boys immediately burst into hysterical laughter. Pete looked offended. "What's wrong with that?"

"Rock Bockner is not a four foot nine, 87-pound ostrich. He's a big, tough guy. With muscles and . . . a cool haircut," somebody responded.

"I can pull it off," Pete said.

"My sister could play Rock Bockner better than you."

This went on for another few minutes until Pete put his director's hat back on and insisted that they move on.

■ ■ ■

Auditions continued for the next couple of hours. The boys all came desiring the role of Rock and had their hopes dashed. But the best girl's part was still up for grabs. It was the role of Ginger, Rock's love interest and leading lady. Pete got to live out the dreams of pretty much every teenage boy in Odyssey—to choose from a long line of girls exactly who got to be his love interest.

At 1:13 that afternoon, the girls who were still standing in line realized they had no hope of being Ginger when they saw Valerie Swanson take her place in the audition chair. Like most of the guys in town, Pete was secretly in love with Valerie. She sat down and read for the part, but he never heard a word she said. He just stared at her with his chin resting sloppily in his hand. After she was done he said, "Wonderful." She smiled, flipped her hair back, and left.

■ ■ ■

After the main characters were cast, Pete held auditions for stuntmen. A dozen boys lined up to do whatever Pete asked, unconcerned with the danger. To refuse a challenge in front of a crowd of other boys would be unthinkable.

At one point Pete said, "All right, line up and jump off this cliff." The drop was about 10 feet. The landing didn't appear to be terribly dangerous, but no one knew if there were rocks beneath the surface of the dirt. "Who's first?" Pete asked as he took his chair and notebook down to the bottom of the cliff. Everyone casually shuffled backwards to allow someone else to go first. "Come on, people!" Pete shouted. "You can't be a stuntman if you're afraid to do what I tell you."

The boys looked at each other. They were hoping to find a hint of fear in one another's eyes so that they knew they were not alone. Finally, Scott, whom everyone knew didn't have a courageous bone in his body, asked a question that everyone would love him for. "Can we have some pillows down there?"

"Pillows?" Pete said.

"Yeah," Scott went on. "Whenever stuntmen jump off buildings and stuff, they always get one of those big balloon things to land on. I figured at least we could get some pillows." Some of the others nodded in agreement, casually shrugging their shoulders. No one wanted to admit that they needed pillows.

Pete rolled his eyes and sent a boy to get pillows. "Does anybody want to really impress me and do it without the pillows?" Pete challenged. But everyone collectively agreed to wait for the pillows.

The boy came back with a pile of laundry. "My mom wouldn't let me have pillows, but she gave me some old beach towels."

Towels? I didn't think towels would absorb much of the shock. It was, after all, a 10-foot drop. Pete laid the towels out on the ground, covering a fairly wide area at the bottom of the cliff. All in all, the towels appeared to provide about an inch and a half of padding.

Pete patted the towels, showing the prospective jumpers just how nice and soft the ground was now. He looked up at them, then backed into his director's chair. "All right. Who's first?"

They all looked at each other. "Scott," Pete said, "you got your padding. Why don't you give it a try?" Scott scratched the back of his neck and took a step forward to look over the cliff. He licked his lips and clenched his teeth.

"All right, everybody back up," Scott said. They obeyed. He backed up 20 feet and took a deep breath. The other boys were in awe. He closed his eyes, took a running start, and hurled himself off the cliff. He let out a small squeal and landed on the edge of the towels, fell awkwardly, and took a violent turn to the right, rolling into the bushes. He screamed in pain. Pete ran over to him, and the other boys peered over the top of the cliff to see what damage had been done.

"Are you okay?" Pete asked. Scott's eyes were closed. He grunted a bit and gingerly pulled a branch away from his face. He wiggled his toes as if to test for paralysis. Pete scanned his body for blood, but saw none. "Do you want me to help you up?"

Scott said with difficulty, "I'm okay."

"Anything broken?" Pete asked.

"I don't think so."

"Here. Let me help you," Pete said, grabbing his arm.

"No!" Scott shouted. "I got the wind knocked out of me. I'll just stay here for now."

"Under the bush?"

"Sure."

"You want me to just leave you here?"

"Yeah. I'll be fine."

Pete looked up at the boys at the top of the cliff. He walked to his chair. "Okay, good. Who's next?"

The boys looked at each other, waved a group good-bye, and went home. Pete went back over to Scott, who hadn't moved. "Congratulations, Scott. You're our stuntman."

■ ■ ■

On the way back into town the next morning, I noticed something very odd and disturbing. Jake's new house was not made of tarp, as I thought it would be. It was made of wood, just like everyone else's. Why would somebody pay top dollar to buy wood from Max when he could have a perfectly good house made of tarp for much less?

I got my answer seconds later. Max came up from be-hind me.

"Hey, Ryan. I met your buddy Jake." I practically bit my tongue in half. "I hear you guys go way back," he said.

"What did he tell you?" I asked, hoping he didn't notice the tremble in my voice.

"Just that you two have a special bond between you that goes back to your kindergarten days. Nice guy."

"Sure is."

"I look forward to getting to know him. In fact, he may just turn out to be one of my best friends." He winked at me and left. The lump in my throat was so large that I couldn't swallow. Max never wanted to get to know anyone. He didn't care about having friends. Why would he want to be Jake's friend? And why did Jake agree to buy Max's wood? Did Max give him the wood at a special price in exchange for . . . *information*? I could handle Max most of the time. Jake would be tougher, but I still thought I could deal with him. But the two of them together . . .

■ ■ ■

I expected the first day of filming to be like a soccer practice for five year olds—one person trying to organize 10 other people who would rather just kick stuff around. But when I got there, I was amazed to see that Pete had everything under control. In fact, he looked as though he knew exactly what he was doing every step of the way.

He had his lead actors in place. Valerie was standing behind the camera, ready to go on set. A boy named Kirk had won the part of the bad guy. He was wearing a black suit and he had a smirk on his face. His longer hair gave him a convincing bad-guy look.

Pete had put the camera tripod on wheels and bought some plywood from Max so that he could easily roll the camera, making a sort of makeshift dolly. He watched through the viewfinder and yelled "Action!"

Kirk was already on the set, sitting at a table in what looked like an outdoor café. Valerie approached him cautiously. She spoke with a hint of fear in her voice. "What do you want?"

"Thanks for coming, Ginger. Have a seat." She sat down. Pete whispered something to his cameraman and motioned to two production assistants standing nearby. They wheeled the dolly slowly to the left.

"I want the computer disk," Kirk said.

"What if I don't have it?"

Kirk laughed. Pete had the cameraman move in slowly. "Well, then . . . I guess I don't have your mother, either."

Valerie gasped. "What have you done with my mother?"

"The question should be, 'What will we do to your mother if you don't comply?' And the answer, for now, is that we haven't done anything . . . yet. She's safe and sound and could remain that way, but that's up to you."

Pete signaled to a guy who was operating a large fan. A fairly heavy breeze suddenly hit the scene and Valerie's hair fluttered. Then Pete motioned to Patty, who was off-camera. She approached with a tray full of food in one hand, and a plastic pitcher of water in the other.

"The shrimp looks good," Kirk said, seeing the tray.

Valerie didn't care about the shrimp. "What's to prevent me from going to the police right now?"

"Oh, I don't think you want to deal with the police. Not with *your* past, Ginger . . . or should I say . . . *Gretchen*." Valerie gasped again. She was really good at that. She exhaled, and then pushed her hair back casually as if to mask her fear. Suddenly, she glanced upward. Her eyes widened when she saw Patty, the waitress. The wind from the fan had blown a large oak leaf into her face, and it had stuck there. She was powerless to do anything because both her hands were full. Valerie snickered a little, but quickly looked away. Patty was jerking her head to the left, trying to get the leaf off, but it remained stuck.

Kirk noticed Valerie's snicker and looked up at Patty. He made a funny noise, then grabbed his water glass and drank. Valerie and Kirk tried to regain their composure and continue with the scene. Charlie, the guy holding the microphone, noticed the leaf and tried to stifle his laughter, but the microphone began shaking above Kirk's head. Pete saw the microphone and the sudden change in the actors, and he looked around. He finally noticed the leaf that appeared to be a part of Patty's face. She swung the pitcher up toward her face to scrape it off, but instead the water flew up out of the pitcher and spilled over the front of her shirt. She remained calm. Pete bowed his head and his body shook with laughter.

Heroically, the actors continued on. "You see, Ginger . . ." Kirk said with a slight smile, "we have many ways of getting that disk, even if you don't give it to us."

Valerie covered her mouth and was barely able to deliver her line. "What are you talking about?"

"Well . . . we could . . . we could . . ." He was starting to lose it. "We could glue a leaf to your face just like we did to her!"

The entire cast and crew burst into hysterics. Patty grinned, threw the plastic pitcher down, and peeled the leaf off her face. Valerie and Kirk laughed until they cried. Pete fell on the ground headfirst. I had to hold my side to keep it from bursting. Valerie stood up and gave Patty a sympathy hug. Patty laughed at herself.

After five full minutes of utter frenzy, Pete began to get everything set up again. The crew went back to their places, Patty reloaded her tray and pitcher, and no one was upset that they had to do the entire scene over again.

It was one of the nicest moments in the history of Kidsboro.

■ ■ ■

I left the set for a while and took a leisurely walk around. There were several people playing on the miniature golf course. Mark had made a few changes in the course. It was actually possible to make a decent score on a couple of the holes.

Nelson, Eugene, and two employees were giving their newest model a road test: a stylish, red pickup truck. He'd gotten several more orders for this model. Nelson had a stack of wood nearby, and the truck had a small stack in its bed. Eugene had a pencil behind his ear and a pad in his hand. He was smiling as though he was impressed. Apparently, they were testing to see how much weight the truck would hold.

I stopped by the bank, and Marcy was signing a few papers. A customer was opening up a new account. Marcy explained the concept behind interest, withdrawals, and deposits. She entered some figures into her computer.

I went into my office, sat back in my chair, and smiled. I was proud of my city. This was how it was supposed to be.

Suddenly, the door crashed open and Scott burst in. "There's been an accident!"

6

THE BEGINNING OF THE END

SEVERAL PEOPLE WERE ALREADY AT the scene when I got there. Jill, the newspaper reporter, was there with her notebook and pen. Roberto, assistant newspaper editor/reporter/photographer, was taking pictures of the scene. And lying on the ground, holding his ankle, was Jake. James, the town doctor, was kneeling down beside him with his medical bag. I suppose I should have asked Jake if he was okay, but I couldn't bring myself to do it.

He offered the information on his own. "I think I pulled something."

James fumbled around in his bag. He had never actually treated anyone, so he looked excited to finally get a chance to use his limited knowledge of first aid. He pulled out an Ace bandage.

"Let's wrap that—"

"Get away from me, you quack!" Jake shouted.

"What happened?" Jill asked.

"I fell on one of Nelson's stupid cars. It came out of nowhere and I tripped over it."

"Can you walk?" Scott asked.

"I haven't tried."

Scott and James helped Jake up, and he tried to walk on his own. His ankle buckled and he almost fell. They gently helped him sit back down.

Nelson ran up. "What's going on?"

"You!" Jake screamed. "You and your stupid cars!"

"My cars?"

"I fell over one! And I might've torn something."

"I'm sorry . . ." Nelson noticed one of his cars upside down on the grass. He turned it over and saw that the entire length of the car had been crushed. He went over to help Jake.

"Don't even come near me! Haven't you done enough?"

"Jake, I'm just trying to help. It's not my fault that you fell on the car."

"And why not?"

"Who was driving it?"

"I don't know. But you're the one who invented these death-mobiles."

"That's irrelevant."

"It's *your* fault. And I'm gonna take you for every penny you've got."

"What?" Nelson asked with his eyes open as big as saucers.

"I'm suing you," Jake said. Nelson stepped back as if he was going to faint. Kidsboro had gotten sue-happy before, and it had hurt the town badly. I didn't want to go through that again.

"Now come on, Jake," Nelson said. "You don't need to sue me."

"What do you care? You're rich."

Scott went to get Mr. Whittaker, who rushed out the back door of his shop, and down the main street of Kidsboro. He bent down at Jake's side. "Can you walk?"

"No."

"Where does it hurt?"

"I'm okay. I just need to get home."

Mr. Whittaker pulled Jake up, threw his arm around him, and half-carried him off. Jake moaned until he was out of earshot.

■ ■ ■

The whole story was in the *Kidsboro Chronicle* the next day, along with a picture of the scene of the accident, some quotes from Jake, "our newest citizen," and comments from Nelson. Jake's threat to sue Nelson "for every penny" was in there too. I was hoping that part of the story wouldn't appear in the paper.

I didn't want anyone to think there was any kind of trouble in paradise during this "golden age" of Kidsboro, as I liked to call it. But now it was out there, and all I could do was hope that it wouldn't lead to anything worse.

■ ■ ■

"Come on! I've been behind the camera for an hour and a half, and I haven't even filmed anything yet!" Pete's cameraman complained. It had been a long day and tempers ap-peared to be running high. This was the fifth day in a row they had been filming.

"Hang on," Pete answered. "I just have to work some things out." Pete was explaining the next scene to Stuntman Scott.

"Okay, you're being chased by Kirk. You've got the disk in your pocket and you're trying to get it to Rock. Over by the creek, you jump on your getaway bike, and you have this high-speed bike chase through the woods. Kirk will be behind you. When you get over here, you lose control of your bike and run into this tree right here."

"What?"

"And make sure you hit the jagged branches."

"You want me to run into a tree?"

"Yes."

"At full speed?"

"Yes."

"On an out-of-control bike?"

"Yes."

"Excuse me for being sane, but are you crazy?"

"Are you not my stuntman?"

"Sure, but . . . don't you think that's kind of dangerous?"

"What? You want me to nail some pillows to the tree?" Pete asked, throwing his arms up in disbelief.

Scott thought a minute, then said quietly, "Yes."

Pete looked disgusted. "We can't put pillows on the trees; the camera will pick them up. Now if you want to remain my stuntman, I suggest you get on that bike and start plummeting headfirst into that tree!"

Scott put his head down and headed for the bike. Several times he turned back and glanced at the tree as though wondering how to escape certain discomfort.

As Scott prepared for his big scene, Valerie came over with a script in her hand. She was as fed up as everyone else seemed to be.

"What is this?" she asked Pete.

Pete looked at where she was pointing on the script, acting as if he had no idea what she was talking about. But he obviously knew what she was going to complain about.

"What?"

She began reading from the script, "'Rock gently pulls her toward him and kisses her on the lips. Ginger knows she must resist, but cannot. She melts into his powerful arms.'" She looked up. "I am *not* kissing you, nor am I melting into your powerful, yet completely unmuscular, arms."

"But . . . Valerie . . ." Pete responded with all the confidence he could muster. "It's very important to the script. This is a turning point for your character. Ginger has never let herself become vulnerable before. Now she's falling in love and has no choice. She has to trust him."

"I think I can communicate that in other ways."

"Like what?"

"I don't know. I'll give Rock a little thumbs-up sign or something."

"Dramatically, that's a little less impressive than what I was going for."

"I know what you were going for," Valerie said suspiciously. "I'm not kissing you, and that's final."

"Do you want this to be a good movie or not?"

"More importantly, I will have a *life* after this movie. And I would like to be able to sleep at night and not have nightmares about your disgusting little lips coming at me."

"You know, I don't want to pull rank, but who's the artist here?"

"Are you kidding me? You call this art?" Valerie turned back a page in the script and pointed to a selection. "This line, right here. This line that you are expecting me to memorize and say on camera. *This* is art?"

Pete scanned it. "That's *beautiful*. It's practically *poetry*!"

"This is garbage! Listen to this, everyone." She began reading, "'Rock, ever since I met you the stars seem to shine brighter, the mountains seem taller . . . flowers seem to smell sweeter. I love you because of the way you make me feel, Rock.'"

"You don't like that?"

"That's *terrible*!"

"You're just so used to your soap operas that when you see a well-written love story, you don't even recognize it."

"I guarantee you I could write better than this."

"Then be my guest, Valerie! *You* rewrite that scene, and we'll see how artistic you and your little soap-opera brain can be."

"Love to." Valerie closed the script and headed off to work on the rewrite. Pete shook his head back and forth violently to illustrate to everyone around him how frustrating actors can be.

With that over, Pete got ready for the bike-chase scene. Scott was ready, and Pete gave the signal for the cameraman to roll.

Scott took a deep breath and started pedaling. He veered toward the tree he was preparing to hit. Kirk started up be-hind him.

"Faster!" Pete called out. Scott stood up on his pedals to gain more speed. Kirk came up behind him.

"You're too close together!" Pete yelled. "Speed up, Scott!"

Scott obeyed again. He clenched his teeth and looked directly at the tree.

"Now look back a couple of times, like you're scared he's catching up!"

Scott glanced toward Kirk and swerved around a rock. There was nothing between him and the tree now.

"Faster!" Pete shouted. Scott pedaled faster, and it really did look like he was starting to lose control. I put my hand over my mouth and prepared for the impact.

Scott closed his eyes, hit a root, and lost control of the handlebars, swerving to the right and crashing into the tree at an angle. His left leg hit sharply against the bark, sending him flying out of the seat. The bike flipped and fell on top of him. The back wheel pinned his leg to the ground. Scott lay motionless, the front wheel still spinning.

Everyone nearby ran toward him.

"Are you okay?" I asked.

Scott opened his eyes. He breathed heavily, glancing around at all the faces staring down at him. "I'm fine," he said.

"Fantastic!" Pete shouted after seeing that Scott was still alive. "Wonderful, Scott. Now let's go to another angle and do it again."

Scott's eyes opened wide. "You're crazy," he said, still lying on his back. "I'm not doing that again."

"We have to get it from another angle, so that we have something to cut to," Pete said, as though Scott should understand this logic.

"Forget it, Pete. I quit."

"Come on, Scott, you did great. I need you."

"You're crazy! You're insane, and I will never do another thing you ask for the rest of my life. Never."

Pete turned back to his cameraman. "He just needs a little time to get over the trauma . . . of running into a tree and all."

I tried to help Scott, but he didn't want to be touched. I did manage to pull the bike off of him.

In the meantime, Valerie had finished her rewrite. "Here you go. I rewrote that scene. You wanna hear it?"

"Sure," Pete said, undoubtedly hoping it wouldn't be as good as his draft.

Valerie cleared her throat and read from the new script, "'Rock, ever since I met you . . . garbage smells more disgusting . . . all men, other than you, seem more handsome . . . and muscles seem to be flabbier . . .'"

"All right, very funny," Pete said. "But this is not a comedy."

"There's where you're wrong, Pete. This *is* a comedy. This is the most hilarious thing I've ever been a part of. I look at this script and I cannot help but laugh my head off."

This went on for several minutes until Nelson came running up to me with a piece of paper. "Look at this." He handed me the paper and I quickly scanned it. "I'm being sued. For 100 starbills."

"One hundred starbills?!"

"Ryan, if I lose this case . . . I'm ruined."

7

THE TRIAL OF THE CENTURY

ONE HUNDRED STARBILLS WAS RIDICULOUS. There was no way that Nelson's "crime" was worth 100 starbills. That amount would ruin anyone.

Nelson tried to get his sister, Valerie, to represent him, but she was busy shooting the movie. Unfortunately, she was the best lawyer in town. The only other lawyer in town was Pete, who was also shooting the movie. So Nelson decided to be his own lawyer. No one had any idea who was going to represent Jake, the "victim."

We found five people to be on the jury. None of them had seen the accident and four of them didn't even know Jake, so they seemed impartial.

- - -

The meeting hall was packed. Almost everyone who wasn't involved with the movie shoot was there. Before taking my seat, I stopped by Nelson's table. "Keep your head up. You can trust the judgment of the people of this town."

"Will you testify for me?" he asked.

"Of course."

Jake made a dramatic entrance into the courtroom. He was on crutches and had a splint on his leg. He groaned just loud enough for everyone to hear him and asked several members of the audience for assistance. I saw Nelson bury his head in his hands. But as bad as Jake's appearance was, things were about to get worse. Right behind Jake, to the horror of everyone there, was the person who was to be his lawyer—Max Darby. A gasp echoed under the roof as they came in together. The loudest gasp came from Nelson.

I didn't think Max's presence was so bad, though. Max was smart and he was mean, and that made him the tougher lawyer. But everyone knew Max was dishonest and cruel. I hoped the jury would keep his reputation in mind.

Many of the jurors themselves had probably been swindled by Max at some point. But there was no telling what Max would say to tear down Nelson's character. Win or lose, Nelson would be hurt by this trial.

Judge Amy called court into session. Nelson was sitting alone at a table in the front. Max moved their table so that Jake could stick his leg out far enough for the jury to see the splint. When the jury entered, that was the first thing they all saw.

The judge asked Jake to tell everyone, in his own words, what happened. Jake told the whole story. He was walking home when the car came out of nowhere and he stepped on it. He fell down and pulled a ligament in his ankle. The judge asked how he knew it was ligament damage. Max submitted a copy of a real doctor's report. It stated that Jake should stay off his feet because he had pulled a ligament in his ankle. The judge had the jury pass the slip of paper around, and then moved on.

Judge Amy asked how much money the plaintiff (Jake) was asking for. Max told her that since the injury had prevented Jake from doing his job (he mowed lawns), Nelson should pay him 100 starbills for lost wages.

"One hundred starbills seems like a lot of money, Mr. Darby," the judge said.

"Yes, Your Honor," Max said in the over-dramatized Southern accent he saved for really important swindles. "But since my client is losing real wages, that is, real money from the real world, we thought 100 starbills, which is, well . . . pretend money . . . would be about the right amount."

Judge Amy nodded her head, and then asked Nelson to begin. Nelson pleaded his case, telling everyone that he never had any intention to do anyone harm, and that it was a freak accident. Then he pointed out that if this had been a real car accident, it would be the fault of the driver, not the manufacturer of the car. I saw a juror nod, so I thought Nelson had made a good point.

Then Nelson called me to the stand. I talked about how I had been friends with Nelson for many years and that I would vouch for his good character. I told the jury that I believed he had only good intentions when he built those cars and that his business had been good for the city. Nelson smiled at me, and then told the judge he had no more questions for me.

I started to go back to my seat when Max suddenly said, "I'd like to cross-examine the witness." What was he going to ask me?

I sat back down in the witness stand and nervously pushed my hair back off my forehead. Max stood up and approached me.

"Mr. Mayor, how long have you known Nelson Swanson?"

"About four years."

"And from what you've seen, what does he do with most of his time?"

"Well . . . he's always building things or coming up with new ideas . . ."

"So, he's an inventor?"

"Yes."

"I declare. Quite a noble profession," he said. "Besides the cars, what else has Nelson invented?"

"Um . . . lots of things. He made a burglar alarm, um . . . an air hockey table, an automatic soccer ball kicker—so goalies could practice keeping goal."

"Go on."

"Well, a couple of smaller things . . . a self-heating frying pan . . ."

"Self-heating frying pan? Now that sounds interesting."

"Yeah, he made it for Sid so he could sell egg and cheese sandwiches in the bakery."

"Mmm. Sounds good."

"It was battery-operated. You didn't need a stove."

"A marvel of technology. Tell me, how long did it take Nelson to make it?"

"I'm not sure. Maybe two months or so."

"Why'd it take so long?"

"He's kind of a perfectionist. It had to be perfect."

"But what was wrong with the first model?"

"The first model?"

"The very first time he tried this self-heating frying pan, did it not work?"

"I guess . . . not the very *first* time."

"What was wrong with it?"

I had no idea where he was going with this, but I figured I should tell the truth as I knew it to be. "I don't know. He could tell you better than I can."

"What happened when he first tried it out?"

I thought about it a second, then I remembered. Suddenly, I knew exactly where Max was going with this. I didn't see how I could avoid admitting something that would be damaging to Nelson's case. I decided to stall. "It . . . didn't work perfectly."

"What makes you say that?"

"The, um . . . wiring was a little off . . ."

"And what happened as a result of the bad wiring?"

"It . . . malfunctioned."

"How?"

"By . . . not working correctly."

He was getting impatient. "Mr. Mayor, isn't it true that the frying pan caught on *fire* in his house?"

"I seem to recall—"

"Mr. Mayor, you are under oath! Did it catch on fire?"

"It was just a small fire . . . and we put it out with an extinguisher."

"Nelson has a fire extinguisher in his house?"

"Yes."

"So apparently this happens to Nelson a lot, huh?"

"I wouldn't say that—"

"Wouldn't you agree that a person who has a fire extinguisher in his house does so because there might be a fire?"

"Oh, come on, Max—"

"Let's go back to the soccer ball kicker. Isn't it true, Mr. Mayor, that the first version of this invention nearly kicked Scott Sanchez's kneecap off?"

"It wasn't that bad."

"Did Scott Sanchez have to go to the doctor because of it?"

"It was Scott's fault—"

He started shouting. "Did Scott Sanchez have to have medical treatment done to his knee because of an invention that Nelson Swanson created, or not?"

He had me. I had no choice. "Yes."

"So, Mr. Mayor, is it fair to say that Nelson Swanson has a history of creating dangerous products?"

Nelson shouted from his chair, "Objection!"

"No further questions, Your Honor," Max said before the judge could answer the objection. All he wanted to do was get the jury thinking that Nelson was dangerous. And he was probably doing a good job of it. I stepped down and gave Nelson an "I'm sorry" look. He didn't respond because he appeared to be thinking up a new strategy.

"Nelson, do you have any more witnesses?" the judge asked.

"Yes," Nelson said. Nelson called a boy named Charlie to the witness stand.

"Charlie, is this your remote-controlled car?" Nelson held up the car that Jake had tripped on. It still had a crushed windshield.

"Yes."

"Were you operating the car on the day that Jake tripped on it?"

"No."

"What were you doing?"

"I was working on the movie shoot all day—holding a microphone."

"So, Charlie, did you loan your car to anyone?"

"No."

"Did you pre-program the car to operate at that specific time of day?"

"No."

"So, who was controlling the car?"

"I don't know."

"Did any of your friends have access to the car?"

"Not that I know of."

"Do you think someone stole your car?"

"Yes, I do."

"Isn't it a possibility that someone might've stolen your car, used it to stage a fake fall in order to sue—"

Max exploded out of his chair. "Objection! He's leading the witness."

"Sustained," Judge Amy said without hesitation.

"No more questions, Your Honor." Brilliant. Just as Max had done minutes earlier, Nelson had planted a seed of doubt in the jury's minds. Was all of this some kind of hoax? No one knew who had been operating the car. Surely this missing bit of information was crucial.

Max had no questions for Charlie, so Nelson continued. "I would like to call Eugene Meltsner to the stand."

Max objected to Nelson calling an adult, stating that because this was a kids' town, adults had no business interfering in the affairs of Kidsboro. Judge Amy overruled him, since one of his pieces of evidence, the doctor's slip, was signed by an adult. Amy was a fine judge.

Eugene stepped to the stand. Reverend Joey was working as the bailiff. He asked Eugene, "Do you promise to tell the truth, the whole truth, and nothing but the truth?"

"Indeed I do," he replied.

Nelson said, "Mr. Meltsner, you helped me build those cars. In your expert opinion, is there anything unsafe about them?"

"Undoubtedly, there are dangers inherent in any manmade mechanism, but I would consider these to be slight in the models created by Nelson Motors."

Confused silence settled upon the audience. Nelson noticed. "And that means?"

"No."

Eugene's testimony went on endlessly, somehow transforming every one-sentence answer into a four- or five-sentence answer. Finally, he was finished.

"The defense rests for now," Nelson said.

"All right, then. Max, do you have any witnesses?" Judge Amy inquired.

"I do, Your Honor." He called Nelson to the stand and asked him one question. "How much money did you make this summer, Mr. Swanson?" Nelson immediately objected, but for some reason, Judge Amy allowed it.

"About 125 starbills. But most of that went back into my company."

"No further questions." I couldn't believe Judge Amy would allow a ploy to get the jury to think, "Let's get the rich guy." It was a despicable strategy on Max's part, but it would probably work.

Max then called Jake to the stand. "Do you know Nelson Swanson, Mr. Randall?"

"Not really. I've met him. I know he's the one who built the car."

"Do you know Jill Segler?"

"I met her once. She interviewed me."

"How about Scott Sanchez?"

"Again, I met him once." Where was he going with this?

"Alice Funderburk."

"Cop, right?"

"That's right. Do you know her very well?"

"Nope."

"How about Mayor Ryan Cummings? Do you know him very well?"

Jake looked over at me with an evil smile. "Oh, yes. I know Ryan."

Nelson objected, "Your Honor, I fail to see the relevance—"

"Thank you, Mr. Randall. That's all," Max said.

Jake stepped down. Then Max pulled another unexpected move. "I'd like to call Ryan Cummings back up to the stand."

I looked at the judge, desperately hoping this was against the rules. But it wasn't. I slowly left my seat and took my place on the stand.

"Mr. Mayor, welcome back," Max said with a smile.

"Thanks," I said, rolling my eyes.

"Mr. Mayor, do you know Jake Randall?" Oh no. He wouldn't. Jake had probably told him something, and now Max was going to blackmail me. Or maybe it was something else. Maybe Max was just trying to scare me. I had to stay calm. If I acted nervous, or if I refused to answer the question, everyone in Kidsboro would know something was up. They'd all be asking me questions. I couldn't deal with that. I had to remain calm.

"Yes," I said.

"How well do you know him?"

"Not that well, really."

"Is he your friend?"

"I don't know if I would call him that. He's an acquaintance."

"Isn't he a little more than that?"

I gulped. "What do you mean?"

"He's a citizen of this town, isn't he?"

"Yes," I said, fearing a bad question was just around the corner. I shifted in my chair.

"It's very strange that he became a citizen. You know why? Because our city charter states that 80 percent of the city council has to approve a new citizen. That means four out of the five members of the city council had to vote for him. And yet . . . Jake just testified that he doesn't even know four out of the five members of the city council. He does, however, know you. Mr. Mayor, if Jake only knows one out of five people on the city council, could you tell us how it is that he became a citizen?"

I glanced over at Jake. He was trying to hide a smile.

"You must've recommended him very highly if they were convinced without ever meeting him."

I didn't answer.

"He must be a very good friend, Mr. Mayor. And we all know how much pride you take in your citizens. We all know you would never want a dishonest, untrustworthy person within the walls of Kidsboro. So, Mr. Mayor, when Jake says that these events took place . . . you know, with the car and all . . . you believe him, don't you?"

He had me again. I couldn't question Jake's character. I took a deep breath and prepared to lie. "If that's what he said . . . I guess it happened."

"And do you think Jake would ever be a part of any hoax, Mr. Mayor?"

"I . . . suppose not."

"Thank you, Mr. Mayor." Thankfully, I got to get off the stand. My heart was pumping against my chest like a bongo drum.

"No further questions," Max said. "We rest our case, Your Honor."

The judge allowed each lawyer to restate his case. Nelson's sounded pretty flimsy up against Max's, I must say. I couldn't quite read the jury's faces. I just hoped they remembered the other scams that Max had pulled in the past. That was probably Nelson's only hope. The jury left to discuss the verdict.

■ ■ ■

Nelson remained in his chair behind the table. I wanted to say I was sorry, but I didn't think it would matter at this point. I would wait until the verdict was in.

I decided to get out of there before anyone asked me any questions about Jake. On my way out, I ran into him. He was maneuvering himself out from under the pavilion roof on his crutches. He smiled and patted me on the back. "Thanks for saying such nice things about me, Ryan."

Fuming, I grabbed him by the arm and led him away from the crowd. "What are you guys doing?" I demanded once we were out of earshot.

"Who?"

"You and Max."

"We're tryin' to win a case."

"What did you tell him?"

"About what?"

"You know about what," I said, fisting the bottom of his shirt up into a wad.

"Man, you're really scared of me." I let go of his shirt. I was giving myself away. "I didn't tell him nothing. Don't worry." He headed back to the meeting hall. "We're pals, remember?"

I watched him walk away. I didn't want to be scared of him. But I was.

■ ■ ■

The jury would probably be out for a while, so I decided to take a break from reality and check out Kidsboro's version of Hollywood. The movie shoot had been in progress for over a week now. The last time I had been there, things weren't going terribly well. I hoped Pete had been able to smooth some things over.

When I got there, Pete was filming at the bottom of the cliff and had apparently just finished a scene. Scott was lying at the base of the cliff, moaning. Lying next to him were three garbage bags filled with couch cushions. The bags were painted to look like rocks. From the looks of things, Scott had just been asked to stand under a cliff while rocks landed on top of him. I guess Pete had misjudged the weight of the couch cushions, because Scott looked to be in quite a daze. He was mumbling something about naptime.

Then Valerie stormed up with a piece of paper in her hand. She went straight to Pete and stuck her finger in his face. Everyone else on the crew stopped what they were doing and filed in behind her. Pete watched them, clueless.

"Mr. Director, the entire cast and crew met last night after we were done taping. We met to discuss how we were feeling about this movie production. As it turns out, Pete, everyone felt pretty much the same way. We're all sick of you!"

"What?"

"You've pushed us way too hard. We're 10 to 14 years old. We shouldn't have to work 60-hour weeks."

"I thought you *liked* doing this," Pete said.

"We *used* to like doing this. But you've completely taken the fun out of it for everyone."

"How?"

"Funny you should ask that. At the meeting last night, we came up with a list of grievances. And from that, a list of demands. We will refuse to work until every last one of these demands is met."

"Refuse to work? You can't do that. You're under contract."

"We're breaking it, unless these demands are met."

"Okay, what demands?"

Valerie cleared her throat and read aloud, "We will get a one-hour lunch break every day."

"All right, I can deal with that," Pete said.

"We will not work past seven o'clock in the evening, unless we are given overtime pay."

"I suppose I could work around the seven o'clock thing. But you're not getting overtime. We're over budget as it is."

Valerie went on. "The cast and crew will be allowed to have as much creative input as they desire."

"What do you mean by that?"

"We can change the script if we want to."

"No way. This is *my* film—"

She ignored him and went back to the list. "The actors will not be required to touch other actors." I was certain this one was Valerie's demand.

"What? You've gotta be kidding! The script has to have—"

"We will not be required to travel over 15 miles an hour and run into solid objects, and we will not be required to have solid objects that are traveling over 15 miles an hour run into *us*." Scott's demand, obviously.

"This is ridiculous."

"We will not be required to do any more method-acting exercises where we have to act like we're a kitchen appliance for an entire day." I could understand this one. Scott was clearly embarrassed one day when he had wrecked trying to ride a bicycle like a toaster oven.

"What gives you guys the right to question my techniques? *I'm* the artist here. Spielberg doesn't have to answer to his actors."

"You're not Spielberg. And you'll give us what we want or we walk."

"No way. I can deal with some of those things, but I can't turn my set into a free-for-all. I have to have control."

"Fine. Then we're officially on strike."

"You can't be serious!"

"Come on, everybody." Valerie dropped the list on the ground in front of Pete. The group filed away quietly. Scott got up from the bottom of the cliff and followed.

"*Nobody's* staying? Oh, come on!" Pete picked up the list. "I'll give you the lunch break . . . and the quitting at seven o'clock deal! Except for night shoots, of course. Okay, no more method-acting exercises! I'll give you that one." Pete continued to yell out at them, but no one even turned around. Pete suddenly turned defiant. "You'll be back! You need this job! A lot of you don't even *have* other jobs! And you know what? I can finish this movie without you!"

I turned to Pete and shrugged my shoulders. "Maybe a little compromise wouldn't hurt."

"Compromise is what makes bad movies," he said, turning and putting his equipment away.

■ ■ ■

I got back to the meeting hall just in time. The jury was in place and ready to read the verdict. I sat down and glanced at Nelson. He was fidgeting in his seat. A juror handed a piece of paper to the judge and she read it.

"Has the jury reached a verdict?" she asked.

The foreman of the jury stood up. "Yes, Your Honor."

"Go ahead."

"We, the jury, find for the plaintiff." Nelson had lost. A gasp went through the crowd and Nelson's head practically dropped to the floor. The foreman went on, "For the entire 100 starbills." Another gasp. Nelson's head bent even further down. I looked around. One person knocked over a chair in anger; another pounded his fist into a post. They were both investors in Nelson's company. All that money they had invested was gone. Another boy shouted "No!" and buried his head in his hands. It was one of Nelson's employees. He was probably out of a job. Until this moment, I hadn't realized just how many people this lawsuit would affect. Max and Jake were giving each other high-fives, and they left the room taunting Nelson. Nelson continued to sit there and stare at the ground. I went over to him.

"I'm finished," he said.

"You can rebuild," I told him. "You've got a good product."

"How am I gonna get any investors after this? I can't build cars anymore. I'm done."

■ ■ ■

A week after the verdict, our two biggest industries were gone. Nelson Motors was bankrupt, and Pete's movie was on hold because of the strike. Investors in both were furious. All of Nelson's employees had to be laid off. Also, some of the investors had their own businesses, and when they lost the money they had put into Nelson Motors, some of *their* employees had to be laid off too. In short, no one in Kidsboro (except for Max and Jake) had any money. And because no one had any money, that meant that no one had any money to spend—so businesses were failing. No one was playing miniature golf anymore or going to the movies. Unemployment was growing and it showed no signs of getting any better.

But it could get worse.

8

THE GREAT DEPRESSION

MARCY CAME TO MY OFFICE after she was done at the bank for the day. She looked rattled. "Ryan, can I talk to you for a minute?"

"Sure." I motioned for her to come in. She sat down and hit my desk with her knee, almost knocking over a clock.

"Sorry."

"That's okay." Her face paled. I felt sorry for her and I didn't even know what was the matter yet.

"We've got a problem. The bank is almost out of money."

"What?"

"You see . . . everybody's broke, and so people are taking their money out of the bank because they suddenly need it. And the people who took out loans to start their new businesses, well . . . they can't pay their loans back because they don't have any customers anymore."

"So, there's all sorts of money going *out* of the bank, but no money coming *in*?"

"Exactly."

"Oh, boy."

"We wouldn't be so low except that Max withdrew all of his money—212 starbills."

"Why did Max take out his money?"

"He said he had some things to buy."

"With 212 starbills? There's nothing in Kidsboro that costs that much."

"I didn't ask him about that. I didn't think it was any of my business."

"Oh, man. This is bad. If this gets out, everybody's going to want to get their money out of the bank as soon as possible," I said. "And if the money runs out, a lot of people are gonna be really angry."

"I know. Some people put everything they owned in the bank."

To be honest, I was tempted to take out my own money. I had almost 20 starbills in that bank and I couldn't afford to lose it. But I couldn't do that to Marcy or to Kidsboro.

"How much do we have left?"

"Twenty-three starbills. And some change."

"Okay." I got up and began to pace around. I had to think. "Okay . . . if anybody wants to take out any money tomorrow, try to convince them not to. Make up any reason."

"I could raise interest rates."

"Yes. Good. Tell them that for this week, and this week only, the interest rate is raised three percentage points. They could earn extra money for keeping it in there for one more week. Figure out exactly how much and tell them."

"Okay."

"And get on these guys who owe the bank money."

"I've already talked to them. No one has anything to pay back."

"I'll go out tomorrow and bring Alice with me. She'll squeeze it out of them."

"Oh, yeah. That might work."

"And most importantly, Marcy . . . don't tell *anyone* about this. Not your best friend, not your mother, not even your teddy bear."

"I won't."

"If this gets out, we're *all* in deep trouble."

■ ■ ■

The next day I asked Alice to help me collect some debts. I knocked on doors and asked people to please pay back the money they owed the bank. Most said they didn't have any money, until Alice stepped inside and threatened to turn them upside down by their ankles. Then they suddenly remembered that they *did* have a little money stashed away somewhere. The plan worked. We were able to retrieve 19 starbills, but that wasn't nearly as much as what was owed. People genuinely had no money, and no amount of being turned upside down could get them to pay up. By the end of the day, I was happy with what we got. I was pretty sure that the 19 starbills we had collected, plus the 23 already in the bank, would hold us for another few days.

■ ■ ■

I was surprised to see Pete with a camera. He was apparently getting ready to film a scene. I walked over, but didn't see any of the regular actors or crew around. It was just Pete and his six-year-old sister, Robin. Robin was sitting at a table facing someone I didn't recognize at first. The face was turned away from me. Maybe Pete was filming something for his family.

"What are you doing, Pete?"

"Making my film."

"What film?"

"The film I've been making for the last few weeks," he said matter-of-factly, as though it was a stupid question.

"I didn't know your sister was in it."

"She is now."

"What role is she playing?"

"Right now she's Ginger." He looked through his viewfinder and dollied the camera a little to his left.

"What do you mean?"

"I told them I could make this film without them. And I will."

"How is Robin going to play Ginger?"

"Robin's a very talented actress. You'd be surprised."

"So, you're just going to throw out all the stuff you filmed with Valerie as Ginger?"

"Nope. I'm keeping it." This was getting tiresome. I wished he would just tell me what was going on.

"How are you going to explain how Ginger suddenly changed from a 14 year old with long, brown hair into a six year old with curly, black hair?"

"With this." Pete held up a plain silver mask, which he took over to Robin. "Here. You can put this on now." She tied it around her head and he came back and looked through the viewfinder. He glanced toward me. "I changed the script a little bit. Now, Ginger has some kind of dental surgery and has to wear this mask for a month."

"So, she's going to wear this thing for the rest of the movie?"

"Yep. You see, it makes perfect sense, because if you'll remember, earlier in the film Ginger talks about being engaged to a dentist."

"So?"

"Well, it's natural to assume that her fiancé would recognize her need for surgery. It's perfectly logical."

"Oh, right," I said.

He looked back toward Robin. "Pull the mask a little toward your right ear."

"Who's that?" I asked, pointing to whoever was sitting in the chair opposite her. I still hadn't seen his face, and he hadn't moved an inch since I got there.

"That's the bad guy."

I walked around where I could see the bad guy's face, and as soon as I saw it, I almost burst out laughing. "A giant teddy bear?"

"All you can see is the back of his clothes. When I change angles, *I'll* play the bad guy."

"With a dental surgery mask on?"

"No. I'll just duck behind flowers and stuff. Wear a hat."

I raised my eyebrows.

"It'll work," Pete insisted.

"No, it *won't* work," came a voice from behind me. Pete and I whirled around and saw Mark, the owner and creator of the miniature golf place. His face was red.

Pete ignored Mark and continued to work.

"You're not going to do this, Pete!"

"Go away, Mark."

"I invested a lot of money in this movie, and you've got your six-year-old sister playing the romantic lead? I don't think so."

"I've got it all figured out. You'll never know the difference."

"Listen to me, Pete." Pete continued to look through the viewfinder.

Mark walked around in front of the camera and spoke into the lens. "Listen to me. I've got a business to run. I've got loans that I can't pay back. This movie needs to be made, and it needs to be made *now*. You will give the actors *everything* they want."

"I can't do that."

"You have to."

"If I give in now, they'll just want more and more."

"I don't care."

"This is my movie!"

"But it's my money you're making this movie *with*!"

"Investors have no say in how a movie is produced."

"I don't know where you're getting all these rules. But you'd better close your little rule book and start negotiating with the actors. Now." Mark pushed on the side of the camera, rolling it to the edge of the flat, wood piece it was sitting on. He took one last angry look at Pete and left. Pete hesitated only a second, then moved his camera back into place.

"You know, Pete, he's probably right," I said.

"Would you mind leaving the set, Ryan? I'm trying to concentrate."

I turned on my heel and left.

■■■

Scott ran up to me, grabbed my arm, and pulled me behind a tree. He looked around to see if anyone was nearby.

"What is it?"

Scott came close and whispered, "You need to go to the bank."

"Why?"

"It's almost out of money."

I suddenly lost feeling in my lips. "How do you know that?"

"A bunch of people are talking about it. I just withdrew everything I had in there. You'd better do the same before it—"

Before he could finish his sentence, I was sprinting toward the bank.

I could hear people yelling before I could even see the bank. When I finally saw it, I came to a complete stop. There was a crowd of people outside the door, demanding to get in. A "Closed" sign hung on the door and Marcy was desperately trying to keep people out. I went to try to make peace, knowing full well I had nothing to tell them that would make anyone feel better.

Valerie was the first to see me, and she ran over to me. "Is this true? Is all our money just . . . gone?"

"Look, Valerie . . ." A couple of people saw us talking and filtered over to me. "There's not much I can do."

"This was your idea, Cummings!" Valerie shouted into my face. "This whole bank thing was your brilliance at work. Now you've got 20 people here who are completely broke!"

"Listen . . . some people are having trouble paying off their loans. As soon as we get that money, we'll be able to give you everything you put in."

"And how are these people going to pay off their loans? They're probably broke too. Right?" I was hoping that nobody would be able to think two steps ahead. I shouldn't have underestimated Valerie.

"I—" I stuttered. "I'll work this out. I just need to talk to Marcy."

"You'd *better* work it out, Cummings! And you'd better do it fast or you'll pay for this." Valerie yelled at me as I moved past her.

I made my way through the crowd. A few people bumped me and a few more said some harsh things to me. I called out to Marcy to open the door. She unlocked it. I pried the door open against the weight of a couple of people leaning on it. I pushed them out of the way, slammed the door, and locked it behind me. Marcy was leaning against the back wall, petrified.

The noise outside was muffled, but still loud. I had to raise my voice for her to hear me.

"What happened? I thought we were going to keep this quiet."

"I didn't tell anyone. I was gonna yell at *you* for telling somebody."

"I didn't tell a soul."

"Then how . . ." she started, but faded.

"Is there any money left at all?"

"Forty-seven tokens."

"Where do you keep the money?"

"In a safe down here. I take it home with me every night. And I'm the only one who knows the combination."

"Let me see your laptop."

"Here."

"Show me how to find out how much money is left."

She punched a few keys, and I looked at the screen.

"Was there any time today when you left this laptop alone?"

"No. I was in here all day."

"How about yesterday?"

"No."

"You never took a break, you never ran an errand? Nothing?"

She thought for a second. "No, I . . . wait a minute. Yes, I guess I did leave it, but it was only for a minute or so."

"What were you doing?"

"I went to help somebody put up a street sign. He needed me to hold it while he—"

"A street sign?"

"Yeah, it was a yield sign. I didn't really understand why we needed one there, but this guy was putting it up."

"Who was it?"

"I don't remember his name, but it was that guy who sued Nelson."

"Jake?"

"Yeah, Jake. That's who it was."

I gritted my teeth. There was something going on here. Someone was trying to destroy the town, and I had a good idea who it was. The only problem was that I had no proof.

■ ■ ■

I remembered in history class when we learned about the Great Depression, which occurred in the United States in the 1920s and 1930s. The banks ran out of money and people lost all their savings. Unemployment was very high, so no one had any money to pay for anything. Businesses failed everywhere. If it was anything like what was happening in Kidsboro, the Great Depression was named well. A dreariness seemed to hang over the city like heavy fog. Half the citizens of Kidsboro lost their savings when the bank went under. A third got fired from their jobs. No one was buying anything; no one was selling anything. I didn't catch very many people even smiling anymore. A once-proud city was now just a couple of steps away from being a ghost town.

9

THE INVESTIGATION

THE ONLY WAY I COULD see us getting out of this depression was to figure out how to prove that Jake's accident was a hoax. I got to work immediately.

I needed to find some place where those guys had slipped up. Something about their testimony in court that didn't make sense. Something that couldn't have possibly happened.

The first place I looked was the newspaper office. I asked Jill to show me the article that she ran about the accident. I knew there was an interview with Jake in there. I also asked to see the article about the trial. I took them both out and laid them side by side on the table, searching for something . . . anything.

As I flipped through the pages, Jill came over. "What are you looking for?"

"I don't know yet," I said.

Then I found it. "Look at this. Right here. Jake changed his story. In his interview with you after the accident, he said he was walking toward the *bakery* when the accident occurred. During the trial, he told everyone that he was going to the *movie shoot*. From where he was standing, that's going in two different directions!"

"Are you sure?"

"Here." I grabbed a piece of paper and a pen and quickly drew a rough sketch of the town. "If he was walking toward the bakery," I drew a dotted line to show the direction Jake was moving, "at that angle, if he went as far as he could go, he'd end up in the creek. The movie shoot was all the way over here." I drew a circle to indicate where the filming was taking place.

"But how do you know he was walking from *here*?" Jill said, pointing to the spot where I'd written "Jake."

"Well . . . didn't he say that?"

"No. He never said where he was before the accident. He only said which direction he was going in."

"But he said two different things. To you, he said he was going to the bakery. In court, he said he was going to the movie shoot."

"No, he told me he was going *toward* the bakery. That's just a *direction*. Going to the movie shoot means he was actually headed there—in *whatever* direction." She was right. I looked down at the map and tried to figure out why she was wrong. But she wasn't.

"What's going on?" she asked.

"Huh?" I replied.

"Why are you doing this?"

"I guess I'm just frustrated with the verdict."

"Do you really think Jake made it all up?"

"I . . . don't know."

"What have you heard? What makes you think he's lying?"

I looked her straight in the face. I knew I could trust Jill, even more than Scott. I couldn't tell her everything, but I had to get my town back. "I just think he is," I told her.

"Why? Did he say something? Look at you in some weird way? What?"

"I just have this feeling . . ."

"That's not good enough!" she suddenly lashed out. I jumped. "What's going on with you, Ryan?"

"What do you mean?"

"What do I mean? You call a city council meeting to nominate Jake to be a citizen. We've never heard of the guy, yet you tell us he could be a real asset to our community. None of us really goes for it, so you ask us to trust you. So we do. We vote him in. I figure he's got to be a great guy if you nominated him, but you never introduce him to any of us. I never even see you *with* him. And now, you're telling me you think he's lying. But you have no reason to believe that. You just think he's lying. Now tell me the truth, Ryan. Is this guy a real asset to our community or is he a liar?" She was standing with her face six inches from mine, glaring into my eyes.

"He's a liar."

"Then why did you make him a citizen?"

"Jill . . ." I pulled out a chair and sat down. I didn't know what to do next. She closed her eyes and knelt down next to me.

"Are you in trouble?" she asked. "Because I've never known you to lie to anybody, much less your friends . . . so something must be seriously wrong here. Did he threaten to beat you up?"

"No."

"Cause if he did, you know you've got Alice."

"He didn't threaten to beat me up."

"Then what?" I turned away from her. She grabbed my chair and turned it forcefully around so that I was looking right at her.

"Ryan . . ." she said quietly. "I'm your friend. And when you ask me to trust you, I do. Every time. You've never given me any reason not to trust you. But now you need to trust *me*." She took my hand between both of hers and held it tightly. I was completely comfortable with her. I always had been, since the day I met her. I had no trouble trusting her with my secret, but this wasn't about trust. It was about putting her in danger. They had told us at the shelter that telling who we were would not only put us in danger, it would put everyone we told in danger too.

"Okay. I can't tell you exactly what's going on because . . . well, I just can't. But I will tell you that he's threatened me with something and I think he's trying to sabotage the city."

"Why?"

"Because of something I did to him a long time ago. He wants to get me back."

She smiled slightly. "Okay. That's a good start. At some point I'd like to know the whole story, but I understand if you don't want to tell me everything. Now . . . what do you want me to do?"

"I'm looking for proof that Jake—and maybe Max—staged the accident in order to win all that money."

I told her the whole story about how Max had taken all his money out of the bank, then sometime afterward, Marcy had gone to help Jake put up a street sign—possibly so Max could get in the bank and look at the computer files. Jill thought it sounded fishy too.

We spent the afternoon in my office, looking through the articles and photos from the crime scene and the trial. One picture caught my eye. I couldn't quite put my finger on it, but something was wrong. It was a picture of the damaged car. I snatched the Kidsboro map off the table and laid it alongside the picture. Jill peered over my shoulder. Suddenly it hit me.

"I've got it. Okay, the car was coming from *this* way, right?" I said, making a straight line with my finger on the map.

"Right."

"And Jake was walking this way."

"Right."

"So look at the way the car is crushed. You can plainly see the shape of a foot."

"Yes."

"But it's backward. If he ran into it head-on, the heel should've landed on the front of the hood, right?"

"I see where you're going," Jill said. "This car is crushed like Jake came up from *behind* it."

"Exactly. And look at how much the car has been damaged. If the car simply tripped him, Jake would've fallen off quickly and his full weight never would've been on top of the car . . ."

"But this looks like somebody just stomped on it."

"That's it. You think this'll hold up in court?" I asked.

"Not a chance. The car could've made a sharp turn right when it came up on Jake, plus he could've turned his body. But this is a start. We need more evidence."

The discovery had given us our second wind. We were onto something, and nothing could stop us now. We hurried back to the newspaper office.

"Listen, Jill." I stopped. "If we do find something, and we take this back to court . . . you have to do it. Jake can't know that I had anything to do with this."

"Gotcha. I'll do it."

■ ■ ■

Late that afternoon, we decided to take a look at the crushed car. We checked first at the police station, because we figured since it had been evidence for the trial, Alice would have it. But Alice told us that she had given it back to Nelson once the trial was over, because he wanted to put it back together. So we walked to Nelson's, hoping he hadn't begun repairing it.

When we got there, we were shocked to discover that Nelson Motors was up and running again. Nelson was inside with his designer, looking at a picture of what would be their next model. Jill and I exchanged confused looks. "What's going on?" I asked.

Nelson glanced up at us, then motioned for us to follow him outside. We did. "Someone donated some money to us," Nelson said. "We're back. We've got eight more cars to build, and I think I can pay off the investors and my employees with the profits."

"Who donated the money?"

Nelson looked at the ground and spread some dirt around with his foot. He said quietly, "Max."

I gave him a stern look. "I know, I know," he said. "It's probably a mistake. But what else was I going to do? I've got people all over the place who want their money back. I have a responsibility to them. Sure, I'll probably have to be Max's slave for a while . . . but at least I'll be able to pay off my debts."

I didn't like the sound of that arrangement. We asked about the car. Nelson had already begun repairing it, so it was useless to look at it.

On our way back to the newspaper office, we noticed someone on the miniature golf course. Mark was watching four people play a round together. There was a big sign on the office door that read, "GRAND REOPENING."

"You're open again?"

"Sure. You wanna play?"

"No thanks. We're on our way somewhere. I thought you had a lot of debts to pay."

"Max took care of it for me."

"Max?"

"Yeah, you know, I owed him most of the money anyway—for the wood to build this thing. But he told me to forget it. And get this: He even gave me some money to hire an employee since I have to go to swimming lessons in the mornings now."

Jill and I exchanged looks. This was not looking good.

"I gotta tell you. After the trial, I kind of thought that Max was a jerk, you know? But he saved me, man. He saved the whole town."

Max was now the town hero.

■ ■ ■

Within a week, all the businesses were back up and running. The bank was back too, since Max had paid off some of the loans that other people couldn't pay. Many people were able to get their savings back. Everywhere I went, people were singing Max's praises.

Max even gave Pete enough money to start filming again. With his investors breathing down his neck, and his sister Robin beginning to make demands of her own, Pete agreed to let the actors have everything they wanted. With everyone happy, Pete put Valerie and Kirk back in front of the camera.

■ ■ ■

That night, Pete opened up the movie theater with a special discount showing of *Rocky*. Twenty-four of Kidsboro's 31 citizens filed in. Pete introduced the movie as a celebration of the rebirth of Kidsboro. Several people clapped, but the applause was slow and halfhearted.

During the movie, the laughter seemed a little forced; the sarcastic comments from the crowd were not quite as sharp as usual. The inspirational scenes in the movie didn't make anyone sit up straight or bounce their knees.

It was almost as if everyone was scared to celebrate.

■ ■ ■

My fears began to be realized the next morning.

"What's with this muffin, Sid?" I asked. I almost always had a muffin at Sid's Bakery in the morning. This one was not up to his usual standards.

Sid rolled his eyes and lowered his voice. "I had to put extra cinnamon in it."

"What do you mean, you *had* to?"

"He likes cinnamon."

"Who?"

"Max, of course. He gave me a loan to start the business up again, so I kind of have to do what he wants. He told me to put more cinnamon in everything. So I did."

"You put more cinnamon in *everything*?" I asked.

"Yep."

"But he's not going to eat everything."

"Doesn't matter. He told me he was making a business decision. And as he said, people like cinnamon."

"But this doesn't taste as good as it usually does."

"No kidding," Sid said.

"Did you tell him that?"

"He's not an easy person to disagree with. I'm sure you've noticed that."

"Yes, I have."

Next, I stopped by the newspaper office to see if Jill had come up with anything else.

"I saw something today that made me a little curious," she said.

"What?"

"It may be nothing, but I saw Max and Barry together."

"What were they doing?"

"Just talking. They were on the other side of the creek, like it was some secret meeting."

"So?"

"I don't think they're friends. And they have nothing in common."

"Right."

"Except for the fact that Max was the lawyer for the trial, and Barry was on the jury."

"You think Max bought him off?"

"I can't prove it . . ."

"Jury tampering would be tough to prove. But I agree. That's really strange."

Jill sat down and bent her head over the mess of papers and photos she had scoured a thousand times before. "There's something we're missing," she said. "I know there's something obvious here, something that'll prove our case without a doubt—but I just can't put my finger on it."

"I know how you feel. I can sense it too."

We brainstormed a while longer, and then I went home to rest my weary brain.

--- ---

I dodged one of Nelson's cars as I was coming back into town. As it passed me, it got stuck on a tree root. Its wheels turned furiously but without success. I was about to reach down and give it some assistance when I heard, "Don't touch it, Ryan." It was Nelson. He and an employee were standing 20 feet behind me. Nelson's arms hung limply at his sides as if he had lost all hope in whatever he was doing.

"It just doesn't work!" Nelson shouted. I had never seen one of Nelson's cars get stuck. I walked over and joined them.

"What's wrong?" I asked.

"The new cars don't work," Nelson said. "We usually put four-wheel drive into all our vehicles. It's a luxury, and if you're going to use it on the street, you don't need it. But when you're in the woods, you've got to get over tree roots, leaves, rocks, branches, grooves in the soil. These things just don't work out here without four-wheel drive."

"I don't understand."

"Max came in yesterday and started watching our operation. He noticed us putting in extra components and asked why. We told him about the four-wheel drive, and he said that the cars don't need it. He said he wants our company to start being more cost-effective, and since we're using his money, he gets to call the shots."

"Oh, boy," I said.

"I argued with him for about an hour, but he wouldn't have it any other way."

"Maybe you could show him that it doesn't work."

"He doesn't care. It makes no difference to him if we sell an inferior product. He just wants us to sell as many as we can as soon as possible. This company's always been known for quality. If we start selling people *this* stuff, what happens next year when I want to start making something else?"

"Maybe you could put in the four-wheel drive and he won't notice."

Nelson shook his head. "He's got a new rule. All cars have to get his approval before they go out to be sold."

"This is bad."

"What exactly am I supposed to do?"

— — —

We were to see much more of this as the days went on. Throughout the city, businesses that sold things now had "price scales," where friends of Max paid less for everything, while everyone else paid top dollar for the same things. For instance, Max's friends got to play a round of golf for five tokens, while *I* had to pay 10 tokens. I knew I needed to call a city council meeting to discuss a new law regarding this practice. This was discrimination or something. Even worse, the course was now called "Putt to the Max," in honor of its new financial backer. There was a huge sign right in front of the course.

But it was at an evening film shoot that things really came to a head. I was sitting on a lawn chair just close enough to the set to observe without being in the way. Pete was getting a scene ready when Max showed up with a script in his hand. "Okay, I've made some changes."

"What?" Pete said.

"I've just made a few small revisions on this scene. I think it works a whole lot better." Pete took the script from Max, gave him a nervous smile, then scanned the pages. His mouth immediately turned down, then his eyes widened in horror. He seemed to calm himself, and then looked back up at Max, faking a smile.

"You know, Max . . . I don't think we can do this."

"Why not?"

"This is . . . um . . . kind of disgusting, and there's some bad language in here."

"Yeah, I know. I thought the character of Ginger needed some more . . . umph. She was too flat."

Hearing her screen name, Valerie immediately wanted the scoop. "Wait a minute. What did you do to Ginger?" Valerie grabbed the script from Pete and started scanning it.

"Max," Pete said, "this is supposed to be a family film. I don't use that kind of language in my films."

"How do you know? You've only made one."

Valerie wasn't yet done reading the page, but she was already shaking her head and saying, "I'm not saying this . . . I'm not doing this . . . I'm definitely not saying *that* . . ."

"Listen to me," Max said. "This will make the movie seem more real. People use this kind of language in real life. You want this movie to be realistic, right?"

"Not if I have to embarrass myself and my family," Pete said.

"Your family? What's your family got to do with it?"

"I've been telling them all about how well this project is going, and they can't wait until they get to see it for the first time. I am *not* going to have them come here and hear that stuff coming out of anybody's mouth."

"No way, Max," Valerie added. "I'm not saying this stuff. Forget it."

"Oh, come on, Val. I've heard you say stuff your momma wouldn't be too proud of."

"Well, I'm not putting it on film," Pete said. "Now get outta here."

Max smiled his evil smile. "You guys don't get it, do you? *I'm* running the show here. Pete might be the director, but there's nothing going on without me. If you don't say what I want you to say, there's no movie."

"Fine. Then there's no movie," Valerie said. Pete snapped a look toward her.

"Wait, wait," Pete said. "Let's just take the script and talk about it for a second. I think we can come to some kind of agreement."

"I think we can too. And I think we'll do it my way."

"But Max . . ."

Max gave him a stern look. "We *will* do it my way."

There was a long pause. Everyone looked at Pete.

"I can't."

"All right," Max snapped. "Then I guess there's no movie." He looked around at the cast and crew. "None of you are getting paid anymore. Which pretty much means, that's a wrap, people! Everybody can go on home!" He left quickly.

Valerie and Pete looked at each other, then Valerie rolled her eyes and packed up her makeup and left. Pete and the rest of the crew soon followed.

■ ■ ■

A day later, we held a scheduled town meeting. Thirty of 31 people showed up. There was nothing on the agenda until Max stood up to make a motion. I had no idea what he was going to suggest, and I was horrified when he finally uncovered his agenda. He wanted to officially change the name of the town to Maxboro. We had no laws regarding the name of the city, so legally he could bring it before the city and call for a vote. All he needed was a majority consensus. He stood up in front of the crowd and took the vote. All the people who owed him money raised their hands. The final vote was a reluctant 16 to 14 in favor of switching the name to Maxboro, but I could see that everyone was fed up with Max's changes.

I was determined to put this on the agenda in the upcoming city council meeting. We had to put a stop to this, but for now, the city was officially named Maxboro.

■ ■ ■

Our church had more people in it than I had ever seen there before. It was practically the only place in Kidsboro that wasn't run by Max, and this apparently appealed to a lot of us. I counted 15 people. I sat between Jill and Scott.

Joey had something to say today. He came out with fire in his eyes. Perhaps he had been inspired by one of his dad's sermons. Perhaps he had read something in the Bible. But more than likely, he had seen what was happening in Kidsboro—and he wanted to say something about it.

He slapped his Bible on the front cover and immediately had us turn to Joshua chapter seven. He told the story of Achan. Joshua commanded the Israelite troops, and he sent 3,000 men out to conquer this tiny little place (with a tiny little army) called Ai. The Israelites got there, and the 3,000 men were defeated. Joshua was shocked, and so he asked God, "Why did you let this happen?" God told him that because Israel had disobeyed Him, He let their army be defeated. Joshua didn't know what God was talking about, so he went back to his men and asked, "Who disobeyed God?" Finally, Achan confessed, saying that he had stolen some things from God.

"Can you believe this?" Joey said, and I could almost hear his father's voice coming out of him. "An entire army was destroyed because of one man!" Joey went on, and though he didn't use the most poetic language or organize his thoughts in the most effective way, he made an excellent point.

"We have an effect on our society. Whether we know it or not, our actions affect others. We have a responsibility to live an honorable life—if not for ourselves, then for the benefit of others." I immediately thought of the lawsuit against Nelson, a selfish act that had ended up causing the entire town to go into a tailspin. One single act.

"Amen!" I heard from behind me. Mr. Whittaker was sitting in the back row, gleaming with pride at Joey's revelation.

Joey went on to tell the story of Jesus feeding the 5,000. "Jesus had no food to offer the people, so He asked around for help from the crowd. One boy came up with just five loaves of bread and two fish. Jesus took what the boy gave, and He performed a miracle, feeding all 5,000 with this little bit of food. Can you see how one small, *un*selfish, honorable act helped the whole crowd?"

Joey finished his spirited sermon, and I wanted to stand and cheer. We sang a hymn, took up an offering, and we all filed out. Before everyone left, I suggested that we get together on Monday and talk—the 15 of us, and anyone else who wanted to come. I wanted to tell them not to invite Max, but I thought that might be rude. Besides, I think that was understood.

■ ■ ■

On Monday, everyone still seemed to be energized by Joey's sermon. We'd all had some time to think things over, and I was hoping this meeting would generate some ideas. All 15 people showed up including, surprisingly, Valerie. Before we even started the meeting, Scott came through the door. "Um . . . " he said with a frown, "I think there's something we need to go see."

The entire group filed out, and Scott led us to the outskirts of the town. We stopped when we saw what Scott was pointing to. There, 30 feet in front of us, were Max and Jake pounding a sign into the ground that read: "Welcome to Maxboro." Underneath, in small letters, it said, "Land of Opportunity." My shoulders drooped. Jill's eyes were glazed over as though she was about to cry. Scott bit his lip. Nelson looked down at the ground with his hand on the back of his neck. Alice cracked her knuckles as if in preparation to hit something. We were completely silent as we all stared at this spectacle, wondering what had become of our city.

Finally, Kirk spoke up, "I'm gonna go home." A couple of others agreed and followed. They drifted toward their individual homes.

"Wait!" I said. They all stopped. "Hang on a second. I've got an idea."

I'd gotten everyone's attention, though they didn't look hopeful. "Why don't we make our movie?"

Pete shook his head. "Ryan, I don't have the money to pay anybody since I won't go along with Max's changes."

"I know, but . . . Kirk? Valerie? What do you say? You can work for free, can't you? Scott? The rest of you guys in the crew? I'll help out too." Everyone sort of stared at me blankly. "Come on, now. We need something to give us our town back."

Scott looked around, and when no one else volunteered, he said, "All right, Pete, I'll be your stuntman for free."

"Thanks, Scott," I said. "Anybody else?"

"I'll do it," Kirk joined in.

"Yeah, me too," Valerie said. Soon, everyone in the cast and crew had agreed to work for free in order to finish the movie.

Pete got a sudden burst of energy and shouted, "All right!" and pumped his fist in the air.

"All right!" I repeated, and suddenly everyone forgot about going home. Instead, they went straight to the movie set. Maybe with this one unselfish act, we could get our town back.

■ ■ ■

That first day of filming again was extraordinary, almost magical. Pete was sharp and creative, while Valerie and Kirk put more energy into their performances than I had seen up to this point. Scott was asked to swing from a tree and crash into a pile of garbage, and he didn't even complain. When he emerged from the bags, he had a banana peel stuck to his shoulder. He laughed right along with the entire crew.

A good portion of the day was taken up filming an intense scene with Kirk, Pete, and Valerie. In it, Kirk was supposed to face off against Rock Bockner for the final time. They attempted to do the scene, but Pete started giggling for no reason at all. Then they tried again, and Pete did it again. Another take, and Pete smiled, making Kirk giggle. Soon, none of the actors could even speak a word without the cast and crew laughing uncontrollably. They did the scene 17 times before they finally got it right. But number 18 was perfect. And no one complained about numbers 1 through 17.

I was still laughing when Jill came up behind me. "I got it!" she exclaimed.

10

COMEBACK CITY OF THE YEAR

JILL PULLED ME INTO HER office and closed the door behind us. "I found the proof." She opened a folder. "I went to Alice to see if she had any of the evidence left from the trial, and she did. This." She held up a sheet of paper and I looked at it.

"The medical instruction sheet?"

"Right. From Dr. Yohman."

"It looks real."

"Sure it does. It's on letterhead, it has a lot of long, medical-sounding words on it, and it even has what looks like an adult's signature on it. But I know one of the secretaries at Dr. Yohman's office, so I called her. She told me that Jake is indeed a patient of theirs, but that he didn't come in at all on the day of the accident."

"Really?"

"And he hasn't been in since that day, either. But listen to this. He was in the office the day *before* the accident."

"For what?"

"She couldn't tell me that. But guess what he could've done while he was at the doctor's office?"

I was catching on. "Stolen some of their stationery."

"Exactly. Then he forged the doctor's signature thinking that nobody would check into it."

"Are you sure Jake never went into the doctor's office that day?"

"Positive."

"All right. Tell you what," I said. "I can't go with you, but go get Alice, then Jake. Then I think you should all pay a visit to Dr. Yohman."

- - -

Later on, I heard about what happened, and I wished I had been there. Alice pulled Jake out of his clubhouse by his ear. Jill said he didn't seem to be having any trouble with his ankle, which was interesting. Alice suggested handcuffs, but Jill thought that was a little over the top. So she simply pulled him by his arm to Dr. Yohman's office, which was only a few blocks away. Jake protested, but a quick ear pull from Alice shut him up. He mumbled something about police brutality, and Jill whispered to her to take it easy on him. He was, after all, someone who liked to sue.

Jill said Jake's eyes got wide when he discovered that their destination was Dr. Yohman's office. He figured out pretty quickly what was going to happen next. Jill asked the secretary if they could see the doctor for a minute. Then they all sat down—one big, happy family—in the waiting room. Jake squirmed in his seat the entire time.

The doctor came out and asked what this was all about.

"Dr. Yohman," Jill said.

"Yes?"

"Do you know Jake here?"

"Oh, yes. Hello, Jake. How are you doing?" Dr. Yohman said with a smile. Jake couldn't seem to return the smile.

"Jake had us believe that you diagnosed his condition as pulled ligaments in his ankle. In fact, he gave us this to prove it."

"This is not my signature."

"It's not?"

"That doesn't look anything like my signature. And what is this diagnosis? This doesn't make any sense. 'A stretched cardiac ligament on the anterior side of the ulna bone.' Cardiac refers to the heart, and the ulna is a bone in your arm."

"So, you didn't write this?"

"No. In fact, whoever *did* write it could be in a lot of trouble. Forging medical documents is against the law."

"Really? Wow."

Dr. Yohman got a call, and went back into his office. Jill looked at Jake. "So, Jake, do you have something to tell us?" Alice stepped forward and leaned down into his face, close enough to bite his nose if she'd wanted to.

— — —

Jake admitted to everything, except Max's involvement. I think he must have been scared of what Max might do to him if he ratted on him.

Alice and Jill interrogated Max anyway. Max told them he was just the lawyer, and lawyers have to defend innocent people, guilty people, and even sometimes people who fake injury to make money. He was "shocked" that Jake had lied to him.

Jake's crime was bad enough to earn him immediate banishment from the city. Jake was gone, never again to be a citizen of Kidsboro, and he had no idea that I had helped do it to him. It was perfect.

However, we couldn't lay any blame on Max. At least we'd discovered that the lawsuit was a fraud. Nelson's money was immediately returned to him, and right away, he went to Max's house to pay back his loan. As he said, "I don't want to be in debt to that snake any longer than I have to be." The next line of cars produced by Nelson Motors had four-wheel drive, air bags, antilock brakes, and even tiny little cup holders. They were the best cars yet.

■ ■ ■

I approached Jake cautiously as he was taking his stuff out of his clubhouse. He sneered at me. "I bet you're happy." I didn't answer.

"You might actually get a decent night's rest for once, huh?" I kept my mouth shut, but he kept talking. "I wouldn't get too comfortable, though. You know what I found out? Your dad left California. About a month ago."

What? My dad loved California. His job was there. *Why would he leave?*

"Nobody knows where he went," he chuckled. "Hey! Maybe he's on his way to find *you*." He turned away and chuckled again to himself. For a moment I had trouble breathing. What if he *was* trying to find us? And what if Jake had contacted him somehow?

Jake turned back around. "And don't worry, Jim. I'll be back."

■ ■ ■

I decided this had gotten too serious to keep to myself anymore, so I told my mom about Jake and his news that Dad had moved from California. I was afraid she would make us pack up and leave right then, but she suggested something else instead.

We got down on our knees next to my bed and prayed together for a long time. We asked for God's protection. We cried a little bit, but afterward I think we both felt better. We felt assured that God would take care of us, and for the first time since I'd seen Jake again, I was able to sleep peacefully.

▬ ▬ ▬

Two weeks later, Kidsboro was back. Loans had been paid off, and the bank had plenty of reserve cash. The city council voted to create our version of a Federal Deposit Insurance Corporation (FDIC), which is a government organization that makes sure that if a bank runs out of money, the people who have their money in it don't lose it all.

The first thing each business owner did, once the business had made enough money, was pay off Max. He now owned only his wood shop. The golf course was renamed "Golf-O-Rama." Pete showed movies every night, and the theater flourished. But it never had a turnout like the night of nights . . .

▬ ▬ ▬

I counted 55 people at the world premiere of *Rock Bockner and the Forest of Pain*. There were 29 citizens of Kidsboro, all except Max who was curiously absent, and 26 people from the outside. When Pete's parents walked between the hanging bed sheets and into the "theater," I introduced myself. They seemed just as excited as everyone else.

Valerie wore what looked like a prom dress, catching the eye of every boy she walked past. She smiled and greeted everybody.

Eugene Meltsner arrived carrying a thermos, and Pete made him leave it outside. No one was allowed to bring in outside drinks.

Connie Kendall, a teenage employee at Whit's End, came in just after Eugene. She said hi to everyone and told Pete how excited she was to see the movie.

Mr. Whittaker hugged a few people on his way in, and then he bought a giant bucket of popcorn at the concession stand to share with anyone who was sitting around him.

I sat down on a stump in the back. It was a gorgeous night. Jill came in and saw me, waved, and joined me on the stump. "This is gonna be so cool," she said.

"Yeah, it is," I agreed.

She looked around at the stars and the trees, and then closed her eyes. Her black hair flowed in the breeze like it was floating on water. She opened her eyes and looked at me. "You're not going to tell me what's going on, are you?" I knew she was talking about my relationship with Jake.

"One day I will."

"Do you need me to tell *you* something personal? Is that it? You want me to go first?"

"No, that's not it—"

"All right, I'll go first," she interrupted. "I think you're perfect."

"Perfect?"

"Pretty much. Except for all those nasty little secrets you keep. Other than that, you're flawless."

"That's . . . quite a compliment."

"It's not a compliment. Just an observation." She shrugged it off.

Pete walked to the front of the crowd, and before he could even start talking, everyone clapped. He blushed. He was wearing a suit. He thanked everyone and began his prepared speech.

"Thank you all for coming. Tonight is the result of all our hard work. So many creative minds came together to pull this off. To be honest, I think this movie ended up better than I ever dreamed it would be—and that's because of the people I worked with. I went into this thinking this was *my* production, *my* project, *my* creative genius that would make it all work . . . but it ended up being yours as well. This is *our* movie, and I'm proud to have been a part of it. I hope you feel the same way."

Everyone clapped, and the projector was flipped on and began to whir. Every eye was focused on Kirk as he came onto the screen and whispered his sinister plot to his partner. Some of the crowd hissed, and Kirk was elbowed by the people next to him near the front row. Valerie came on in the second scene and various whistles and cheers filtered through the audience. I could hear Valerie giggling.

The movie was 45 minutes long. The crowd laughed at the jokes that were only remotely funny and clapped at the points that were even barely inspirational. And when Rock Bockner defeated the evil villain, the audience sent up a loud roar of approval.

The acting was pretty bad, the script was weak, and the stunts were pitiful, but it was us, doing our thing.

Afterward, Pete led a discussion about the movie and declared it a classic. Everyone agreed, though many people did point out some of the less than logical things in the movie. Pete took it all in stride. We talked and laughed well into the night.

And no one wanted to go home.

THE END

For Paityn,
my second-born,
who smiles for no reason,
except to make my day.

■ ■ ■

BOOK 3

The
Creek War

POETIC JUSTICE

I SAT AND WATCHED Max squirm in his chair. For him, every second was more painful than the one before. I wished I could videotape the moment and watch it over and over at home, and maybe invite people over to have a "watch Max squirm" party. But I was told I couldn't bring a camera into the courtroom.

"Guilty!" Pete, the prosecuting attorney, shouted, banging his hand on the table. He winced a little bit. Clearly he had hurt himself, but knowing the jury was watching, he clenched his teeth and went on. "That is the perfect word to describe Max Darby—not just today but throughout his entire life. He has been guilty of so many crimes within the walls of this town that it would be impossible to count them. But in this court case, right here, today, we're going to attempt to do just that—count how many people have been ripped off by Max Darby."

The jury was visibly nodding, as well as everyone else in the jam-packed meeting hall pavilion, which doubled as our courtroom. Max sat at the defendant's table, nervously tapping his pencil on his knuckles. He had on his best suit and his favorite cowboy boots. I think he felt the boots made him look more rural and, therefore, more friendly. But today they made him seem like a dishonest used-car salesman who wanted you to *believe* he was friendly.

It was obvious he knew the end was near. Twenty-nine people had shown up to watch Max get trounced—the entire population of Kidsboro. As for me, Ryan Cummings, mayor of Kidsboro, I couldn't have been happier.

I reclined in my chair and prepared for an entertaining show. This was something I'd anticipated for a long time. Max Darby had burned so many people with so many tricks that I doubted he had a friend left in all of Kidsboro. For nine months I had tried to get him thrown out of town, but he always had some legal loophole that made him technically innocent of his scams. Plus, the city council—made up of the five original members of Kidsboro, myself included—had always been afraid to throw him out because his father owned a construction company, and Max had access to large amounts of wood—the wood with which we built our clubhouses. But now our hesitation to throw him out was over. A boy named Mark had become a citizen during the summer, and he'd shown us all how to make clubhouses out of tarp—so we didn't need Max's wood anymore.

After that, I had led an effort to throw Max out. I contacted all of the people who had ever been cheated by Max and asked them to testify at a trial. Legally, I figured Max had a technicality to stand on for every scheme he pulled, but put them all together and a jury might decide to throw the book at him. After I had a list of people who would testify, I just waited for Max to strike again—and he did.

This is what the trial was about: Max had bought a plot of land on the shore of the creek and had built very nice, two-story clubhouses on it. Each was furnished with a bed, chairs, and even a recliner that Nelson, our town inventor, had made for him. The nicest feature, though, was siding. None of the other clubhouses in Kidsboro had siding, and I had to admit, it looked really sharp. Most of our walls were slabs of uneven wood boards. But the siding in Max's clubhouses made the new models look almost like real houses. Max sold two of these houses to citizens of Kidsboro. Little did they know that the siding was made out of painted cardboard. The first time it rained the roofs sagged in and large pieces of siding drooped and fell off the houses. It was a classic Max scheme. So the owners of the houses were now suing, with Pete as their lawyer.

"The defendant, Mr. Max Darby," Pete said, "is going to come up here and tell you that the people he sold houses to bought them *knowing* that their siding was made out of cardboard. After all, it's in the contract, and since these people signed the contract stating that they had read through the entire thing, they must have known. Ladies and gentlemen of the jury, he is telling the truth. Technically, Max is right in saying that the fact that the siding was made out of cardboard is, indeed, in the contract. But let's have a look at this contract."

Pete walked quickly to his table and grabbed a thick stack of papers. He held it up for the jury to see and slammed it back down on the table. The legs wobbled and the people in the front row jumped back. "This is the contract: 38 single-spaced pages of impossible reading material. Legal jargon, 14-letter words, and enough Latin to choke a Trojan horse. Allow me to read an excerpt from page 16: '*Pluribus equus caput capitis es horridus plebeius.*' Translated from Latin this very loosely means: 'Many horse heads are scary and uneducated.' The point I'm trying to make here is that none of this contract makes sense. It's just thousands and thousands of words thrown together for the purpose of boring the reader out of his mind. There are very few people in the world who would be willing to read through the entire thing."

The jury was smiling at the Latin translation. Pete went on. "And why, you ask, does Max not want you to read the entire thing? Let me read an excerpt from this contract, buried on page 27, in the middle of a 573-word paragraph. It reads, and I quote: 'Without limiting the generality of the foregoing, the party of the second part, hereafter referred to as The Seller, will indemnify the non-excepted payments. The siding is made out of cardboard. Whenever any claim or demand is instituted in order to defray expenses . . .' " Pete's voice trailed off. He'd made his point.

"So, yes, the siding material is in the contract. But you and I both know that Max had no intention of anyone actually reading through this entire contract to get to that one fact. It's a scheme—a scheme that we all know too well. For this case, I will parade witness after witness before you to show you a pattern of this type of behavior. You will be amazed at how many people in this community have been ripped off by Max Darby."

One by one, Pete called witnesses up to the stand to testify how Max had tricked them out of their money or property. And every time someone stepped down, Max sank a little bit lower in his seat.

Then, as if wanting to go out on his own terms, he suddenly flew up in the middle of someone's testimony and yelled, "Forget it! No more of this! This is ridiculous, and I don't even care! I don't need this town! You guys are a bunch of whining little twirps, and I'm sick of being a citizen here." I guess he had given up on trying to appear friendly. "Don't bother kicking me out. I quit!" He stormed out.

Nobody was quite sure what to do at this point. Pete had six more witnesses that he was ready to call to the stand, plus he had a closing argument I'm sure he was dying to wow the jury with. He turned to Judge Amy, who probably thought she ought to rule something. But did she need to rule anything? Pete and I exchanged looks, and then Amy shrugged her shoulders and lifted her gavel.

"Court's adjourned," she said, pounding the gavel on the table. Everyone sat silently for a moment, and then I heard someone snickering. It was Scott Sanchez, my best friend and one of the many who'd been tricked by Max before. Suddenly, he let out a burst of joyful laughter, followed by the laughter of others. People around him started clapping, including me, and soon everyone in the assembly hall was smiling and giggling and high-fiving each other. The place was oozing with joy. We had rid the evil king! We had bested the giant troll! Ding dong, the witch was dead! Kidsboro was free at last!

It was a revival of sorts, but as it turned out, it was a short-lived one. For at that moment, no one could have dreamed of what Max would do for revenge.

2

THE COMPETITION

THE GRASS CRUNCHED UNDER my feet, evidence of the first frost of the year. It was a weekend morning in late October. Cold weather came early in Odyssey. I was on my way to a city council meeting where we would discuss who would replace Max and become our newest citizen. The Kidsboro city charter stated that whenever someone left the city, a new person could immediately be brought in to fill the spot. There was a small problem involved with this situation, however. Max had built an incredible six-room clubhouse, the largest house in Kidsboro. It didn't seem fair that a brand-new citizen would be able to move into his home. There were people who had been in Kidsboro since the beginning who still owned only small, one-room clubhouses. So this meeting was also about who would get Max's house.

The five members of the city council were at the meeting hall pavilion promptly, though not all of them were fully awake. Scott let out an enormous yawn. "Good morning, Scott," I said.

He mumbled back, "Morning, Ryan." His dark hair was sticking up out of the side of his head in an involuntary ponytail.

Jill Segler came in with a soda, knowing full well it was a questionable health choice, but justifying herself by saying, "All journalists have caffeine in the morning, and I'm not into coffee yet."

Police Chief Alice Funderburk was in her warm-up suit, leaning against a pole. The pole and the section of roof held up by it appeared to be ready to collapse under the weight of Alice. She was the only one who looked awake. I figured she had been up for over two hours already, lifting weights and jogging her usual two miles before breakfast.

Nelson Swanson was dazed, and I couldn't tell if he was trying to wake up, or if he was in that little world of his where he hears nothing and sees nothing around him. He was usually in this state when he was dreaming up a new invention. His glasses had a big white stain in the middle of one lens, and I couldn't imagine how he could see through it. He didn't seem to notice.

I sat down and opened a notebook that contained a list of possible candidates to take Max's place.

"Anybody got a name that sticks out?" I asked. They acted as if they hadn't heard me. The silence was broken by a distant hammering. I seemed to be the only one intrigued by the question of who would be hammering in Kidsboro this early in the morning. I scanned the main road of the town and saw no one. Ignoring the noise, I went back to my list.

"How about Monica Sertich? She's pretty nice." Silence. Scott's face wrinkled up as though he was trying to remember who Monica Sertich was, even though I knew that he'd known her for eight years. Alice was the only one who wasn't dazed, but she very rarely voiced an opinion about anything. The hammering stopped, and a power drill started up.

I was much too curious to stay in the pavilion with my catatonic friends. Alice followed me, apparently curious as well. The noise was coming from a strange distance. It was too far away to have been anywhere in Kidsboro, yet it wasn't far enough to be construction on a real house. Alice and I strolled farther and farther without a word, and the drilling gave way to hammering again. A few steps more, and we could hear voices. The hammering was now doubled, as if someone were helping. We both saw it at the same time. There, across the creek, were Max and a friend, building a clubhouse. I moved in to get a closer look.

"What are you doing, Max?" I called.

He smiled and gave a half-salute. "Howdy, neighbor."

"What's going on?"

"Just building me a house," he said in his Southern accent, an accent that came and went as he pleased.

"Why?"

"Well, since I can't live in Kidsboro anymore, I figured I'd start my own little town." Alice and I exchanged looks.

"Your own town?" I asked.

"Sure. This isn't Kidsboro property over here across the creek. I didn't think anybody'd mind if I just settled right here. Hey, a little later on, I'm gonna need some help moving my house over here from Kidsboro. You think you could help out?"

"That's not your house anymore, Max," I said.

"Oh, I beg to differ," he said with a smile. "I built that house myself. It's a nice one too. I wouldn't dream of leaving it behind."

"You want me to take him out?" Alice whispered, feeling her right hip as if she wished she had a weapon there. I didn't encourage her.

I was desperate for an ingenious reply to Max, but all I came up with was, "You can't do this."

His more-than-adequate reply: "Why not?"

In my mind, I scrambled for any reason. As far as I knew, he was right—the Kidsboro property line stopped at the creek, so if he wanted to start his own town, he was perfectly within his rights to do so. And he did build the house himself with his own materials, so he could do whatever he wanted with it.

The three other members of the city council joined us and stared across the creek at Max as well.

"What is *he* doing?" Scott asked.

"He's starting his own town."

Scott was offended. "He can't do that!"

"Why not?" I asked.

"Because he's . . . He can't just . . . It's got to be in the city charter somewhere."

"The Kidsboro city limits end at the creek, Scott," I said. "As long as he's not on Kidsboro property, Max doesn't have to pay any attention to our laws."

Nelson shook his head. "This is not good."

"No kidding," Scott replied.

"No telling what kind of town it's gonna be. And the citizens? Probably the dregs of society—ignoring all the laws and constantly harassing us. It'll be like living near one of those high-crime suburbs that nobody likes to talk about."

"Are they out of my jurisdiction if they commit a crime over there?" Alice asked.

"I wonder how he plans to destroy us," Jill said, taking out her reporter's notebook and jotting something down.

"Listen," I began, "maybe he was . . . just unsatisfied with the way we ran things over here, so he's exercising his constitutional right to secede from the union and create his own state."

Jill stepped toward the creek. "Hey, Max!" she called.

"Yeah?"

"What's the name of your new city?"

"Bettertown," he said, smiling. Everybody looked at me and raised their eyebrows. I think they all knew, and I suppose *I* knew deep down in my heart, that we had a fight on our hands.

■ ■ ■

I left Kidsboro without any more thought to our scheduled city council meeting and headed to Whit's End, Odyssey's ice cream shop and discovery emporium. I was certain that Mr. Whittaker, the owner and operator of the place and the founder of Kidsboro, would have something to say about Max starting his own town. Mr. Whittaker owned the woods behind Whit's End, where both Kidsboro and Bettertown were situated. If he said Max had to go, his word would be final.

Before I even sat down at the counter, I was already into my story. "Max is starting his own town!" I said to Mr. Whittaker.

"I know."

"He's across the creek, building a . . . what?"

"I know, Ryan," Mr. Whittaker said. "He was in here last night and asked permission." My face burned. This was typical Max. He was always a step ahead of everyone else.

"And you said yes?" I asked weakly.

"I didn't see any reason why not."

"But . . . don't you know Max? The only reason he's building this town is to tear ours down! He just wants to get even because we forced him out. His only purpose is to destroy Kidsboro!"

"Oh, I don't think there's really anything Max could do to destroy Kidsboro. I'm actually thinking it could be good for you."

"What?"

"Healthy competition. I'm sure he'll create new businesses. It'll force your business owners to make better products and lower prices so that they can compete with Max's businesses. It'll give you a taste of the real world."

I didn't want a taste of the real world. I was very happy in my imaginary one, a world that for about 12 hours didn't include Max. "He doesn't want healthy competition, Mr. Whittaker."

"Ryan, I know Max. I know what he's like. I know he's schemed his way to the top, and if things go the way they usually do, he'll scheme his way back to the bottom. But I also know that there's hardly anyone more capable of being the leader of a town that could compete with Kidsboro. He's smart, he's ambitious, and he knows how to get things done. I wouldn't do this unless I thought it would be good for you. Who knows? Just like different countries of the world, you may end up needing each other."

"I'm sorry for saying so, Mr. Whittaker, but I can't imagine this being good for us."

"I guess you'll soon see."

I walked out the door of Whit's End, my shoulders drooping. I reached down, picked up a rock, and threw it at a tree. How could Mr. Whittaker show no loyalty to Kidsboro? The town was his idea. He had helped write the laws and set up the government. And now he was going to let it be taken over. I couldn't understand it.

■ ■ ■

For the next month, we could barely hear ourselves think with all the construction going on in Max's new town. Eight of his friends were working, and, from the looks of it, not all of the structures they were building were houses. Max was mum on what he was creating, which had Jill fuming, of course. She had tried to interview him a number of times, but he kept answering questions such as, "What kinds of things will you have in your town?" with comebacks like, "Good things." The construction workers didn't know anything either—they were just following orders.

I was watching them work on an odd-shaped, three-story building (I'm not sure I would have the guts to go up to the third story) when Nelson came up from behind me.

"Look at this," he said, handing me a piece of paper. It was a flyer.

GRAND OPENING!!!

BETTERTOWN
COME SEE THE ATTRACTIONS! EAT THE FOOD!
LIVE THE EXCITEMENT! ALL FOR FREE! ALL FOR FUN!
THE DAY AFTER THANKSGIVING

"Our location is just across the creek,
but our attitude is miles away."
Sponsored by Max Darby, King of Bettertown

Nelson watched my reaction as I read it. "These flyers are all over Odyssey. I guess he's inviting pretty much anyone," he said.

I decided right then and there that this was going to be for real, and I could not show others that I was scared of it. People were going to look to me for leadership, and I had to convince them with my actions that I was not threatened by Max's new town.

I swallowed and said unconvincingly, "Good. I'm looking forward to going."

"You're going?"

"Sure. They're our new neighbors. We need to be neighborly."

"This town is obviously a direct attempt to bring us down. I mean, look at their slogan. 'Our attitude is miles away.' That's a slam on Kidsboro, and you know it."

"There's nothing like competitive juices to stimulate people."

Of course, I was unable to look Nelson in the eye when I said that.

■ ■ ■

Jill, Scott, and I went to the grand opening together. I encouraged everyone in town to go, though I didn't really have to twist anyone's arm. Max had done well to keep everything secret, and now people were brimming with anticipation. Plus, there was free food.

Max had spared no expense getting his town ready. There were flags, balloons, and streamers everywhere. The smell of barbecue was in the air, music was playing, and in every direction there was a beehive of activity. Max was decked out in a shirt and tie (one of those string ties that country singers wear) and dress slacks, greeting everyone with a welcome smile as they came across the bridge to Bettertown. I think mine was more of a welcome sneer.

The first thing I noticed was the housing district. It was the Beverly Hills of the woods. Two-story clubhouses were lined up, majestically overlooking the creek. They all had "For Sale" signs hanging on posts in the front yards. The three of us went into one of the houses, and Jill almost choked on her tongue. Smooth, painted walls and ceilings, plywood floors (the floors in Kidsboro were dirt), and two soft chairs decorated the first floor. A ladder led up to the second floor where there was a 10-foot cathedral ceiling, a small balcony, and—most impressive to Scott and me—electricity. Max had put outlets in each of the houses. They were connected to mammoth extension cords, which disappeared underground outside the houses. He had dug a trench from the town and wired the cords through a pipe under the bridge, through Kidsboro, and all the way to Whit's End.

I wondered if Mr. Whittaker had helped Max just as he had helped us build Kidsboro. Kidsboro had electrical access, with the same underground cables, but it was only hooked up in certain places like the meeting hall and the movie theater. If Mr. Whittaker had helped Max out, that meant he had gone to greater lengths to help Bettertown than he had to help Kidsboro. My teeth clenched as I bent down to look at the trench.

Mr. Whittaker's work, I was sure of it.

Max had proudly placed an electric appliance in each of the houses—a radio, a fan, a CD player—to demonstrate the possibilities with a house hooked up to electricity. Scott was mesmerized by the working radio, as if he'd never seen one before. "Excuse me for saying so, but this is awesome."

Jill was enchanted by the balcony and the painted walls. I tried to act like it was nothing special, but to be honest, I was impressed.

The business district was no less impressive. The crowd seemed to be flocking to a large meeting area inland. It was a building much larger than the meeting pavilion in Kidsboro, and it turned out to be a hangout. There was a sign on the door that said "Max's Room." We rolled our eyes as we went in. Tables and chairs were set up. People were mingling and eating popcorn and chips and drinking sodas. There was a concession stand with a line of people waiting to get free food.

The front four tables were arranged so that people could watch Charlie Metzger, a boy from Odyssey Middle School, perform magic tricks on a stage that was raised about six inches off the ground. To his left was a large, white poster board on an easel with the schedule of performances for the day. "Jim Jones, the Junior High Juggler" would perform at noon.

At one o'clock, "The Vocal Stylings of Margaret Piloscowitz" was scheduled. So she was either a singer, or she made funny noises. I probably wouldn't attend in either case.

At two o'clock, Slugfest, an alternative band from our school that consisted of four electric guitars and a guy who played a tambourine and sang every now and then, was playing. The school newspaper had done a story on them once. The reporter had asked them why their songs didn't rhyme, make sense, or contain any complete sentences. The guy with the tambourine had answered that it was because *life* didn't rhyme, make sense, or contain complete sentences. I asked around, and nobody knew what that meant, but everyone thought it was a totally cool thing to say.

Then at three o'clock was "The Rip-Roaring Comedy of Herb Martin." Herb had done a comedy act at a school talent show once and he wasn't funny, but he could pop any joint in his body at will. His routine was pretty much centered around this talent.

"We gotta come back at three," Scott said. "Herb Martin is hilarious."

Jill seemed hesitant to say anything complimentary, probably fearing she'd hurt my feelings. But she did note, "Interesting place."

"It's great," I said, stating the obvious. If I'd said, "This is five times better than anything we have in Kidsboro," that would've been a little more accurate.

Charlie the magician pulled a yardstick out of his hat, and the trick was met with a decent amount of applause. He bowed and said, "Thank you! I'll be here throughout the holidays. Also, if you'd like to learn how to be a magician yourself, starting December third I'll be teaching a class called 'Beginning Magic' at the Bettertown Community School. Thank you."

Jill and I looked at each other. "They have a school?"

■ ■ ■

The school wasn't nearly as nice as anything else we had seen, probably because Max had run out of his seemingly endless supply of wood. The classrooms were divided up by bed sheets hanging from the trees. Each classroom had blankets for the pupils to sit on, and a desk and blackboard for the teacher. There was no ceiling.

"Education always gets the least amount of money, huh?" Jill said, her political commentary for the day.

Outside of the school, a table was set up with a list of the classes that would be offered. A girl I had never seen before was behind the table, taking applications and answering questions. I looked at the list of subjects: Beginning Magic, Bowling, Extreme Sports, Basic Guitar, Wizards and Warlocks (a popular card game that our school had banned because of its references to the occult), Juggling, and a class titled, "Figuring Out Girls." There was a note informing us that more classes would be offered at a later date.

Next to the class names were the names of the teachers of each. I didn't recognize some of the names, but Charlie Metzger was going to teach magic, Jim Jones juggling, one of the members of Slugfest was to teach guitar, and Paul Isringhausen, the Odyssey teen bowling champ, was going to teach bowling. I couldn't believe that Max actually got Paul Isringhausen to teach a class. He was practically a celebrity.

"Figuring Out Girls" was going to be taught by Ted Russo, a junior who had dated 6 of the 10 most beautiful girls at Odyssey High School (according to an informal poll taken by the football team). He was one of the most popular guys in the school. How did Max, a middle schooler, get someone like Ted to come to his little clubhouse town in the woods?

When I asked Jill this question, she gave me an immediate answer. "*That's* how he got those guys to teach," she said, pointing to a small building that looked like a photo booth. The sign said, "Money Exchange," and it was a place where you could exchange real money for the currency used in Bettertown. There was no one in the building, probably because everything was free this day, so no one needed any Bettertown money. I looked inside, and posted on the back wall was the exchange rate: the number of "darbles" you could get for a dollar. Jill and I exchanged another roll of the eyes, noting that Max had again named something after himself ("darbles": Darby).

"You see," Jill said, "he's making money off of tourists coming in, so he can get outside people to teach by offering them real money."

Across from each teacher's name was how much the class would cost. The bowling class was $15 for non-residents of Bettertown and 400 darbles for residents. The "Figuring Out Girls" class was about the same. They were easily the most expensive ones. It appeared that Jill was right.

■ ■ ■

We were weaving our way through the quickly thickening crowd when I saw Sid staring into space, kneading his hands like he was washing them with imaginary soap. Sid owned Sid's Bakery in Kidsboro and was a master chef.

"What's the matter?" I asked him.

He didn't say a word, only pointed his chin slightly forward. We all looked and saw a store with a sign that said "Le Bakeria." It was a full-service bakery. Sid looked at me and shook his head. I assured him that no one could beat his donuts, and he said he knew that. But these appeared to be cheaper (apparently he had already calculated how many of our tokens would equal a darble), and most kids didn't care about the quality of their food. So he figured he was in trouble.

Scott stepped forward, obviously wanting to taste one since they were free, but he looked at Sid and, out of loyalty, did not grab one. Jill tried to make Sid feel better by saying that the words *Le Bakeria* were not French or Spanish or anything for bakery, but Sid was inconsolable.

There were a few more businesses that seemed to be mirror images of attractions in Kidsboro, only claiming to be of higher quality or having lower prices. Mark, the owner and operator of the miniature golf place in Kidsboro, had the same reaction that Sid had to the bakery when he laid his eyes on the Bettertown recreation center. This indoor/outdoor facility had an arcade-like area with carnival games like basketball pop-a-shot and football throw, two dart boards, an archery range, a weight bench, and an outdoor bowling alley with three lanes. Mark was not pleased. I had been repeating Mr. Whittaker's words and telling everyone that the competition would be good for us. I'm not sure getting blown away by your competition is all that good for anyone.

■ ■ ■

On our way back to the bridge, we passed a table set up with applications for Bettertown citizenship. There was an illustrated brochure showing all the highlights. It looked like something from Disney World. So far, Bettertown was exactly what its name implied. In every conceivable way, it made Kidsboro look pitiful. I was starting to feel a little sorry for myself.

On our way over the bridge, we met Mr. Whittaker, who was heading over to Bettertown. He caught my eye, and I quickly looked away. My reaction was too obvious, though, so I looked at him again. He smiled at me, and I tried to smile back.

"Hi, Ryan," he said.

"Hi, Mr. Whittaker." We passed each other with nothing to say. I didn't want to feel this way about Mr. Whittaker, but I couldn't help it. I felt the knife in my back.

3

THE BETTERTOWN ADVANTAGE

THE ONE SAVING GRACE in all of this was that I couldn't imagine how Max was going to get anyone to live in his town. I figured tourists would flock to Bettertown because of all of its attractions. People might even go to school there since some interesting classes were being offered. But who would live in those houses? I knew Max would charge an arm and a leg for them. Plus, knowing his greedy nature, I figured that the prices of everything else would be high too. But the main disadvantage was this: What would it be like to live in a place where Max had proclaimed himself king? Everyone knew he was a con artist. Who would voluntarily live in a place where he made the laws?

After school on Monday, I grabbed my copy of the *Kidsboro Chronicle* off the ground and went to Scott's clubhouse. I skimmed through the paper on the way. The entire newspaper was dedicated to the opening of Bettertown. Jill had written most of the stories, including a full-page interview with Max, an in-depth article about all of the attractions, and a story about the school. Roberto, Jill's assistant, had taken photographs and written a few articles himself. According to the statistics on page three, 104 people had passed over the bridge to attend the grand opening, and two had applied for citizenship. It was exactly as I'd expected—everyone wanted to visit, but no one wanted to live there.

Scott was reading a comic book when I went into his house. His eyes focused on my newspaper the second I passed through the door. "Oh, let me see your paper," he said, snatching it from me. He looked with great interest at the front page.

"The whole thing is about Bettertown," I said. "The grand opening was a huge success. Of course, Max is having a hard time getting people to live there."

"Yeah, I bet," Scott said, with an unnatural chuckle.

As he read on, lips moving, I glanced at his desk and noticed a Better-town brochure. I hadn't seen Scott pick one up when we were there, so I wondered if he went back for it. I lifted it, and Scott looked horrified.

"I, uh," he stumbled, "I didn't . . . somebody gave that to me. I was going to throw it away."

He saw my face and must have sensed a look of disapproval. I tried to hide it. "It's okay, Scott. Go ahead and be curious. *I* am. And don't worry about going over, spending time there, whatever. It's a fun place. I'm even thinking of taking a class at the school. I've always wanted to learn how to do magic tricks." Actually, the thought *had* crossed my mind to learn magic, but I was hesitant to spend even one dime in Bettertown. Far be it from me to help their economy.

Scott's shoulders were still tense, as though he felt no relief that I wasn't mad at him. He stared at me like he expected me to do something, and then opened the newspaper back up.

I glanced through the brochure, and then I noticed something on the back page of the newspaper. I sat down on the opposite side of the desk and read it while Scott read a page in the middle.

It was a full-page advertisement, paid for by Max. It read:

Are you tired of being a lower-class citizen?
Living in a run-down clubhouse?
Having trouble making ends meet?
THEN BE A CITIZEN OF
***** **BETTERTOWN** *****
WHERE
EVERYONE IS RICH!!!
Come to an informational meeting at the meeting hall in Bettertown
5:30 P.M. Tuesday night
See a multimedia presentation about
THE TOWN OF THE FUTURE
*******BETTERTOWN*******
PAID FOR BY KING MAX I OF BETTERTOWN

The first thing that struck me was the appeal to the lower class—the people who didn't have much money to spend. Kidsboro did sort of have a lower class, though there weren't too many people in it. These were the people who had trouble finding work for themselves. They didn't have their own businesses, or if they did, their businesses weren't very profitable. These people either had to work for someone else, or they had to get by on small incomes.

Kidsboro had had an economic boom the summer before, with new businesses springing up everywhere, but these businesses could employ only a few. Scott was one of the people who didn't have a real job. He ran a detective agency, but he had only investigated two cases since we'd started Kidsboro eleven months earlier. Other jobs had come and gone, but Scott usually had no money. He also made poor choices about spending what money he did have. I guess you could say he was part of the Kidsboro lower class.

But how would Max eliminate the lower class? What did he mean by saying that everyone would be rich? That was impossible. How in the world did he think he would get people to believe this?

Something told me that I needed to show up at this meeting.

■ ■ ■

Obviously, I didn't want anyone to see me at the meeting. Max would think I was spying and change his presentation. I wanted to hear it just as it was, with no editing. I looked at the advertisement again, and noticed that it was going to be a multimedia presentation. I had seen Max's computer presentations before, and the lights were always turned off. I figured I would wait until the lights were down, and then sneak in and watch from the back. I would sneak out before the lights went back up.

I went in just as someone turned the lights down, and I peered around the room. I couldn't make out many of the faces, but I could see silhouettes . . . lots of them. The place was packed! Max moved to his computer and began typing things in. His presentation began.

A thundering *boom!* shook the whole building, and everybody jumped in their seats. It was followed by embarrassed laughter. Fireworks filled the screen, and red, white, and blue letters swooped down from the upper right and, with majestic fanfare, spelled out "BETTERTOWN." Max's voice echoed, saying, "Bettertown. The town of the future."

Very impressive.

After a lot more of the echoing stuff, a short video came on. On-screen, Edward, a boy from Odyssey Middle School, came out of his Bettertown creek-view house. Edward was a loner. He didn't have many friends at school. In fact, he sat alone at lunch every day. I always thought it was kind of sad, and that if I ever had the same lunch period he did, I would sit next to him.

But here he was in Max's video. I couldn't believe Max got him to do it. Edward didn't seem to be the dramatic type.

Then Valerie Swanson came on-screen. Valerie was Nelson's sister and a citizen of Kidsboro, though not a very loyal one. It didn't surprise me that she was doing a video for Max. Valerie will be a shoo-in for the football team's annual "Most Beautiful Girls" poll when she gets to high school. She'll probably take the top spot as a freshman and hold onto it until she graduates. She flipped her long, brown hair away from her face as she turned toward Edward. Max must have paid her an awful lot to get her to be in this video with him.

Edward awkwardly looked past the camera, as if a director was behind it urging him to say his line. He cleared his throat and began, "Hi, Honey."

"Hi, Sweetie," Valerie said, and they patted each other on the back.

This was beyond unrealistic. This was science fiction. Edward and Valerie?

A girl I didn't recognize came on-screen looking surprised. "Joe? Is that you?"

Edward looked surprised that someone called him "Joe." His name was, in fact, Edward. Edward glanced toward the director again, and then said to the girl, "Yes. Is that you, Marcia?"

"Yes. I can't believe it. Are you and Grace together?"

Valerie smiled and flipped her hair back again. "That's right, Marcia. Joe and I are a couple." That line alone had probably cost Max 30 bucks.

"Wow, Joe," Marcia said. "You used to be such a geek. What happened?"

"I'll tell you what happened, Tara . . . I mean, Marcia," Edward said. "I became a citizen of Bettertown."

"Really?" Marcia said. "So did I." Then she went on about how she had been broke, hungry, and lying in the gutter when Max Darby came along and told her about Bettertown. Now she had a house with a balcony, she was continuing her education at the Bettertown Community School (to be a juggler, maybe?), and she felt like she had a future.

Then Edward smiled at Valerie and said, "I used to be the laughingstock of my school. But now, I'm the envy. In fact, I've got the entire eighth-grade class coming over for a barbecue tomorrow. I'm so thankful for Bettertown."

Then they both looked into the camera, and, with big cheesy smiles, they said in unison, "Thanks, King Max."

Finally, the real message of the presentation came on: the explanation of how Bettertown would work, how there were no social classes, and how everyone was equal.

Max's voice narrated, accompanied by words flying onto the screen in different colors and fonts.

The gist of it was this: Everyone would get a *free* house. The house would be owned by the city, but no one would pay rent. Everyone would work in Bettertown—whether at the bakery, the recreation center, the school, or wherever—for the exact same wage. No one received more for doing a harder or more complicated job. This way, there would be no class system, no low-income people, and everyone would be a team.

At the end of the presentation, a magnificent shot of the creek filled the background, and the flag of Bettertown—five red stick figures holding hands as a show of unity, with a green star above them (probably representing Max, though he didn't say it)—dissolved up into the foreground. The music stopped.

I quickly stood up and reached for the door. Nobody had seen me. But before I could get out, the lights came back on, and I saw a few of the people inside. And just before I closed the door, I saw something I couldn't believe. Sitting in the front of the meeting room, with a pen and paper . . . was Scott.

4

BETRAYAL

I WANTED TO GIVE Scott the benefit of the doubt. Maybe he was there for the same reason I was there—to find out what Max was up to. Maybe he was just curious. But he had seemed awfully guilty when I'd found that brochure in his clubhouse. And why would he have a pen and paper with him, apparently taking notes?

I met Nelson at Whit's End, and I told him about the meeting. He called Eugene Meltsner over. Eugene was a college student and Odyssey's resident genius. Nelson and I told him about Bettertown's economic system.

"That's communism," Eugene said, pushing his glasses up on the bridge of his nose. "Or at least a rudimentary version of it. It is based on the notion that there's no such thing as personal property. Everything is owned by the government, and everyone is paid exactly what they need, no more, no less. It's Marxism."

I had heard of communism before, but all that I remembered was that it was a bad thing, as if people who were communists were evil.

"There's nothing wrong with communism in theory," Eugene said. "Its goal is to create a society in which the working class operates the government. But it also limits freedom. Citizens cannot own anything or start their own businesses. It opens itself up to corruption because the government officials control everything, and they can become power-hungry and start ruling for their *own* benefit, as opposed to the people's."

Nelson and I both raised our eyebrows. Max was the government, and if there was ever a leader who was capable of corruption, it was him. Bettertown and its people were doomed.

"Scott was at the meeting," I told them.

"Why? To spy?" Nelson asked.

"I don't know. I didn't know he was going to be there. But he took notes, like he was interested in it."

"In becoming a citizen?"

"I don't know."

"You gotta talk to him."

■ ■ ■

A special edition of the *Chronicle* reported that 17 people had applied for citizenship in Bettertown. I was surprised at the high number, so I went to Jill to find out who they were. She said that Max wouldn't give her specific names. I wondered how many of the 17 were Kidsborians who were defecting.

The traffic in Kidsboro was high, but it was mainly because tourists were heading through to get to Bettertown. I stopped at Sid's Bakery, and he was visibly miffed by the potential customers who passed by his store without even a whiff. Signs in front of his bakery advertised muffins. Prices had been slashed twice, from five tokens to four tokens to two tokens. Sid had a marker at the ready when I came up; apparently ready to make the muffins two for a token.

"Did you taste those donuts over there?" he asked.

"No."

"They're dry and way too sweet. Whoever bakes those things needs to take it easy on the sugar."

"Your customers will figure it out at some point, Sid."

"I'm practically giving these muffins away. I'm making no profit. I sent a spy over there an hour ago, and he hasn't come back yet. He's probably sampling their cream puffs—which, by the way, are much too flaky."

"Well, Sid, you've been the only bakery business around since we started. Now you have some competition. Maybe this'll force you to work a little harder. Present a better product. Advertise a little."

"Well, I'll tell you what. I'm not going down without a fight."

"That's the spirit!"

■ ■ ■

As I passed Le Bakeria, I got a few whiffs of something, and I was tempted to try whatever it was that smelled so good. But I couldn't do that to Sid. I noticed that there was a fan running behind the counter. Mind you, it was early December and about 40 degrees out, so the fan wasn't there for cooling purposes. It was there to send the smell wafting out to the masses, and it seemed to be working. People were being drawn like bees to pollen. Sid was going to have to do something special to get his customers back, though

I didn't doubt for a second that Sid's food was better than anything they served at Le Bakeria.

I noticed a number of Kidsborians there, and when they saw me looking at them, a few ducked out of sight. Apparently, they didn't want to explain their presence in Bettertown.

But then I saw something that bothered me much more than that. I passed the recreation area, and there, resetting the bowling pins, was Scott. He didn't see me; he was busy trying to keep up with the bowlers, running from lane to lane, setting the pins back up after they were knocked down. Sweat was running down his face despite the 40 degree temperature, and he looked a little flustered.

I stood there watching, not wanting him to see me, but knowing that at some point there had to be a confrontation. Max came up from behind me.

"Good kid," he said, seeing the direction of my gaze. "Hard worker. Must be tough for you to lose him." He smiled at me, knowing how much this dug in. He left to go annoy someone else.

I walked around aimlessly for a few minutes, and then headed for the housing district. Sure enough, there was a mailbox in front of one of the houses that read "Sanchez," Scott's last name. I heard footsteps and turned. Scott froze, seeing that I had noticed the mailbox and knowing there was no rational explanation he could give for it. We stared at each other for a few moments, and then I couldn't help but speak.

"What are you doing here?"

"I'm just . . . I decided to . . . I live here," he said, looking at his shoes.

"Why?"

"I figured I needed a change of scenery. I mean, I *like* Kidsboro and all, but . . ." his eyes fixed on his house. "Well, I've only got a 10-minute break, I have to get back to work."

"What? Setting up bowling pins?"

He looked surprised and a little embarrassed that I already knew about his new profession. "Look, it's a job. At least I'm doing *something*. A lot more than I was doing over there," he said as he pointed across the creek.

"But Scott, you're working for *Max*. Don't you know he's gonna burn you?"

"He hasn't burned me yet. So far, he's given me a job, a living wage, and a house with electricity—none of which I had in Kidsboro."

"But you've got *friends* over there."

"I've got friends *here*. We had a rally yesterday, and we're a team. It's a family. I like these people."

He was making too much sense, so I resorted to a lower blow. "How could you turn on us like this? You're a charter member of Kidsboro."

"Oh, and that's really taken me far in 11 months," he said sarcastically. "You know what, Ryan?" He stepped toward me and pointed in my face. "You have no right to say that. You have no idea what it's like to be me. You're the mayor. You're the leader of the whole place. You *have* a job. You *make* a difference. Me? I'm the town fool. I have a detective agency that no one goes to, even if by some miracle they actually *have* a case to be solved. No one respects me there, Ryan. But *here*? Here, I'm a part of something. They need me. In Kidsboro, I go on vacation for two weeks and no one even knows I'm gone."

"You're on the city council in Kidsboro! You count for 20 percent of the vote."

"I'll tell you what. *You* can have my 20 percent. You pretty much had it anyway."

"What is that supposed to mean?"

"Oh, come on, Ryan. You know that whatever you voted, I voted the same. And if I didn't, you let me hear about it."

"What?"

"I mean, you always made it *sound* like you were just reasoning with me, but really you *expected* me to vote with you. You controlled me, and that's probably the problem here too. You've lost your control, and you're mad."

I was flabbergasted. "What in the world are you talking about, Scott?"

"Are you just jealous that I have a nicer house than you, Ryan? You don't think I deserve it?"

"Scott—"

"Or maybe you're having trouble dealing with the fact that there may be something over here that's better than Kidsboro. Well, for me there's no choice. In Bettertown, I'm equal with everybody else. In Kidsboro, I'm a pitiful, poor boy with a failed business and a lucky connection in city council."

He slowly dropped his finger and let out a few exasperated breaths. I caught a glimpse of a smile, like he was proud of himself for standing up to me. His resolve shocked me, and I could do nothing but drop my shoulders—and my defenses.

"Well, Scott," I said, stiffening my upper lip. "I hope you're very happy here." I walked past him.

■ ■ ■

Scott's feelings about Kidsboro troubled me. I hadn't realized that there were people in our town who were unhappy. And I'd had no idea that one of the unhappy people was my best friend. On my way back into town, I noticed Mark, the owner of the miniature golf course, playing on his own course. Well, at least he appeared to be playing, but in actuality, he was firing his shots into trees outside the course boundaries. No one else was around.

"Why would anybody play here?" he asked before he even looked at me. "There's a bowling alley over there—and darts, and archery and . . . fun. There's *fun* over there. And here? We've got a guy knocking golf balls into trees with a putter."

I told him the novelty of Bettertown would wear off, and I believed that was true, but at this point, its downfall couldn't come fast enough for me.

■ ■ ■

Usually I met with Mr. Whittaker once a week to give him an update on what was happening in Kidsboro. I wanted to meet with him this week and let him know how many problems he had caused, but I could never say that to Mr. Whittaker. Instead, I decided to avoid it completely and not meet with him at all. I went to Whit's End and was glad that he wasn't in the front. Connie Kendall was behind the counter.

"Mr. Whittaker's not here?" I asked.

"No, he's in the back. You want me to go get him?" Connie asked.

"No, could you just give him a message?"

"He's right in the back. I can get him."

"No, just a message, please. Tell him I won't be able to meet with him today."

"Well . . . okay, Ryan."

"Thanks."

■ ■ ■

I called a city council meeting to figure out what we were going to do. Pride in our town had been lost. Suddenly, no one had any reason to go to Kidsboro. We had to do something.

We started with a damage report. "We've lost six people," Jill said. This meant six Kidsborians had left and joined Bettertown. So 11 of the 17 new citizens were from elsewhere. We decided to wait to fill up those empty houses, since none of us believed that Bettertown would stand for long. At least, that's what we hoped.

"Since Bettertown's grand opening a week ago, Kidsboro businesses are down in profits by 65 percent," Nelson continued with the bad news. "Sid's Bakery has taken the biggest hit."

"The crime rate's about the same," Alice said proudly, as if Kidsboro had crime, much less a rate to keep track of.

We briefly discussed the ramifications of losing one member of the city council, and we decided we had to fill the spot. Since having a voting group of four members would result in a lot of ties, we needed a tie-breaker. But this was not first on our agenda. We had to come up with a way to drum up new interest in our city.

"Let's have a 'Pride in Kidsboro' day," Jill declared. "Like a Fourth of July thing, where everybody celebrates the country."

"That sounds great," I said. "Tell us more." The rest of the council members sat up in their chairs and took notice. Jill began slowly, giving us her ideas, then Nelson added a few of his own, and, as if new life had been breathed into us, it became an incredible brainstorming session with fresh and exciting things to add to our celebration.

By the end of the meeting, we had come up with some pretty interesting ideas. Jill was going to do a *History of Kidsboro* collector's book, outlining how Kidsboro came to be and events that had shaped Kidsboro along the way. Nelson suggested that Jill include a short biography of every citizen who had ever settled here. He reasoned that people would be more apt to buy the book if they could see their own names in print.

We were also going to have refreshments. We all agreed to bring food from home, plus, we would ask Sid to offer his cooking expertise and make a smorgasbord of pastries especially for the event. (As it turned out, Sid agreed to make the pastries and sell them for half price, but our end of the deal was that we had to advertise his bakery as much as was humanly possible. Sid was a hard sell.)

We also decided to create a flag, though admittedly, it wasn't an original idea. The Bettertown flag flew high across the creek, in full view from Kidsboro. Jill suggested that we ask Roberto to come up with some ideas because he was a pretty good artist. I told her that we needed something that symbolized what Kidsboro was all about—freedom, loyalty, peace, justice, responsibility, fun—and she said that to get all those things into one flag, we would have to fly a copy of our city charter on a pole. I told her that if he got any two of those things on the flag, I'd be happy. She said she would talk to Roberto.

Alice said that she would take care of security, "just in case things get out of hand." We all knew that things rarely got out of hand, but we nodded to support Alice's one and only contribution to the meeting.

But the one idea that we all got excited about came from Nelson.

"I've got a new invention I've been looking forward to unveiling. Eugene and I are almost done. Maybe I could do it at this thing."

"A new invention?" I said.

"Yeah. We've been working on it for about a month now, and I think we've got it just about right."

"What is it?" Jill asked.

"It's . . . in the entertainment field," he said.

Nelson's inventions were always extremely popular. Everyone loved the idea of playing with something that no one else in the world had. His last invention, a computer-programmable car, had sold 51 units in only three months. The fact that he had a new creation was not only a magnet to draw people to our celebration, but it was also good for Kidsboro. It would set us apart from Bettertown because we had something they didn't—ingenuity. Yes, they had a bowling alley, but we had Nelson. And he would bring Kidsboro back.

We decided that the celebration would be in four days, on December 10.

■ ■ ■

I stopped counting after it became clear that we were not going to get as big a crowd as Max's grand opening had. But it wasn't bad. After the rest of the town got word of the celebration, a few people got into it and created attractions of their own. Pete, our resident movie buff, made a short video presentation that was a reenactment of the settling of Kidsboro, 11 months before. It started out with the words "Birth of a Town" in big bold letters in the foreground, then in smaller letters, "Brought to you by Sid's Bakery." It was part of the deal.

In one scene, the boy playing me said to four people standing around, "What shall we do, my friends? We have fought oppression and slavery, and won. And now, I yearn for a land of freedom." And then I planted a flag in the ground. Not only did we not have a flag back then, but we never faced any oppression or slavery, nor do I ever remember having used the word *yearn*, and I most certainly didn't have a British accent, as this actor did. So, the facts were a little exaggerated, but it was still fun.

Speaking of the flag, Roberto came up with what I thought was a great symbol. It looked a lot like the American flag, with a blue field in the upper left hand corner, but instead of stars, there was a white silhouette of a big oak tree, and the trunk formed the vertical line of a *K*, for Kidsboro. The red and white stripes were the same, except the red stripes were thinner. He told me that this represented us, in that we were smaller, yes, but that we still wanted the same things that America did—freedom, peace, and so on. I thought it was pretty cool. He and Jill had printed out about 20 copies of the flag, and they were flying them all over town. And at the bottom of each flag, there was the fine print that read, "This flag sponsored by Sid's Bakery."

As predicted, many people bought the *History of Kidsboro* collector's book simply because it contained their names. The facts in it were more accurate than Pete's film, but it still sparked some controversy over who actually came up with some of the ideas for the town. The layout was sharp. Jill had scanned color photos and placed designer borders around the edges. The quality was only slightly marred by the Sid's Bakery ads on every other page.

Sid outdid himself with the food. He baked every pastry known to man—donuts, bagels, Danishes, coffee cakes, cheesecakes, pies, breads, muffins, cinnamon rolls, sweet rolls—and it was all delicious. I had forgotten what an asset Sid was to our community, but he proved himself once again.

Mark had lowered the price on rounds for the day, and his miniature golf course was packed. He'd even added two holes. On one you had to pretend you were crossing a city street with the ball. There were tiny plastic pedestrians walking across the street, and if you hit one, you got a one-stroke penalty. This was the type of ingenuity I was talking about.

But the highlight of the day was, of course, the unveiling of Nelson's new invention, which would occur near the creek. All day people were stopping to gaze at the large quilts that were covering the invention, curiosity oozing out their eyeballs. There was a sign next to it that read, "Nelson Swanson's new invention to be unveiled at three o'clock."

At 2:51, when I got there, there was already a crowd of at least 30 people gathered around the quilts. Nelson and Eugene walked up at exactly three o'clock with their chins raised in the air a little. Eugene had invented some very impressive things himself, most of them having to do with computer programs. He often helped Nelson with his more elementary inventions. Eugene's pride was more in Nelson, instead of their inventions. He took a couple of steps to the side of the quilts, letting Nelson have the spotlight.

Nelson smiled as he checked his watch. He looked up and breathed in heavily, as if trying to smell the anticipation of the crowd. It grew quiet. He glanced at Eugene, who nodded back.

"Ladies and gentlemen, for many years, this creek has been impossible to navigate with any kind of watercraft. Boats didn't work because, during most times of the year, the creek was too shallow, and a boat would scrape the bottom. But three months ago, I saw something that made me change my outlook regarding this impossible task. It was a water moccasin—skimming across the top of the water. I asked myself, 'Why couldn't we do that? Why couldn't we float on *top* of the water instead of sinking slightly below the surface?' And that is the reason I decided to create something that will revolutionize the way we view creek navigation.

"I present to you . . . the Water Moccasin 250!" Eugene jerked away the quilts to reveal something that looked like a go-cart without wheels. It had two seats, a steering column, a propeller on the underside, and four inflatable inner tubes serving as "wheels" on the bottom. There was a Sid's Bakery bumper sticker on the back. The crowd stepped closer and peered inside, and we saw two pairs of bicycle pedals attached to axles in front of both seats. It was very impressive.

Nelson, Eugene, and two other boys took the invention to the edge of the creek and placed it in the water. Nelson would be the first to try it, just to show the others that there was no risk of drowning. Without hesitation, he plopped down into the Moccasin and began pedaling. Sure enough, the craft floated on the water with no problem.

Eugene cleared his throat. "Notice the rubber bumpers on each side of the craft, so that rocks can't damage the sides." Nelson bounced a little as he maneuvered upstream. He pedaled frantically, the propeller twirling behind him, and the craft inched up the creek in slow motion. The amount of work Nelson had to do to get the thing to move that slowly didn't seem worthwhile.

"Now," Eugene said, "the craft's velocity will increase when another passenger is added."

Nelson ducked his head as he went under the bridge, and he continued upstream. The crowd cheered.

Nelson floated back downstream a few minutes later. He didn't even have to pedal as he went with the current. But one thing was certain: No one would be taking this thing any farther downstream, no matter how easy it was. There was a five-foot waterfall only 100 feet downstream from the bridge, and no one would risk the fall.

The crowd cheered again, and Nelson waved to the fans. No one had ever gone that far upstream before because there was a tall fence put up by the city of Odyssey that prevented anyone from walking along the shore. But this watercraft would enable people to go upstream in the water. No one even knew what was up there. I knew this would be a popular attraction.

■ ■ ■

That day, Nelson gave everyone free five-minute rides. The passengers couldn't really get very far in five minutes, so this was a smart strategy. It made people want to try it the next day, when they would have to pay four tokens per ride but could go for 10 minutes. The crowds were lined up all day. Nelson was beaming the entire time, giving a history of the invention, and the history of boats, and the history of all things that floated, to people standing on shore while passengers took the Moccasin out.

At one point, I glanced across the creek and saw Max. He was watching the crowds line up to try Nelson's invention, stroking his chin as if he had a beard. Bettertown was noticeably quiet, and it appeared that the tide had turned. Kidsboro was the place to be on this day.

But I had seen that look in Max's eyes before. He was plotting something.

5

THE WALL

I WAS ON THE way out of my real house, heading toward Kidsboro, when my mom stopped me. "Can I talk to you for a minute?"

I followed her into the living room, and she grabbed a cup of coffee off of the end table. The fingers that held the handle shook slightly, and the coffee jostled back and forth in the cup.

"What's the matter, Mom?" I asked.

"Sit down," she said, taking a sip and then placing the cup back on the end table. She paced back and forth.

"It's your father. He may be looking for us."

When I was eight years old, my mother and I left our house in California in the middle of the night to escape my abusive, alcoholic father. An abuse center helped us start our lives over. We changed our names and moved to Odyssey, where we'd been ever since. We didn't tell anyone in California where we'd gone. My father was a dangerous, violent man, and we knew that when he discovered we were gone, he would be furious.

For several years now, we had been able to hide from him, but then we discovered a chink in the armor. An old friend of mine (well, pretty much an old enemy of mine) from California had found me and was threatening to blow our cover. His name was Jake, and he would be visiting his grandmother every summer in Odyssey. Because it was now wintertime, Jake was back in California. So, if he was able to communicate with my father, he might have told him where we were. Jake had been mad at me for years for turning him in for possession of a weapon. He'd had to go to a juvenile detention center, and I was sure he blamed me. I didn't doubt that he wouldn't think twice about putting my mom and me in danger, so my mother's news wasn't all that surprising.

"Mr. Henson called me today," she said. Mr. Henson was one of the agents who was assigned to keep us hidden. "Your father's been traveling. He hasn't moved anywhere, settled down in a house, or anything. He's just driving around the country, asking lots of questions."

"Does Mr. Henson think he's gotten any clues?"

"No, not yet. He's been going to all the obvious places. Like Louisiana." My mom was from Louisiana originally, and her family was still there. This probably meant Jake hadn't told him anything yet. "So, Mr. Henson doesn't think your dad has any leads."

"Did you tell Mr. Henson about Jake?"

"Yes," she said. "He knows about Jake. He can't tell if Jake is a threat or not. But he'll have someone keep an eye on him."

"What are we gonna do?"

"Just keep your eyes open. If you see your dad anywhere, you call the police immediately. Here," she said, handing me a cell phone. "You take this wherever you go—to school, to Kidsboro—everywhere. The speed dial is set. If you see him, you just press this button, and you'll get Mr. Henson. Okay?"

I nodded and stared at the cell phone. My eyes watered, and Mom noticed.

"It's gonna be okay," she said and hugged me.

We knelt on the floor and prayed together, a defense we never had when we were in California. But now that we were Christians, we had a God who was bigger than any danger we might face. I was calmer when I stood up, and so was my mom.

■ ■ ■

On my way to Kidsboro, I wanted to stop by Whit's End to tell Mr. Whittaker about everything. He was the only person in Odyssey besides my mom and me who knew the truth about our situation. He had helped us through painful times before, and I wanted to talk to him now.

I walked up to the door of Whit's End, but couldn't bring myself to walk through it. I was still angry with him.

■ ■ ■

I made it to Kidsboro after lunch and immediately noticed a crowd on the shore of the creek. Nelson had created a game out of the Water Moccasin trips. Every team of two had 10 minutes to get as far as they could. At the 10-minute mark, Nelson blew his whistle, and the team had to retreat. So far, only one team, two boys with muscular legs, had made it beyond the borders of the tall fence upstream. Eventually, when the crowds waned, I imagined that Nelson would let somebody explore for a while and go as far as they wanted. But for now, with the crowds lined up, there had to be a limit.

Everyone was having a good time, except for the people and business owners of Bettertown. The bowling alley was empty. Scott was standing around with no pins to reset.

Max was talking to Rodney Rathbone, a school bully who had, for a short time, been a citizen of Kidsboro. Rodney was a pretty tough guy, and I wondered if Max was having him perform a little bouncer duty—though I couldn't imagine who he would be kicking out of what. There was no one in the whole town.

Suddenly, they both turned and walked purposefully toward the bridge. Nelson looked up and caught Max's gaze. Everyone must have wondered what Max was up to.

There was a noticeable smirk on Max's face as he crossed the bridge and stormed toward Nelson. He had a manila folder in his hand. A team had just parked so the vessel was halfway on the shore.

"Okay," Max said loudly. "Everybody off my property."

"What?" Nelson said.

"I own this land, and I want everyone off of it."

"This is Kidsboro, not Bettertown."

"I still own part of Kidsboro, and this deed proves it." Max pulled a contract out of his folder. I wove through the crowd to see what he was talking about. "As you can read here, I bought this land two months ago and built these houses on it." He pointed to four houses, the ones with cardboard siding, the "Creekview Estates."

I looked at the deed. My signature was on the bottom, along with the other four members of city council. We had, indeed, sold him the land.

"Take it," Max said, pointing to Rodney. Rodney grabbed the Moccasin and pulled it out of the water. He dragged it across the grass toward Nelson's house.

"You can't do this," Nelson said. "You don't even live here anymore."

"Sir, you need to hush up and get off my property," Max said, pointing a finger in Nelson's face.

This was the only place in Kidsboro where Nelson could launch his boat. There was a drop-off everywhere else. Max had successfully ruined the Moccasin business, and there was nothing we could do about it.

■ ■ ■

Later that afternoon, Nelson walked into my office without knocking. "He's imposing tariffs on all goods made in Kidsboro," he stated. Tariffs, in the real world, are taxes placed on things made in another country. For example, if you import something from France, you have to pay extra—a tariff. It encourages people to buy things from their own country, instead of a foreign country.

"If anyone from Bettertown buys something over here, they have to pay a tax on it before they can go back over the bridge. Max even stationed a guard there to make sure they're not smuggling anything in."

I walked out my door and saw a boy standing on the bridge, checking the jacket pockets of an innocent pedestrian just trying to get across the creek.

"This means," Nelson continued, as if I didn't understand what it meant, "that we'll be buying stuff over there, but they'll probably stop buying stuff over here because of the tax." I knew this affected Nelson more than anyone, because he sold his inventions every day.

■ ■ ■

The city council met within an hour to discuss our strategy for dealing with Max's scheme. He had already dismantled our best industry, and he had chiseled little holes in the rest of them. We had to do something, or Bettertown would overtake us.

Nelson had an idea. "Why is Kidsboro better than Bettertown?" This was a fair question, and it was a little disconcerting how long it took us to come up with an answer.

"We don't have Max," Jill said.

"Exactly. And what is Max doing over there?"

"He's putting everything under his control."

"Precisely. Bettertown is run by a power-hungry dictator, but in Kidsboro, there's freedom. We can do whatever we want. We have the freedom to make a life for ourselves. We can follow the American dream, get an education, create a business, and own a home," Nelson said proudly.

"What're you getting at?" Jill asked, having heard enough of the patriotic speech.

"Let's make those people realize that there's a better life over here. That there's more to life than feeding and pampering tourists."

"How?"

"We offer them a chance to follow the American dream."

"Could you be a little more specific?" Jill said, glancing at her watch for effect.

"We go over to Bettertown and tell them what they're missing."

By the end of the meeting, Nelson had explained his strategy. Kidsboro would offer a "Starting Your Own Business" course. We had a fantastic teacher, Nelson, so we just needed students.

We headed out, just like a group of army recruiters. All we needed was a few good men.

■ ■ ■

We all watched as Nelson gave an incredible sales pitch to a boy named Jerry, the Bettertown garbageman. Then, trying to imitate the master we had just seen at work, we went out on our own.

The first person I ran into, unfortunately, was Scott. There was one person bowling, and Scott was setting up the pins for him. When he stood back up, he saw me and immediately looked the other way. I approached him.

I knew that the best way for me to open up to him would be to apologize. But I still thought he was making a big mistake, and I think my ego got in the way of my brain when I started off with the sarcastic remark, "Looks like you're having a blast."

"Why don't you go home?" he rolled his eyes.

"You're being stubborn."

"You still think you own me."

"I can understand you being mad at me, but how can you pick this place over Kidsboro?"

"Pardon me for taking up space, but I hope Kidsboro goes down the toilet. I really do. I think you guys need to be taken down a few notches."

"Why are you talking like that? This is not you. It's like . . . you've been brainwashed."

"Why? Because Max has told me that I can have a better life *here* than over there? Sounds familiar. Who's really doing the brainwashing, Ryan?"

I stared at him for a few seconds, and then put my head down and turned away.

■ ■ ■

Nelson and Jill had recruited one Bettertownian (or "Maxite" as many liked to call them) each to come to our seminar. I had struck out on my three tries.

Max had penetrated their brains with too much propaganda, so there was no hope in getting them to come to the seminar. Alice bullied two kids into coming. I'm sure they were there for fear of their very lives.

Nelson and I, along with the four potential recruits, arrived in the meeting hall. Nelson would handle the presentation, and I would offer my two cents, though Nelson had much more experience than I did in starting a business.

Nelson was well prepared, in spite of having come up with this idea only the day before. He presented a strong case for owning your own business, as opposed to working for someone else. Then he offered some ideas for possible business ventures in Kidsboro. Two of the heads in the group nodded vigorously, as if they were seriously considering every word Nelson spoke. Jerry the garbageman looked especially interested.

Near the end of the meeting, when Jerry was practically ready to jump out of his chair and start building his new office, the door suddenly burst open. It was Max.

He looked at the Maxites. "What are you guys doing here?"

Jerry looked up innocently, apparently unaware that he was doing something wrong. "We were learning how to start our own business."

"Your own business?" Max asked in utter disbelief. "Did you ask permission to do this?"

"Permission?"

"Yes. You can't start your own business without my consent."

"What?" Jerry was offended.

"I might let you, but you *do* know that all your profits will be pumped right back into the government."

"You mean I can't keep any of my own profits?"

"Of course not. That's not the way our government works. You work for the city."

"But what if my business is in Kidsboro?"

"You can't live in Bettertown and work in Kidsboro."

"Why not?"

"Because it's against the law."

"What law?"

"Mine."

Jerry looked around at the rest of us, perhaps expecting us to defend him. But in the next moment, he seemed to muster the strength to do it himself. He faced Max. "Forget it! I'm not living my life to serve you!"

"You have no life without me!"

"What are you talking about?"

"In Bettertown, you have a nice house. You have a job. You're working for a team. When I found you, you were nothing," Max said.

"Yeah, and now I'm the garbageman."

"I can give you a promotion."

"To what? Bowling pin setter-upper?"

"You're violating the loyalty laws."

"I've got nothing to be loyal to. I'm moving to Kidsboro!"

"You move here, and you'll be broke before the spring thaw."

"I'd rather be broke than have to serve you."

Just then another voice of reason checked in. Harry, a Maxite, raised his hand. "Yeah, I'm moving to Kidsboro too." The other two Maxites lowered their heads, uncommitted to either side.

"You traitors!" Max yelled. "I'll get you back for this. Every one of you." I knew this message was directed at me as well as the others. Max stormed out and slammed the door.

■ ■ ■

That night as I was heading out of Kidsboro to go home, I noticed that Max and about 10 of his citizens were on the Kidsboro side of the creek. He had floodlights illuminating the area, as if they were preparing for a long night. There was a pile of wood and wire to the side, and Max was ordering his subjects around. Scott was with them, looking cold, tired, and sick of working for Max.

What were they building?

■ ■ ■

I was in my real home eating breakfast the next morning when there was a knock at my door. Jill's face was pressed up against the screen door, and she was frantically knocking on the metal at the bottom.

Once I opened the door, she practically pulled my arm out of its socket. "Come on. You have to see this."

She dragged me through Kidsboro, toward the creek. Once we got there, my mouth fell open. I beheld a magnificent, yet horrifying, sight. Before me, on the edge of the creek, was a wall. Constructed out of wood and wire, it went around the circumference of the Creekview Estates. There were openings in the wall—well guarded by the wire—so I could see through it. Max and his merry band of Maxites were on the other side, taunting any Kidsborian they could see.

Max saw me and took the opportunity to anoint this structure as a tribute to himself. He turned to his flock, though I suspected the speech was really meant for me, and said, "This wall represents the hard work and dedication of a land that is driven by a desire to succeed. We constructed this wall because we will have nothing to do with failure, and we feel that the land on the other side of this wall represents the failure of government, and the failure of people. We are a separate, greater nation than Kidsboro! And from this moment forward, we will not allow Kidsborians on our land! They have infected us with the disease of greed and laziness. Now we will move on without them dragging us down to their level. We will rise as a new, independent nation—the nation of Bettertown!"

The crowd cheered with all the patriotism they could muster after a late night of building the monstrosity in front of them.

The wall was six feet high and about 30 feet long. On both ends there were perpendicular walls connected to it, which ran down to the creek side. All of it was well within the borders of the Creekview Estates. Max now controlled the bridge. There was an opening in the middle of the front wall, and I was sure that he would place a guard there at every moment of the day and would have a list of people who could and couldn't pass through it.

Of course, Kidsboro residents would be on the "no" list.

There was no good way to go *around* the wall. The drop-off down to the creek bed was fairly treacherous (except along the area where Nelson had sailed his Water Moccasin, which was also now controlled by Max). Plus, I was sure the guard that would be placed at the wall would also be in charge of keeping an eye on the bridge and anyone who tried to climb it from the underside.

In history class, we'd studied about how East and West Germany used to be separated by the Berlin Wall. For 28 years, those two countries were bitter toward one another, mainly because of their differences in opinion about government. I never understood why they would just cut themselves off from each other. I understood a little better now.

■ ■ ■

There was a lot of hurtful talk in Kidsboro the rest of the day: "We don't need them!" "Maxites are such idiots!" "I hate those guys!" "I'd like to knock that wall right on top of them!" Even people who were normally very rational, like Nelson, had their better judgment impaired by anger. Nelson spent the day inventing a catapult that would hurl things at the wall. Of course, Max had pulled the rug out from under Nelson's Water Moccasin, so quite possibly he had more to be angry about than most. But I didn't like how things were shaping up in our town.

6

BAD BLOOD

ON THE FIRST DAY of Christmas break, it all came to a head.

The first snow of the year had fallen on Odyssey, and about two inches covered the ground and rooftops. When I had left Kidsboro the night before, there was a guard at the wall. The same guard was there the next morning, as if he had stayed through the night. But I was pretty sure he was wearing different clothes.

My office door was blocked by a four-inch snowdrift, and I had to kick it out of the way to get inside. But as I was halfway through the door, I heard yelling. I turned and ran toward it.

Pete was standing on the Kidsboro side of the creek, about 20 feet downstream from the wall, and across the water was his friend Kirk. Kirk had been one of the Kidsboro defectors. He had joined Bettertown and seemed to be enjoying the change. But now it appeared that these two friends had become adversaries.

"What am I gonna do with this stuff?" Pete asked.

"I don't know. That's *your* problem," Kirk yelled back.

"What's going on?" I said as I approached Pete.

"I've got all this Bettertown money." He unfolded about 30 darbles. "And I can't use it anymore since I'm not allowed over there." He turned back to Kirk. "You have to exchange it for me," he yelled.

"We don't do that anymore. We don't give out tokens."

"Then I want real money!"

"Forget it!"

"Why not?"

"'Cause we don't have anything to do with you people anymore. We don't deal with your money; we don't deal with *you*."

"I spent good money for this, and you guys are gonna pay me back!"

"Make us!"

At this challenge, a number of Maxites gathered around Kirk, backing him up. Upon seeing the confrontation, several Kidsborians that were in the area filed in behind Pete.

"Come on over . . . or are you scared?" Kirk shouted.

"Why don't you come on over here, or won't your Mommy Max let you?"

Pete and Kirk stared at each other without blinking. Pete slowly bent down and grabbed a handful of snow. Kirk did the same. They packed it in their hands, making it more solid and easier to throw.

The rest of the group behind Kirk also reached down and filled their gloves with snow and purposefully began molding it together. Pete's group did the same.

Still, no one blinked.

Now it was five against five, each armed and dangerous, each one prepared for a battle but no one willing to throw the first snowball.

Deep down they must have all known, just like I did, that this would be the beginning of something bigger, something none of them could control. It would be war.

But for now . . . silence. No one dared move a muscle or even breathe suddenly. The rush of the creek was the only sound for 45 seconds.

The snowballs in their hands were as hard as they were going to get. Yet they continued to pack them, as if they knew that if the first hit didn't do its damage, all would be lost. The first hit was the crucial one.

Then it happened. A breeze blew in and shook the tree above the Maxites, blowing snow off one of its branches and sending it down Kirk's collar. Kirk scrambled to get it out. But Pete, who was concentrating on Kirk and not seeing the snow, interpreted the sudden movement as an act of aggression and panicked.

Pete threw his snowball, and it splattered on Kirk's left shin. Kirk seethed, and then the Maxites began machine-gunning their snowballs, pelting the group of Kidsborians. Kidsboro fought back, and I backed away from the fight, which was getting more and more intense.

Pete got smacked in the face and was stunned for a second, but then, with more determination than ever, he ran four steps closer to the creek and gunned his snowball into a Maxite stomach. His advance made him an easy target, and he was pummeled by three snowballs. He retreated.

The Maxites made use of their advantage and hid behind trees, coming out only to fire. Kidsboro was losing.

I had to stop it. I didn't know if anyone would listen to me, but Pete's face was as red as a cherry Popsicle, and the rest of the Kidsborians weren't looking much better. I ran out in the middle of fire.

"Stop!" I yelled. No one even heard me. The Maxites, sensing victory, had come out from behind their trees and were on the very edge of the creek. "Cease fire!" Still, no one listened. Suddenly, Mark, a Kidsborian, got smacked hard in the ear. He felt the side of his head for blood, and then he angrily charged the creek, eyeball-to-eyeball with the enemy. He was lambasted, one snowball hitting him so hard that it knocked him off balance. He lost his footing on the slippery snow and fell down, sliding over the four-foot embankment and into the creek!

He flailed around in the cold water, and Pete and I ran down to help him. The Maxites laughed but had enough sense to know that Mark could catch pneumonia, so they held their fire. Pete and I stepped down into the water and grabbed his arms. Mark found his footing on a rock and pushed himself up, and we pulled him onto the bank. He was soaked. His lips were already turning blue, and his entire body was shaking. Pete and I helped him toward home, and as we left, I looked back at the Maxites with a furious glare.

They smirked as if they had won.

■ ■ ■

This had gone too far. Surely Max had enough sense to realize that a war would not benefit anyone. As soon as I changed my pants and socks and returned to Kidsboro, I stormed directly to the wall. The guard stopped me.

"I'm sorry, but do you have any identification?"

"You know who I am, and I wanna get across."

"What was your name again?"

I rolled my eyes. "Ryan Cummings."

The guard picked up a clipboard with a list of names on it. He scanned it, and then shook his head. "I'm sorry. But you're not on the list."

"I'm talking to Max," I said, as I shoved past him.

He grabbed my arm fiercely and jumped in front of me. "First of all, you will address him as King Max. Second, you're not welcome in Bettertown. Now, turn around and go home."

"That's okay, Frank," Max said, crossing the bridge. "Let him pass. I'll talk with him."

"Yes, sir," the guard said, letting go of my arm and backing away. We headed to Max's clubhouse, or "palace" as the sign on the outside referred to it. We went into his enormous living area. It was almost as big as the meeting hall in Kidsboro. We sat down on cushioned chairs. I began to understand why people were drawn to living here.

"What's the problem?" Max asked.

"What's the problem? You didn't see the snowball fiasco this morning?"

"Oh, yeah, I caught the tail end of it. Shame about Mark. He shouldn't have charged the creek like that, very poor strategy."

"So, what are we gonna do about it?" I asked.

"Do?"

"Yes. We *have* to do something about this."

"Oh, I'm not sure that we do. I mean, I would hate to disrupt the natural order of things."

"What are you talking about?"

"People fight, that's a rule of life. This might be a good lesson for all of us."

"What kind of lesson—"

"Wasn't it you, Ryan," he interrupted, "who said that you liked the idea of having us around so that you could experience competition?"

"This is not competition. This is war."

"War is the greatest form of competition there is."

"Mark could've really gotten hurt, and he still might get sick."

"That's one of the hazards of war, Ryan. An excellent teaching point, don't you think?"

"No, I don't think! We have two towns here, and even though we have different philosophies of government, we don't have to fight about it. We could coexist. We could help each other; we could trade or barter. We could even combine our city councils and have common functions."

"Coexist? Oh, how boring. I'd much rather defeat you and take over the whole thing myself."

"Defeat us? What're you gonna do? Invade?"

"I could do anything I wanted to. You can't protect yourselves against me."

"What makes you so sure?"

"I've got more on my side than you think," he said with a wink. I had no idea what this meant, but it scared me.

"You've got nothing on your side but a bunch of robots who don't care anything about you or your town. They just like their balconies."

"And that's not worth fighting for?"

"They have no loyalty to you. My people? They're proud. They love their city. And they'll protect it with all they're worth."

"Well, your people may have pride, but we've got the strength." He smiled, and then pointed to the door. "It was nice talking to you," he said.

What did he mean he had the strength? Kidsboro had more people than Bettertown. And none of his population was especially athletic. Apparently, he had a plan.

■ ■ ■

On my way back into Kidsboro, I saw Pete and Nelson pounding a post into the ground at the site of the morning's snowball battle. I got a closer look and saw that the post had the day's date, then "The Battle of Snowy Creek," and Mark's name as the lone casualty.

"What is this?" I asked

"Something to help us remember," Pete said. "We might need this for motivation later." It seemed that everyone on both sides of the creek was preparing for the inevitable.

■ ■ ■

Nelson was hyperventilating when he got to my office in the early afternoon.

"What's the matter?" I asked.

"I can't find my plans."

"What plans?"

He took a deep breath. "The catapult. You know that device I'm building to hurl things at the wall?"

"Right."

"Eugene and I drew a sketch before we started it. It had all the measurements, diagrams of every element. The sketch showed where everything would go. I even calculated angles, trajectory . . . Now it's all gone."

"Did you take it home with you?"

He shook his head. "It never left my clubhouse."

"You think somebody stole it."

He nodded.

■ ■ ■

I spent the rest of the day in my office, listening. I don't know what I was expecting to hear—another snowball fight, maybe an attack from the Maxites, or some sort of weapons testing from across the creek—but I was continually raising my eyebrows at any foreign sound. Being on edge like that was tiring. I usually stayed in Kidsboro until dinnertime, but on this day, I was worn out from worry. I headed home early.

When I went through my back door, I noticed that my mom had already decorated the Christmas tree. I had always helped her with that before, but with everything that was happening in Kidsboro, I hadn't had time. I felt bad, knowing that I had broken tradition. I'd barely even remembered that Christmas was coming up.

The phone rang. My mom wasn't anywhere to be seen.

"Mom?" I called. I heard the shower running upstairs, so I picked up the phone.

"Hello."

"Jim?" the voice on the other end of the line said.

It was my father.

"Jim, is that you?"

My instinct told me to hang up immediately. Talking to the man we had been hiding from for years was a dangerous thing to do. But for some reason, I stayed on the line.

"Jim, this is your dad. Don't hang up. I promise I'm not gonna hurt you."

"Why are you calling us?" I asked, a quiver in my voice.

"I just wanted to talk to you. My, you sound like a man. I miss you." He paused, as if he wanted me to return the sentiment. I didn't.

"Listen, I just wanted to tell you that I understand why you left. And . . . I don't know if you're gonna believe this or not, but I've changed. I'm not the man you knew when you were eight. And I don't expect your forgiveness, but I did want to let you know that I'm sorry."

The "I'm sorry" speech. I'd heard it many times as a child. He usually said those words as he surveyed the broken windows and lamps that he had destroyed the night before. I couldn't listen anymore. It hurt too much to hear those words again. It brought back too many bad memories. I hung up the phone.

My hand remained on the receiver, as though holding it down tightly would prevent him from calling back.

Mom came downstairs in a sweatshirt and jeans, drying her hair with a towel. "What's the matter? Are you calling somebody?"

I shook out of my trance and noticed my hand still on the phone. "It was Dad."

The towel dropped to the floor. Her mouth fell open; she was unable to speak for a full minute.

"What did he say to you?"

"He said he was sorry, and that he's changed."

"He knows where we are," she said under her breath.

"I guess I should've hung up."

"That's okay," she said. Her eyes darted around, then lit on me. "Why didn't you?"

"Hang up?"

"Yes."

"I don't know." This was true, though there was a voice inside that was telling me I enjoyed hearing his voice for some reason. Maybe I missed him.

My mom shook out of her own trance and got on the phone. She called Mr. Henson. He said he'd be right over.

■ ■ ■

Mr. Henson asked me more questions than I could answer. He peppered me with: "Did your father sound aggravated?" "Did it sound like long distance?" "Did you pick up any background sounds?" Seeing as how I was in total shock during the entire phone conversation, I couldn't imagine how he could think that I would pay attention to background sounds.

During this interrogation, my mom was sitting balled up on the couch, holding a pillow tightly to her chest. The phone rang, and everyone jumped. Mr. Henson ran to get on the extension upstairs and told my mom to answer it. As it turned out, it was just my mom's friend Margaret, wanting to know if Mom wanted to join her in a garage sale. Mr. Henson came back downstairs, quite agitated with Margaret.

Mr. Henson then called us together in the living room and gave us our options.

"You can move away if you want to," he said. "We'll protect you. We'll change your names again and move you somewhere in the Southeast, I think. Or you could stay here under our supervision, and if he comes back and provokes you in any way, we'll have him arrested on the spot. The fact that he knows your phone number doesn't mean he knows your whereabouts. We gave you a special number that gives callers no indication of your location. It's up to you."

Mr. Henson gave us a few more instructions on how to keep ourselves safe, and then headed for the door. He turned around momentarily. "It's a good sign that he called. If he were going to hurt you, he probably would've just shown up and done it. He knows that by calling, you have a chance to leave. So maybe he's being truthful. People do change sometimes."

We knew this was true. *We* had changed a lot over the course of the last few years. But my dad? I wasn't sure he was capable of it.

We stayed in a friend's basement that night. Still, I lay awake until three o'clock, worrying that the locked doors wouldn't be enough to stop a man motivated to hurt someone. I'm sure my mom stayed awake too.

7

BASIC TRAINING

Oddly enough, the next morning I found solace in Kidsboro, even though we were on the brink of war. Maybe I felt that this was something I could control, or at least try to. In fact, I was in my office working on a proposal that would give me more control over the situation.

I was proposing an amendment to the city charter on how we would conduct war. Obviously, there was nothing in the original city charter about it, since there was no one around to have a war with when it was written. But an amendment was needed now. I would present this before the city council.

In the American government, the Congress has the responsibility to declare war. This is smart, making it a law that a lot of people have to agree on a decision as important as this one. So I figured it needed to be an overwhelming vote in the city council for Kidsboro to declare war. My proposal stated that 80 percent of the city council had to vote yes, which meant that four out of five of us had to vote in favor of war. Of course, with Scott being on the other side now, that meant it had to be unanimous. If the question were to come up right now, I would vote no. War could only end in disaster. But if we were forced to fight . . .

While I was scribbling away, the door opened and a person walked in with his or her jacket pulled over their head. I didn't think it was quite cold enough to be bundling up this much, so I immediately asked, "Who is it? What are you doing?"

The person took a quick peek outside to see if anyone was watching, then shut the door and lowered the coat. It was Marcy Watson, one of Jill's friends. Marcy had lived in Kidsboro almost from its beginning and had eventually become our banker. But she seemed to have grown bored with her job and was reeled in by Max's multimedia presentation. She was now a citizen of Bettertown and seemed to like it there. Jill was disappointed that she had moved away, but she understood Marcy's point of view. This was a mature way of handling it, of course, unlike my feelings toward Scott. Me? I had driven him away with my accusations that he was a traitor.

Marcy's eyes darted around the office until she found two tacks, and then she pounded her jacket into the wall, covering the window. This made it quite dark in my clubhouse. She definitely had my attention.

"What are you doing, Marcy?"

"I have to tell you something," she said.

"Okay."

"I'm sorry for abandoning Kidsboro, but that's over and done with now, and I have to deal with it. But I don't like what they're doing, so I have to tell you something."

"Okay."

"Because I don't want any of you guys to get hurt, I'm be-traying my own city to lend you some important information."

"Okay."

"They're building an arsenal."

"Max?"

"Everyone. Max has got people working around the clock making snow-balls. They've got a big pile four feet high. It's over by the school, blocked off by bed sheets so you can't see it. Plus, they have a weapon."

"Weapon?"

"A big catapult thing." The case of the missing catapult plans was solved. "It can heave big blocks of snow, about 10 pounds worth. It'll bury you."

"When do they plan on using it?"

"I don't know. Max has his own plans, and he's not telling anyone about them."

I swallowed a lump in my throat.

"I don't like what Max is doing, so I had to tell you this. Not that I think there's any way for you to stop him."

"Thanks," I said.

"I better get outta here," Marcy said, pulling her jacket off the window and draping it back over her head. She opened the door slowly and slith-ered out.

I had to call a city council meeting.

— — —

"We have to start an army," Alice said, pounding the table with her palm.

"She's right," Nelson said.

"We can't let these bozos push us around," Alice said. These two sentences equaled the most words she had ever spoken in a city council meeting. In war, she finally saw an opportunity to really inflict pain on someone without being accused of police brutality, which happened about every other week in Kidsboro.

I spoke up. "I don't want war."

"We have no choice," Jill said. "They're coming. You heard what Marcy said. Why would they be building up their arsenal if they weren't going to attack?"

"We have to prepare to defend ourselves," Nelson said. This made sense. There was no reason why we should just let them run over us.

"I don't want anybody to get hurt."

"That's what an army is for," Nelson said. "Listen, Ryan. An army is not there just to attack other people. An army is there to show other people that they can't attack *you*. At least, not without a fight."

I got up and paced around the room. The others were looking at me, silently pleading that this was the only solution.

"Okay, what do we do?" I asked.

"We recruit soldiers," Nelson said.

"We won't get enough people that way," Jill said. "If you haven't noticed, our city is made up of wimps. With the exception of Alice, we have a bunch of future figure skaters. They won't wanna fight. We need to have a draft."

A draft is when the government makes a law that every able man must serve in the army. It's only done during times of war.

"No," I said. "I don't want anyone in our army whose heart isn't in it. I'd feel guilty if something happened. We'll just have to depend on the patriotism of our people."

Jill didn't agree, but she nodded.

"Alice, I think you should be in charge of the army," I said. She straightened up and stood at attention. Nelson and Jill seconded this idea. "But," I pointed to Alice, "you will not train this army to attack. We're *not* going to be on the offensive here. You're only training them to defend themselves and their property." Alice's face turned down. For a split second she had probably envisioned storming the bridge. Her vision of greatness had just been erased.

"Nelson, I'd like you to build some kind of anti-missile device. We'll need to have something in case they use the catapult."

"Got it."

"Jill, you and I need to start recruiting."

"Okay."

"Let's go!"

■ ■ ■

Nelson advised us to get groups of people together and then start asking them to join our army, because no one would want to wimp out in front of his friends. This plan worked, and we recruited almost everyone in town. Jill and I also joined up and reported to boot camp just hours after we'd concocted this idea.

Alice, or "General Funderburk" as we were told to call her, was in top form that day. She lined us all up, and we stood at attention. She walked back and forth in front of us, inspecting whether or not we were standing up straight enough.

"You people are the sorriest looking soldiers I've ever seen," she said, shaking her head. She had seen dozens of army movies, and this was a scene that was in just about all of them. However, in this case it was probably true. I couldn't imagine a group of soldiers looking any sorrier. I peered down the line at our troops, and I didn't see much military promise.

There was Corey, the Kidsboro garbageman, who, when picking up the garbage, had to make twice the trips as most people because he had, as he put it, "a lifting problem."

There was James, the town doctor, who probably thought he was there to provide medical attention to injured troops. But we would all prefer to live with serious injury rather than let him treat us.

There was Roberto, who was born in the Dominican Republic and was not used to these cold temperatures. He was dressed in about eight layers of clothing, and this restricted his movement to the point where he really couldn't bend down to even form a snowball.

There was Pete, who held the record in our school for the most consecutive hours in front of a television—an amazing 23 hours. It was a weekend "Charlie Blue: Bird Lawyer" marathon.

There was Mark, who had no business being out after his traumatic creek accident but didn't want to be left out of the big war. His face was pale, and his lips were quivering.

There was Valerie, who didn't really want to be there, but had developed a crush on one of the boys in Bettertown and wanted to impress him with her military experience. Of course, Valerie was more of a liability than an asset because she would distract our entire company, as practically every male in it had a crush on her. Also, if the temperature ever dipped below 20 degrees, she wouldn't risk possibly cracking her skin.

The others in line weren't much better. We weren't much of a fighting machine, but I was confident that Alice would get the best she could out of us.

■ ■ ■

Alice marched us to an area deeper in the woods, where Maxite spies couldn't watch us prepare. Then she had us run around with weights tied to our ankles.

"Come on, people! Move! This will prepare you for running through deep snow."

Then she had us crawl in groups of three. We had to fall to our knees in the snow, crawl a hundred feet to a tree, and then head back. My turn came, and I fell to the ground. A hundred feet suddenly looked like a mile. By the time I had neared the tree, my gloves were soaked through. My hands froze up on the turn. By the end of the course, I had to watch my hands carefully because I couldn't feel where I was putting them. I stood up and went back to the end of the line. I looked at Jill as if to say, "When are we ever going to need to crawl through the snow?"

By the time Pete had finished his round, his face was caked with snow. He acted as if he didn't notice. The entire company had collapsed by the end of the exercise.

Next, we did snowball-throwing exercises. Alice had placed five targets on trees. Each soldier had to make snowballs, throw them, and hit all five targets in 25 seconds. Those who didn't make it would be pelted mercilessly by the rest of the company.

"Roberto! You're first!" Alice yelled. Roberto stepped forward reluctantly. The rest of us bent down and retrieved handfuls of snow. He watched us all very closely and cleared his throat.

So far, the exercises had been much harder for Roberto because of his eight layers of clothing. For him, crawling through the snow meant pretty much rolling through the snow. He dropped to his knees with a heavy plop and wiped the sweat off his forehead with the back of his soggy glove. He looked down at the snow and waited for the signal.

"Go!" Alice yelled. Roberto frantically grabbed a handful of snow and began packing it with his already numb hands. He packed it four times and created a loose ball. He turned, ready to throw his ammunition, but he got in too big a hurry. His follow-through was awkward because he couldn't lift his arm over his head, and he missed the target by four feet.

"Miss!" Alice shouted.

Time to panic.

He rolled over on his knees to make a new snowball and pounded it between his hands.

"The enemy's coming! Hurry up!" Alice yelled.

Roberto threw a desperation shot from his knees.

"Miss!"

No time to pack now. Roberto frantically clutched some snow in between his hands and threw it loose toward the target. The wind blew it back in his face.

"That's not gonna hurt anyone, come on!"

He lunged at the ground.

"They're coming at you with a catapult!"

He packed with reckless abandon.

"They're gonna bury you!"

He threw.

"Five seconds!"

Hit.

"They're on top of you!"

Too late.

"Time!" We all threw our snowballs, and Roberto was hit on every side of his body. Driven every direction by the force, he fell prostrate onto the ground. It grew quiet as we all looked down at Roberto, flat on his back as if he were about to make a snow angel. Alice shook her head and walked slowly toward him. She stood over him and stared down into his face.

"You're dead, soldier."

▬ ▬ ▬

After we all took turns suffering the humiliation of that drill (Valerie was the only one who beat the timer), Alice took us over to our command post where we would make and store our arsenal of snowballs hidden behind two club-houses and a bed sheet. Making snowballs and putting them in a pile was a welcome diversion from the workout we had just been put through, even though none of us could really feel our hands.

As I laboriously packed and stacked, Nelson came over to show me his plans.

"Here's my anti-missile device." He showed me a picture. It was a map of Kidsboro with something that looked like a net over it. "A mesh screen," he said. "We hang this in the trees over strategic targets—our houses, the base, and anything they catapult over here will be sifted into harmless flakes when it hits this."

"That looks good. How are we gonna get the mesh?"

"I'm working on it. Now, look at this." He showed me a rough sketch of some kind of launching device. "This is a salt shooter. I have bags of snow salt at my house. This device will send them—a few salt pellets at a time—into enemy territory and into their arsenal of snowballs. Now, it'll take a while, but after a couple of hours, the salt should have melted a good portion of the pile, or at least the snow will stick together and be worthless for throwing."

"How are you going to get it to be that accurate?"

"I'm working on that, too. I'll test it in my backyard before I bring it over. But listen, this way we can deplete their arsenal virtually undetected, since we're doing it just a few salt pellets at a time."

"That's brilliant," I said, holding the plans with both hands.

"Cummings!" Alice shouted at me. "Get back to work!" I guess she figured that she outranked me now that we were at war.

"You'd better show these plans to Alice," I told Nelson.

"All right."

■ ■ ■

After we had made a pile of snowballs about three feet high and seven feet wide, Alice marched us to the little league baseball field in McAlister Park and had us climb the backstop. She told us it was good training for climbing the wall between Kidsboro and Bettertown. I had no idea why we would need to do that, since I had told her that we weren't going to attack, but she seemed to think it was necessary.

This exercise was especially difficult because our hands were numb. But everyone managed to climb it anyway.

After that, we went back to the 25-second snowball drill, and this time, Roberto hit three of the targets before his time ran out. Eight people, instead of one, actually hit all five, and everyone came a little closer than they had before. Alice looked satisfied for the first time all day.

Alice dismissed us to our homes as the sun went down. Strangely enough, no one complained about the day, and no one hung his head low. Perhaps surviving the training exercises made us feel as if we had accomplished something.

Maybe we felt like we were ready.

— — —

The success of the day before may have been the reason I was a little too cocky for my own good the next morning. Max was reclined in my office chair when I walked in.

"Get any sleep last night?" he asked, smiling.

"Plenty." This was true. I had slept like a baby after the workout Alice had given me.

"Didn't stare at the ceiling last night, wondering when we're gonna strike and annihilate your little town?"

"Not at all."

"That's surprising, Ryan. You being so worried about your citizens like you always are. I figured you'd be a little more concerned about their well-being."

"I think you ought to be a little concerned yourself."

"Oh, really?" He sat up, ready to get down to business. "Do you enjoy war, Ryan?"

"Of course not," I replied.

"Of course not, no. You're a man of peace, aren't you? So, what would you say if I told you we could prevent this inevitable conflict between our two fair cities?"

"How?"

"I'll make you a deal. I'll call off my dogs, we sign a treaty, and the two of us live in peace and harmony."

"If?"

"If you give me back my wood."

I wasn't surprised by this request. Ever since I'd noticed that his "school" was made out of bed sheets instead of wood, I knew that Max was getting low on building material. Of course, across the creek, he saw our houses made of wood that used to be his. Naturally, he would ask for it back.

"Are you crazy?"

"It's *my* wood."

"We bought that wood from you."

"You don't need it now anyway. You've got your tarp and all that. Why don't you just use that?"

"That's not the point. You're talking about our houses. They belong to us."

"But isn't it a small price to pay for peace?"

I stiffened. "You're not taking our wood."

He stood up and smiled again. He acted as if he had come as an instrument of peace and had been thwarted by a war-mongering dictator. He shook his head and said, "Then I'm sorry to say this, but . . . I'm afraid we're at war." He slapped me gently on the shoulder, and then turned and left.

8

THE RESCUE SQUAD

ABOUT THREE MORE INCHES of snow had fallen during the night, so our arsenal had to be dug out a bit. The footprints from the day before were gone. Evidence of our training had been buried.

Alice put us through more drills. We all ached from the day before, but none of us cared. We all seemed a little sharper, a little more determined, a little more excited about being there. Every person—except James the doctor—hit all five targets before time ran out. We were suddenly a well-oiled machine, a team of trained soldiers taught to protect each other with every freezing, pained bone in our bodies.

Halfway through target practice, I heard a *psst!* I was apparently the only one who had heard it. I looked around, but didn't see anyone. Thinking I had imagined it, I went back to the drill. Then I heard it again: "*Psst!*" I turned again and saw a small bit of a black jacket sticking out from behind a tree. I glanced around to see if anyone noticed me, and then I went to investigate.

It was Marcy.

"What's wrong?" I asked.

"You gotta call this off," she said, her eyes darting all around her.

"Call what off?"

"The war. Just give Max whatever he wants and forget it."

"Why?"

"He's brought in ringers."

"What?"

"He went around town yesterday and recruited a bunch of hoodlums—Rodney Rathbone, Luke Antonelli, Jerry Wilmott, and lots of others." Jerry and Luke were pitchers on the Odyssey Middle School baseball team. Rodney wasn't the athletic type, but he could probably give the Bettertown army some tips on cheating.

"What do those guys have to do with this? Why did they even want to be involved?"

"Are you kidding? This is a war. There might be an opportunity to pound someone. You think they'd pass that up?"

"I guess not." I looked at the troops, loyally preparing to defend their city, and I knew in my heart that we didn't have a chance against those guys. At least, not if we pitted strength against strength.

"Would you do me a favor, Marcy?"

"Sure. Anything."

"Keep an eye on 'em. Let me know if they're planning an attack."

"Okay."

"Thanks."

Marcy hurried off for fear of being discovered. I rejoined my unit.

We still had one advantage over them. With Nelson on our side, we were smarter. If we could out-strategize them, we had a chance. I casually went over to Nelson, who was watching the drill.

"How much longer before that salt shooter is up and running?"

"It's ready."

■ ■ ■

We set it up under the tree that was closest to the creek, where we could still escape detection. The salt shooter looked like a narrow-barreled cannon. Nelson poured an entire 10-pound bag of salt in the back of it, and then motioned for me to climb the tree. I took a pair of binoculars with me to scout out the guards around the snowball pile while we shot the salt at it.

I started up the tree. Nelson checked the wind, and there was none. I continued to climb until I could just see the guards' heads over the sheets, shielding the snowball pile. The pile was higher than they were. I nodded to Nelson, and he turned the machine on. It revved up for a couple of seconds, and then it made a *phht!* sound, like an air pump. A dozen or so pellets flew out, and I quickly put the binoculars to my eyes to see where they landed. The sheet puckered all over.

"You hit the sheet. Aim it farther," I said. "You'd better go real far so you don't hit the guards."

"Gotcha," Nelson said, adjusting the machine. The cannon rose up a bit, and he was ready again. Another dozen pellets flew out with a *phht!* I looked through the binoculars and saw the pellets hit the snow behind the pile.

"About 10 feet back this way."

Two adjustments later and Nelson had it. I saw the pellets hit the snowball pile. The guard in front looked up as if he'd heard the sound of rain. The sky was perfectly clear, so his eyebrows rose a bit. Then he seemed to brush it off. Nelson shot another round. Bulls-eye. The guard looked around again, thoroughly confused. I chuckled at this funny sight.

Nelson hit the target fairly consistently with the next five shots, and every time the guard looked around, he saw nothing and probably thought he was going crazy. He went over to talk to someone else and . . .

Suddenly I saw something through the binoculars that I wasn't expecting. In front of the sheet were several guards pulling someone forcefully toward Max's office. The person they were pulling was struggling to get away, like a dog being taken to the vet. The struggle continued until the victim came out of the jacket and fell to the ground. It was a black jacket.

Marcy.

They'd captured our spy.

I hurried down out of the tree and gave the binoculars to Nelson.

"What's wrong?"

I didn't answer. I went straight to Alice.

■ ■ ■

"We have to form a rescue team," Alice said without hesitation.

"How are we gonna rescue her? We can't even get through the wall." This was barely even a question to Alice. The wall, the bridge, and the creek were not obstacles to her.

The bridge was the only legitimate way to get across the creek. The water was from three to six feet deep. During the summer, it was possible to wade through it, but the cold was a factor now. Upstream from the bridge, the drop-off was too extreme. It was like falling off a cliff. Downstream from the creek, there was the threat of getting caught in the current and going over the waterfall. This was the reason that control of the bridge was so crucial to this war. There was no other way across.

"We'll get across," Alice said. I thought that maybe she was thinking of taking out the guard at the wall, but now that Max had recruited the thugs of the school, he had a guy even bigger than Alice there, plus another one on the other side of the bridge.

"How?" I asked.

"We'll get across," she repeated. We went to the troops.

"Men," Alice said to the unit, "I have a dangerous mission that we must undertake. One of our brave soldiers has been captured by the enemy."

Everyone started looking around, trying to see who was missing. "We have to form a rescue team, go into hostile territory, and bring her back."

"*Her?*" Pete asked. "Who?"

"Marcy," Alice said.

"Marcy's a Maxite."

"She was spying for us. Now she's been found out. No telling what kind of torture they're putting her through over there. We have to go. I need two good men."

The problem of getting over the creek probably never even crossed anyone's mind. The thought of wandering be-hind enemy lines did. There were no immediate volunteers.

"I think I should go," I said. I felt responsible, since I was the one who had asked her to be our spy. She might have been trying to get information for me when she was captured.

"Good," Alice said. "We need one more."

Jill stepped forward. "Marcy's my friend. I'll go."

"All right. We have our team. Come on." Alice motioned for us to follow her. The rest of the unit went back to their stations.

■ ■ ■

Alice took us back to her real house. We followed her into the garage, where she pulled out a toboggan. She also pulled out two large pieces of wood and a long rope, and then handed them to us. I saw Jill's eyes widen, as if she were wondering, as I was, what in the world we were going to do with this stuff.

"Put these on," she said, handing us white parkas. "It'll camouflage us against the snow." She also made us put white stuff that looked like cold cream on our faces.

Without a word, she led us back into the woods, to a point well east of Kidsboro. We were far downstream of the bridge, past the waterfall, nearing the farm owned by Tom Riley, a friend of Mr. Whittaker's. As Alice stopped, I had an inkling of what she had in mind—and it terrified me.

At this point in the creek, there was a steep hill that led to the creek bed. The cliff on the other side of the creek was five feet lower than on this side.

She wanted us to jump it.

She went down to the cliff edge and set up a ramp with the two pieces of wood we had brought. Jill and I stayed back and contemplated our certain death.

"Is she crazy?" Jill asked.

"I think so," I said. It was a seven-foot drop into freezing water if we didn't make it.

Alice covered the ramp with snow and then tied the long rope to a tree. She threw the other end of the rope across the creek. It landed on the other side. I presumed this was how we would get back across once we had made the daring rescue.

She headed back up the hill. She wouldn't look either of us in the eye.

"Have you ever done this before?" I asked.

"No," Alice said, apparently finding no relevance to this question. "Lean forward as we're going over. And wrap your legs around the waist of the person in front of you." She casually hopped into the toboggan and held the reins. Jill and I exchanged looks.

"What's wrong?" Alice asked.

I had no feeling in my legs, but somehow I managed to climb in behind Jill. I grabbed tightly to the ropes along the side of the toboggan and stared down at our doom. I turned away quickly. Jill was shaking in front of me. Alice was a rock.

"Push off," she said, and we did, as hard as we could, believing speed was our friend.

We picked up speed . . . faster . . . faster . . . the creek came on like an on-coming train. The cold wind tore at my face. I couldn't watch, but I couldn't *not* watch.

I looked ahead and suddenly realized that we had veered too far right. We were going to miss the ramp!

Alice leaned to her left, and we went with her. Jill lifted her head, realized what was happening, and screamed. We weren't going left.

The cliff was 40 feet away . . . 30 . . . 20 . . . 15 . . .

"Bail!" Alice screamed and dropped off the left side, taking us with her. The impact drove my face into the snow, and I went into an uncontrolled roll. Jill flipped over onto her head, kicking me in the face. Before I stopped, I saw Alice lunge for the toboggan, grab one of the side ropes, and save it before it plummeted off the cliff.

Jill was face down.

"You okay?" I asked. She lifted her head long enough to say "yes," and then buried it again. I felt a lump forming on the side of my head.

Alice was already up and ready to do it again. She said, "My fault. I misread the terrain."

Jill rolled over and looked straight up into the sky. "She's not going back up the hill, is she? Please tell me she's not going back up the hill."

"She's going back up the hill."

Alice gave us a few moments to catch our breath, and then she yelled down to us from the top of the hill. "Come on, let's go!" We both shook our heads and trudged back up.

I was a little firmer with her this time. "Are you *sure* this is gonna work?"

"Yeah," she said, grabbing the reins. Jill and I took our places on the sled. Without any hesitation, Alice pushed off, and we joined her.

The toboggan gained speed . . . faster . . . The ramp ap-proached, only this time we were straight on. We were going to do it.

I prepared to lean forward, the snow kicking in my face. I clenched my teeth, peeked at the ramp, and suddenly . . .

Woosh! We were airborne! The toboggan tipped up ever so slightly, but then lost speed at the zenith and plummeted back down. The front of the to-boggan dipped at a severe angle. I squeezed the side ropes with all my might. The sled swooped down and . . . *Wham!* The curled wood at the front slammed into the bank. The back flipped over the top of us, sending us headlong into the snow. The jarring knocked the wind out of me.

My face was pinched between the ground and the topside of the tobog-gan. Jill was pretzeled up beneath me. Alice de-tached herself from the side ropes and quickly stood up.

We'd made it.

"Are you okay?" I asked Jill. She lifted the ski cap off her face and looked at me. She chuckled.

"I'm fine."

I started laughing too. Soon we were in hysterics, simply happy to be alive.

Alice was on to business, of course. By the time Jill and I had stopped laughing, Alice had tied the loose end of the rope to another tree. She pulled it taut and hung underneath it to make sure it would hold us when we came back and needed to get across. She was satisfied and was ready to rescue somebody.

She led us the long way around Bettertown. She felt it would be best to move in from the back.

As we got close enough to see the clubhouses of Bettertown, Alice mo-tioned for us to get down. The closer we got, the slower we moved and the more we relied on trees to shield us. "Okay, I'm going to that tree. Jill, you follow along, exactly one tree behind me. Ryan, you're one tree behind her."

"Got it," we said at the same time.

Alice moved with quick, smooth steps to the next tree, then the next. I watched Jill do the same, and I followed along behind as I'd been told to do. Soon, I could hear voices. Luke Antonelli was giving orders to a smaller kid who I didn't recognize from this distance.

Then I saw it: their arsenal. A huge pyramid of snowballs, standing six feet tall and as wide as a minivan. It was more ammunition than they would need for a dozen wars.

Then I saw something even more frightening—the weapon. They'd obviously taken Nelson's plans and ex-panded on them, like doubling the recipe for a cake. The catapult looked exactly like Nelson's, only it was three times bigger. The springs that would fling the snow were made out of iron coils as thick as watermelons. Nelson had intended to use a mop bucket to hold the ammunition on his catapult. On this one, it was an outdoor garbage can.

They could probably bomb Indiana with it.

I listened carefully, trying to hear what the enemy was saying while still trying to keep up with Jill and Alice. I could make out some of the conversation. Max was talking with Rodney Rathbone.

"What do you want me to do with her?" Rodney asked him. I assumed they were talking about Marcy.

"Move her into the rec center. I'm tired of listening to her whine." I could tell that Alice heard the conversation as well, because she changed directions and headed toward the rec center.

I was 10 feet away from the snowball mountain and could clearly see the checkered pattern on the guard's ski hat. Alice moved along, undetected, and Jill followed.

Then something strange happened. I felt something hit me . . . like tiny grains of hail. A few seconds later, I was hit by another batch. This time, I could hear them falling all around me. The guard turned to see what had made the noise.

It was the salt pellets!

I quickly ducked back behind my tree, held my breath, and hoped the guard hadn't caught a glimpse of me. The pellets again rained against the tree I was hiding behind. I heard the guard shuffle around and move closer. The footsteps got louder. More pellets. The wind must have changed and carried the pellets farther than Nelson was aiming. The guard, curious about this strange noise, continued coming. I pressed myself as flat as I could against the tree, wishing I could climb inside of it.

I turned my head . . . and he was there. His face was inches from mine, his nostrils flaring.

"Rodney!" he shouted. I tried to run, but it was too late. The guy grabbed me and forced my arm behind my back. Rodney ran up, discovered Jill, and went after her, too. A couple of other guards went for Alice, who fled the scene and headed back from where we had come.

Jill and I were taken with rough hands to the rec center, where Marcy sat quietly. Her hands were tied behind her back, and Rodney ordered the same to be done to us. Neither Jill nor I struggled. We knew we were outnumbered.

I looked at Marcy, who didn't seem to have been tortured, but I asked anyway. "Are you all right?"

"Yeah."

"I'm sorry."

"That's okay."

A couple of Maxite thugs tied our hands behind our backs and around the wooden supports that helped hold up the roof. Marcy's hands were wrapped around another one. The three of us sat on the ground.

"Have they been bad to you?" I asked her.

"Every 10 minutes they come in and put snow down my back. I'm starting to get used to it."

The icy ground was beginning to penetrate my pants and numb up my legs. I could tell the same thing was happening to Jill because she shifted a few times and then settled on a bent knee approach to sitting. Apparently Marcy's legs were already numb because she sat still.

Over the next few minutes, I had fleeting thoughts of trying to escape, but I knew it was probably not possible. Even if I did manage to free all of us without anyone noticing, we would still have to get past several guards, all of whom outweighed me by about 20 or 30 pounds. So I sat quietly, being the model prisoner.

Suddenly Marcy said with glee, "Hey, this is just like your dream, Jill. The one where you and Ryan get stuck in a room together all alone." Jill's eyes widened.

"Marcy—" she said through clenched teeth, trying to sound both serious for Marcy's sake and indifferent for my sake.

Marcy went on, ignoring Jill's objections. "Of course, *I* wasn't there. And in your dream, didn't Ryan put his arm around you and try to comfort you? Guess he can't do that now, with his hands tied . . ."

Jill's face turned hot pink. She turned and gave me a nervous smile. "Marcy, nobody cares," she said, again trying to sound indifferent.

She dreams about me?

Much to Jill's obvious relief, the tension broke when the door opened and Kirk walked in. He stopped suddenly, as if he wasn't aware that I would be in there. He looked at me. Kirk was a former Kidsborian. I was the one who had put him up for a vote in the city council, and now he was my enemy.

He had a handful of snow. He had probably been ordered to put it down our backs. He looked only at me. But not as an enemy. He was looking at me as the one who gave him his start in Kidsboro.

He crushed the snow in his fist and dropped it on the ground. Then he turned around and went out the door.

■ ■ ■

An hour passed, and the three of us had said very little to each other. Jill could barely even look at me after Marcy's embarrassing revelation. Activity outside the door seemed to be growing, and I wondered if an attack was imminent. My town was on the brink of being shelled, and here I was, stuck in this room, unable to help. My frustration was growing.

The door burst open, and Max came in. He chuckled upon seeing us, helpless, our rear ends frozen to the ground. Then he approached me.

"Feeling beaten, Ryan?" I didn't respond. "Well, you are." He crouched down and looked me in the face. "That was a nice little rescue attempt. I commend you. Very brave, too. But I hope you noticed something about your attempt. It was a failure. Just like everything you've done lately. And yet, everything I've laid my hands on has turned to gold. Did you see that arsenal I've got? Have you looked at the size of my guards? How about that catapult? We're stronger than you. We're better, faster, and smarter. And if you know what's good for you, you'll stop this little war we've got going before it even starts."

"We're not giving back the wood," I said with a stiff upper lip, which wasn't difficult since it was frozen.

"Ryan!" Max laughed. "I'm surprised at you. You're going to willingly put your town through a devastating war, when you could just swallow your pride and get it over with now."

I stared at the ground in front of me. Was I being prideful?

Max moved even closer to my face and got serious. "You've got until Monday to give me back my wood. At three o'clock on Monday afternoon, we attack and take the wood by force." He stood up and headed out the door. I swallowed a lump in my throat and exhaled. I turned to Jill, who seemed to empathize with my dilemma.

Crash!

Suddenly the wall caved in, almost landing on the three of us. Jill and Marcy screamed. The ground shook under us. Alice cracked her knuckles and stepped over the wall that she had just pushed in.

I could hear the Maxite army come to life as Alice jerked the support beams out of the ground with ease and freed us. Rodney and some others burst through the door, looked a little stunned as they saw the room had one less wall, and then came after us.

In true Hollywood fashion, Alice smiled at Rodney and said, "Sorry to bust in on your little party."

We ran. Jill and I led the way, with Marcy right behind us and Alice falling back on purpose to deter anyone from chasing us.

It was difficult to run with our hands still tied behind our backs, but on we sped, toward the rope that was hopefully still tied across the creek. I looked back and saw that there were six Maxites behind us, but none of them seemed to be running their hardest for fear they would actually catch up to Alice.

By the time we reached the creek, we had lost them. The rope was still there. Alice untied us, and we made it back across. Out of breath, Marcy thanked us. It was sort of a weird rescue, but a rescue nonetheless.

9

WAR

WHEN MR. WHITTAKER FOUNDED Kidsboro, he told us that he would be available to answer questions and give advice. I rarely asked for advice because I wanted to figure things out on my own. But this was a problem I didn't know how to handle. Still, I wasn't sure I could trust him anymore. I didn't know whose side he would be on in a war. So I missed my weekly meeting with him again.

I did know that going to war against Bettertown should not be my decision alone. Technically, it was a decision for the city council, but I thought this was too important to bring before only four citizens out of 25. I had to bring this up before the entire town. It was their houses and their town that were at stake.

We held an emergency meeting in the pavilion. Everyone was there. When I walked in, I noticed that there wasn't the usual hubbub that a group of 25 adolescents and pre-adolescents makes. People spoke in low tones with furrowed brows. Others shook their heads in disbelief at what was happening.

I took my place in front. I didn't have to call them to order. They were already staring up at me like little children waiting for their parents to make the bad dreams go away. I wished I could.

I breathed a long sigh and began. "We have a decision to make, and I think everyone in town should be here to help make it. Max has threatened to attack and rip apart our houses if we don't agree to give him back his wood by three o'clock Monday. I've been over there and seen their arsenal. This is the situation: They have a snowball pile twice as big as ours. They have recruited some of the toughest guys in our school to be in their army—including Luke Antonelli, Rodney Rathbone, and Jerry Wilmott." I saw a few people exchange concerned looks when I mentioned those names.

"I know that it would be a pain to take apart our houses, but we do have tarp now, and I think we could get by with that. It's just something to think about." I stopped to get input from them, but they didn't take the hint. They just sat there, as if they were expecting me to list our assets alongside the large list of liabilities I had just rattled off. Actually, I didn't see too many assets. "I'd like your input," I told them.

"Let 'em come," came a voice from the back. It was Alice. "We're ready." A few people clapped in agreement.

"We'll never win, no matter how ready we are," said Valerie, an unwelcome voice of reason. "We can rebuild the town. Let's just give him the wood, get rid of all memories of Max, and move on with our lives."

"But we can't get rid of him," Nelson said. I was surprised that he would contradict his sister. "We all know Max. We know he'll never quit wanting more. If we give him the wood, what is he going to want next? Will he try to expand his kingdom and take the land to the east and west of us? How many more businesses can he run into the ground just because he's there and he hates us? We can't get rid of him. I say we fight him."

"I agree," said Mark. "We can't just let Max and his friends run over us whenever they want to."

"And Nelson's right," Marcy said. "They *will* want to. Every chance they get, they'll try to invade, especially if they know they can just plow over us."

People were nodding their heads furiously, and I tried to restore reason. "Do you understand what you're saying? You actually want to stay here and try to protect our houses while Max and his troops come over here and attack? I'm sorry to say this, but . . . they're *stronger* than we are. Some of those guys are athletes—they're huge! I'm not sure we stand a chance."

"You're wrong," Jill said. She walked up to me, and I took a step backward. "We've got one thing those guys don't have. We've got pride. We've got loyal citizens. We've got a country worth fighting for."

The crowd cheered, ignoring the fact that we weren't a country.

"Our army has been working hard, not because we have to, but because we love our freedom. Nelson knows what he's talking about. If we give the Maxites this victory, we'll never be free from Max's rule. We might as well crown him king. Are you people ready to make Max king of Kidsboro?" Jill asked loudly.

"No!" the crowd unanimously declared.

"Then we have to fight."

"Yes!"

Everyone looked up at me. I was glad that it had been taken out of my hands. It had become their decision. "Okay. On Monday, we go to war."

The troops cried out in agreement, many standing to applaud. There was no more tension, no more fear. Kidsboro would not be Bettertown's doormat anymore. We would fight.

■ ■ ■

The crowd filed out of the building and headed for the creek, half wanting to tell the Maxites about our decision and half wanting to attack right away. There were eight Maxites on the other side of the creek, downstream of the wall, and several Kidsborians mirroring them on our side. The Kidsborians taunted them. The Maxites bent down and made snowballs just in case. Our people did the same. Names were thrown over from both sides—hatred at its worst.

Then I saw Scott. He was behind the line of eight, and he made a snowball and joined in the name-calling. The yelling became so fierce that no one could even decipher any of the words. There was just a lot of pointing and clenched fists. Scott looked at me, his teeth clenched. We stared at each other for a few moments, and my only thought was that I couldn't wait to deck him with a snowball. I imagine he was thinking the very same thing.

■ ■ ■

I thought it was curious that Max made his threat on a Friday, and then gave us the weekend to think about it. But I figured it had less to do with him respecting the Sabbath and more to do with people on his side leaving town for the weekend. Whatever the reason, we had the next two days to think about things.

One thing I did during the weekend was go to the Kidsboro Community Church. It was made up of a group of wooden benches along the creek, upstream from the wall. Very few people ever attended, but I had gotten some good things out of it before, especially when I had decisions to make.

Joey, the preacher, was one of the two African-American citizens in Kidsboro. He was also the son of a real minister, and, though he didn't have quite the speaking gifts of his father, he poured out his heart and soul every week. I admired that.

Joey smiled at me as I approached. Once again, I was the only one present. In the front, next to the music stand he used for a pulpit, was a nativity scene. It had all the characters—Mary, Joseph, shepherds, wise men, angels, donkeys, and the baby Jesus lying in a manger.

I had seen nativity scenes before—we had one ourselves—but for some reason, this one looked different. More beautiful somehow. I couldn't quite put my finger on it at first, but then I realized that this was the first time during this Christmas season that I had even thought about the birth of Jesus. I glanced down at my watch. Today was December 22. Christmas had come and was almost gone, and I hadn't even paid attention.

None of the characters were talking—the shepherds, the wise men, none of them. Nobody was saying, "Boy, that was some trip," or "I hope you like this myrrh," or "Move your head! I can't see the baby!" This was the first time I had ever noticed that the only thing they were doing was staring at the baby Jesus. All those people, yet there was such peace on that night.

I sat down on the hard wooden bench, and Joey took out a hymnal. We sang three verses of "Silent Night." Neither one of us had much in the way of a singing voice, so we could barely be heard above the rush of the creek.

After the hymn, Joey made a couple of announcements. There was going to be a church-wide prayer vigil early Monday morning to pray about the war, and then a potluck dinner after the war was over. He put me down on the list to bring a vegetable dish and napkins.

He prayed, calling the war "an atrocity" and "needless," and asking God to intervene and make sure that no one got hurt. I repeated his "Amen."

Joey handed me the offering plate, and I saw him look up at something behind me. I turned around to look.

It was Scott.

He came up quietly, sneering my way a little, and sat down on the farthest possible seat from me. I stood up and carried the offering plate to him. He took it without making eye contact, and I returned to my seat. Joey seemed a little disappointed that neither of us gave anything, and when he was ready to speak, he looked at both of us with disdain, as if he had the perfect sermon with which to nail us.

He was right.

He read from Matthew 9 about how Jesus, the Savior of the world and King of Kings, didn't hang out with other kings and princes and military heroes. "His friends were fishermen," Joey began. "And he spent time with tax collectors and sinners—people that were hated back then. The religious leaders asked his disciples, 'Why does your teacher eat with tax collectors and sinners?' Jesus loved these people and wanted to be their friends and help them change their lives.

"You see, Jesus didn't think of any group of people as his enemies. He didn't say, 'That guy hangs out with this group or that group, so I hate him.' He treated people as individuals." Joey cleared his throat and raised his voice,

"How many times at school do we put people in groups? Oh, those are the jocks, or the bullies, or the stuck-up princesses, or the geeks . . . and so I don't like them. They're not jocks, or bullies, or princesses, or geeks. They're people. People who have feelings."

He glanced at both of us. "And now friends have turned into enemies, simply because they live in different places? What's up with that?

"Jesus told us to love our enemies because they're people, just like us. And if we give them a chance, they might even be our friends. You guys are making a mockery of the Christmas season. Jesus came as the Prince of Peace. The least you can do is give it a try yourselves."

Joey put down his Bible and waited for us to respond. I imagine he wanted us to kiss and make up, but we didn't. I don't know why. That was my best friend sitting over there, as far away as he could get from me. I'd slept over at his house dozens of times. We'd had dreams of one day being college roommates. I'd seen him in his Spiderman pajamas. He was my best friend, and I had placed him in a group because of where he lived, just like Joey said, and now I was supposed to hate him.

But I didn't.

Perhaps Kirk was a better man than I was, dropping the snow that was meant to go down my shirt. At least he knew that the value of friendship was more important than victory over an enemy.

Joey gave up and prayed a benediction. We stood up. Scott and I looked at each other, this time without hatred, and then he turned and walked away.

▬ ▬ ▬

I got up Monday morning, and the first thing I heard outside the house was the sound of dripping. I stepped outside. The icicles were melting, and the temperature was getting warmer. I smiled, thinking this might mean a postponement of the war. We couldn't throw snowballs if there was no snow.

But my mother told me it was supposed to get colder in the afternoon and snow some more. I chose to believe the icicles.

Kidsboro was in full motion when I got there. Alice was in the meeting hall (now army headquarters), giving a briefing on the military strategy for the day. She'd put up an easel with a well-drawn map of Kidsboro and Bettertown on it. There were arrows and X's and little silhouettes of bombs on it. I certainly hoped she didn't really have any bombs for this battle.

I should have stayed to hear the strategy since I was in the army, but at the moment, I was clamoring and praying for another way out of this. I went to the creek side where I saw six people lined up on either side of the creek, just staring at each other. Every now and then, an insult was hurled, but for now, no snowballs. I went to the wall and tried to get past. The guard stopped me.

"What do you want?"

"I wanna talk to Max."

"About what?"

"Ending this war."

"You're giving him his wood?"

"No, I just want to—"

"I was told not to let you through unless you are offering to give him his wood."

"Let me talk to him."

"Sorry."

I took a sharp move to his right, trying to shove past him, but he stopped me and turned me around. I walked back to Kidsboro.

— — —

As it turned out, my mother was right. By one o'clock, it was starting to get colder, and it was snowing again. Ominous clouds gathered overhead.

I sat in on another of Alice's strategy sessions. She had a plan to storm Bettertown's arsenal and destroy their pile of snowballs. I still didn't like the idea of being the attacker, but this wasn't exactly attacking *them*, so I didn't object.

Afterward, I went outside and saw several people taking last minute target practice. Nelson was up in a tree, spying on the Maxites with his binoculars.

"What are they doing?" I called up.

"They're moving the catapult closer to the creek, and they're transporting some of their snowballs with it. Plus, the troops are getting fitted with their gear—special backpacks that they're filling with snowballs."

Nelson came down and started putting his mesh up over the clubhouses. I helped him. He had stopped shooting the salt, seeing that it hadn't had much of an impact. It would be impossible to control the shots anyway, with the wind swirling around as fiercely as it was right now.

All this busy work was being done, but at this point, it was really just a waiting game.

■ ■ ■

At 2:45, the troops were already crouched down into position, with a pile of snowballs at each foot. Alice had people stationed in every area of town. The whole place was surrounded, most heavily around our arsenal. Even though each person in the army had his or her own set of snowballs, the big pile was hardly even dented. Running out of ammunition would not be likely.

The weather, however, might be a problem. The wind was kicking up and sleet was blowing horizontally into our faces. Because of the thick clouds flying overhead, it was dark—almost like dusk—even though it was the middle of the afternoon.

I knelt in position, with my pile of snowballs nearby, and peered around at the tense faces.

Jill wiped her face with her sleeve quickly, so as not to block her eyesight for more than a split second, in case they decided to attack early.

Nelson was our lookout man in the trees, his eyes buried in the binoculars. I could see him shivering because of the wind. The tree he was in swayed dangerously back and forth, but he didn't seem to notice.

Mark was making more snowballs, thoughtlessly increasing his pile. Just to make sure.

Alice stood closest to the creek, staring the enemy in the face, daring them to come. She had no ammunition.

I could barely see the Maxites across the creek because of the darkness and snow, but I could tell they were preparing to come across. They were getting into a double-file line.

The wind howled around us. Other than that . . . silence.

Ring!

What was that? It was coming from my jacket. My cell phone was ringing—the one my mother had given to me so I could call for help if I saw my father. But it had never rung before. I reached into my pocket and pulled it out. I pushed the talk button.

"Hello?"

It was my mom. The connection was bad. I could barely make out "Ryan, get home now—" *Click.* What had happened? Had the phones gone out? It was probably the weather. But maybe not.

Maybe somebody had grabbed the phone out of her hand.

Maybe my father had hung up the phone.

"I gotta go." I stood up and ran as fast as my numb legs could carry me.

The troops couldn't believe I was chickening out. I didn't care. I had to get to my mom.

■ ■ ■

I got there in record time. The lights were on. I looked inside and didn't see anyone. I pushed open the door and ran inside. My mom was in the kitchen, trying to get the phone to work. I breathed a sigh of relief. "Are you okay?"

"I'm fine. The phones are out. Why didn't you come home earlier?"

"For what?"

"It's a blizzard out there, Ryan! Didn't you notice? The forecast says it's going to get worse. Frozen rain, sleet, hail—it's dangerous. They're telling everyone to take cover. We're going into the basement. Come on."

"I can't," I said, still out of breath.

"What?"

"I have to go back."

"No, you're not."

"I have to tell the others. They'll stay out there. I need to go get 'em."

"They don't have enough sense to go home themselves?"

"Not right now, they don't. Can I go?"

"Okay. But you make sure you're back in this house in five minutes. I'll call some of the other parents if I can get the phone to work."

"Got it."

I was out the door before I could take another breath.

10

THE BRIDGE

THE STORM HAD GOTTEN EVEN worse since I'd left just 10 minutes before. Visibility was down to about 30 feet. I couldn't even see the creek, much less the people on the other side of it. None of our troops appeared to have moved from their stations. Nelson was still in his tree; everyone else was in their crouched positions. They were going through with this, no matter what.

I shouted, "Go home! There's a storm coming!" But no one listened. They were soldiers, protecting their land. If they left, the Maxites would destroy their houses without a fight. They could not back down now.

I ran to Alice. "Alice! Tell them to retreat. We have to get out of here!"

"It's too late," she said. "I've already sent a Green Beret team out."

"What?"

"Three of our men snuck around the wall and are taking out the bridge at this very moment."

"What?!" The bridge was made out of heavy chains and wooden slats, and it was fastened onto the bank with screws into wooden planks. A heavy-duty wrench could free the chains and drop the bridge into the water.

"No!" I yelled, running toward the creek. The Maxite army was marching double-file toward the bridge, their snowball bags at the ready. I plunged through the opening in the wall and saw that I was one moment too late. The first man was about to cross when—"Now!" I heard from below the bridge, and suddenly, the chains fell and the bridge collapsed into the rushing creek. Several pieces of wood broke in half on the rocks, destroying any chance of ever using the bridge again. The Maxite first in line nearly fell in, but then he found his balance and scrambled back onto the bank.

Max ran up to see what was happening and saw that there was no way for them to get across the creek. The water rushed past us, out of control and rising. To cross it on foot would be too dangerous in such a current.

The Green Beret team high-fived each other, but no one else found this very funny. The Maxites were in trouble. The driving ice and rain hurt our faces. We had to get these people to safety. No longer were these people our enemies, they were people in grave danger.

"How are we gonna get outta here?" a Maxite yelled.

Alice rushed up to me, realizing the same thing I did. We had to help them. "The rope!" she shouted. "I put a rope upstream. You can go across on that!"

"No," Max yelled. "We found that rope and cut it in half."

Nelson ran up. "Try this." He squeezed his Moccasin through the door in the wall.

We lowered the craft into the water, and Alice held it as steady as she could. There were launching ropes on both sides of the boat. People on either side could hold the ropes tight so the watercraft wouldn't get swept away in the current. Nelson and I held one end, and a couple of Maxites held the other end.

Slowly, the first two Maxites got into the boat. Their weight, plus the current, made holding onto the rope difficult. With all the strength we had, we pulled them across and they stepped onto the bank.

Hey, this was working! A crowd of Kidsborians had gathered on the banks and were clapping.

The Moccasin threatened to get away from us in the swift current, and the Maxites on the other shore started to panic. Four of them scrambled to get on at once.

"No! Two at a time!" Nelson shouted. The four fought each other to make room, and the weight was enormous. Mark came up behind us to help pull them in, but it was too much.

The boat capsized, sending all four into the water. Two of them leaped onto the shore, but two more were caught by the current. I let go of the rope and jumped into the freezing water. Alice jumped in after me. I grabbed hold of a hand—I'm not sure whose—and battled the current, but it was too strong. Nelson had my feet. The water was pouring over my face, but I briefly saw that Alice had rescued one person, and she was coming after me. I felt a strong arm grasp under my arms and pull me onto the bank. The boy I tried to rescue was on the shore with me. We all watched as the Moccasin was taken by the current. It plummeted down the waterfall.

I turned to anyone who was listening. "Run to Whit's End! Get Mr. Whittaker! And call the fire department!"

But the fire department was 10 minutes away, and with the roads as icy as they were, it might even take 20. These people needed to get across now. But the fire department gave me an idea . . . fire truck . . . ladder . . .

"The wall!" I shouted, rising to my feet. "We'll take down the wall and lay it across. They can crawl across it."

Everyone seemed to like this idea, or at least they weren't sure they could come up with anything else, so we scrambled to the wall. Alice knocked it down with one heave, and 10 of us picked it up and took it to the edge of the creek. Slowly, we inched it across, until it made a bridge.

The first Maxite, Luke Antonelli, tried it out. Before he ventured across, he pounded the wood into the ground on the other bank. He was trying to make sure it was sturdy. It wasn't. Max had obviously built a shoddy wall. Luke inched across one wooden plank, but it cracked in the middle. He backed off and tried another one.

Three planks later, he found one that held. But he had to take it slowly. He shifted to place some of his weight on a wire that stretched across. If this piece of wood broke, the wall would be worthless.

Everyone on both sides of the creek held their breath as Luke inched like a caterpillar across the makeshift bridge. I reached out my hand for him, and he stuck out his own. We connected, and three of us pulled him across.

The next Maxite was ready, and with more confidence after seeing it done, he crawled more quickly.

With every person, the wood seemed to groan a little more. Finally, it was Max's turn, the last Maxite to go.

He started across. The wood creaked. Panicking, he burst forward.

Too fast.

The wood cracked, bent, and shattered underneath him. As he fell toward the water, he flung out his hand—and found mine. I grasped with all my might and held him for a split second until I felt a strong hand reach across me and grab Max's wrist. It was Mr. Whittaker.

Max dangled from his hand for a moment, then with one big heave, we pulled him ashore.

We caught our breath, and then we all ran through Kidsboro toward Whit's End.

■ ■ ■

Most of the people ran on to their own homes, but some went to Whit's End because it was closer. Five Maxites and four Kidsborians took shelter under its roof. Mr. Whittaker called everybody's parents to tell them we were okay and would be welcome to stay until the storm passed. Two of the people who had to stay were Max and Scott. Max never said thank you, but he nodded to me once, and that was enough. I could expect no more from him.

Mr. Whittaker had some clean clothes he kept on hand for Little Theater productions. I chose some clothes like Joseph from the Christmas story. I put them on and sat in front of the fireplace. I saw Scott on my way from the bathroom, and he smiled at me and said, "So, you think you're Aquaman now?"

I smiled back and said, "Pretty much."

Mr. Whittaker ran around serving everyone hot chocolate. I took a cup and said, "Thank you." Our eyes met.

"I'm sorry, Mr. Whittaker. I was mad at you, and you were just trying to teach me something."

"That's okay, Ryan. Sometimes people pay a price to learn a lesson, and sometimes people pay a price to teach one. The important thing is that the lesson was learned."

"Yeah. I guess so."

"Merry Christmas, Ryan," he said.

"Merry Christmas, Mr. Whittaker."

It was the eve of Christmas Eve, and for the first time, it felt like it. There was peace inside Whit's End. There was a nativity scene on the mantle above the fireplace. I moved one of the shepherds so that he could clearly see the baby Jesus. Scott did the same for a donkey.

The smiles all around and Christmas decorations made it seem like a party. Imagine that—mortal enemies having a party together.

■ ■ ■

The storm lasted through the night, and we all slept at Whit's End. No one seemed to mind. When morning broke, a bunch of us, both Kidsborians and Maxites, trudged through the two feet of new snow toward our clubhouses.

The wall was still there, except it was no longer dividing our two cities. Instead, it was the bridge between them. The first thing Max did was start tearing down the rest of the wall. Since he had been too proud the night before to thank me for saving his life, I figured this was his way of saying that the days of two separate nations were over. Kidsboro and Bettertown would live on as cities of peace. The other three Maxites helped him.

Scott stayed behind in Kidsboro, which was half buried in snow. The icy rain had fused our arsenal of snowballs together, so now it was one big, solid mountain. They were never even used . . . until now.

Scott found a Kidsborian flag and pulled it out of the ground. He walked over to the mountain and began to climb it, all the way up, six feet high. He looked around at all the people watching him, and then he raised his hand and plunged the flagpole into the mountain. It stuck firm and waved majestically in the breeze.

We claim this land for Kidsboro.

THE END

For Kristyn,
my third-born.
I can still make you laugh
at any given moment,
even though I haven't come up with
any new jokes since 2003.
I wish more people were like you.

■ ■ ■

BOOK 4

The
Risky Reunion

A REALLY BAD PARADE

I PRESSED MY LIPS tightly together and tried to force the laughter from my ears. It was worse than when I thought of something funny during church. I glanced over and noticed that Scott Sanchez, my best friend, was about to burst as well. I exchanged covert smiles with Nelson Swanson and Jill Segler. Alice Funderburk, the only member of the Kidsboro city council who was taking this performance seriously, was listening intently.

The Clean Up Kidsboro group continued their presentation, as passionate about the environment as they could be. Mark was the leader of the group of three, and he dramatically pulled a prop out of a garbage bag. It was a picture of a large, ripe, perfect pumpkin. The picture was on a stand, and he propped it up on the table.

"This," Mark said, "is the human lung." Scott snickered at the thought. I had no idea what Mark meant. Mark reached back into the bag and pulled out an actual pumpkin, cut in half so we could see the inside. We turned our noses away in unison. It was rotted out and black with fungus. He placed it on the table next to the picture. "This," Mark continued, "is the human lung after it has been exposed to just two weeks of air pollution. Disgusting, isn't it?" He was right. I'd never be able to eat pumpkin pie again.

Mark went on. "Pollution in Kidsboro is out of control. We are in a crisis situation, and if we do not respond to it right now, we are forfeiting the futures of our children and our children's children."

I could hear Scott chuckling. I dared not look at him. Mark glared in his direction, and Scott buried his head in his hands as if he were crying—mourning the thought of our children's children having lungs like rotten pumpkins. I don't think Mark was fooled, but he continued with his presentation anyway.

It was budget time in Kidsboro, the only town I know of that's completely run by kids. It was May, a year and three months after Kidsboro had first opened its doors, so to speak. Our first budget had been done pretty randomly, so we had decided we needed to be more organized this year and write out a complete budget for the entire year. In Kidsboro, everything was paid for with Kidsboro money—starbills and tokens.

We were meeting to decide what kinds of things the Kidsboro government would pay for with the people's taxes. The first year we'd had only three government employees—Alice, the chief of police, Corey, the garbageman, and me, Ryan Cummings, the mayor. The three of us were paid through taxes. The only other things that were paid for with taxes were city buildings, such as the meeting hall pavilion.

But this year was turning out to be different. People had the idea to try to squeeze as much money as they could out of the government for their own causes. Today we were to hear arguments from groups like Clean Up Kidsboro, trying to convince us to give them money. It was supposed to be a serious time of deciding where our citizens' tax money was going to go, but groups like this made it a circus.

I tried my hardest not to laugh. The people who were representing causes really cared about their issues and expected wise, informed decisions from their government. I cared about the environment too; I just didn't think Kidsboro had a big pollution problem. And that rotten pumpkin was enough to make a dead man giggle.

Despite Scott's stifled laughter, Mark continued straight-faced.

"Listen to this. A poll taken of Kidsboro citizens shows that 85 percent of our population don't want our city to become a scummy pothole of pollution and filth."

Wow. Did that mean 15 percent of our people *did* want our city to become a scummy pothole?

"I think this statistic speaks for itself," he continued. "Kidsboro wants you to do something. Kidsboro *needs* you to do something." He pushed the Stop button on his tape player to put an end to the patriotic background music. He took a deep breath and looked at us like a puppy begging for table scraps.

"What exactly do you want?" I asked him.

Mark picked up some pieces of paper from his notebook and handed them out to each member of the city council. "On these handouts, I have outlined exactly how much money we'll need for each project that we'll be leading during the upcoming year." We all looked at the paper in front of us. He wanted 30 starbills? That was ridiculous! Very few people made 30 starbills in an entire summer!

"The first project we would like to see approved is the building of an outdoor bathroom. We have noticed some of our citizens—boys—relieving themselves in the creek. This is unacceptable."

An outdoor bathroom was actually not such a bad idea. The nearest building to Kidsboro was Whit's End, the ice cream shop and discovery emporium owned by Mr. Whittaker, or "Whit" as most adults called him. Whit's End was a long way to walk to go to the bathroom in an emergency. But an outdoor bathroom would not cost 30 starbills. And we were all at least nine years old. In my opinion, we could hold it.

"We also need money to increase pollution awareness. Not many people even know there is a problem."

Including me.

Mark continued, "We would also like tougher penalties on littering."

"Is that all?" I asked.

"Yes," he answered.

"All right," I said. "We'll discuss it and get back to you, Mark. Thanks."

"Thank you, Mayor Ryan. Thank you, Scott, Nelson, Alice, Jill," he said, nodding his head toward each council member in turn. "The future of Kidsboro depends on you."

Mark, his two assistants, and his pumpkin left. As soon as they were out of earshot, Scott's cheeks burst open with laughter, as if he'd been holding his breath for 10 minutes. The rest of us laughed with him.

"I thought I was gonna explode when he brought out the pumpkin!" Scott said.

"Has he been saving that thing since Thanksgiving?" Jill asked.

"What kind of poll was that?" Nelson asked. "How unscientific can you get? You might as well ask a hundred people if they'd like to be eaten by a mountain lion."

The next group approached, and we had to stifle our giggling. But it didn't get any better throughout the rest of the day. More groups came, all so passionate about what they believed in that it almost brought tears to our eyes—especially Scott's eyes, which were about to cry from laughter.

The next group was the farmers, led by Kidsboro's only doctor, James. James had probably joined a special-interest group because he had nothing else to do, since no one trusted him to treat even their slightest wound. I supposed he picked farming because it was the closest thing to medical work, as it dealt with health and nutrition.

The farmers had planted a garden the summer before, but they didn't make any money from it because of a very important premise that they forgot and continued to ignore: Kids don't buy vegetables. In fact, kids usually avoid the vegetable aisle when they go to grocery stores. But the Kidsboro farmers were determined to make us all eat vegetables.

They came to the meeting with charts and graphs showing why it's so important for people to eat healthy foods. I agreed, of course, but I still didn't think kids would *buy* vegetables. The farmers must have had some doubts too, because they wanted the government to subsidize their garden. That meant they wanted the government to buy all of their produce since there was no demand for it from the customers.

Next was Corey, our garbageman, who wanted to be paid as much as Alice and me. We had intended to give him a raise, but he certainly didn't deserve as much as he was asking for. After all, he only worked once a week! And it wasn't as if people were throwing away heavy things like old televisions or charcoal grills. All he had to do was go around collecting candy wrappers, apple cores, soft drink cans, and paper. That was about it. Everything he collected would fit in a small grocery bag.

Next was an animal rights group that wanted dogs and cats to have the same rights in Kidsboro as humans—including citizenship and their own houses. A newer citizen of Kidsboro named Melissa told us a tear-jerking "true" story about a cat that wanted to be an actor in cat food commercials but kept getting thrown off buses. He could never get to Hollywood.

Unless we had some blind citizens or created a fire department, I couldn't fathom what a dog would do for a living in our town. Much less a cat, unless a big hairball fad suddenly swept the city.

The next group was the Legalize Slingshots group, who wanted to put an end to the law in our city charter forbidding slingshots anywhere within the Kidsboro city limits. I thought this was a common-sense law, but the group did their best to shoot holes in it. A boy named Ben stood up and said with all sincerity, "We have a right to protect ourselves against nature. Do you have any idea how many bears there are in this part of the country?" He was right—I didn't have any idea. And I was pretty sure Ben didn't either. The group brought out different kinds of slingshots—some large, some small, some built to fling rocks, some made to fling things like rubber balls. They wanted us to consider each type, noting the ones that were perfectly harmless. But what good would harmless slingshots be against a bear?

Finally, the slingshot guys collected their weapons and displays and headed home. Again, the second they were out of earshot, we all had a big laugh about it. I was still laughing when the next group came up from behind me. Suddenly, everyone else stopped laughing. They looked over my shoulder with faces of stone, not cracking a smile. I turned around.

It was Valerie Swanson, Nelson's sister. She was accompanied by two other girls, and the looks on their faces told us they meant business. Suddenly, things were not so jovial in the meeting hall. Valerie always got what she wanted, and I shivered to think about what she could possibly want now. Everyone else had come to us like desperate souls, worried about the status of the world. Valerie came with a demanding look that said, "I have no concern for you or your city. I just want what I want, and I will get it." Her long, brown hair was pulled back in clips, and I was momentarily distracted by her good looks. I quickly shook it off, knowing that I needed to be at the top of my game to deal with her.

The three girls walked in sync as they approached the front of the meeting hall. They had no charts, no diagrams, no visual aids—just themselves and whatever frightening cause they were about to stand for.

Valerie, of course, was the spokesperson. "Good afternoon, council members. We represent Girls Against Discrimination." (GAD?) "We have noticed certain inconsistencies with the way our city council, and specifically, our mayor, makes decisions. Our research team has documented evidence that boys are given special privileges in this town. There are more boys than girls in Kidsboro. There are three boys but only two girls on the city council. Boys get better pay. And boys are hired for government jobs before girls. We want these things changed."

There was a short pause. Apparently, this was all she felt she needed to say. She wanted it. Now we were expected to do it. I wouldn't let her get away with this, but I had to act reasonable at the same time. "Valerie," I said calmly, "I've never noticed a pattern of special treatment or consideration given to boys over girls."

"Of course you haven't. You're a boy."

This was her response? I was looking for something more along the lines of this documented evidence she was talking about. "Well . . . Valerie . . ." I continued, sounding a bit too much like I was talking to a three year old, "you've got to have more solid evidence than vague accusations. You need to make an argument."

"Oh, I will. Just not here."

"Then where?"

Valerie reached into her back pocket and pulled out a folded sheet of paper. She handed it to me. I unfolded it, and across the top of the page was the word *Subpoena*, which meant she was taking me to court. "I'm suing you," she said.

"For what?"

"Discrimination."

I looked around at the rest of the city council, trying to feel their support. But all I got were looks that said, "You're on your own, buddy."

I stiffened my upper lip. "Is this supposed to scare me into giving you whatever you want?"

"Oh, I'll get what I want."

"And what's that?"

"More government jobs for girls. Another girl on the city council. Equal pay for equal work. And no more new boys will come in as citizens until there are just as many girls here as there are boys."

I chuckled and hoped the rest of the city council would follow my lead and chuckle with me. They didn't. "Valerie . . . you know, I would love to . . . but there's not much I can do about—"

"See you in court," she said, gesturing to the other girls to follow her out. They were gone before I could get another word out.

I looked at the other council members. I started laughing again, just like I had laughed at all the others. "Does she really think that . . . Ha! She's so . . . silly . . . " I scanned their faces, but no one was laughing with me this time.

Jill stared at me with a scrunched up nose. "Why *are* there three boys but only two girls on the city council?"

I gulped hard.

Alice glanced at me with the same look. "How much money do you and Corey make?"

■ ■ ■

I wasn't paying much attention to what Mr. Whittaker and Nelson were working on, but whatever it was, I knew it would be amazing when it was done. It was things like this that made Whit's End more than just an ice cream place. Mr. Whittaker was a great inventor who taught all the kids who came into his shop about the Bible (and life in general) through his machines. He and Nelson were working on the Imagination Station, which was sort of like a time machine that let you live in other times. At the moment, they were working on a Bible program for the story of Joshua.

"Could you read off those numbers, Nelson?" Mr. Whittaker asked.

"Sure."

"Thanks."

Nelson read off a list of numbers from a sheet of paper. The list made no sense to me, but Mr. Whittaker pounded them all into the keyboard.

I waited for Nelson to finish, and then asked the question that had been dominating my thoughts ever since Valerie and her friends had made their announcement. "Do you think I discriminate against girls?"

Nelson took off his glasses and put one earpiece in his mouth. He looked thoughtful for a few moments, and then said without a doubt, "No." He looked back at the computer screen, where Mr. Whittaker's program was loading.

"That's it? No explanation?"

"My response doesn't require an explanation. If I had answered 'Yes, I do think you discriminate,' then it would require an explanation. But I said no." He was beginning to sound more and more like Eugene Meltsner, Odyssey's resident genius and Nelson's mentor.

"May I ask why you're asking that question, Ryan?" Mr. Whittaker asked. I told him about Valerie's new feminist group.

"I've never known you to make any decisions that discriminated against girls," Mr. Whittaker said.

"Yeah," Nelson said, "you're always suggesting girls when we vote on new citizens."

"And you seem to get along with most of them," Mr. Whittaker added.

"Yeah," I said, my head raised a little higher. "I *do* get along with girls. I don't discriminate. I'm very fair. Right?"

"Right," Nelson said, his attention back on the computer.

"I don't have to just sit here and accept what Valerie says. I've got plenty of evidence on my side. I can beat her in court!"

"Sure you can."

"I need to write some stuff down," I said, but before I could find any paper, Scott walked up.

"Hey, did you meet the guy from the *Odyssey Times*?" he asked excitedly.

"No."

"He came out to Kidsboro today and asked me a bunch of questions."

"About what?"

"The town, how it worked . . . he asked a lot of questions about you."

"Really?"

"Wouldn't that be cool if there was an article in the paper about Kidsboro?"

"That would be great," Mr. Whittaker said.

"Hey, he'll probably want to interview both of you," Scott said, referring to Mr. Whittaker and me.

"Yeah, that's right, Mr. Whittaker," I said. "He'll want to know how the place started." Having a town run by kids had been Mr. Whittaker's idea. He'd founded Kidsboro and had helped us build the town.

I coached Mr. Whittaker on some of the things to talk about when the *Odyssey Times* reporter came to him. Mr. Whittaker chuckled, knowing exactly what to say. He always did.

2

JUSTICE IS SERVED

ALL COURT CASES TOOK place in the meeting hall pavilion, the same place where the city council met. Kidsboro had 36 citizens now, and it seemed like every one of them was there. There were people crammed in under the roof, plus there were more than a dozen outside looking in. A few outsiders were also there either because they were interested in our justice system, or they were just bored. The chance to see somebody get sued always seemed to draw a crowd, but this was an even bigger event. The mayor was getting sued.

Because no crime had been committed, this was considered a civil case. Civil cases that required an interpretation of the law were not heard before a jury, only a judge. Judge Amy came out in the long, black robe that her brother had used for his high-school graduation. She looked very official but a little intimidating. Still, I wasn't worried by the fact that this was a "boy versus girl" case and Amy was a girl. She had always been fair. In matters of justice, I didn't trust anyone as much as I trusted Judge Amy.

Valerie was wearing a business suit and had her hair up in a bun on top of her head. I knew her strategy. She wanted to look as much like a boy as possible, so that people would begin to see fewer differences between girls and boys. She wanted everyone to know that the two were equal. This was one of the few times in Kidsboro history that anyone had worn a suit within its city limits. I wore jeans with a hole in the knee.

Valerie winked at me when she sat down at the opposite table. I hated it when girls flirted with me and didn't mean it.

Judge Amy called the place to attention with her gavel. Everyone fell silent. "All right, state your cases," she said. "Valerie, you go first."

Valerie stood up. If there had been a jury at this point, she would've smiled at them and flung her hair back. Of course, every boy on the jury would have immediately been on her side when she did that. But since there was only Amy to impress, her face remained rock-hard and serious. "Your Honor, I'm here to state my case against Ryan Cummings, who I believe has discriminated against girls during his tenure as mayor here in Kidsboro. I have documented evidence that proves he has given special privileges to boys."

"Documented evidence?" Amy asked.

"Yes. May I approach the bench, Your Honor?" I knew this won her big points with the judge—asking permission to approach the bench. Wow.

"Yes."

Valerie walked up to where Amy was sitting and held out a cassette tape and a stack of papers for her to see. Then she turned and spoke loudly so that the crowd could hear. "In these documents, I have statistics that prove an obvious imbalance in Mayor Ryan's nominations for citizens of Kidsboro, as well as how he hands out government jobs. As you can see here, there are 36 citizens of Kidsboro, and 23 of them are boys—or 63 percent. The government has developed a number of city projects in which it hired workers for a couple of weeks at a time. They hired 27 workers for all of these projects. Twenty-two of them were boys." There was some murmuring from the crowd. But she wasn't done.

"On average, boys make eight starbills a month more than girls in Kidsboro." More murmuring, and this time I noticed that most of it was female murmurs. I didn't want to turn around in case every girl in the place was staring at me. Valerie went on. "And, of course, I find it very convenient that there are three boys on the city council but only two girls. Mayor Cummings is obviously anti-girl."

Valerie glanced at me with a smirk on her face and reached behind her chair. She pulled out a tape player. "Let me show you just how anti-girl he is."

What did she have on that tape?

"On this tape, I have the voice of Ryan Cummings, our mayor. I'm sure you'll recognize it immediately. You will hear Ryan share his true feelings about girls. This is a taped interview that Ryan did with the *Kidsboro Chronicle* last winter when Jill did an article on the Kidsboro military. Listen carefully, if you will." I shot a look at Jill, who had her head down. She refused to make eye contact.

Valerie pressed Play, and out came Jill's voice. "Ryan, there are many girls who have volunteered to be in our army. What do you think their role will be?"

The next voice was mine. "Oh, the girls will play a vital role in our military. They'll be right there when the fighting starts . . . serving the guys hot chocolate."

Valerie quickly pressed Stop and looked out at the audience. I was too shocked to look around, but I could feel the red-hot stares of all the girls, plus the utter disbelief of all the boys.

I had only been making a joke, and Jill knew that.

Valerie continued. "A person who thinks this way about girls can't make decisions without his bias getting in the way. And indeed, I believe it *does* get in the way. Ryan runs a city where girls are in the minority, where girls make less money, and where boys get more and better jobs in the government. I cannot just sit back and watch this happen to my gender."

There was some female applause from the back. I glanced over, and Scott was doing sort of a half-clap, which meant that he didn't exactly agree with Valerie, but he also didn't want to get attacked by a bunch of angry girls afterward either.

I had to admit that Valerie was well prepared. I'd had no idea she was going to have statistics and a tape, and for a few moments, I wondered if I really was a girl hater. But I had to go ahead and state my case. I knew in my heart that I wasn't a girl hater, and I had to prove it.

"Is that all?" Amy asked Valerie.

"Yes."

"All right. Your turn, Ryan."

I stood up and tucked my shirt into my pants. Nothing I could do would make me look as professional as Valerie, but I also didn't want to be a slob. Sloppiness might somehow make me look like a girl-hating man.

"I would like to answer all these claims, Your Honor. May I approach the bench?"

"Yes."

I approached, but then I realized I had nothing to give to her and no reason to approach the bench. I just wanted to extend to her the same respect that Valerie had. I got up there and immediately took a couple of steps back. "First, I'd like to talk about this '63 percent of all Kidsborians are boys' thing. Now, if you ask anyone on the city council, I am always suggesting girls as new citizens. But for some reason, girls are less likely to want to join our town than boys. Maybe they think that clubhouses are boy kinds of things."

I sensed some seething behind me, like I had just offended somebody, but I went on. "In fact, in the history of Kidsboro, only six boys have turned down our offers to become citizens, while 13 girls have declined to become citizens. I have the city council records . . ." I whirled around and realized I hadn't planned as well as I thought I had. "I have them on my computer at home. I'll get you a copy. Second, I want to talk about the government projects Valerie mentioned. Let me list those projects: rebuilding the bridge this spring, paving the roads in the middle of town last summer, moving those huge rocks on the edge of town so that we could create a sports field—all of these projects required hard, manual labor that girls are not built for." I heard hissing from the back.

"I'm sorry, but except for Alice, I don't think there are any girls in here who could've moved those rocks." Male clapping and female hissing.

"Order," Amy called out.

"As for the salaries, how can Valerie bring up salaries? This town has business owners and independent workers. Their salaries are based on how much they sell and how much work they do. The government has nothing to do with the salaries of anyone but Alice, Corey, and me. And Alice makes more than Corey. I don't doubt that boys make more money—just look at Nelson, for example. Nelson's inventions always sell like hotcakes. He's very rich. He raises the average all by himself. Of course the boys' average is gonna be more. Nelson makes as much as 10 boys!"

The boys' applause drowned out the girls' hissing.

"Valerie's statistics are misleading. I believe that I have made very fair decisions in my time here, and I will continue to do so. As for that tape . . . I was clearly making a joke! If Valerie had let that tape play just a few seconds longer, I'm sure I said the words 'just kidding' and laughed or something. I don't feel that way at all about girls. Just look at my record." I sat down to some mild applause.

"Okay. Thank you, Ryan." Judge Amy's face wrinkled up, and she tapped her gavel on the table several times. "All right," she said, "I'd like to listen to the entire tape."

Valerie stood up in instant protest. "Why, Your Honor?"

"I want to hear context. I want to hear what Ryan said right after he made the comment about girls."

"Your Honor, with all due respect, the context makes no difference. The fact is he said it, whether he was joking or not."

"I'll make that call, not you," she said. I liked Judge Amy.

Valerie breathed a heavy breath of protest, and then re-trieved her tape player.

"Rewind back to the beginning of Jill's question," Amy said.

Valerie obeyed. The tape came on in the middle of Jill's question.

". . . girls who have volunteered to be in our army. What do you think their role will be?"

"Oh, the girls will play a vital role in our military. They'll be right there when the fighting starts . . . serving the guys hot chocolate." I laughed. "Just kidding. You're not gonna print that, are you?" Valerie stopped the tape.

"Wait," Amy said. "Let it go. I want to hear how he really answered the question." Valerie let out another breath of protest and pressed Play. I loved Judge Amy.

I continued. "I don't really see any different roles for girls. They're just as capable as boys are of doing the things that army training calls for."

"Okay, stop the tape," Amy said. Valerie rolled her eyes. She stopped the tape but didn't sit down.

"Your Honor, this was a newspaper interview. He was just saying what he thought the readers wanted him to say. His true feelings are the things that remain unpublished."

"That's not for you to say, Valerie. Now, I'm going to leave for a few minutes and make my decision. Court is in recess." She banged her gavel.

I believed I was out of trouble. But one thing really bothered me. Why did Jill give her that tape?

I turned around to look at her, but she was no longer there. I whirled around and saw her practically running toward her clubhouse. I went after her.

"Jill!" I shouted before she made it inside her office. She stopped suddenly, but she didn't turn around.

I had to walk around her to get her attention, because she stubbornly refused to turn around. I looked straight at her. "Why did you give Valerie that tape?"

"I remembered that joke."

"You knew I was joking."

"Maybe I didn't think it was that funny."

"You know me, Jill. You know I don't hate girls."

"Maybe not. But I'm starting to see what Valerie is talking about."

"What?"

"Government jobs usually do go to boys. You definitely suggest boys for citizenship more often than girls."

"Are you actually joining Valerie's GAD group?"

"No, of course not. I know better than to follow Valerie. But I'm just trying to make sure our world doesn't work like the real world."

"What do you mean?"

"Women are sometimes discriminated against. There are women who get paid less for doing the same jobs men do. I think Kidsboro should be different."

I fumed. "Did you think of that yourself, or did Valerie come up with that?"

She fumed right back. "Believe it or not, Ryan, girls can think for themselves. Even me." She stormed off back toward the meeting hall; obviously, she didn't really need to go to her office. I followed 30 steps behind her.

Judge Amy sat down in her seat. The crowd was as quiet as 40 adolescents and preadolescents could get. She folded her hands and peered out over the audience.

"Mayor Cummings," she began, fixing her gaze on me, "your joke wasn't funny. Boys are not smarter than girls, and girls are not less capable than boys. Whether you were joking or not, the attitude that girls are not as valuable as boys are should be avoided at all times. You should know better, being in the public eye. If I were you, I would watch what I say, on and off the record."

She stopped looking at me and directed her attention to the audience again. "But I do believe it was a joke. I don't believe that this joke is evidence that Ryan truly feels that way. I also don't believe that any of the other evidence Valerie presented shows he feels that way either."

She turned toward Valerie, who had her arms crossed and her teeth clinched. "Valerie, you presented a strong case, but I must rule in favor of the mayor. Court's adjourned."

She banged the gavel, and the whole place erupted with opinions. A number of the girls were livid, and some of the boys were relieved. I heard the word "appeal" come from Valerie's lips, but Kidsboro had no court for her to appeal to. We only had one court, and it had just ruled in my favor. Whether or not she had a court to appeal to, though, I knew very well that Valerie was not through with me.

Jill was gone the second Amy's gavel hit the table.

■ ■ ■

There aren't very many people who get the best of Valerie Swanson. So as I strolled into Kidsboro the next morning, I held my head a little higher than normal. I probably walked a little more quickly, my feet a little lighter. I greeted everyone I saw. "Hi, Marcy. Hey, Mark. Hi, Pete. How's it goin', Sid?"

But there was something strange going on. No one was saying hi back. They all just stared at me, like I had an extra nose this morning. My inner joy turned to inner confusion as I was a one-man parade through a crowd of people turning to each other and whispering. No one spoke to me, but everyone seemed to be speaking *about* me.

What was going on?

I asked this question of a few of the gawkers, but no one would answer. I guess no one wanted to be the one to tell me what was so terribly wrong.

I ducked into my office, eager to be out of the spotlight. Scott was at my desk, reading a newspaper.

"Why is everybody acting so weird?" I asked.

Scott looked at me in shock. "Is any of this true?" he said.

"Is any of what true?"

He slid the paper across the table. It was the *Barnacle*, the weekly newspaper printed in Bettertown, the rival town across the creek. The *Barnacle* always made fun of the *Kidsboro Chronicle* and everything about Kidsboro.

On the front page, in big bold letters, were the words: "Kidsboro Mayor Has Secret Past."

I started sweating.

3

THE SECRET REVEALED

THERE IT WAS FOR everyone to see—my secret past. And whoever had written the article hadn't missed many details.

KIDSBORO MAYOR HAS SECRET PAST

Kidsboro—Ryan Cummings, mayor of Kidsboro, is not who he appears to be. According to a source who wishes to remain anonymous, Ryan Cummings is actually Jim Bowers, a former resident of the San Francisco area. He and his mother ran from California and changed their names for "personal reasons." Also, in direct contrast to the mayor's claims over the last five years is the resurrection of his father, who Ryan (or is that Jim?) said was dead. The source explained that Ryan's father is very much alive.

The article went on about some other lies I'd told. There was a picture of me from my third-grade yearbook. The caption read "Jim Bowers." I hadn't changed much since the third grade. That was me, all right. The truth was that my mom and I had left California to escape my abusive, alcoholic father.

My second biggest fear—after my dad finding my mom and me—had always been that my friends would find out who I really was. And here it was, in black and white. Scott saw that I was done reading the article. "What's this all about?" he asked.

I looked at him, but couldn't answer. I crumpled up the paper, threw it down, and ran out of my office.

Jill was right outside the door. I switched directions to get past her, but she stuck her arm out. "Ryan, what's going on?" I didn't want to talk to her, even though I knew she probably wouldn't put anything I said in the paper. I kept going.

I heard footsteps running up behind me, and I glanced back. It was Valerie.

She had the biggest smile on her face. I sped up, but not before she got some verbal shots in. "Hey, Ryan," she said, "you remember in our election last year, how you told everyone that you had never lied to them? I was just wondering: Does that include the time when you lied about everything?"

Done digging in her heels, she slowed down and let me go. Dozens of people were watching. I didn't know where I was running. I was just furious with everyone and everything right now.

But then something dawned on me. I stopped and addressed the onlookers. "Has anyone seen Jake?"

Jake Randall was the one who had told my story. I just knew it. He'd been a neighbor of mine in California before we had moved. He'd visited his grandmother in Odyssey last summer and had a stranglehold on me because of what he knew about my past. I believed he had just returned to Odyssey for summer vacation. I was going after him.

Someone in the crowd answered my question. "I just saw Jake at Whit's End about 20 minutes ago," he said. I was gone before he could finish his sentence.

■■■

Whit's End was crowded when I burst through the door, but I barely even noticed. Jake was standing in a corner of the shop, next to a tall indoor plant. I went straight for him. He saw me coming and must have known why I was there, because he stopped talking to Max.

"You just couldn't keep your fat mouth shut, could you?" I said.

"I didn't tell him nothing, man."

"Liar!"

"You've got the wrong guy, dude," he said with a smirk. I hated that look, and somehow it sparked an uncontrollable anger in me. I wasn't going to look at that face anymore. Suddenly, my fist clenched up and I let it fly. I hit him square in the jaw. He was caught off-balance and fell backward into the plant. The sides of the pot broke apart underneath him, sending dirt in all directions. The crowd fell silent as I looked at him. That wasn't me that had just punched someone. I didn't hit people. Jake looked up at me with blood streaming from his chin, more shocked than hurt.

Mr. Whittaker ran up just as Jake got to his feet and charged at me. Mr. Whittaker grabbed Jake by the chest, and his punch missed me by a foot. Mr. Whittaker forced him to the wall.

"What's going on?" Mr. Whittaker asked.

Max spoke up with shocked glee. "Ryan clocked him."

"What?"

"Right in the jaw."

Mr. Whittaker looked at me in disbelief, and then he looked at Jake. "Are you okay?"

"Yeah. Just caught me off guard," he said, loosening up to show that he wasn't going to charge me again. He pointed at me. "If that punch woulda hurt, you'd be lyin' in a ditch sometime tomorrow."

"That's enough, Jake," said Mr. Whittaker.

"I never said a word to that reporter," Jake continued.

"Let me see your face," Mr. Whittaker insisted. Jake moved his hand and Mr. Whittaker looked it over. "I don't think it needs stitches. You want a ride home?"

Jake shook his head. "I'm okay."

Mr. Whittaker turned his attention to me. His face was rock-hard. "I *am* taking *you* home, Ryan."

■ ■ ■

"You want to tell me what that was all about?" Mr. Whittaker asked in his car on the way to my house. I had seen him angry before, but never at me.

"I don't feel like talking about it," I said, not looking at him. I didn't want to hear any advice. I wanted to be mad for a while. I didn't want him to make me regret hitting Jake. I knew I would probably feel bad about it later, but right now I was enjoying the memory of his bloody chin. He was trying to ruin my life. I was glad I had at least ruined his chin for a moment.

Mr. Whittaker must have known what I was thinking, because he allowed me to keep my feelings to myself. He probably knew that I would tell him everything in time.

My mother wasn't quite as understanding. The second Mr. Whittaker and I walked through the door, she wanted to know exactly what had happened.

"You hit him?" she exclaimed.

"I'm sorry." It was all I could say.

"Why did you do it?"

I glanced at Mr. Whittaker, who I knew was anxious to hear my explanation. "You don't have to say why in front of me, Ryan," he said.

"No, you can stay," I replied. I looked at my mother, whose face had an odd expression—somewhere between fury and sympathy—knowing something heavy was going to come out of my mouth. "Jake told a reporter all about us. It's in the Bettertown newspaper. Everyone knows everything."

My mom put her hand over her mouth, and her fury instantly vanished. "Everything?"

"Except for Dad. He wasn't mentioned, except to say that he's alive."

"I should call Mr. Henson." Mr. Henson was the agent assigned to keep us safe. We knew my dad was close by, because he had called our house the previous winter. He knew what state we were in but possibly nothing more. He could narrow it down to an area code, but our next three digits didn't give away anything. The local exchange numbers Mr. Henson had given to us weren't found anywhere else in the state. But the more word got out about us, the easier it would be for him to find us.

■ ■ ■

Mr. Henson came by to talk to all of us. My mother asked Mr. Whittaker to stay for emotional support, and he did.

"We'll confiscate all copies of the newspaper," he said.

"There's a reporter for the *Odyssey Times* that's been asking questions in Kidsboro," I said. "What if the *Times* gets it?"

"I can talk to Dale Jacobs," Mr. Whittaker said. Dale Jacobs was the editor. "I'll make sure he doesn't print this."

"Good," Mr. Henson said. He sighed and looked at my mom and me. "Listen, I want to give you this option one more time. I know you like Odyssey, but we can safely move you away. We can change your names again, change everything."

I loved Odyssey, and I never wanted to move. Mom and I exchanged pitiful looks. I was sure she was feeling the same way I was. "I'm tired of running, Mr. Henson," she told him. "This is the place I want to be. I'm not going to let him dictate our lives anymore."

"Ms. Cummings," Mr. Henson said, looking to Mr. Whittaker to see if he would back him up, "this is for your own safety."

"I know it is, and I appreciate your concern. But we need to put an end to this now. If he finds us once, he'll find us again."

Mr. Henson breathed heavily and stood up from the couch. "I'll put the police on alert. We have his picture up at the station. Everybody knows who to look for. But if you change your mind . . ." He looked at my mom and must have decided not to finish his sentence. She would not change her mind.

He glanced at me before he went out the door. "The article didn't mention the abuse. Don't tell your friends about it. The more you tell, the more danger you put them in if he comes around asking questions." He nodded to Mr. Whittaker and left.

——— ■ ■ ■ ———

There was no pretending it never happened. Everywhere I went I was reminded that I was no longer Ryan, mayor of Kidsboro. I was now Jim, the fraud who punches people. I tried to slink to my office unnoticed, but all my friends wanted to know if the *Barnacle* story was true, and all my enemies wanted to dig their nails into my skin.

The last person I wanted to see, Max, ran over from Bettertown to see me. "Jimbo! Hey, buddy!"

"Go away, Max."

"Wow. It's true. You really are a new man. I like it. You're not gonna punch me, are you? You know, I'm definitely voting for you in the next election."

"You don't get a vote."

"Oh, I'll get my vote in there somehow."

"I've got stuff to do."

"Oh, that's right. Mayor stuff. Bills to sign, laws to write, people to send to the hospital . . ."

"Go back to your own town."

"You know, you've inspired me. I'm thinking about completely changing my image too. Hey, you'd know this. Where would I go for a fake ID card?"

"Max—"

"No, just call me Dirk from now on. I think I look more like a Dirk."

"I have a meeting."

"It must be so cool to be able to reinvent yourself like that. Nobody even knows who you are anymore. Not even your friends. The only thing we all know for sure is that you're a liar and a thug."

I had tried my best to ignore him, but his last statement struck me. Did my *friends* really feel this way?

——— ■ ■ ■ ———

We held a scheduled city council meeting to discuss the new budget, but when I got to the meeting hall, the only item on anyone's agenda was getting to the bottom of the whole Jim Bowers story.

I sat down and took out my notes. No one was there to discuss the budget. They all just stared at me like I didn't belong anymore. I needed to get this over with.

"It's all true," I said. "I lied about my past because I had to. I can't really tell you any more than that. It's about my family, and it's very personal, and I hope you can understand that I . . . I just can't talk about it. I was upset that the information got out, and that's why I hit Jake. I shouldn't have done it, but I did. I'll apologize as soon as I see him. Could we please not mention it again?"

I could tell from their faces that they were not satisfied with my answer. They probably felt betrayed because I didn't trust them, but apparently nobody trusted *me*, either.

No one said anything for a solid minute. I stared at my hands. My city council sat there frustrated, not allowed to ask any of the hundred questions that must have been on their lips.

Finally, Scott asked a pretty harmless one. "Do you want us to call you Jim?"

"No," I said firmly. "I'm Ryan."

After another few quiet moments, Police Chief Alice spoke up. "Mayor, I must ask you this. Are you and your mother fugitives from the law?"

"No," I said, even more firmly. "Absolutely not."

"I had to ask," she said. I rolled my eyes.

Then Jill said, "Ryan, look . . . I know you have to keep this whole thing secret, but I'm afraid you're going to have to say *something*."

"Why, so you can get a juicy story?" I said, more harshly than I probably should have.

"You have an image problem, Ryan. Nobody trusts you anymore."

"What do you mean?"

"I did a poll for tomorrow's edition of the *Chronicle*. Your approval numbers are way down. From 78 percent to 33 percent. You lied to everybody, Ryan."

"Well, what was I supposed to do?"

"I don't know, but you need to fix it."

"It would be nice if I had some help from the press. It would be nice if the press didn't print that my approval numbers are down to 33 percent. Maybe if my closest friends didn't think I was a fugitive from the law, I could convince other people to trust me. You think that might make it easier?"

I threw my papers down, and they scattered across the floor. Without looking at any of them, I stomped off and left Kidsboro.

4

KISSING AND MAKING UP

I THREW OPEN THE door to my room and slammed my notebook on the desk. I could stay in my room for the summer. I didn't have to go back to Kidsboro. Maybe Mr. Henson was right. Maybe we could leave Odyssey and just start over again. I could make new friends—ones who would trust me. I could start a new Kidsboro in . . . I don't know, Florida or someplace. Maybe I could be this new kid in Florida like Max was talking about. One that hits people. I hadn't had much luck lately being the nice, fair, leader type.

I laid down on my bed with my arms crossed, ready to give up on everything. I wanted to lay here until all this was over.

I gazed around. My room was littered with Kidsboro stuff. On my wall was the Kidsboro flag, which looked just like the American flag, only with thinner stripes and a tree in the field of blue instead of stars. There was a framed copy of the *Kidsboro Chronicle* in which Jill had interviewed me, the brand new mayor, just a year before. The city charter was bound and sitting on my bookshelf. I'd helped write it, and I was very proud of what we had written.

My desk had folders of paperwork scattered across it. I got up and was about to throw it all away when something caught my eye. The proposal from Valerie's feminist group lay on top. The farmers' budget was underneath it, followed by the Clean Up Kidsboro plan to save the Earth.

I shouldn't have laughed at them. They all had concerns and needs and looked to their government to help them. There was nothing wrong with that. If I had been a true leader, I would've compromised. I would've found a way to make their plans work.

Perhaps I wasn't a good leader at all. Maybe that was the real problem. Maybe I couldn't be trusted because there was nothing in me that was worthy of trust.

I sat down at my desk and began leafing through all the proposals. For some reason, I suddenly didn't see anything so unreasonable in these requests. These people had probably worked just as hard on their proposals as I had worked putting together the city charter. Was it right for me to just shoot them down?

I grabbed a pencil and my notebook with new energy and started writing furiously. I could make this work. They would all see that I hadn't lost my ability to lead. A 33 percent approval rating indeed! I would double that number by the weekend.

■ ■ ■

People were still whispering about me as I passed them on the way into Kidsboro the next day, but I didn't care. I had five copies of my 10-page proposal under my arm and I was ready to present it to the city council. I had worked on it until 11:30 the night before. It was well thought out, organized, and in my eyes, un-rejectable.

I was the first one in the meeting hall, but the other four members filed in just after me.

"You're here?" Scott asked, as if he expected my hasty exit from the last meeting to have been my last.

"Yep," I said with a smile.

"You're happy?"

"Yep."

Everyone arrived with pretty much the same response. They were all unsure, even hesitant to sit down. Was this the same person who'd stomped out of the city council meeting just the day before?

I got right to it. "I wrote a budget plan last night. I reconsidered the proposals given to us by all of the groups that made their presentations the other day, and I think I've come up with some good compromises."

"Compromises?" Nelson asked as he took a proposal and handed another to Jill.

"Yes. I think we were too quick to turn these people away. Some of the things they asked for were quite reasonable—"

"Which ones?" Nelson asked.

"You can read it all right there. I haven't given in to every demand, just the ones that make sense."

They all looked at the plan with their mouths wide open.

"You're giving money to Clean Up Kidsboro?" Jill asked.

"Not as much as they wanted, but yes. We should care about the environment. And I think the outdoor bathroom was a good idea."

"You want to legalize slingshots?" Alice asked, probably because she had never been allowed to carry a weapon herself, yet other people were going to get to.

"On a limited basis: only the small slingshots and not within the city limits. Only in designated slingshot areas."

"Wow. You're giving the feminists everything?" Jill asked.

"Not everything. I think we should agree to give girls more government jobs. And we'll look into equal salaries for boys and girls. I'm still against adding another girl to the city council because that would make six people, which will create a lot of ties. But I'm open to the possibility."

Alice turned to the feminist page and her eyes widened. She apparently liked what she saw.

It was Scott's turn. "You're doubling Corey's salary? He's a garbageman! He's making more than me!" This was a weak comparison since Scott barely made any money from his detective agency.

"He has to pick up garbage. It's disgusting, and he should be paid well for it. I'm not giving him what he asked for, only part."

They continued to read through the proposal, glued to every word. Their heads nodded, except for Nelson's. "We can't do this," he said. "This is going to cost too much. We don't have this kind of money."

"That's not for us to decide. That's for the taxpayers to decide. They're the ones who are going to be paying for all of it."

"Taxes are going to go through the roof."

"It'll be a sacrifice."

"It'll be a suicide. They'll be paying half their salaries in taxes," Nelson said.

"When we bring this proposal before the town, we'll explain all of that. It's up to them," I insisted.

"We can't bring this before the town."

"That's what we're here to vote on. The city council votes on what we present to the town. If you don't like it, don't vote for it."

"This is insane!" Nelson said loudly.

"That's fine if you think that, but the rest of us might not agree with you. Has everybody had a chance to read it?" I asked.

They all nodded.

"Okay, then I say we vote on it. Who votes that we present this budget plan to the town? Raise your hands."

I raised my hand immediately. Alice, Jill, and Scott leafed through the plan, skimming the main points before they made their decision. Nelson had his hands on his hips, amazed that we were even considering this. Scott flipped over the last page and raised his hand. I knew his reasoning. He didn't care about high taxes because he made so little money that it wouldn't affect him that much. He was probably excited about using a slingshot.

Jill breathed a heavy sigh and raised her hand. She was probably pleased that I was giving in to the feminist group and would vote for it based solely on that.

Alice liked the part about equal salaries for girls. The Clean Up Kidsboro section mentioned harsher penalties for litterers. I'm sure the vision of throwing litterers to the ground and handcuffing them flashed before her eyes. She lived for moments like that. She raised her hand without hesitation.

Nelson bowed his head in his hand. "This is a mistake," he said.

"The town doesn't have to vote for it."

"Can I campaign against it?" he asked.

"Go right ahead," I said, even though I didn't like the idea of the town seeing that the city council was divided.

■ ■ ■

Jill printed a special edition of the *Kidsboro Chronicle*, which included the entire budget in chart form and a written explanation of what each of the items in the chart meant. Jill also wrote up a point/counterpoint-type article in which she interviewed both Nelson and me to show the opposing sides to the issue. Nelson's essay on tax increases and government waste was well written, scary, and probably very effective. I wrote my essay on the government's responsibility to take care of its citizens and the citizens' responsibility to take care of each other. Both gave the reader something to think about, which was the point. The article ended by informing everyone that we would vote on the budget in a citywide vote the next day at four o'clock at the meeting hall.

One very nice thing happened after this article came out. People started looking me in the eye again, especially people who were members of the groups that would benefit from this budget. Mark, head of Clean Up Kidsboro, smiled at me as I walked past him. The farmers were reading the article as I passed them, and they gave me a thumbs-up sign. Even Valerie gave me a slight grin.

Suddenly, I felt like the mayor again. I had made them forget about Jim Bowers.

■ ■ ■

I would stack Kidsboro's voting record against that of any country. In the United States, only about 50 percent of registered voters vote. But in Kidsboro, everybody votes. I like to think it's because we care about the issues that affect our city and our lives. But if I wanted to be honest about it, it's probably because we have such a small number of citizens. Everyone knows exactly how important his or her vote is.

Maybe people must have thought that this vote was going to be close, because everyone showed up at the ballot box the next day. The meeting hall was packed. I looked around at all the people and tried to figure it out. Valerie's group, plus the Clean Up Kidsboro group, plus the farmers, plus the slingshotters, plus the animal rights guys . . . It appeared that there were about 16 or so people in the hall who were in at least one of these groups. If I had all of their votes, I would need only a few more people to agree to the budget for it to pass.

There was a big box on the front table with a hole in the top. Everyone waited for the polls to open. We'd agreed that there would be a brief discussion time before we started.

Jill was the moderator. She stood up and called for attention. "Does anyone have anything they want to say before we start the voting?"

Nelson popped up immediately. "This budget plan would send taxes soaring. The economy wouldn't be able to handle it."

A boy stood up in the back. "He's right. And what are we spending our money on? We don't need slingshots and bathrooms. We especially don't need vegetables."

Nelson raised his hand. "I have a suggestion. Can we at least vote on all these items separately? One vote for the slingshots, another for the farmers . . ."

Mark stood up and addressed Nelson directly. "No! Then everybody would just vote for their own cause, and nothing would get passed. It's all or nothing."

"This budget could bankrupt us," Nelson stated.

"The only reason you care so much is that you're rich. You'll have to pay the most in taxes," Mark said.

Everybody started speaking at once, and none of it was audible. Mark was right. Nelson was the richest person in town, and if we took a percentage of income from each person in Kidsboro, the rich would have to pay a lot more than anyone else.

Jill yelled at the top of her lungs, but couldn't restore order. After a few moments of utter mayhem, she stood up on the table. "Quiet!!!"

The noise subsided. She cleared her throat. "Does anyone have anything constructive to say?" I raised my hand. "Yes, Ryan?" She nodded at me.

I stood up and turned to face as many people as I could. "I understand how Nelson feels. But I think we should always be looking for ways to make this city better. The only way we can do that is through the sacrifices of our people. It will be a sacrifice for us, yes. No doubt about it, taxes will increase, but the rewards could be great." This was followed by the applause of about half of those present.

"Why do we need more girls in this town?" an unidentified boy shouted from the back. "We've got too many as it is!"

If this kid had set off a bomb, it would've caused less of a stir. There wasn't a closed mouth in the whole place. Girls were yelling at boys, boys were yelling at girls, farmers were yelling at meat-eaters, environmentalists were yelling at big-business polluters. It took Jill a full five minutes to calm everyone down.

"Okay, no more discussion! We're just gonna vote on this thing! Form a single-file line at the box. Alice will give you a piece of paper. Write down your vote and put it into the box."

The process was remarkably civilized, considering that everyone had been at each other's throats just moments before. Everybody cast his or her vote, and then the polls closed. Jill and Alice voted last, and then they took the box to be counted. It didn't take long to count 36 votes, so I knew we would get the results almost immediately.

Alice and Jill came back with a piece of paper. Alice held it in her hand as she stood at the table. The crowd was motionless as she unfolded the paper. Not one for dramatics, Alice came right out with it. "The budget passes, 20 to 16."

The place erupted with simultaneous joy and pain. Nelson buried his head in his hands. Valerie's feminists jumped up and down and hugged. The farmers pulled metal trowels out of their pockets and started waving them back and forth. The animal rights group barked like dogs.

Nelson looked up long enough to make eye contact with me. He shook his head and left.

■ ■ ■

The new laws went into effect immediately. My first order of business was to deal with Valerie and the feminists, because I knew they would make a big fuss over getting what they wanted before anybody else did. I thought about government jobs, and the one that came to mind as I stared out at my big list of things to do was to get myself a secretary. Of course, I would have to call her an "administrative assistant" to please the feminists. An assistant would take a lot of the burden off of me.

I looked over my list of citizens, and one name stood out: Lauren Luzinski. She had never held a steady job, so she was definitely available to work. She had never done anything to catch my attention in either a good way or a bad way, so perhaps this would be a chance for her to stand out for once. She could sit in on city council meetings and take notes.

I informed Valerie that I was going to hire Lauren, and she was pleased. Lauren had not been a member of Valerie's feminist group, but she was a girl and that was enough.

Lauren was surprised when I asked her. "You want me to be your administrative assistant?"

"Yep."

"Why?"

"Because . . . I think you'd do a good job."

"Really?" she said, her eyes sparkling.

"Sure. You interested?"

"Well . . . yeah. I'd love to."

"Then you're hired."

"Wow." I felt like I had just told her she'd won the lottery.

"Come on, then. I'll show you everything."

■ ■ ■

"I believe a new day has dawned in Kidsboro. We are now not just—"

"Too fast."

"Oh. Sorry." I was dictating a press release to Lauren. She was writing down everything that came out of my mouth and would deliver it to Jill later.

"That's really good," she said, writing down the first sentence.

"What's good?"

"That first sentence: 'A new day has dawned.' That's nice."

We smiled at each other. "Thanks," I said.

I waited for her to give me a signal that she was done. She nodded.

"We are now not just a government by the people—"

"This pen's out of ink."

"Oh. Here. Try mine."

As I bent down to give her the pen, I noticed that she smelled really good. When I backed away, we looked at each other, and I noticed something I'd never noticed before. She had freckles on her nose. Possibly the most perfectly circular freckles I'd ever seen.

"Okay, we are now a government of people . . ." she started.

"No, no. We are now not just a government by the people."

"Oh, I see. That's different. And a lot better."

"Thanks. But your way was good too."

— — —

No one was wasting any time using the money they'd received from the government. I strolled around town just to see if anything had changed, and there was more activity than there had been in months. The farmers were busy in their garden.

"What are you planting?" I asked them.

"Oh, just the standards. Cucumbers, beans, tomatoes, carrots, turnips."

The government was buying turnips from them?

They continued to hoe, looking very much like they knew what they were doing.

The Clean Up Kidsboro group was making a trash run. They had been at it for a couple of hours by the time I walked by, so they had pretty much cleared the entire town of any trash. But still they searched.

"The place looks really good," I said to Mark.

"I know," he replied. His eyes darted wildly as he continued to scan the ground.

"So, why are you still looking?"

He stopped suddenly and looked at me as if I had just told him I thought the capital of Florida was France. "Ryan, litter is thrown on the ground every two seconds in this country. This is not a one-time clean-up project. It is an ongoing quest. It is a lifestyle. Our land is too important to ignore for even one minute."

I felt like standing at attention and covering my heart. "Then by all means, get back to it," I said. I wanted to tell him that 27 people had littered while we were having that conversation, but I felt that would put too much pressure on him.

"Would you get that dog out of my house!" I heard someone yell from across town. It sounded like Valerie. I rushed over to her clubhouse. She was trying to drag a big German shepherd out of her house by the collar. "Get over here and get your dog!" she shouted. The dog's owner, Melissa, the leader of the animal rights group, came over slowly, as if to torture Valerie for as long as possible.

"Why do we have all these mangy animals here?" Valerie pointed to several dogs and cats being held by their owners. "They should be chained up."

"What?" Melissa said.

"They're a nuisance. We should have a law saying that if they're going to be here, they have to be chained up."

"No way!"

Valerie turned to me. "Ryan, I think you should bring this up at the next city council meeting."

"I guess I could."

"No!" Melissa shouted. "You gave animals equal rights. People aren't chained up. Why should animals have to be?"

"Um . . ."

"Oh, perfect. Nice decisive answer there, Ryan," Valerie said. "Meanwhile, this place has turned into a pound."

"Don't say 'pound' in front of them," Melissa said in a harsh whisper.

"If this dog gets into my house again, I'm grabbing one of those slingshots," she said, pointing away from us.

I looked in the direction she was pointing, and saw that the slingshot boys were meeting in a group not too far from the dogs and cats. They were comparing their equipment, and every now and then, they would fling a nut away from town. I could tell the animal owners were getting nervous with these flying nuts, even though it looked like the slingshotters were being careful. Scott was with them, looking anxious to learn some slingshot skills.

A squirrel ran by, and I saw one boy aim at it but stop as soon as he saw me looking at him. Or maybe it was just my imagination. The animal rights group was keeping a close eye on the slingshotters.

The groups may not have been getting along with each other, but they were all happy about getting the chance to do something they believed in. I was proud I'd given them the opportunity, but now came the hard part: collecting taxes.

5

REALITY SETS IN

A FEW WEEKS BEFORE the budget debate, we had passed out an income tax form to all residents of Kidsboro. Everyone was supposed to keep good records of the money they had made over the year. People could try to lie, but in a town as small as Kidsboro, it was hard to hide how much money was spent where. We had records of most transactions.

When we added up everyone's salary and how much the new budget was going to cost, we figured out that the tax rate for this year had to be 19 percent. I knew this was a little high, but we had a lot of new programs to pay for. People were not going to be very happy about having to give up 19 percent of everything they made, but it was something that had to be done, and they all knew it was time for sacrifice.

When we came up with the 19 percent figure in the city council meeting, Nelson had almost fainted. He would have to fork over a huge amount of money. "I'm so glad I'm paying for vegetables I'm not gonna eat and a bathroom I'm not gonna use," he said as he stormed out.

We calculated what everyone would have to hand over, and then Alice and I went door-to-door to collect. Usually she went alone, since she had no trouble squeezing money out of people—sometimes literally—by herself. But I went along this time to offer an explanation.

The first door we knocked on was Roberto's. Roberto was Jill's assistant at the *Chronicle*. He usually had very little to say about anything. But he had yet to see how much he owed.

"Eleven starbills?" he asked.

"Yes. That's what you owe in taxes for the year," I told him.

"I don't have that much money," he said with a Hispanic accent.

"I'm sorry, that's why we told everyone to save up. This is tax day."

"I don't understand the taxes."

"The tax rate is 19 percent, which means you owe the government 11 starbills. This was all explained in the memo we sent out to everyone."

"I cannot pay that much."

"Then we may have to set you up on a payment plan. Give us what you have now."

"I have nothing."

"You don't have anything?"

"No."

"Well . . . then . . . you'll have to give us your full salary every week until you pay us back."

"My full salary?"

"Yeah. How much do you make?"

"About three starbills in two weeks."

"Okay, then it'll take about nine weeks for you to pay off your taxes."

"Oh," he said, the impact of this finally dawning on him, "almost the whole summer."

I wasn't sure what to say. I'd always liked Roberto. He had been compliant with all our laws, he worked hard at the *Chronicle*, and he was a model citizen. I wanted to give him a break, but that would've been unfair. I wouldn't be giving a break to anyone else.

"Thank you very much," he said, disappearing into his clubhouse. His shoulders were sagging.

Alice and I looked at each other. We had to do this 33 more times.

— — —

After crushing the hopes and dreams of 34 people, I went back to my office to take a break. Jill walked in as soon as I closed the door behind me.

"What is this?" she asked before she was even all the way inside. She was holding up a piece of paper.

"What is what?"

"Were you sleepwalking when you wrote this press release?"

"What do you mean?"

"It's got all sorts of spelling errors and incomplete sentences. I can't even tell what you're trying to say sometimes."

"Oh," I said with a slight chuckle. "That's my new secretary . . . er . . . administrative assistant."

"Administrative assistant?"

"Yeah, this was her first dictation. She's still learning."

"Why do you need an assistant?"

"I've got a lot of paperwork. And it's a government job."

"Who is it?"

Right on cue, Lauren walked in with a handheld pencil sharpener. "I'm having . . . oh, I'm sorry. I didn't know you had a visitor. Hi, Jill."

"Lauren? You're his new assistant?"

"Yes. It's a great job, very challenging."

"Really?"

"Ryan, I'm done sharpening pencils," Lauren said. She handed over a shoebox full of sharp pencils.

"Thank you. Good job."

We looked at each other as she moved away. She briefly touched my arm and said, "Thanks. You're welcome."

"No problem."

I watched her leave the room. She gave me a little wave as she turned out. Jill had her hands on her hips. "Lauren's your assistant?"

"She'll be fine. She just needs some time."

"I'm so glad my tax dollars are being used this well."

- - -

Ten minutes after Jill left, Scott walked in. He was wearing his detective outfit—a Sherlock Holmes coat with matching hat, a magnifying glass sticking out of his pocket, and a bubble pipe that he claimed helped him think when he was on a case. I figured he was on one right now.

"What are you doing?" I asked.

"I'm on a case."

"What case?"

"I talked to Jake this morning at Whit's End. He told me that he wasn't the one who spilled the information about you to the *Barnacle*."

"Yeah. Right," I said sarcastically.

"Pardon me for walking the earth, but don't you think that's weird? I mean, if Jake really did do it, wouldn't he love to tell everyone? He would love it if everyone knew he'd exposed you."

That was true.

"Plus, you let him into Kidsboro because he knew about your past. That's how he got you to do everything for him—blackmail. So why would he play the only card he had? Seems like he would've tried to hold on to it to get something else out of you."

Maybe the bubble pipe really did work; all of this made sense. "Who else could it be? No one else knew that stuff."

"I don't know, but it could be worth some investigation. I say we head over to the *Barnacle*."

I was tired of thinking about taxes and the budget, so I decided to follow him. I couldn't imagine that we would turn up anything.

■ ■ ■

The *Barnacle* office was a regular clubhouse, only bigger than any of the ones in Kidsboro. Max Darby was King of Bettertown, and he wanted his town to be bigger and better than Kidsboro in every possible way.

For whatever reason, there were very few people in town. On most days, tourism was high, and the place was buzzing with activity. *Maybe they're all someplace shedding their skins*, I thought to myself with a mischievous grin.

Scott knocked on the door of the *Barnacle*, but no one answered. Neither of us heard any rustling inside, so Scott took a quick glance around to see if anyone was looking, and then he opened the door.

I followed him but immediately protested, "This is breaking and entering."

"I'm just visiting the newspaper office."

"Max will hang me if we get caught breaking a law on his turf!"

"Don't worry about it. We'll be in and out in 10 seconds." He scanned the room. It was littered with papers—all over the desk, on the floor, tacked to the walls. A filing cabinet in the corner was half open. I had no idea what we were looking for, but Scott seemed to think the filing cabinet was a good place to start.

He opened one drawer and flipped through the labeled tabs on top. "Nothing," he said, moving on to the next drawer.

I scanned the table. There were handwritten notes on yellow sticky paper everywhere. The notes said things like "Kidsboro police corruption," "Kidsboro lawyers corrupt," and "Judge Amy paid off?" The *Barnacle* specialized in scandal.

"Bingo," Scott said in true TV-detective fashion. He pulled out a file labeled "Cummings" and leafed through it. He gave me a stack of papers from inside and took the rest himself. I didn't hesitate to look at it, even though this was surely illegal.

"Look at this," Scott said. "Notes from the interview."

"Let me see that."

He turned so we could look at it together. It was hard to read the chicken scratch. It looked as if someone had written quickly to keep up with someone talking. It was a list of random facts about me. I read some of the things that appeared in the article—where I lived, my real name, the names of my pets . . . Wait a minute.

"Something's wrong," I said. "There's information here that wasn't in the article."

"They probably decided not to print everything."

"The name of my cat when I was little is in here."

"Not very print-worthy."

"This is impossible. The cat was dead before I ever knew Jake. He couldn't have known about it."

"Did you ever talk about your cat?"

"I was three. I barely remember it. I doubt I ever mentioned it, and if I did, I can't imagine Jake remembering it."

I scanned more of the page. "There's more stuff in here that he couldn't have known."

"So you don't think it was Jake?" Scott asked.

"Not unless he talked to my dad."

"Does he know where your dad is?"

I shook my head. "Nobody does."

"Then who?"

I stormed out of the *Barnacle*, not caring who saw me. We had to find the writer of that article. I just might have punched the wrong guy.

■ ■ ■

The reporter's name wasn't on the article. The *Barnacle* kept its authors secret because if the facts in the article were proven incorrect, which they almost always were, then the person who was offended by the article didn't know who to be mad at. But I did know the editor: a boy named Leo, who'd been a citizen of Bettertown since it began the previous fall. He had wanted to be a citizen of Kidsboro, but all he'd wanted to do was be the editor of a newspaper. There were no openings at the *Kidsboro Chronicle* since Jill was already the editor and she had a reporter, Roberto. So when Bettertown opened up, Leo pounced on the opportunity, even though working for the *Barnacle* meant he would have to publish garbage. I don't think this was what he really wanted, but in Bettertown, everybody did what Max told them to do, or they were thrown out. Leo had started the *Barnacle* reluctantly, but I got the feeling that he was starting to enjoy publishing scandals because the articles were getting more and more mean.

We found Leo at Whit's End, talking to Eugene Meltsner. Eugene was trying to work on a computer program, and Leo was obviously interrupting him. Leo was holding his reporter's notebook—a legal pad of paper exactly like the kind we'd found in my file at the *Barnacle*.

"Yes, he conceives of all of the inventions himself," Eugene said, agitated. "I simply assist him in the process of research and development."

"So, all he comes up with are the ideas?" Leo asked.

"No, we work together. I believe we went over this once already."

"I just find it hard to believe that a 12-year-old kid could come up with some of this stuff on his own."

He was obviously trying to dig up dirt on Nelson.

Eugene had clearly had enough. "I apologize if I cannot give you the answer that you want. The truth is all that I can offer you." He looked at us as if we might be able to save him.

"Hey, Leo," I said. "I need to talk to you."

"What do you want?" he asked sharply. I don't think he'd ever forgiven me for not letting him into Kidsboro.

"Did you write that article about me?"

"Sorry. Can't reveal that information."

"Why not?"

"*Barnacle* policy."

"Who wrote the policy?"

"Me," he said with pride.

"Then you can change it. I need to know who wrote that article."

"Never mind, Ryan," Scott jumped in. "Come here." He motioned for me to follow him, and we walked 10 feet away, out of earshot.

"Leo wrote it," he whispered.

"How do you know?"

"While you guys were talking, I checked out the notes on that legal pad he's holding. Same handwriting as we saw on that paper at the *Barnacle*." Scott's detective agency really should have been more successful. The kid had a knack for this stuff.

We walked back over to Leo, armed with this new information. "I need to know who you interviewed to get that story."

"I thought you knew it was Jake."

"Well, now I know it wasn't."

"You mean you punched the guy in the face for nothing?"

"Yes. Could you at least tell me if I'm right? It wasn't Jake, was it?"

"No can do. A good reporter never gives away his source."

"A good reporter? That's what you call yourself?" Scott said. I gave

Scott a sharp look. We were trying to convince him to help us; insulting him wouldn't help matters.

"How about this," Scott said. "I was at Miller's Ravine a month ago when Charlie Metzger got hurt. Tell us what we want to know, and I'll give you an interview and tell you everything."

"That's right. You were there, weren't you?"

"Yep."

A month before, Charlie Metzger and Scott had been playing around at Miller's Ravine, and Charlie fell in and had to go to the hospital. But the rumor got around school that it wasn't an accident, because just the day before Charlie's fall, he had told on Rodney Rathbone, leader of the worst gang in Odyssey, the Bones of Rath. Rodney got into trouble with the school principal, so after he found out that Charlie had ratted on him, everyone expected Rodney to seek revenge. Of course, when Charlie had to go to the hospital, word got around that the Bones of Rath did it, even though Scott was there and told the doctors that it was an accident. But the kids at school didn't believe Scott or Charlie, thinking that the two were just making up the story because they feared that the Bones of Rath would come after them again.

Scott had told me the whole story of how Charlie had simply slipped and fell. Now he was using the incident to tempt Leo to give away his information about me.

"You'll tell me everything?" Leo said.

"Everything," Scott replied. Of course, Leo didn't realize that Scott had already told everyone everything. This article would definitely be weak.

Leo licked his lips, scanned the room to see if anyone was watching, and then let it all spill. "The guy I interviewed was a reporter for the *Odyssey Times*."

"The guy that's been asking people about Kidsboro?" I asked.

"That's the one. We traded stories. He gave me the story about you, and I answered questions about Kidsboro. Now, give me the scoop, Scott."

"Later, I promise," he called out as we rushed off.

▬ ▬ ▬

The *Odyssey Times* was a maze of gray cubicles, copy machines, and wastebaskets filled with bad ideas. I only knew one person at the *Times*—Dale Jacobs, the editor. I figured he was busy, but we would wait for him to have a quiet moment.

He was in a glassed-in office along the back wall. I could see him inside.

He was on the phone and the door was closed. I waved, and he lifted a finger to tell us that he would be with us in a minute. We waited outside on a bench. A secretary approached us. "Can I help you?"

"I just need to ask Mr. Jacobs a question," I said.

"Does he know you?"

"Yes. My name's Ryan Cummings."

"I'll tell him you're here."

"Thank you."

Ten minutes later, Mr. Jacobs poked his head out the door of his office. "Hi, Ryan, Scott. Did you guys need me for something?"

"Just to ask one question. Who's doing the story on Kidsboro?"

"What story?"

"There was a reporter in Kidsboro a little while ago, asking questions. I figured you were doing a story on us."

"I've been thinking about doing a story on Kidsboro, but I haven't assigned a reporter to it yet."

Scott piped up. "Could a reporter do a story on his own, without you knowing about it?"

"If a reporter was doing the story for us, I would know about it."

Scott and I exchanged confused looks.

"What makes you think this person was from the *Odyssey Times*?" Mr. Jacobs asked.

I had never thought about that possibility. What if this person was not really a reporter? Maybe it was someone who was just trying to get information about me. But who would know all of that stuff about my past? There were only two people—my mom, who I knew wouldn't reveal any of that stuff . . . and my dad.

Could my dad be in Odyssey?

"What did he look like?" I asked Scott.

"The reporter?"

"Yeah."

"Um . . . he had black, spiky hair, kind of short. And he had a mustache."

I breathed a sigh of relief. My dad had red hair and was rather tall.

"No," Mr. Jacobs said. "That doesn't fit the description of anybody here."

It didn't fit the description of anyone I knew either. Who could it be?

6

THE DANGEROUS
REUNION

As much as I despised the thought, I knew there was something I had to do before I returned to Kidsboro.

I found Jake at Whit's End again. He was sitting in a booth with Max. He saw me approach and sat up in his seat. Maybe he was expecting me to deck him again. I stopped in front of him.

"What do you want?" he growled.

"You didn't leak my story."

"I know."

"I thought you did," I said, hating every minute of this. "I was wrong. I shouldn't have hit you. I'm sorry."

"How considerate of you, Jim. You always were the polite one on our street. My mother always said, 'Why can't you be nice like Jim Bowers?' I always told her that no one can be nice like Jim Bowers. Jim Bowers is not real. Jim is fictional. Hitting me in the face was the only real thing you've ever done. In a weird way, I was proud of you."

"I didn't come here to be made fun of; I came here to ask for your forgiveness."

"Oh, I'll more than forgive you. I'll shake your hand in congratulations. I mean, I won't forget what you did. I'll definitely get you back for that. But I congratulate you because you deserve congratulations. You split open my chin. Let's just say I was impressed."

I turned around and headed for the door. I wasn't really expecting the forgiveness part, but the apology had to happen. As humiliating as that had been, at least now I could get on with my life.

■ ■ ■

The moment I stepped onto Kidsboro property, I could hear an argument going on. Then I saw three people outside Nelson Industries, yelling at each other. Nelson was one of them.

"I was here until six o'clock every night last week!" said one boy.

"I know. I'm sorry," Nelson replied.

"We had a contract!" the other boy said.

"There was no contract," Nelson argued.

"Well, there was an understanding!"

"Look, I'm sorry. I just can't afford you anymore," Nelson said.

"You can't afford two more employees?"

"Not with so much of our profits going to taxes."

"You could keep us on if you really wanted to."

"No, I can't. I've crunched the numbers every way I know how. I simply can't afford four employees anymore."

"Great."

"Listen," Nelson said, pleading, "maybe I'll be able to hire you back someday. You'll be the first people I call."

"No, thanks. I'd like a job that I can count on."

The two boys left. I didn't want to look Nelson in the face, because I knew he would blame this on me.

"You had to fire them?" I asked.

"Yes."

I knew this would be devastating for them. Working for Nelson Industries was one of the best jobs anyone could have. Nelson was always very fair in paying his employees.

"I can't pay the taxes," Nelson said, glaring at me, then turning to his two remaining employees. "Okay, guys. We've got work to do."

"Are you kidding me?" One of them said. "We could barely keep up with all the orders with five of us. Now we have to do it with only three?"

"Don't worry about it. With everyone else in town having to pay taxes too, there've been cancellations." He glanced at me one more time, and then disappeared into his clubhouse.

This was bad. Nelson Industries was the most successful business in town. If it was in trouble, the whole town was in trouble.

■ ■ ■

A crowd of people was gathered on the edge of town, and I ran over to see what was going on. Joey, the African-American preacher at Kidsboro Community Church, was on the ground in the middle of a two-layered circle of people. I could barely see him through their legs.

"What's going on?" I asked whoever might be listening.

"Joey's been blinded!" came the reply from an unknown source.

"What?" I scrambled in between the bodies and made it to the center where James, the doctor, was trying to look at Joey's eye, while Joey was covering it with his hand. There was blood on the top of Joey's shirt and on the back of his hand.

"What happened?" I demanded.

"He was hit in the eye by a rock," said James, the expert at the scene.

"It's not my eye," Joey said, without looking up. "It's my forehead."

"Let me see, Joey," I said, kneeling down.

"I'll move my hand if he promises not to touch me," Joey said, pointing to James.

"Step back, James," I said.

"I took a first aid course!" James shouted. "I know what I'm doing!"

"Just step back."

James rolled his eyes and moved back six inches on his haunches. Joey lifted his hand. The crowd pressed in to get a closer look. There was a gash above his left eye. It had bled some but was stopped for now.

"Does anybody have a tissue or something?"

"I've got bandages!" James yelled before anyone else could even process the question. He opened his black doctor bag, and, for the first time in his medical career, he was able to use something from it for a real medical purpose. In two seconds he'd found a package of sterile gauze and flipped it to me.

I carefully opened the package and gave the gauze to Joey. "Just press this against the wound. It may need stitches. We should get you to a doctor." Looking up I said, "Somebody go to Whit's End and call his mom."

I heard someone run off. "Come on, Joey." I helped him up. He swayed a little bit when he got to his feet, as if he were dizzy, so I didn't push him too fast.

"Okay, how was he hit with a rock?" I asked the crowd.

"Slingshot," said Scott, who I now noticed was part of the crowd.

I felt my face get hot. "Whose?"

"Ben's."

"It was an accident," I heard Ben say. "It got away from me."

"This is not a designated slingshot area."

"It was *shot* from one," he said. "It just didn't *land* in one."

"That's no excuse," Pete, the lawyer said. He stepped to the front of the crowd. "This is an outrage. Joey, you need to sue this man!" he said, pointing to Ben.

"We don't need this, Pete," I said.

"Joey's gonna need stitches. He's entitled to damages."

"Stop it!"

Pete turned to Joey. "You could sue this pea brain for all he's worth."

"Hey!" shouted Ben. "Get outta here."

"I'm not going anywhere, Ben. And I would suggest you get your own lawyer."

Ben made a swim move past two bodies in front of him and came at Pete. Pete dropped his briefcase and lifted his arms to defend himself. Ben pushed him, sending Pete sprawling to the ground.

"Stop!" I shouted.

"Come on, Pete," Ben yelled. "You want to sue somebody? How much do you think you can get if I break both your arms?" The crowd egged both of them on.

Pete didn't get up. "Oh, real smart. Pushing me in front of 15 witnesses. I could take you for everything."

Ben moved to kick him, and I stepped in front. "Ben!" Scott and I grabbed him and pulled him back. He wasn't a very big guy, so it wasn't terribly difficult to get him away from the scene.

"That's it!" I shouted. "Ben, go home and take your slingshot with you. Pete, no one's suing anybody. You can go home too. Everybody, mind your own business. I'm taking Joey to Whit's End now."

I turned to Joey, who didn't seem to be taking any of this in. "You okay?" He nodded. "Ready to go?" He nodded again.

I put my arm around him and led him away. As we walked away, I turned around briefly. The crowd had not dispersed. They just stared at the two of us. I couldn't tell if they were concerned for Joey, or if they blamed me for the whole thing happening in the first place.

■ ■ ■

We met Joey's mother at Whit's End. Mr. Whittaker looked at the wound and kept pressure on it until he was ready to go. Then Joey's mom took him to the doctor.

When I got back into town, there was still an uneasy buzz in the air. The walls of a strong city were beginning to crumble, and it felt like it was only the beginning.

I picked up a copy of the *Kidsboro Chronicle*, which had just come out, and skimmed through the first few pages. There was a lot about the changes the city council had made, as well as the effects of the changes. Jill had written the articles and usually she was very fair in her writing. But there was an edge to these, as if she disagreed with every decision that had been handed down. I knew this couldn't be true, though, because she had been involved in those decisions herself.

I turned the page and discovered that I wasn't imagining things. The headline on the editorial page was "Mayor and City Council Give In to Special Interests," by Jill Segler. What? Give in?

In the article, she took responsibility for herself in saying that she was a member of the city council, and she'd made a mistake when she allowed the budget to pass. But she kept referring to it as "the mayor's proposal" and "the mayor's budget plan." One line that particularly bothered me was, "The mayor's budget plan ignored the true needs of the city in order to please a few people." She went on to criticize "the mayor's decision to hire an assistant that he doesn't need."

I couldn't read on. I threw the paper down and stormed over to the newspaper office. I pushed open the door without knocking. Jill was sitting at her desk.

"What are you doing?" I asked harshly.

"You think you're the first political leader to get criticized in the press?" she replied calmly.

"But those things you wrote—"

"Were all true."

"Mine was not the only vote in the city council."

"I messed up too, but it's your name on the budget proposal."

"You're on the city council. You're supposed to back me up."

"I have to print the truth. There's no loyalty in journalism."

"What kind of a motto is that?"

"I have a responsibility to my readers to print the truth. We caved in to all those groups. Slingshots? Vegetables? Why are we paying for these things? And why do you need an assistant?"

"You're a supporter of the group that wanted me to create more government jobs for girls. You wanted me to hire an assistant!"

"But why did you listen to me?"

I was all ready with my next response, but her question caught me by surprise. All I could come up with was a quiet "What?"

"You used to be strong. You used to stand up to people. You didn't care about popularity or making everybody happy. You did what you thought was best. I don't know what happened to you, but you'd better find your spine or this town is going down the tubes."

I was quieter, but no less angry. "You didn't have to vote for this proposal. I wrote it, and I handed it to you. This town is just as much your responsibility as it is mine. If I'm going down, you're going with me. I'm writing a rebuttal to your article, and I expect you to print it."

I didn't wait for her to respond. I left, slamming the door behind me. Smoke was coming out my ears. She was irresponsible, thoughtless, reckless, wishy-washy . . .

And right.

■ ■ ■

I was still going to write my rebuttal, even though in my heart, I knew Jill's article was accurate. I just wanted to deflect some of the blame off of me.

I sat down at my desk and pulled out a pencil and my notebook. Lauren had noticed me walking by and poked her head in. "Do you need me for anything?"

"No, thanks."

"You want me to take dictation?"

"No, I'll just write this one by myself." I wondered if she had read the article and wanted to make sure that I still felt like I needed her. Not that her actions were any different than they had been in the weeks before. She had been a faithful, helpful employee.

She backed out of my office, and I got down to writing. Halfway through my first sentence, I suddenly became distracted. There was a feeling in the air that was so strong it forced me to stand up. My stomach dropped like the time I woke up and thought I heard someone breaking into the house. There was an intruder nearby. Obviously, he wasn't inside right then. It was a small clubhouse and there was nowhere for anyone to hide. But there was a presence there, and I could almost feel it choking me. It was a sense . . . or a smell . . . or . . .

I backed up against the wall, suddenly needing air desperately. I had to prop myself up with the desk as I anxiously moved for the door. I lunged out. Lauren was sitting at a desk outside my door. I was gasping.

"What's wrong?" she asked.

"I . . . I'm just going for a walk." But walking wouldn't do the trick. After a few steps, I found myself running. I headed straight for home, the feeling of dread melting away with every stride. I ran out of breath, not from running, but from this strange horror that had overtaken me. I slowed down and caught my breath. The feeling was gone. I wasn't being strangled anymore, and I felt like I could breathe again.

Was I going crazy?

■ ■ ■

I went home. It was much earlier than usual for me to go home for the day, but I didn't want to be anywhere near my clubhouse. I figured I would go up to my room and read for a while. I'd get lost in another world for an hour or two, and I'd forget the one I had just run from.

"Mom?" I called out when I opened the back door and went into the kitchen. She didn't answer, and I remembered that she'd had an afternoon meeting at work. I opened the refrigerator and pulled out some orange juice. As I reached for a glass, I felt a draft. I was suddenly very aware of sounds outside—birds, cars driving by on the street. I peered into the living room and saw that a window was open. Strange, I thought, since the air conditioning was on. The thin drapes were billowing in the wind. I closed the window.

As soon as the wood of the window touched the wood of the sill, I felt it again—the same presence I'd felt in my clubhouse. The cup dropped from my hand as my entire body went numb.

It finally hit me which sense was being heightened—the sense of smell. There was a familiar scent in the air: the smell of dread and fear and a time I wanted to forget. I managed to move my legs enough to maneuver past the dining room table and toward the stairs. I was walking in slow motion, dreading each step but desperately wanting to know who or what was there in my house, alone with me.

I heard and saw nothing. But the smell was getting stronger. It sickened me but also drew me. I walked on, my eyes darting but my head not moving, for fear that I would make a noise and awaken something I wanted to remain asleep. As I started up the stairs, something caught my eye. On an end table by the couch was a set of keys. Not my mom's keys, not my keys . . . but a set of keys with a picture-frame keychain on it. Taking a closer look, I saw that in the picture frame was a photo of me—when I was seven.

I whipped around and headed for the door. Frantically, I scrambled for the doorknob, but my sweaty hands slipped off it. Trying to unlock the door was suddenly like trying to disarm a bomb before it went off.

"Jim."

I screamed and threw myself against the wall in one motion. It was my dad. I tried to scream again but nothing came out. He was just standing there, 15 feet away, smiling but obviously nervous. I pressed myself against the wall harder, trying to put as much distance between him and me as possible.

"I'm sorry. I didn't mean to scare you. I didn't think you'd be home yet. I thought you'd stay in Kidsboro longer."

He looked exactly the same except for a few things. He had dyed his hair black, probably because he was a fugitive from the law, and, for some reason, he seemed much shorter than he had before. Maybe because the last time I had seen him *I* was much shorter.

He appeared sober, and that was encouraging. He also didn't move toward me, which made me feel better. But he had always been very good at getting people to trust him.

Tears welled up in his eyes. "You're so big. You look just like I did at your age."

My lips were trembling, but I managed a question. "Why are you here?"

"Well, I know you're not gonna believe this, but . . . I missed you. I wanted to see my family again. I promise I won't hurt you. I know you've heard that before, Jim, but I've changed. Really. You guys leaving just killed me. I didn't even want to go on. There was a time when all I did was think about my life, and how I'd messed it up so bad. So I turned to God, Jim. Just like you. About a year ago I became a Christian. Jesus helped me get back on my feet. I've stopped drinking, I've stopped . . . well, a lot of stuff. I have a new life now. I want the chance to prove to you that I've changed, because I want my family back."

I was still pressed up against the wall. "If you're a Christian," I said, "why did you break into our house?"

"I know I shouldn't have done that. But I wanted to know you again, and I was still scared that you wouldn't want to know me. That's why I went to Kidsboro and asked all those questions. I wanted to meet my boy again, even if it was through his friends. You've got some great friends, Jim. They love you. They think you're the best, even the ones who disagree with you. I'm so proud to be your father. Do you think it would ever be possible for you to forgive me for all I've done to you?"

I didn't move a muscle. He had convinced me many times before that he was a "new man," and I was always devastated when I soon realized that he wasn't. "I don't believe you," I said.

My dad closed his eyes and dropped his head. "I don't blame you."

When he closed his eyes, I subconsciously planned my escape. My hand drifted up toward the doorknob.

"I know we can never be a family again," he said, "but I'd like to be able to visit, you know? I don't know if I can handle being out of your life forever."

Our next door neighbor pulled into his driveway. My dad was distracted for a moment, maybe thinking it could be my mom. I saw an opening and took it. I bounded up the stairs and ran into Mom's room—the only inside door in the house with a lock.

"Jim!"

My heart was beating so loudly that I couldn't tell if there were footsteps behind me or not.

I burst through my mom's bedroom door and spun around to reach the lock. I slammed the door, knocking two pictures off the walls. I turned the lock and ran for the phone by her bed.

Mr. Henson was on speed-dial, so I punched two numbers and waited for his phone to ring.

It wasn't a dead-bolt lock, and it wasn't a steel door. I knew he could get in if he really wanted to. I watched the knob carefully, waiting for it to turn.

One ring.

It was happening just like it had before. When my dad was on a tirade, I would sit up in my room, huddled up on my bed. I would sit and wait for it to be over, praying to God that the door wouldn't open, and that he wouldn't turn his anger on me.

Two rings.

It felt like I had been on this phone for hours. *Please be there!* I heard a noise and locked my eyes on the knob. Still, it didn't turn. Maybe he was grabbing a bat or something to knock the door in. He might have been scouting the house out for days, he probably knew where my room was, and my closet, and . . .

I jerked my head around to the window. He could've gone out my window and walked across on the porch roof! He could be right outside, ready to bash in the window with my aluminum bat.

"Hello?" It was Mr. Henson on the line.

"It's my dad. He's here in my house!"

"I'll be right there." I heard him yell to somebody, "Get over to the

Cummings house! Now!" He came back on the line about 10 times calmer. "Where are you?"

"In my mom's bedroom."

"Where is he?"

"I don't know. I haven't heard anything since I ran away from him."

"So he knows you're there?"

"Yeah."

"Is the door locked?"

"Yes."

"Okay. Stay right where you are until we get there. Somebody should pull up in two minutes. Stay on the line."

I didn't know if I had two minutes. My eyes darted back and forth from the doorknob to the window, but I saw no signs of my dad. Outside the door, it was silent, as if I were alone. I didn't trust the silence.

Finally finding my head, I examined the room for an escape route in case he did come through the door. I could jump out the window, climb down the porch roof, and jump down into my front yard. Nothing else came to me, though I continued to scan. Then I saw the master bathroom. If I went in there and locked the door, it could buy me some time. If I only had to kill two minutes . . .

I glanced at my watch. I only cared about the second hand.

I thought I saw the doorknob move, but after 10 eternal seconds, decided it was my imagination.

My entire body was shaking, my shirt dripping with sweat. I checked my watch again. It had barely moved. I made a dash for the bathroom, ignoring Mr. Henson's orders to stay on the line.

I locked the door behind me and climbed into the bathtub. I was desperate for every second—perhaps the extra second it would take him to find me behind the shower curtain would be all I needed. I crouched down on the ceramic and bit my fingers.

Suddenly, off in the distance I could hear a siren. It was coming closer and closer . . . and then it stopped in front of my house.

I could hear at least two officers burst through the front door. One shouted something to the other, and I heard footsteps running up the stairs. An officer slammed his body on the bedroom door. "Is anyone in there?"

I managed a weak, "Yes." I jumped out of the tub and ran into the bedroom. I unlocked the door and let the officer in.

"Is he still here?" I asked.

"I don't think so. Did you see where he went?"

"No. I was running away from him."

"Was he armed?"

"I don't think so."

"How long were you up here?"

It seemed like four days. But I took a wild stab at the answer. "Maybe five or 10 minutes."

"How did he act? Was he angry?"

"No. He wanted me to forgive him."

"Okay, come on." He took me to the squad car. I sat in the back behind a locked door while three officers searched the house and all around it.

After they had searched everywhere, the officer who had come upstairs got into the front seat. "I'm gonna take you to your mother."

"Is anyone going to be looking for him?"

"We'll have a few squad cars and some officers on foot searching. We'll find him."

SHOCKING NEWS

My MOM AND I went to Mr. Whittaker's house. We were planning on staying with one of Mom's friends overnight, but we wanted to spend the
evening with Mr. Whittaker. I always felt safe at his house.

He poured me a glass of lemonade. As I lifted the glass to my mouth, I
noticed my hand was still shaking. We were silent for a long time, not really
knowing what to say to each other.

"Do you think he's changed, Mom?" I finally asked.

"No," she said. I guess she saw my head drop, because she seemed to
sense my disappointment. "Ryan, your father's very tricky. He's good at
making people believe in him. But he always ends up disappointing them.
I don't know if he could ever change."

I stared at my lemonade and asked the question again, only this time of
Mr. Whittaker. "Do you think he could change?"

"God's changed worse people than your father, Ryan. I know it's possible. I hope your dad has changed, I really do. But I understand how your
mom feels. It would be tough to ever trust him again."

"Impossible, you mean," Mom interjected.

We sipped lemonade for a few more minutes, silent. "You do think
they'll find him, don't you?" I asked.

"Yes, I do," Mr. Whittaker said. "He couldn't have gotten far."

"Because I don't want to move again," I said. "I like it here."

"I hope you don't have to move either."

▬ ▬ ▬

I called Scott and told him I wouldn't be in Kidsboro the next day, and that
I was handing over the reins to him. He was to be the mayor for the day. He
sounded way too excited. He asked me if he would get my salary for the

day, and I said yes. He finally got around to asking me why I wasn't coming. I told him I was taking a personal day off from work.

■ ■ ■

Mom and I slept in the same room that night at her friend's house. I was on a sofa, and she got the bed. Actually, not much sleeping occurred at all. I laid awake almost all night, staring at the ceiling. Every now and then, I glanced over at Mom. She was pretty much doing the same thing. There was a tree branch hitting the window outside. I knew it was a tree, but I still had trouble convincing myself of that. In my imagination, it was always my father trying to break in. If he could track us down to Odyssey, he could find us here. In fact, he could probably find us anywhere. I knew we'd have to go into hiding again, but I couldn't imagine ever feeling safe, no matter where we were.

"Ryan, are you awake?" Mom called softly.

"Yeah."

"I've been thinking. I hate it, but if they don't catch him, we're going to have to move again. Maybe to Canada or something."

I didn't want to hear those words, but I'd known they were coming. "I know."

"I'm sorry," she said.

"It's not your fault."

After a few moments of silence, I could hear her crying. I got off the sofa and snuggled up to her. She put her arm around my head and stroked my hair, we prayed together, and, finally, I was able to sleep.

■ ■ ■

It felt like I had just fallen asleep when there was a knock at our door. Mom's friend poked her head in the room we were staying in. "Hey." We both woke up. "There's a policeman here to see you."

It wasn't quite daylight yet, and I looked at the clock—5:54. This had to be important. We ran up the stairs and met the policeman just inside the front door.

"Sorry to wake you up, but I thought you should know this as soon as you could," he said.

"That's okay. What's going on?"

"We have your husband in custody. He's in the Richland jail right now." My mom gasped and covered her mouth with her hand. She hugged me as tightly as she ever had. I felt a hot tear running down my face. It was as if an anchor had just been unchained from my heart.

After we'd cried on each other for a few moments, Mom talked with the policeman. "How did you catch him?" she asked.

"We didn't," he said. "He turned himself in."

"Really?" I said. "He must've known there was no way out."

The policeman shook his head. "That wasn't it. He turned himself in in Richland, which is about two hours away from here. He must've caught a ride or hopped on a bus or something. We probably wouldn't have caught him all the way out there. He could have gotten off scot-free."

My mom looked at the officer as if his nose had just melted off his face. I must have looked the same way because he said, "You folks need to sit down?" We were too numb to move.

"What did he confess to?" Mom asked.

"Enough to keep him in prison for quite a while."

"I can't believe it."

"He's at the Richland sheriff's office if you want to go see for yourselves. A lot of folks want that."

"Yes," Mom said. "I think I need to see him behind bars for myself."

■ ■ ■

We took our time getting ready, even though I think Mom was anxious to get on the road for the two-hour trip. We ate breakfast, got dressed, and walked out the door into the bright sunlight. I noticed that Mom didn't put on any makeup, and though she may not have thought about it herself, I considered this important. My dad always wanted her to wear lots of makeup. Now she was going to see him for the first time in five years, and she didn't care anything about what she looked like to him. He was not going to tell her what to do anymore. Or maybe her mind was in other places and she forgot. I liked the first reason better.

We didn't talk much on the road. My head was filled with all sorts of emotions—mainly just relief. I couldn't believe it was finally over. But I was also a bit confused by the whole thing. As the road flew by, I came up with a theory.

"Mom," I said, the first word out of either of our mouths in 20 minutes.

"Yes?"

"Dad said something to me in the living room, and I was just thinking about it."

"What did he say?"

"He said that he wanted to prove to me that he had changed. Do you think maybe this was his way of doing that?"

"Turning himself in?"

"Yeah."

"Could be."

"I mean, why would he go all the way to Richland to turn himself in? I think he was trying to show us that he did it because he wanted to, not because he had to."

"You may be right."

She turned left and merged onto the interstate. There was little traffic. "Do you think he's changed?" I asked.

She chuckled under her breath, but then seemed to think it over. She glanced at me with sympathy. "You'd like that, wouldn't you? To know he had changed?"

"Yeah, sure."

"Why?"

"I guess . . . well, sometimes . . . I miss him."

She breathed a long, difficult breath. "Me too. And I wish he would change; I really do. But Ryan, I don't think there's anything he could do to prove it to me. There are just too many scars."

I adjusted myself in the seat and pretended I was very interested in the trees passing by the window. I didn't want her to see me cry.

∎ ∎ ∎

An officer sat alone at a big desk at the sheriff's office. He seemed to be expecting us. "Ms. Cummings?"

"Yes."

"Why don't you come on back with me?"

We followed him through a steel door and back into a damp, concrete-walled area that felt like my uncle's unfinished basement. Along the far wall were two jail cells—one empty and one holding my father. I could see Dad stand up from his cot. We approached him slowly as the officer pulled two chairs over from the opposite wall. He placed them in front of the cell for my mom and me, and then stood by the door. I was glad he was there. Mom pulled her chair back a little farther away from the cell, and then sat down.

Dad gave a half-smile to Mom. "You look nice." She didn't answer. "Both of you look so nice." I didn't answer either. After an awkward pause, he stepped toward the bars and leaned against them. "I did some research last week at the law library. With all the stuff I've done, it looks like I'll get a minimum of five years." He smiled, probably wondering if we wished it were more. "Guess that'll give me some time to think. . . . Give you guys some time to think too."

"I don't need any time to think," Mom said, stone-faced. She sat up straight in her chair, seemingly determined not to show any emotion but complete indifference.

"I understand that. I do. I can't blame you for all the things you feel about me right now. I'm not expecting any miracles. Maybe just a letter every now and then." He pressed his face between two bars and looked at us like a puppy dog about to be left in the pound. "I miss you so much."

There was another awkward pause. He studied us. I guess Mom had gotten her closure—she saw him behind bars and was satisfied—because she stood up quickly and scooted her chair back against the wall. "I'm ready to go. Come on, Ryan."

Seeing him behind bars was not what I came to do, though. I wasn't through yet, and I didn't quite know why. "Can I stay for a few minutes?"

She looked surprised that I'd asked, but then softened for the first time since we had walked through the door. "I'll be out here," she said, and without looking at Dad again, she headed out.

The heavy door clanged shut behind her, leaving only Dad and me and the police officer. I had no idea what to say and was grateful when Dad finally started talking. "Do you hate me?" he asked, his face looking as if he were preparing for someone to punch him.

"Sometimes," I said. "But not right now."

He chuckled a little bit. "I guess I'll take what I can get. Do you know why I turned myself in?"

"Why?"

"Because I didn't care about anything. I didn't care about being stuck behind bars for five years; I didn't care if I never made another dime; I didn't care if I ever lived another day in the sun. The only thing I wanted was a chance to be your dad again, and I knew you'd never let me do that unless there were steel bars between us. And at least five years for both of us to think about . . . each other." He ducked his head and pressed his hair against the bars, looking at the ground.

"I'm so proud of you. The way you've grown. You're so smart and kind and . . . I was actually kind of jealous talking to your friends in Kidsboro, because you've got something now that I never had: respect. You've made enough good decisions that people respect you. I never made any good decisions—always selfish ones." He lifted his head and looked at me again.

"Don't ever lose that, Jim. Don't ever do anything that would make others lose respect for you. Trust is a hard thing to get. Pretty easy to lose, though. Look at me. I'm gonna be working a lifetime trying to get you to trust me again. It may take even longer than that."

"It may not take as long as you think," I said. His eyes gleamed a bit. It was probably his first ray of hope in a long time. "I'll write to you, Dad."

"I'd like that. And I'll write to you, too."

I turned and looked at the door. "I'd better get going."

"Okay."

I scooted the chair against the wall and headed for the steel door.

"I love you," he said, again acting like he was waiting for someone to punch him. My lips formed the words to tell him I loved him too, but they got stuck in the back of my throat. All I could manage was a nod and a smile. I pushed the door open and joined my mother.

8

THE GREATEST SHOW
ON EARTH

I DIDN'T FEEL READY to go back to Kidsboro the next day, but I did want to do one thing. I went to the services at Kidsboro Community Church at least twice a month, mainly to show my support for Pastor Joey, who always tried hard to say something meaningful.

Mr. Whittaker attended services almost every week and sat in the same place: front row on the right. I saw him before he sat down. "How's your mom?" he asked.

"She's not ready to have a party yet, but she's getting there. She's taking off work for a few days."

"Good. I've been praying for you guys."

"I know. Thanks." He smiled and nodded, and then we sat down for the service.

There were only five of us there—Mr. Whittaker, myself, a young African-American boy whom I had never seen before, Marcy, who sat in the back, and Joey, who had a large bandage above his eye. "Healing okay?" Mr. Whittaker whispered, pointing to his head.

"Yeah." He'd had to get three stitches.

Joey started the service with announcements. He began reading from a sheet of paper. "We have choir rehearsal this Wednesday at 5:30. I could really use more tenors . . . and basses . . . and sopranos. Last week only one person showed up, so I guess we need just about anybody." Mr. Whittaker and I exchanged looks, wondering if we should volunteer for the choir.

"Also, we only had three people sign up for the church softball team. We really need more than that, especially if the other team hits any balls to the outfield. I put the sign-up sheet on the meeting hall bulletin board, but all I got were three names." He read the names off. "So far we have Lou Gehrig, Ken Griffey Junior, and Gen . . . Geng . . ." He showed the name to Mr. Whittaker to get help pronouncing it.

"Genghis Khan," Mr. Whittaker said, rolling his eyes.

"Thank you. Um . . . I don't know any of those people. If you happen to see them, they didn't put phone numbers down, so tell them we'll practice next week if we have enough people for a team."

I was sure Mr. Whittaker would give him the bad news later.

"Now, for the special music, my little brother Terry is going to play his xylophone."

The little boy that I'd never met before stood up and pulled out a toy xylophone. The mallet was attached by a string. Without looking up at anyone, he started playing the slowest version of "Amazing Grace" I had ever heard. He missed a few notes, but it was still very moving. After he played the last note, he slid the xylophone under his seat and sat down, still without looking at anyone. "Thank you, Terry," Joey said.

"Let's turn to Second Corinthians, chapter 11." I had forgotten my Bible, but Mr. Whittaker let me share his.

I couldn't imagine Joey ever winning any contests in public speaking. He did not have a very polished delivery, and his content usually sounded like it was meant for a five year old. But Joey had a knack for picking the right sermon at the right time. This time, as always, he had something to say to me personally.

"How many of you have heard of the apostle Paul?" he said, asking for a show of hands. His father, also a preacher, did this in his own sermons to get people's attention and to get them involved. Joey didn't do it with quite as much flair, but it did get us involved. Mr. Whittaker and I both raised our hands.

"Paul was a missionary for Jesus. And he had a real bad time of it. Wherever he went, he was in danger. He was beaten, robbed, and stoned. He was in three shipwrecks and thrown into jail a bunch of times. He hardly ever slept. He had to fight against lots of people who didn't want the gospel spread. But he did it anyway. He did what he had to do, even though it made him unpopular, sent him to jail, and all that other stuff.

"Like it says in First Peter 3:14, 'But even if you should suffer for what is right, you are blessed.' Paul stood up for what was right," Joey said, "and he was blessed, because he became probably the greatest missionary ever and wrote more books of the Bible than anyone else."

Joey was right once again. The apostle Paul stood up for what was right, even though it made him unpopular. Suddenly it occurred to me that if you do the right things long enough, not only will God bless you, but you will win the respect of other people. I realized that my decisions should never be based on what I think will make me more popular. They should be based on what is right. I wanted to jump out of my chair and clap. I now knew what I had to do. Actually, there were two things I had to do. I would start on number one immediately.

■ ■ ■

I called everyone that I could find together. I grabbed people off the streets of Kidsboro and asked them to join me in the meeting hall. I was glad that Scott, Nelson, and Jill were among them.

They gathered at my invitation, and I stood in front of a lot of confused faces. This was something I'd wanted to do for five years.

"I called you all here to publicly apologize. I lied to each and every one of you, and I'm sorry. I ask for your forgiveness. I lied to you about my life in California because my mother and I had to escape my abusive father. We changed our names because we didn't want him to find us. I will answer any questions you ask, because now it's finally over. My dad is in prison and will be there for a while." I scanned the faces and could sense that no one blamed me.

"My name is Jim Bowers, but that's a name I'd rather forget. I'd like you to keep calling me Ryan. Other than my name and my past, I'd like to believe I'm the same person you've always known me to be. Please don't treat me any differently."

I noticed Jill among the faces. I had promised her that someday I would reveal my deep secret. From the look on her face, I could tell that she forgave me, just like everyone else.

■ ■ ■

After the crowd cleared out, Jill approached me. "So that's your big secret."

"That's it."

"I was kind of hoping you were a criminal. It'd make better headlines."

I chuckled.

"Listen," she said. "I want to apologize for that nasty article I wrote about you."

"No, you were right," I said. "I caved in."

"I did too. We really made a mess of things, didn't we?"

"Yeah . . . but I don't think it'll last much longer."

"Why do you say that?"

"I have a plan. Let's get a city council meeting together."

- - -

The city council agreed on what we had to do. We had to make the special-interest groups accountable for the money we'd given them. We made appointments with all of them, and they all came, group by group, to hear the bad news. The five city council members sat on one side of a table, while the members of the different groups stood on the other side and heard their sentences.

"You have three days to prove to us that your group is good for our society and not dangerous," I said to the slingshot group. They looked worried. "We want to see the benefits of having slingshots in our town."

They all looked at each other as if to say, "Are there any benefits?" But they tried to act as confident as they could.

"We will have another meeting in three days—72 hours from right now—and if you can't prove that slingshots are truly useful, we will take away your designated slingshot area and make slingshots illegal again. Got it?"

They nodded slowly, and then realized they needed to look positive about finding benefits to having slingshots in Kidsboro. "No problem. Three days."

"We'll have lots of stuff by then."

"We don't even really need three days."

"I can already think of 10 or 12 benefits right off the top of my head."

We all waved good-bye, and as soon as they got out of earshot, we could see them having a panic meeting.

The other groups paraded in as well. The farmers were told that in three days we would check out their garden to see whether it was making progress, and they would also have to submit a written plan for making sure the produce was all eaten. They left arguing about who would write the plan. I don't think any of them really believed the vegetables would actually be eaten by people.

The animal rights group had to prove to us that their animals could contribute something positive to our city. If humans were required to take their places in society, then animals had to as well. They all had to find jobs in three days. I had a feeling that if any of the dogs became respected physicians, James would scream.

The Clean Up Kidsboro group had three days to show us that their goals were being accomplished. Otherwise, they would lose their funding. Kidsboro had to be virtually litter and pollution-free, and they had to make sure the outdoor bathroom was built.

"Who's going to build it?" one of the group members asked. I just smiled.

▬ ▬ ▬

Valerie's feminist group came in, expecting us to start fulfilling our promises to them. They got what they asked for—sort of.

"I'm giving your group a government project."

Valerie and the two other girls high-fived each other.

"You will be paid, as a group, to build an outdoor bathroom."

"I'm sorry. A what?" Valerie said.

"An outdoor bathroom. A latrine."

"Oh."

"I thought you'd appreciate that since you said you wanted jobs that were usually given to boys," I told them. They stared at me with their mouths open. They had to make a toilet?

"Okay," Valerie said, putting on a brave face. "We'll do it."

"Yes, you will," I said. "Because if it's not done in three days, you'll lose all your funding."

"Three days . . . great. We'll get right on it." This was supposed to be what they wanted. They had to be determined to do it.

They turned around, their eyes still wide with shock.

The feminist group was the last of the day, and the city council members began gathering up our things. Scott snickered, and Nelson joined him. All these groups had come in with their heads held high, and had left with their tails between their legs.

I was interested in seeing the results of this challenge. Scott and I planned to watch everyone very carefully. But there was one thing I had to do before I started. And I was dreading it.

▬ ▬ ▬

"You called for me, Mr. Mayor?"

"Yes, Lauren. Have a seat, please," I told her.

She hesitated before she sat, as if she wondered if my asking her to sit was a sign that I was going to say something bad.

"You don't want to sit?" I asked.

"Did I do something wrong?"

"No."

"I've been working on my spelling, I really have."

"It's not your spelling."

"Is it something else I did?"

"You didn't do anything, Lauren. I just need to talk to you." She finally sat down, though she didn't look like she believed me.

"Lauren . . ." I knew immediately that I shouldn't have started off saying her name, because she closed her eyes and prepared for the blow. "You know that we've had some economic problems in Kidsboro lately."

"Yes."

"It's because of these new taxes. A lot of extra money is going out this year to different groups of people, and because we're having so many problems with the economy, the city council and I believe that we need to hold these groups accountable. You also know that I've been under some criticism for hiring you, right?"

She suddenly stood up and started crying. "I'll have my desk cleaned out this afternoon, Mr. Mayor."

"Lauren, I'm not firing you."

"You're not?"

"You have to pass a test. To prove that you're worth your salary."

"A test?"

"Yes. It's a project, and you have to have it done in three days."

"Okay," she said, wiping away the tears.

I pulled out a thick stack of papers. "This is the city charter. Every law that we've ever come up with for Kidsboro is in it. We've added a lot to it since we started, so it's very disorganized. There are laws stuck in here at random, and they need to be put in categories. Like laws that have to do with the court system, laws about conduct in the town, laws about money—stuff like that. It all needs to be retyped and look very professional by the time your three days are up." She had a blank look on her face. "Do you understand?" I asked.

She nodded slowly, but I wasn't convinced.

"I'm not allowed to give you help on this. It has to be your project."

She took the stack of papers and looked at it as if it were written in Swahili. I had sympathy for her. "I'm sorry."

"It's not your fault."

"Do your best."

"I will." She turned and headed for the door, hunched over like an old woman with a bad back.

This was a project that I felt would be challenging, but could be done by most people my age. I had serious doubts about Lauren being able to handle it, though. I felt like I had just given out my first pink slip.

■ ■ ■

Over the next two days, Scott and I ducked behind bushes and trees, watching the special-interest groups unravel like a bad sweater.

Valerie and her clan were gathered at the spot where they'd been told to build the bathroom. They all had their shovels out, but no one was digging. Scott and I crouched behind some bushes to listen to what they were saying.

"Come on, we have to do this," Valerie said.

"I think I'd be better at helping build the walls," Patty said.

"What's the big deal? It's just a hole."

"Yeah, but it's the thought of what it's going to be," another girl said. "And how are we going to be able to walk down the halls of our school ever again? Everybody'll call us the Toilet Girls."

"Yeah," Patty agreed.

"It's just gross."

"Nobody will even come near us."

"I can't do it."

"Okay, okay," Valerie said. "This is silly. We need to do it. This will prove once and for all that we're equal to boys—that we can do anything they can do. There's nothing in there but dirt. We don't have to ever use it, we just have to dig it."

"Then you do it," Patty said.

"No way," Valerie said. "It's disgusting."

■ ■ ■

The slingshot guys were having a powwow in one of their designated areas. Scott and I crept up behind the group, ducking behind a couple of trees.

"I can't come up with anything," one said.

"Why do we have to prove we're a benefit to society? We just want to be able to use slingshots," another said.

"Look, I don't agree with this ruling any more than you do, but we have to think of something. We have to show we have some purpose. Now everybody think!" Ben, their leader, ordered.

They all bowed their heads and squinted their eyes shut, clearly trying to squeeze every ounce of intelligence out of their brains.

"What are we here for?" Ben said. "What's our purpose?"

"Protection. We're here so that Kidsborians can feel safe in their homes."

"Right. Protection. But from what?"

They all looked at each other, and then one said, "Bears?"

"How can we prove that, though?"

"Man, if only a bear would attack or something."

"Oh, that would be perfect."

"Maybe we could lure one here. Put out some food or something."

"I've never seen any bears around here."

"We'll have to go deeper in the woods."

"Yeah. There's tons of bears out there."

"That's it. We go find a bear, shoot it with a slingshot, then drag it back here and tell everybody we saved them from certain death."

"Yeah!"

"That's it!"

"Let's do it!"

They picked up their slingshots and marched onward, heads held high. They all high-fived each other, whooping and hollering as they headed deeper into the woods as a group. Scott was holding his hand over his mouth to keep from laughing.

Suddenly, one of the slingshotters stopped. "Wait a minute."

"What?"

"We're gonna shoot a bear?"

They all halted, and it suddenly dawned on them what they had decided to do. They exchanged frightened looks.

"We can do this," Ben said. No one else seemed convinced, but no one wanted to admit his fear. They moved on into the woods, though there was no more hollering, and their steps weren't quite so quick.

■ ■ ■

Scott and I were pretending to casually walk past the farmers' garden. We slowed our steps to overhear Mark and the Clean Up Kidsboro group having a feud with the farmers. "What is that?" Mark said to farmer/doctor James. "What are you putting on your plants?"

"It's bug killer," James replied.

"That stuff pollutes the environment. You can't use it."

"If we don't use this, the bugs'll eat everything. These beetle things are all over the place."

"I guess they're gonna have a feast then."

"Sorry, but you'll have to fight pollution somewhere else. This is our garden, and it's got to look a lot better than this in three days if we're gonna keep our funding."

"You keep using that death spray, and you won't have a garden to show."

"What do you mean?"

"You put one drop of it on your plants, and we'll rip 'em all out by the roots."

"What?"

■ ■ ■

We passed by the feminists, and they had begun work on the latrine walls. I imagined they were doing this to put off having to dig, which was much more offensive. They had built a frame of wood, and it looked rather good.

■ ■ ■

Scott and I were kneeling behind some tall bushes, watching Melissa and the animal rights group attempt to train their dogs to pick up rocks in the middle of Kidsboro's main street and take them to the creek. Apparently, this would be the way they would show that their dogs benefited Kidsboro— by getting rid of dangerous rocks that people could trip over.

The trainers weren't having much success. "Come on, Tornado," an owner said to his terrier. "Pick up the rock. Pick it up, boy." The owner looked around to see if anyone was watching, then got down on all fours and demonstrated the technique to his dog. He picked up a rock in his mouth and carried it away, then turned around to see if his dog would do it. At this point, Scott and I were both stuffing our fists in our mouths to keep from bursting out laughing.

The dog just looked at his owner as if to say, "Well, if *you're* going to pick up the rocks, then there's no sense in me doing it. You can take them to the creek. And while you're there, would you mind filling my water dish? It's kind of a long walk."

■ ■ ■

Two days later there was panic in the air. None of the groups were making much progress with their assignments, and they had only 24 hours left. I was nearby the designated slingshot area as the guys returned from another unsuccessful bear-hunting trip. They came back with a couple of dead crickets.

"But crickets are gross," one of them said. "They spit this tobacco-like stuff, and they jump on you. The government should pay us big bucks to rid our town of these pesky marauders of freedom." The rest of the guys weren't buying it. They must have known that two dead crickets were not enough to pass the test. I found out later that it had taken 14 shots from four different people to hit the first cricket with their slingshots. The other one they had just stepped on.

■ ■ ■

The feminists were holding a six-person rally at the meeting hall pavilion to psyche themselves up for digging the hole. The walls were complete, but they had yet to break ground with their shovels. Scott and I peeked in.

Valerie was at the front, her fist waving madly. "We can do this, girls!" Wild cheers. "We are entering a new age where there is no difference between boys and girls!" More applause. "An age where we can do anything boys can do! I have a dream! I have a dream that one day boys will be cleaning the kitchen cabinets, and girls will be choosing the president's cabinet. I have a dream that girls will be found within the capitol walls and boys in the shopping malls!" The girls were now in a frenzy. "I have a dream that one day there will be girls and boys standing side by side, kings and queens, dresses and jeans, Chrises and Christines, using all their means, to dig latrines!"

Valerie had them going crazy, and didn't want to lose them. She grabbed a shovel and raised it above her head. "This is the symbol of girls now! We use shovels! We dig dirt! We do construction! We get dirty!" They all raised their shovels.

Valerie reached up and pulled off her earrings. "These are no longer a symbol of us!" she said, and threw the earrings into the grass behind her. Another girl joined her and started raising her own symbols in the air. She picked up a pair of pantyhose and threw them away. Another girl threw her purse about 30 feet. They'd obviously been told beforehand to bring all the symbols of girlhood because everyone seemed to have something to throw away—jewelry, acrylic nails, perfume, and makeup.

Patty raised up a can of hairspray and shot it out into the air, waving it to show the stream. Just then, Mark, head of Clean Up Kidsboro, flew out of a nearby bush. He had obviously been watching them to make sure they finished the bathroom. But now, I had a feeling he thought the feminists had gone too far.

"Hey! Stop that!" he yelled. Most of the girls ignored him, including Patty, who continued spraying. "Those are harmful chemicals!" he protested.

She continued to ignore him. "Stop spraying!" he yelled, jumping up and snatching the can from her hand. Some of the girls finally noticed that there was a boy present, and their frenzy came to an abrupt halt. "What are you people doing?" Mark shouted. "You're killing us! My organization is relying on you. You're supposed to be digging a latrine, not spraying deadly chemicals in the air!"

"We're just about to dig," Patty said.

"Well, get started, then! You've only got 24 hours, or we lose our funding!"

"How about it, girls?" Valerie shouted, trying to regain the momentum.

"Yeah!" they shouted.

"Then let's go!" she shouted, raising her shovel in the air. Each girl grabbed her shovel. Like angry villagers ready to lynch somebody, they marched out to the latrine construction site, shouting as they went. Mark followed them to see that the job would actually be done this time. Scott and I went along too.

The feminists all circled around the spot where the bathroom was going to be built. "Let's make a toilet, girls!" They all cheered, but something about the words *toilet girls* hit them. A couple glanced around and could see that there were several boys in the distance, watching them carefully as they prepared to break ground. I think each of them had their own vision of walking down the halls of the school, with boys all around them pointing and saying, "There goes one of the toilet girls." Somehow this vision seemed to drain their enthusiasm. Valerie stood with her shovel poised above the ground, ready to strike down on the earth. Then she looked around and saw more boys watching her from across the creek. She scanned the faces of her followers and realized that they had lost their fervor. They suddenly wanted their makeup and hairspray back.

"Come on!" Mark said, noticing the sudden change of attitude. "Dig! Come on! It's only a hole!"

Valerie handed him the shovel. "Then you do it."

"No way; that's disgusting."

■ ■ ■

James marched over to where the animal rights group was busy trying to train their cats to rake leaves. One cat carried a small rake on its back like a plow horse. *This is animal rights?* I asked myself.

James was irate. "Your dogs are destroying our garden," he shouted.

"How?"

"You've trained them to pick up rocks and take them to the creek, and now they're doing it to my unripe tomatoes!"

"Really?" one of them said with glee. They were excited that the dogs were using what they'd learned.

"Keep your dogs out of my garden."

"Well, if you haven't noticed," the animal lover replied, "we have laws now that say that animals can roam freely, just like humans. The dogs can go anywhere they want."

"So, you're not gonna keep them out?"

"Nope."

"All right, then." James left. He walked away so quickly it was obvious that he had a plan. Scott and I followed quietly behind him.

He went to see the slingshotters. "I have a job for you," he said.

Their eyes lit up. "What?"

"I want to keep the dogs out of our garden. I'll hire you to stand guard. If any of those dogs come near it, open fire."

"Really?" the slingshotters said in unison. They huddled up. "This is our chance. We can show we're useful to the farmers." They all nodded in agreement and broke the huddle.

"We'll do it," they said. James smiled.

■ ■ ■

Later that day, the slingshotters had the garden surrounded, waiting for the dogs to make one false move. It was like a police stakeout. They sat there for an hour without a single animal in sight, their trigger fingers itching to fire away.

Suddenly, one of the slingshotters got hit. A stray nut from out of nowhere pelted him on the back of the head. He turned around. It was Melissa, holding a slingshot of her own.

"What are you doing?" the slingshotter asked, his buddies giving up their positions and gathering around him.

"How does that feel?" Melissa said. "What if the dogs just suddenly started shooting at you? Doesn't feel so good, does it?"

All at once, three more animal rights people appeared from behind the trees. They all had slingshots. Melissa signaled them forward. "It's hunting season, boys." They advanced on the slingshotters with an entire arsenal of nuts and hard objects in their pockets. The slingshotters, who had left their weapons at their posts, backed away and started to run. The animal rights people ran after them, shooting at will. The slingshotters retreated into the woods until we couldn't see them anymore.

9

TIME'S UP

A MISCHIEVOUS GRIN CROSSED my face as I headed into Kidsboro the next morning. The 72 hours was up for all the special-interest groups, and I could already tell that some of them were going to fall short. I passed the garden on my way to the office; the bugs and animals had destroyed it. It didn't even resemble a garden anymore, it looked more like a greenhouse that had been bombed. One of the farmers was sitting beside it and waved sheepishly at me. He was caressing a perfect unripe tomato. Maybe it was the only one left.

Along the way, I saw that garbage was strewn everywhere, down the main street all the way across the creek and into Bettertown. Scott was noticing it as well.

"What happened here?" I asked him.

"Corey overslept, and the animals had a party." This was the garbageman who had just gotten a raise because he thought he deserved as much money as the mayor and the chief of police.

The city council met in the meeting hall; we were all curious as to what we were going to see today.

The slingshotters came in first. They dropped three dead crickets and a snail on the table. Half-heartedly, Ben said, "We have to rid the woods of these." He looked at us to see if there was even a hint that we were taking him seriously. He gave up in about five seconds. "Never mind. Let's go," he said, and the others followed.

Clean Up Kidsboro was next. Mark stood in front of me with all the pride he could muster. The rest of his group stood behind him.

"Let's see here," I said, reading over their contract. "You were supposed to make Kidsboro litter-free."

Mark raised his eyebrows and chuckled under his breath. "It was the dogs."

"Part of your job was to keep Kidsboro clean, despite dogs running around," I said.

"Yeah. We know." Mark turned and left.

■ ■ ■

Melissa and the animal rights people strolled in with just one dog.

"Melissa, we asked that you make sure these animals had jobs. Could you please show us what they're doing now?"

"Well, Bowzer here is going to show you how he can deliver things directly to someone's door."

"Really?" I said, looking forward to this demonstration.

"Okay, boy," she said to the basset hound, who lay prostrate on the ground. "Take this ball to Nelson's house." She handed him a ball, but he failed to grab it. She dropped the ball on the ground in front of him. He sniffed it. It was obvious that he was one of the dogs that had gone through the garbage and had such a full stomach that he had no desire to get up.

"Come on, boy. Come on, Bowzer." She glanced at me sheepishly. I tried to hide my grin. Bowzer burped and closed his eyes.

"They just need more training," she said.

"I've been around dogs. I know dogs. Training a dog not to tear through garbage is like training a fish not to swim," I said. Scott snickered, and Nelson elbowed him.

■ ■ ■

The farmers came in with the remains of a watermelon plant. It had been chewed through by beetles. "I could almost taste this watermelon," James said and laid it down on the table in front of us.

■ ■ ■

Valerie came in with her shovel. She was covered in dirt from head to toe. "You got your bathroom. But do me a favor. Don't give us any more government jobs," she said, spearing the ground with the shovel and walking away.

The city council members exchanged looks and started chuckling.

"We gotta do this again sometime," Scott said.

"Absolutely," Nelson said.

"Next time, I'll bring the popcorn," Jill said.

Alice just smiled with her arms crossed. For Alice, who rarely even smiled, much less laughed, this was like rolling on the floor.

We all laughed and talked for 20 minutes or so, and then remembered that we had jobs to do. Mainly, we had to vote to change the budget plan to exclude the groups who failed to pass their tests. It was unanimous. The budget would be amended.

— — —

I couldn't really get any work done on the budget when I got back to my office. I was too distracted thinking about how this was going to benefit Kidsboro. The special-interest groups had lost their funding, taxes were back to normal, and Nelson would be able to hire his employees back. I sat at my desk with my hands folded behind my head, very proud of myself.

There was a knock at my door, and Lauren came in. I had completely forgotten that I had given her an assignment, and that it was due. My glee suddenly turned sour because I knew I was going to have to fire her.

"Mr. Mayor?" she said, stepping in anxiously.

"Lauren, come in." She did, and then she sat down. I swallowed a lump in my throat and asked, "How did you do?"

"I don't know. I hope I did okay."

"You finished it?"

"Yes."

She handed me her work. It was hardbound like a textbook and much thicker than the city charter I had given her. I opened it, and my chin dropped to the floor. Inside were beautiful computer graphics, illustrations, and big ornate fonts. Written in gold calligraphy on the first page, were the words: *The City Charter of Kidsboro*. It almost made me weep. On the sides were category dividers—the divisions were perfect: judicial, legislative, and executive branches of government, just like in the Constitution of the United States.

There was a table of contents on page three, dividing up the book into sections, such as the government; the courts; elections; rights of citizens; selection of citizens—every word spelled correctly, every punctuation mark in the right place.

It was beautiful.

"Lauren . . . this is fantastic!"

"Really? You like it?"

"I can't believe this. You did a great job! How many hours did you spend?"

"All day every day. I've slept a total of seven hours over the last two nights."

"But, why?"

She seemed stunned by the question. "Because I love this job. I love working here. I love . . . working with you."

I smiled, and we looked at each other for a long moment. Even with an average of three-and-a-half hours of sleep the past two nights, she was radiant.

We were interrupted by a knock on the door. "Come in," I said.

It was Jill. "Oh, Lauren. Hi." She looked at me. I think she thought I was in the middle of firing Lauren. "Oh, I'm sorry. I guess you're . . . I'd better get going."

"No. Wait, Jill. I was just about to send Lauren home to get some sleep," I said.

"Thank you," Lauren said, smiling.

"Oh. I see," Jill said, then looked at Lauren sympathetically. "Hey, I'm sorry about . . . you know . . . But with the taxes . . ."

"Jill, Lauren did a great job on the charter."

"What?"

"Here."

She looked at the charter and her jaw dropped even farther than mine had. "This is great."

"Thanks," Lauren said.

"Why don't you go home now?" I said.

"Okay. Thanks. I'll see you first thing tomorrow."

"Bright and early," I called after her. She left.

"You're really gonna keep her on?" Jill asked, shutting the book.

"Look at what she did."

"One project. Big deal. Can she be consistent?"

"I don't know. But we're gonna see."

"Yeah, I guess we will."

"Jill," I said, "What's your problem with her? You've been really focused on getting her out of here. Why?"

"I don't have a problem with her," she said.

I smiled at her because I knew she was lying. She always looked over my shoulder instead of at my face when she was telling me something that she knew was untrue.

She smiled back because she knew I knew. "Maybe I just don't think she's good enough for you."

"She's my assistant, not my fiancée."

"Maybe I can sense a little office romance budding between you two."

"And why would that bother you?"

She chuckled and looked away from me. "You deserve a good speller."

"Yeah. You're right. I do."

■ ■ ■

Dear Dad,

One of my favorite memories of you is when you taught me how to make a soapbox derby car. You were so set on me learning to do it right that you made me repeat all of your instructions, and you had me do all the work myself so that I could get a feel for it. I never told you this, but I had no interest in soapbox derby cars. I didn't care about making one, and I've never made one since. I've probably forgotten all you told me. But I always loved learning from you. You were a good teacher.

And I hadn't realized how much I missed listening to you teach until last week. Last week I made an unpopular decision in Kidsboro, and I had half the people in town hating me. A lot of groups lost their government funding because of me, and everybody was pretty sore. They might not like me right now, but you taught me that at least they respect me now. And they trust me. I'll try very hard not to break that trust.

Anyway, I just wanted to let you know that you are still teaching me. Even if you're behind bars, miles away, you're still showing me what it takes to be a man.

I would be lying if I told you I wasn't glad you're behind bars. I am finally able to sleep at night. You deserve to be in prison, and I don't know if I'll ever be able to forgive you for what you did to Mom and me. But there's also a part of me that knows you're still my dad and wishes that we could one day be a family again. I know that's not likely, but I do want you to know that there were times when you were a good father. I still love that part of you very much.

I'll see you again sometime.

Your son,

Jim

THE END

PASSAGES™

What if history repeated itself—with you in it? Passages takes familiar stories and retells them from a kid's perspective. Loosely based on the popular Adventures in Odyssey® series, Passages books begin in Odyssey and take you to a fantasyland, where true belief becomes the adventure of a lifetime! Look for these exciting Passages adventures, including *Darien's Rise*, *Arin's Judgment*, *Annison's Risk*, *Glennall's Betrayal*, *Draven's Defiance*, and *Fendar's Legacy*.